FIRST TEMPTATION

"But I think it was the light in Venice that I remember most," Tye said, leaning forward, and Ophelia wondered if he meant to kiss her.

She'd been kissed before, of course. Grabbed and forced to endure the sloppy smacks of men who had believed she could have been had with a fine phrase. They'd always paid for it. Usually a slap across the face had made her point. She'd never, ever returned their desire. Had never, ever particularly wanted to be kissed.

Never, ever. Until now.

"Was it, do you think?" she said softly, drawing closer to him. "Made for lovers?"

"I'm certain of it." He leaned forward precariously, tipped her chin up and stared into her eyes. Her breath caught at the blatant desire she saw there and her own shocking yearning. For the first time in her life she wanted what she knew this man was about to offer. "And Venice is lovely this time of year."

"Lovely," she whispered. He was going to kiss her. And Lord help her, she was going to kiss him back.

By Victoria Alexander

VICTORIA ALEXANDER

The Emperor's New Clothes

AVON

An Imprint of HarperCollinsPublishers

This is a work of fiction. Names, characters, places, and incidents are products of the author's imagination or are used fictitiously and are not to be construed as real. Any resemblance to actual events, locales, organizations, or persons, living or dead, is entirely coincidental.

AVON BOOKS
An Imprint of HarperCollins*Publishers*
10 East 53rd Street
New York, New York 10022-5299

Copyright © 2004, 2013 by Cheryl Griffin
ISBN 978-0-06-201926-4
www.avonromance.com

First Avon Books mass market printing: April 2013

Avon Trademark Reg. U.S. Pat. Off. and in Other Countries, Marca Registrada, Hecho en U.S.A.
HarperCollins® is a registered trademark of HarperCollins Publishers.

Printed in the U.S.A.

10 9 8 7 6 5 4 3 2 1

*This book is dedicated to my dear friend
Carol Schrader,
who has always helped me see what
was right in front of me
all along.*

The Emperor's New Clothes

Chapter 1

"**W**E'VE got to get the hell out of this town!" Ophelia Kendrake yanked open the hotel dresser drawer, snatched up her meager belongings and threw them into the oversized carpetbag that served as valise, catchall and home-away-from-home, wrapped up in one slightly faded package.

Jenny Kendrake bolted upright in bed and blinked in the abrupt glow of the gas lamp and the utter confusion of one roused out of a sound sleep in the middle of the night. "What is it? What on earth is going on?"

"We just have to get out of here, that's all." Ophelia grabbed her sister's lone presentable traveling dress and tossed it at the bewildered girl. "Get dressed. Now."

Jenny stared for a moment, then her eyes widened in understanding. She raised her arm and aimed her finger dramatically at her sister. "You've been cheating, haven't you?"

Ophelia drew herself up to her full, and somewhat impressive, height of five feet six inches and regarded the younger girl with a lofty glare. "Well, I certainly wouldn't call it cheating."

Jenny's eyes narrowed suspiciously. "Would somebody else call it cheating?"

"Somebody already has," Ophelia said sharply. "He's a vile, nasty and downright disgusting man, and that's why we have to get out of here." She strode across the room to a beat-up wardrobe and flung open the door, muttering all the while. "I wasn't cheating."

"Then why do we have to leave?" Jenny said smugly.

Ophelia glared. "Because he thinks I was cheating. I frankly don't know what happened." She shook her head, still trying to sort out exactly what had transpired. "But it seems there were a few too many aces in the deck and several of them—through no fault of my own, mind you—were in my hand."

Jenny groaned and fell back on the bed. "You *were* cheating."

"No, honestly." Ophelia drew her brows together in puzzlement. "It wasn't me. Someone else must have done it."

Jenny raised up on her elbows. "Who?"

"I have a rather horrible suspicion about that." Ophelia plopped down beside her sister. "When this little discrepancy in the cards became apparent, the loathsome beast I referred to earlier gave me the choice of rotting in jail or acquiescing to his demands of a relatively personal nature."

Jenny clapped her hands over her mouth. "Goodness."

"Goodness has nothing to do with this proposition," Ophelia said wryly. "Although, to give the revolting creature his due, he did offer to marry me. He said it was about time he settled down and got him a wife. 'Got him a wife.'" She snorted with disdain. "Like he was purchasing a pack mule."

Jenny brightened. "But marriage—"

"But marriage, nothing. The man had"—Ophelia shuddered at the thought—"hair on his knuckles."

"Oh my," Jenny said faintly.

"And that's why we have to get going." Ophelia bounded from the bed and continued collecting the various bits and pieces that comprised their few possessions and total worth on earth. Jenny had finally realized the seriousness of the situation and was dressing with appropriate speed.

Dear, sweet Jenny. Just sixteen, the girl was a vision of purity with white-blonde hair, a delicate figure and the face of an angel. Ophelia was determined to keep it that way.

Jenny was as much a legacy of Ophelia's father as were Ophelia's own unruly dark red hair, instinctive gift for gambling and diabolically clever, creative mind. Edwin Kendrake was a great—at least according to his own personal reviews—Shakespearean actor who had toured the country with various troupes of entertainers, hauling his daughters behind him like so much excess baggage. When he died six years ago, Ophelia found herself, at age seventeen, the sole support of a ten-year-old girl.

Jenny was her sister in every way except blood. Edwin found her abandoned at a backstage door when the child was less than two years old and took her in as his own. Edwin Kendrake had more character flaws than any man had a right to, but in one area he was a saint: he loved children and treated them as gifts from God. Ophelia often wondered if that alone got him into heaven. Nothing else in his life would have.

"Are you ready?" Ophelia scanned the tiny hotel room, looking for any articles they might have missed.

Jenny jammed an old, tattered rag doll and a frayed, deteriorating book into her bag, a smaller version of her sister's. "I suppose so. But where can we go in the middle of the night?"

Ophelia threw up the window sash. "It's not the middle of the night, it's nearly dawn. And there's a train through here at daybreak."

"Then you did win some money tonight?"

"Not exactly," Ophelia hedged. "But I did manage to procure two train tickets for us."

Jenny studied her carefully. "You won tickets?"

"Let's just say I have the tickets and leave it at that." Ophelia glanced up and down the street below their window. All was still quiet in this dusty, little frontier town.

Jenny sighed and rolled her eyes heavenward. "You stole them, didn't you?"

"Stole!" Ophelia mustered her best indignant look. "I am appalled you would even think such a thing."

Jenny planted her hands on her hips and glared. "Just tell me if you won the tickets or stole them."

"Very well." Ophelia shrugged. "I took the opportunity to liberate the tickets when the chance presented itself, but I would have won them if the game hadn't broken up when it did. The previous owner of the tickets, an English gentleman, quite refined, was no doubt about to wager them." She leaned toward her sister in a confidential manner. "The man was extremely charming in a Continental sort of way, but a lousy card player. The vouchers would have been mine if Hairy Knuckles hadn't interfered."

"Was that really his name?" Curiosity tinged Jenny's voice.

"No, but"—Ophelia sighed with a theatrical flair

that would have made her father proud—"he'll always be Hairy Knuckles to me."

Jenny laughed and Ophelia grinned. "Now," she said briskly, nodding toward the window. "Let's go."

"We have money for the room, though, don't we?" Jenny said hopefully.

"Nope." Ophelia tossed her bag through the window, a muted thump signaling its landing below.

Jenny paled. "Not out the window again. I can't abide going out the window."

Ophelia swung one leg over the sill. "There really isn't any other choice. Come on."

"Can't we just sneak out through the front door?" Jenny said hopefully.

"Absolutely not." Ophelia glanced down, estimating the drop to the ground. They were on the second floor, in a room facing the back alley. A simple leap out the window could well result in a broken limb or worse. A narrow ledge, perhaps a foot in width, no more, ran around the building. If they could inch their way along the ledge to the corner of the hotel, they'd meet the porch. From there it was a simple matter to slide down the post supporting the roof. Ophelia nodded with satisfaction. "This will do quite nicely."

She swung her other leg over the sill, stood up cautiously and tossed her sister a reassuring smile. "It's just like a stroll in a park."

Jenny opened her mouth as if she was about to protest, then seemed to think better of it and sighed in the manner of a martyr being led to the stake. She tossed her bag out the window, then gritted her teeth and climbed out, following carefully behind her sister.

Ophelia reached the corner and shinnied down the post, landing on the dusty ground with a soft thud.

"Oof." She glanced up, speaking in her best stage whisper. "That wasn't so bad. Your turn."

Even in the dark she could see the glimmer of fear in Jenny's eyes, and guilt twinged through her. This was no life for an impressionable young girl. Ophelia stared at the frightened child, and a concern that had been growing for months abruptly crystallized into a solid determination. She had to find a way—or rather, she corrected herself, she had to find the money—to allow the two of them to settle down in some nice, respectable community. Jenny's budding beauty was increasingly difficult to hide, and Ophelia wasn't sure how she'd protect her sister from the advances of bawdy men in the free-for-all atmosphere of the booming frontier towns the girls passed through.

"Here I come," Jenny whispered.

"Watch out." Ophelia eyed her sister with apprehension. Jenny was not at all fond of heights. Even as a child, she had never taken to climbing the rafters and catwalks above the stage the way Ophelia had. The dear girl was pretty and sweet and kind but had simply no physical agility beyond the coordination it took to balance a parasol and walk at the same time. "Be careful. No, Jen! Climb! Don't let g—"

It was too late. Jenny landed on Ophelia with all the subtlety of a bag of bricks, knocking her breath from her lungs and her body to the ground. Both sisters lay winded in the dirt, Jenny slightly atop Ophelia.

"Are you alive?" Jenny said cautiously.

"Yes, dear," Ophelia said, hoping she was indeed still alive. Goodness, for such a delicate little thing, Jenny certainly packed a rather impressive wallop when dropped like a stone from above. "Now, if you would just get off me . . ."

"Sorry." Jenny scrambled to her feet and helped her sister up.

Ophelia stifled a groan and rubbed hard at her stinging posterior, which had obviously taken the brunt of Jenny's landing. Ophelia sighed in acute discomfort. "It could be worse, I suppose. I could have broken something." She dusted her skirt with a disgusted slap. "Still, the very idea of having to sit on a train for the next day or so . . ."

"Day?" Surprise colored Jenny's voice. "Where are we going, anyway?"

"I'm really not certain exactly." Ophelia spotted their bags and headed toward them. She grabbed her valise, handed Jenny her satchel and took off in the general direction of the train station. "Anywhere is just fine with me as long as we get as far as possible as fast as possible."

Jenny struggled to keep up with her sister's long stride. "Don't you have any idea where we're heading?"

"I can't remember the name of the town." Ophelia shrugged. "Somewhere in Wyoming, I think."

"We've never been to Wyoming," Jenny said wistfully. "It sounds lovely."

"Doesn't it, though?" Ophelia forced a cheerful tone to her voice, but her heart sank. She'd meant to get to Wyoming for years, but somehow the opportunity had never presented itself. It would indeed be lovely if this little town could provide her with the means to acquire the home and life Jenny so badly wanted and needed. But it would probably be no better, and hopefully no worse, than the dozens of frontier villages the girls had seen in recent years.

The sisters trudged toward the train station. Ophelia had to come up with a plan for Jenny's future.

Maybe she could figure something out in Wyoming. No doubt it was as good a place as any.

Still, the name of the community listed on the ticket flashed through her mind, and she grimaced to herself. It was unlikely they'd find any kind of future there.

After all, how much faith could one have in a place that bore the depressingly prophetic name of Dead End, Wyoming?

"Now THE FIRST thing we have to do . . ." Randolph Watson paused dramatically, and everyone else sitting around the table in the back room of his bank held their breath. "We have to change the name of the town."

Tyler Matthews groaned to himself and rubbed his forehead. He knew that something was up as soon as what passed for civic leaders in Dead End asked him to attend this little meeting. He didn't really care one way or another what the town was called, but he suspected renaming the community was only the beginning. He had a bad feeling about this. A real bad feeling.

Tye looked up and found six pairs of expectant eyes trained on him.

"I see," he said with a pleasant, if somewhat forced, smile. "What have you got in mind?"

The gathering breathed a collective sigh of relief, and he realized at once his initial suspicions were correct. There was much more going on here than a simple name change.

"At first, we thought about naming it for your uncle," Randolph said. "Big Jack Matthews owns a good chunk of the land around here, and it seemed fitting. He's always pretty much run things in town anyway."

Henrietta Watson nodded vigorously. "It would have been quite an honor."

"But it sounded too damn biblical." Joe Simmons snorted, while his wife, Anna Rose, bobbed her head in agreement.

"Not good for business." Anna Rose's unnaturally raven black curls bounced up and down. "Not good at all."

"Don't know how you'd expect me to run a proper saloon in a place called Matthew City," Joe grumbled.

"I hardly think the word *proper* has any connection whatsoever with the goings-on in that so-called business of yours." Maize Johnson cast a disdainful glance at the saloon keeper, who returned the stare of the widowed general store owner with a sneer of his own.

Tye rolled his eyes heavenward. It apparently didn't matter how long he'd been gone; some things never changed.

"Knock it off, Joe. Maize." Sheriff Sam Parker nodded at the widow and turned to Tye. "The point is, son, it's 1888, and we think it's high time that we made some changes in this town."

"Time we became respectable," the banker said.

"Sophisticated," his wife added.

"Civilized," the widow chimed in.

"Yeah," the saloon keeper said reluctantly, "civilized."

The hair on the back of Tye's neck bristled. His voice was cautious. "And you can do that by changing the name of the town?"

Sam shrugged. "To start with."

"Well, I don't see anything wrong with Dead End." Tye shook his head. "It's really rather historical, when you think about it, and damned appropriate. This is the spot where construction on the railroad stopped for that bad winter back in the sixties and the town sprang up around the camp. Dead End fits."

"Times have changed, Tyler," Randolph said briskly.

Henrietta nodded. "We're at the dawn of a whole new world."

"Why, in less than a dozen years we'll be in a brand-new century." Maize's voice rang out with the fervor of a church bell tolling the new year, and Tye suppressed a grin.

"So," he said, biting his lip to keep from laughing. "What are you going to call the town?"

The group exchanged glances.

"We wanted something that sounded civilized," Randolph added. "And impressive."

"We thought about Presidents City," Henrietta said.

"I liked that one," Joe muttered.

Maize ignored him. "We also considered King City."

"Liked that, too," Joe said under his breath.

Sam slanted him a quelling glance. "We still approve of the idea of naming it after Big Jack."

"As long as it ain't too Bible-like." Anna Rose compressed her fleshy lips together in a firm line.

Randolph drew a deep breath. "So we decided to call it"—he paused like an actor waiting for a drum roll—"Empire City."

"Empire City?" Tye choked on the words. "Isn't that a little high-flown? I mean, you can call it Dead End or Empire City or Paradise on Earth if you want, but it's still the same old town."

"It won't be for long," Randolph said confidently.

"What do you mean?" Apprehension nipped at the back of Tye's mind.

"We've appointed a Community Betterment Committee," Maize said eagerly.

"We *are* the Community Betterment Committee," Sam corrected.

"That's what I said," Maize snapped.

Sam gazed upward as if questioning a higher power about the wisdom of including women in this particular venture, or even possibly questioning their very existence.

"And the committee has decided . . ." Again Randolph paused as if to heighten the drama of the moment.

His wife rushed ahead. "The committee has decided a respectable town—"

"A sophisticated town," Maize jumped in.

"A proper town," Joe groaned.

"A civilized town." Sam nodded.

Randolph pushed back into the conversation. "—would have a mayor."

"A mayor?" Tye pulled his brows together in a puzzled frown.

"That's right." Randolph beamed. "A mayor."

"So . . ." Tye narrowed his eyes in confusion. "Elect one."

For the first time since the meeting began, Joe smiled smugly. "Already did."

"What do you mean, you already did?" Tye said.

"Tyler, we've never felt the need for a mayor before." Maize sighed as if the lack of such an official made them all somewhat illegitimate. "So we've never had to hold an actual election. And at this particular point it seems much more important to have a genuine mayor already in office than to go through all the fuss and bother of a complicated election."

Tye thrust his hands out in front of him. "Wait. Hold it. Stop." He shook his head. "I thought you said you already elected a mayor."

The group exchanged glances.

"We did." Randolph shrugged. "More or less. At least we talked to a lot of folks around town. Everyone agreed the committee should choose the first mayor."

"It's really pretty simple, Tye," Sam said patiently. "Before we can become a proper city—"

"Civilized," Maize chanted.

"Respectable," Henrietta chimed.

"—we need to get all these little details ironed out," Sam continued. "Like a mayor and whatever else comes along."

"I see," Tye said slowly. He feared he was indeed getting an inkling of what was going on. And he didn't like it one bit. "What does all this have to do with me?"

Again the gathering traded looks.

Randolph drew a deep breath. "Tyler, my boy, we think—"

"Or rather, it's our considered opinion," Henrietta said.

"After a great deal of thought—," Maize added.

"Oh, just spit it out." Joe glared at Maize, then turned to Tye. "We want you to be the damned mayor."

"'Damned mayor' is probably the most appropriate term I've heard here," Tye said under his breath. He studied the faces eyeing him expectantly. "I am honored. Thanks . . . but no thanks."

Joe groaned.

The ladies gasped.

Randolph sighed heavily.

Sam narrowed his eyes. "Why not?"

"Why not?" A hundred reasons, a thousand legitimate excuses, flew through his mind. "First of all, I haven't been home for years."

"That's exactly why we want you," Henrietta said. "You've spent all that time back East, going to school—"

"You got more book learning than anyone in the county," Joe said with a look that made it clear exactly what he thought of book learning.

"What about the schoolteacher? Mr. Robinson?" Tye said, a note of triumph in his voice.

Sam snorted. "No backbone."

Randolph shrugged. "No spirit."

Maize lowered her voice confidentially. "And he's not really one of us."

"Okay, but there must be someone else." Tye searched his mind for another likely candidate. "What about Maize? She's a respected member of the community and a good businesswoman, besides."

"Why, Tyler, how sweet." Blotches of pale red blossomed on Maize's cheeks.

Joe shook his head in disgust. "She's a woman, Tye."

Tye winced at the look on Maize's face.

"What does that have to do with anything?" she snapped, the blush of embarrassment quickly turning into a flush of anger. "Need I remind you, Mr. Simmons, woman have been voting in this state for nearly twenty years."

"Dammed foolishness, too," Joe muttered.

"Now, Maize." Randolph's tone was conciliatory. "No one is saying women aren't qualified to handle a job like this." A snicker erupted from Joe, and Randolph threw him a warning glare. "But we did all agree Tyler is the right person for this position."

"Sorry, folks." Tye rose to his feet and paced the

short distance across the room. "I've been away from here for five long years. First I wasted my time going to college, then traveling Europe, all at the insistence of my aunt and uncle." He stopped, placed his hands on the table and leaned forward. "The only thing I've ever wanted was to ranch the land my folks left me. Now I'm back, and that's exactly what I'm going to do."

"Big Jack thought you'd be the right man for the job," Sam said quietly.

Tye groaned and sank back into his chair. If his uncle was behind this, Tye didn't stand a chance. Big Jack and Aunt Lorelie gave him a home after his parents died when he was twelve, right after they lost their own child. They treated him like a son. Which was exactly why, after years of fighting, he gave into the idea of attending a snooty, Ivy League university. The grand tour of Europe after graduation was yet another part of his doting guardians' plan for his life. He loved his aunt and uncle, and even though he was a grown man, he was willing to set aside his own wishes for their happiness. But this latest proposal . . .

"No." Tye shook his head vehemently. "I don't get it, anyway. Why this sudden desire for respectability and civilization?"

"Can't say I care one way or the other," Joe mumbled.

"We're heading into a new century. Miracles are being invented every day. The world itself is getting smaller," Sam explained.

Randolph nodded in agreement. "Once people recognize the benefits to be found in our wide-open spaces, mark my words, the population of the West will boom. Why, in a year or two, Wyoming will even be a state."

Henrietta sniffed. "Just as good a state as any in the East."

Maize nodded. "We need to show residents of the big cities that civilization doesn't stop at the Mississippi."

"We want to attract new business and new people," Randolph added.

"It's a question of progress," Sam said.

"A matter of growth," Henrietta said.

"Business," Maize added.

"Pride." Randolph pounded the table with his fist. "And . . . respectability."

"And we got to have a mayor to be respectable," Anna Rose said.

"I don't want to be mayor," Tye said through gritted teeth. "You said it yourself, my uncle's always pretty much run things. Why change?"

"Jack agrees with us," Randolph said firmly.

"We need you, son." Sam smiled in a matter-of-fact manner.

Tye stared at the gathering. He'd known these people his entire life. Tye also knew that if this was what his uncle wished, he could put up a struggle all he wanted, but it would be a waste of time.

Big Jack was a powerful force in this part of the territory, and he'd never arbitrarily impose his will on his nephew. But Tye knew as well that his uncle—and his aunt too, for that matter—would work on him with the dedication of a dog worrying a bone. The same way they wore down his resistance to going off to school until Tye threw up his hands in defeat. Tye had a will of iron, but no one could beat the combined efforts of Jack and Lorelie Matthews. And they were his soft spot. It was easier to give in now and accept the inevitable.

Tye leaned back in his chair and considered his options. There weren't any. Well, hell, how bad could it be, anyway?

He heaved a defeated sigh. "What exactly would I have to do?"

Sam grinned broadly.

Randolph smiled benevolently.

The ladies twittered.

And Joe emitted a grunt that might have passed for approval.

"There's any number of things this community needs to start working on," Maize said.

"But that's in the future," Randolph added quickly. "For now, we just need you to represent the town at official civic functions."

"And present the key to the city to distinguished visitors." Excitement colored Henrietta's voice.

"What key?" Tye laughed. "What distinguished visitors? Just who do you think is coming to Dead End?"

"Empire City," Maize corrected.

"Well . . ." Randolph hedged, and Tye narrowed his eyes in curiosity.

"Well . . . ," Randolph repeated.

"You said that." Tye studied the older man. What was going on now?

"For heaven's sake, Randolph, just tell him." Henrietta sighed with exasperation. "I don't know why you don't say it outright." She turned to Tye with sparkling eyes. "It's quite the most delightful thing that's ever happened to Dead End."

"Empire City," Sam amended.

"What is?" Tye's tone was cautious.

"Royalty, Tyler." Maize flushed with excitement. "A real live English countess is coming here. To Dead End."

"Empire City," Tye said absently, his mind struggling with the absurdity of her statement. "Why would a countess be coming here?"

Randolph grinned. "She's touring the West. We got a letter a month or so ago asking about accommodations in Dead End." Pride puffed out the banker's chest. "It seems someone in her party heard about the beauty of the territory and she wanted to see for herself."

"The hotel really isn't up to royal standards, so they're going to stay at Big Jack's place," Maize said.

"I got rooms," Joe muttered.

"Hah." Maize cast him a lethal glance. "No respectable human being, let alone an English countess, would consider setting one foot into that . . . that . . . that brothel of yours."

"It's not a brothel," Joe said loftily, "it's a saloon."

Maize snorted her disbelief. "And I suppose those girls of yours are all waitresses?"

Joe narrowed his eyes in an unspoken threat. "My girls are—"

"Stop it now, both of you." Sam cast them a stern glance.

Tye sighed to himself. The public debate about the actual duties of Joe and Anna Rose's girls was nothing new. But privately, everyone knew exactly what the girls did and how they earned their money.

Sam turned to Tye. "At any rate, Tye, the countess is arriving tomorrow. We've got a big welcoming ceremony planned, with a band—"

Tye scoffed. "A band? Where did you round up a band?"

"Well, it's not an actual band," Henrietta admitted.

"More like an accordion, a couple of fiddles and a mouth organ." Joe shook his head contemptuously.

"And tomorrow night," Sam ignored the interruption and continued, "Big Jack is hosting a huge celebration for the countess and her party."

"We thought you could bring that English friend of yours." Eagerness underlay Maize's tone.

Tye stared at the group. "Why haven't I heard anything about this?"

"Tyler, you've been home for two months now," Randolph said. "And you've spent all your time on your ranch. Today is, what, the second time you've come to town?"

"Third," Tye muttered. If he'd known about this scheme, he wouldn't have come in today.

Or ever.

"Tyler." Randolph leaned forward to emphasize his words. "The point is, we see this visit as the first step toward the changes we want in this community. If this woman is impressed, we could get a lot more visitors, which would lead to business and growth and prosperity. Why, we could be the Chicago of the West."

"The St. Louis," Henrietta added.

"The Boston," Maize said dreamily.

"The Abilene." Joe glared defensively at the others. "I like Abilene."

Tye ran his fingers through his hair in frustration. He had so much work to do to get the ranch going again that he hated the idea of wasting his time playing mayor to impress some foreign snob. Maybe he could enlist Sedge's help. The man was from England, the second son of a titled family; surely he knew how to entertain a countess. Tye brightened at the thought. Sedge might even take over some of the hosting chores that were no doubt planned for him by the diabolical minds of the Betterment Committee.

Tye held out his hands in a gesture of surrender. "When do I start?"

Randolph grinned triumphantly. "She arrives on the afternoon train. It's just the beginning of a new way of life for us, my boy, just the beginning."

Tye rolled his eyes toward the ceiling. "And the finish of Dead End."

The group chorused together. "Empire City."

"WHAT DO WE do now?" Jenny said with a weary sigh.

"I'm not certain yet." Ophelia forced a brightness she didn't feel to her voice. "But let's sit here and think for a minute."

What were they going to do? Ophelia adjusted her parasol and sank onto the huge pile of trunks and traveling cases stacked on the train siding. The heap of obviously expensive luggage had been unloaded from their train, but she and Jenny had been the only passengers to disembark. Jenny settled in beside her.

Ophelia glanced around the tiny station, and her gaze fell on a weathered sign propped up against the wall. It proclaimed this wide spot in the road to be Dead End, Wyoming. She wondered if the sign had fallen and no one had bothered to put it back where it belonged. She wouldn't be at all surprised. Anyone who lived in a place called Dead End no doubt had little ambition or civic pride.

Her gaze wandered upward, and she stared in surprise. The sign apparently hadn't fallen after all, it had been replaced. A newly painted plaque announced a new name.

"Empire City," she said under her breath. For some odd reason, the new name lifted her spirits. Surely a community called Empire City had far more to offer an enterprising young woman such as herself than anything called Dead End. Why, if there was a decent gambling parlor here, she could probably make enough to get them back on their feet and headed once again toward the distant goal of settling down.

"Oh, dear! We thought you weren't coming." A short, balding man came out of the office and scurried toward them. "What I mean to say is we got your telegram a few hours ago and canceled everything."

Ophelia and Jenny traded glances. Ophelia eyed the clerk cautiously. "You canceled . . . everything?"

"Yes, indeed." The bald head bobbed up and down. "Although I am delighted to see your plans have changed."

"Yes, well," Ophelia said vaguely. What on earth was this man talking about? "Plans do tend to do that now and then."

"Everyone will be so thrilled." The little man fairly beamed with excitement.

"They will?" Confusion colored Jenny's words. Ophelia threw her a warning glance. Best not to say too much until she figured out what was going on here.

"Of course. Why, the whole town has been planning this since we first heard you were coming." The clerk stopped abruptly and gasped. "Dear Lord, I'm sure I'm not doing this right." He swept low in an odd imitation of a bow or a curtsy or possibly something never before seen. What kind of strange town had they stumbled into? "Your Majesty."

"Your Majesty?" Apparently the man had mistaken Ophelia for someone else.

"That's not right, is it?" He shook his head in a worried manner. "None of us was quite sure how to address a countess."

"A countess," Ophelia repeated slowly. Jenny nudged her and glanced toward one of the trunks. Ophelia followed her gaze and for the first time noted that a crest marked each piece of baggage. Below the crest was the name Bridgewater. She extended her hand in a gracious manner. " 'My lady' is acceptable."

Jenny threw her a sharp glance. Ophelia smiled a silent admonition for her to keep still. The clerk grasped her hand and babbled incoherently, apparently caught up in the thrill of being the only one in Dead End or Empire City or wherever they were to greet the arriving countess.

Eventually, sanity seemed to return to the little man, and he glanced curiously around the station. "Where is the rest of your party?"

Ophelia shrugged and sighed. "They were delayed." Jenny's brows rose at Ophelia's newly acquired English accent. "I daresay we will meet up with them at a later date. For now"—she rose with as majestic a manner as she could muster and favored the man with a beneficent smile—"I assume our accommodations are still available?"

"Yes, of course. You were going to stay at Big Jack's place, just a short drive out of town." He cast a questioning glance at Jenny.

"This is my . . . my lady's maid," Ophelia said quickly. "I assume arrangements can be made for her to be lodged as close to my own quarters as possible?"

"Of course, my lady." The clerk executed his odd bow once more, turned to leave, then turned back. "If you'll pardon me for just a minute, my lady, I'll arrange for your ride." He bobbed again and took off, his enthusiastic mutterings trailing behind him. "Imagine, she's actually here. And I met her first. Who's going to believe . . ."

"Your maid!" Sparks of outrage shot from Jenny's eyes. "You get to be the countess and I have to be the maid?"

"Well, you couldn't be the count, dear," Ophelia said absently, her gaze following the flustered clerk.

"But the maid." Jenny moaned.

"This may well be the opportunity I've been waiting for," Ophelia murmured.

"What opportunity?" Jenny's eyes narrowed. "You're not really going to pretend to be this woman, are you?"

"Jenny, one can't turn up one's nose when fate thrusts one into the chance of a lifetime."

"You're not serious." Disbelief washed over Jenny's face. "You'll never carry it off."

"Of course I will." Ophelia smiled serenely. "Didn't Papa always say I was a born actress?"

"But you hate acting," Jenny wailed.

"No, darling," Ophelia corrected. "I hate actors. But I adore acting. There is a distinct difference."

"But . . ." A glimmer of panic shone in the younger girl's eyes. "What if the real countess shows up?"

Ophelia shrugged. "She won't. You heard the gentleman say she sent a telegram canceling her visit."

"What about her luggage?" Jenny waved at the pile of bags.

"A happy coincidence, nothing more." Ophelia considered the stacked trunks. "I suspect this is just a small portion of what she travels with, anyway. I doubt if she'll even miss these for quite some time. And then tracking them down will be next to impossible in this part of the country." She gazed thoughtfully at the luggage. "I do hope we're of a similar size."

"You'll get caught. We'll get caught." Jenny shook her head. "You can't fool a whole town."

Ophelia cast her a condescending smile. The girl was such an innocent. "Jenny, dear, look around you. We are literally in the middle of nowhere. It's not the ends of the earth, but I imagine you can see them from here. The creatures who inhabit such a community, while no doubt honest, hardworking folk, are simply not terribly sophisticated. They have no idea what to expect from a countess."

"Can you act like a countess?" Doubt sounded in Jenny's voice.

Ophelia laughed. "We were raised on the kings and queens and various and sundry nobility inhabiting the works of Shakespeare himself. I daresay impersonating a countess will be child's play."

"All right." Jenny sighed in resignation. "How long do you plan on this little farce of yours running?"

"As long as it takes to make a decent amount of money. I suspect the good people of"—she glanced upward—"Empire City enjoy an occasional evening of cards. One or two substantial games and the Countess of Baywater can be on the next train out of town."

"Bridgewater." Jenny groaned.

"I will make it a point to study my lines," Ophelia murmured. "At any rate, if nothing else, our stay here, with room and board at no expense, will provide me with some time to determine our next move and, hopefully, make some definitive plans for the future."

"Plans about settling down somewhere?" A wistful note sounded in Jenny's voice.

Determination washed through Ophelia. She had to find them a permanent home. "Yes, darling. But for now." Ophelia squared her shoulders and smiled graciously at the clerk hurrying back down the dusty street toward them. "For now, I am the Countess of Backwater."

"Bridgewater," Jenny said in a furious whisper.

Ophelia nodded and favored the approaching man with her most charming expression. It scarcely mattered if she called herself the Countess of Bridgewater or the Queen of Sheba. Instinct honed in the years of trying to protect her sister and keep body and soul together told her, even though she wasn't sure how right now, this time she just might have hit the jackpot.

And Dead End could be just the beginning.

Chapter 2

". . . and I'm the damned mayor." Tye shook his head in disgust.

"That's a bloody inconvenience," Sedge said solemnly, but the irritating twinkle in his eye belied the agreement with his friend.

"It's not funny," Tye muttered.

Sedge laughed. "Actually, old man, it's quite amusing."

Tye glared sullenly. Usually he appreciated Sedge's uniquely British way of looking at life, but today he saw nothing whatsoever humorous in his predicament.

The two men stood on the porch of Tye's modest home on the ranch his parents had run until their deaths. Uncle Jack had kept the place up more or less through the years, but a house left too long unoccupied required a fair amount of work to bring it back to decent living conditions. That was just one of a long list of chores demanding Tye's attention. He didn't have time for this mayor nonsense.

"When do your official duties begin?" Sedge's manner was casual, but Tye read a smirk behind the words.

"Tonight." He sighed in surrender. "It's not much, but it's kind of a reprieve. I was supposed to appear this afternoon until we got word the countess wouldn't be coming. Then the blasted women showed up anyway, so all the festivities are back on."

"Countess?" Sedge raised a curious brow. "We have a countess in Dead End?"

"Empire City."

"Empire City?" Sedge laughed again. "Apparently, Tye, you've failed to give me all the fascinating details of your trip to town."

"It's the details that muddy the water," Tye said grudgingly. In retrospect, everything did seem a bit preposterous, and even he could see the humor. "Let me lay it all out for you. If you want to be a civilized town, you need a mayor."

"And that, naturally, is you."

"That's me, all right. Next you need a respectable name."

"I gather Dead End did not come up to the standards of respectability?" Amusement colored Sedge's tone.

Tye snorted. "No, but I suppose they could have come up with something even more ridiculous. To put the icing on the cake, some damned countess is stopping by on her tour of the West."

"I see," Sedge said slowly. "And I gather you, as mayor, of course, are the official host for the town."

"Something like that," Tye grumbled. He crossed his arms over his chest, leaned against the porch and eyed his friend.

He'd first met Sedgewick Montgomery at school. The two were a bit older than the other students, owing to their individual reluctance to submit to higher learning, and both were far from home. It was only natural that they'd become fast friends in spite of the vast difference in their backgrounds: Tye, fresh from the wide-open spaces of Wyoming, and Sedge, the black sheep second son of an English lord. The men had backed each other up more than once, and each knew the other could be counted on.

Tye had to count on him now. "I need a little favor."

Sedge narrowed his eyes. "What kind of favor?"

"I need you to come with me to Big Jack's party tonight for the countess."

Sedge grinned. "I daresay I can use a bit of amusement. I've been working far too hard as it is." He aimed an accusing finger. "You didn't warn me how bloody difficult this ranching business would be when you talked me into abandoning home and country and purchasing property here."

It was Tye's turn to grin. "You didn't ask me. Anyway . . ." Tye shrugged. "If I remember right, it wasn't so much a case of you abandoning England as England abandoning you."

"It really quite depends on your point of view." Sedge spread his hands out before him in a gesture of resignation. "I prefer to think of my unfortunate departure as simply an opportune twist of fate." He waved at the land around him. "I have the chance here to create a life of my own making. There's something to be said for that." He smiled wryly. "At this moment I'm not sure exactly what, but something, no doubt."

"No doubt." Tye laughed.

"Who is this countess?"

"Name's Bridgewater. Ever heard of her?"

Sedge shook his head. "No, but I have been out of British social circles for some time." He cast Tye a wicked grin. "I only pop in, you know, to create a certain amount of chaos and scandal."

Tye slanted him a stern glance. "Let's try and avoid that for the time being. I was hoping you'd help me out with this woman. I haven't had a lot of experience with countesses."

"And I have had a great deal of experience, in every sense of the word, with women of noble blood." Sedge swept low in a mocking bow. "I shall be by your side every minute tonight, my lord."

"Great. But that's not all." Tye drew a deep breath. "She's going to be here for at least a week, maybe more. Folks in town are planning all kinds of festivities. I know you're as busy as I am, but there's no way I want to be stuck with this woman all by myself. If you could see your way clear to . . . well . . . share the escorting duties . . ."

The British brow rose again. "You want me to share this woman with you?"

Tye threw him a lopsided grin. "When you say it that way it sounds so . . ."

"Crass? Crude? Callous?"

Tye laughed. "Yeah."

"I rather suspect it is." Sedge raised his shoulders in a casual shrug. "I would, of course, do anything within my power to help you out, but before I make any firm commitments, what do you know about this countess? Is she old or young? Pretty or hideous? And, most importantly, does she have money?"

Tye shook his head. "I don't know for sure. I know she's a widow, so I imagine she's old. She's traveling the West, so she's probably rich. All I really know is that her whim to visit this part of the world is going to be a real pain in the ass."

"A *royal* pain in the ass."

"I'd bet the ranch on that," Tye said glumly.

"Cheer up, old chap, I'll do it, but on one condition."

Relief washed through Tye. "Name it."

"If she's young and pretty and rich, I reserve the right to keep her for myself." Sedge grinned. "I may not want to share at all."

"Hey, even if she's young and pretty and rich you can have her."

"What?" Sedge gasped in mock surprise. "No competing for the same fair lady? No attempts to seduce a woman I'm attempting to seduce as well? No games, no contests, no wagers?"

"Not this time," Tye said firmly.

Sedge cast him a suspicious stare. "Are you certain you're feeling well, Tye? All this fresh air hasn't rendered you insane, has it?"

"I'm fine." Tye tossed him a rueful smile. "But the one thing I don't need in my life these days is a woman. Any woman. They're too damned much trouble. You want her, friend, you can have her."

"Excellent. I must say, it's something of a relief to know I shall have a clear field with this countess if, of course, she warrants it. Although it might not be as much of a challenge without you in the fray."

Tye laughed. "I'm sure you'll manage somehow."

Sedge nodded and stepped off the porch toward his waiting horse. "I shall see you at Big Jack's tonight, then?"

"Oh, I'll definitely be there." Tye tossed Sedge a sharp salute. "Whether I want to be or not."

Sedge waved in response and rode off. Tye watched his friend thoughtfully. While Tye had met any number of Englishmen in Europe, Sedge was the only one he could claim a friendship with. And even Tye realized that Sedge was not typical of his countrymen.

What would this countess be like? Tye hadn't much cared one way or another until Sedge had brought it up. How would he feel if indeed she did turn out to be young and pretty and rich?

He shook his head and started toward the barn. He didn't much care about money, even though wealth would come in handy right now. These were tough times for cattle ranches. Big Jack had invested heavily in the railroads and built a fortune that kept his cattle empire going, but the money left from Tye's parents was dwindling fast. If he couldn't make a go of the ranch . . . well, failure was one thing he preferred not to dwell on. And a rich wife would make life a lot easier.

Tye laughed out loud at the notion. There was no way he was ready to get involved with any female, wealthy or otherwise. He had far too many other things demanding his attention. Besides, she was more than likely old and unattractive, and probably an aristocratic snob as well. If not . . . even then, Sedge was welcome to her.

Tye strode into the barn and put all thoughts of the countess out of his head. He had a dozen jobs to complete before he could clean up for tonight's party. Still . . . the thought lingered in the back of his mind.

What if she was pretty?

"WELL, WHERE IS she?" Tye growled.

"I haven't seen her yet," Sedge said idly and raised his glass, studying the sparkling wine it held. "My, this is an occasion. Big Jack has broken out the champagne." He took a sip. "And it's a decent vintage as well."

"Swell." Tye drew a long sip from his glass. Champagne. How absurd. Jack and Lorelie had pulled out all the stops for this little shindig.

"Relax, old man. You look like you're going to a hanging instead of a ball. Besides, I am still willing to assist you in showing your countess our fair community."

"She's not my countess." Tye narrowed his eyes in annoyance. How had he let himself be roped into this, anyway?

"Tyler, my dear." Lorelie bustled up to him and enveloped him in a warm hug. "Good evening, Mr. Montgomery."

Sedge nodded politely. "Mrs. Matthews."

"And as for you . . ." She turned to Tye with a chastising air about her. "Why, we've barely seen you since you moved out to your folks' place. How are you doing?"

Tye's irritation melted at the sight of his aunt's loving face. Lorelie Matthews was tiny in stature, her blonde head barely hitting the middle of his chest. She tended to be flighty and frivolous and scatterbrained, with a rather vague way of coping with the world around her, to the point that strangers sometimes wondered if she wasn't like a house whose walls didn't quite reach completely to the roof. But beneath it all, she was good and kind and even smart in her own, unique manner. Tye loved her with all the protective passion of a son.

He kissed the rosy cheek she presented to him. "Aunt Lorelie." He gestured at the huge parlor festooned with flowers and ribbons and tiny British and American flags. Most of the furniture had been moved out to provide space for dancing, and a group of musicians tuned up at the far end of the room. "I don't think I've ever seen the house done up like this before."

"Well, it isn't every day we entertain royalty." Lorelie dimpled a smile. "It's wonderful, isn't it? Jack wanted the house, I mean the hall—"

Tye choked back a laugh. "The hall?"

"Oh yes, dear, didn't you know?" Lorelie beamed. "It's no longer just a house. Now it's a hall. Matthews Hall." She nodded at Sedge. "You have halls in England, you know."

"Yes, ma'am." Sedge's tone was serious, but Tye could see the glint of amusement in his eye. "And manor houses and abbeys and even an occasional castle or two."

"A castle," she said with a dreamy smile. "Jack would dearly love a castle."

"What do you call this?" Tye waved at the immense room. "Your house is probably the biggest place between Chicago and San Francisco."

"Well, it is nice, dear, and we did want it to be impressive when we built it, but . . ." Lorelie gestured vaguely. "It doesn't have that . . . that . . ."

"Ambiance?" Sedge suggested.

"That's it." Lorelie nodded. "Jack was talking about getting one of those architects from back East, or maybe even Europe, to come out here and see what can be done to add a bit more ambiance."

"Make it more in keeping with its new name?" Sarcasm colored Tye's words.

Lorelie ignored the tone of his comments. "Exactly. Now." She gazed around the room. It was already crowded with townspeople and local ranchers, all dressed in their Sunday best, the women obviously excited, the men distinctly uncomfortable.

"I don't see Jack anywhere, and I don't believe the countess has come down yet. Perhaps they're still in her room."

"Together?" Tye said cautiously.

"My, that is hospitable." Sedge cast her an innocent smile.

"Oh, we're very hospitable and friendly." Sincerity rang in her voice. "You'll learn that the longer you live here, Mr. Montgomery."

"Call me Sedge, please." Sedge nodded at Tye. "I've rather become used to the congeniality and informality of your country. And I must say I like it."

"To tell you the truth, so do I." She leaned toward him confidentially. "I don't mind telling you that's the very reason why I was a little worried about having this countess staying here. You never know what people, especially foreigners, are used to. And I fear our ways can be a bit overwhelming."

"Which ways are those?" As usual, Tye's head swam with the difficulty of following his aunt's conversation from one thought to the next. "The informality? Hospitality? Friendliness?"

"Everything, of course." She sighed. "You just never know what royalty is going to expect, and I do so want to avoid disappointing her."

"By the by, what is she like?" Sedge asked as if the answer didn't matter.

"Oh, she's wonderful." Lorelie fairly gushed with enthusiasm. "Of course, we didn't have much of an opportunity to talk. They arrived very late this afternoon and needed a rest—"

"They?" Tye asked.

"Yes, the countess and her maid."

"No one else?" Sedge said.

"No, just them." Lorelie shook her head. "The countess—her name is Ophelia, by the way—is very charming and quite friendly too. I was worried for nothing. At any rate, she said the rest of her party decided to go on to California and she arranged to meet them there." Lorelie glowed with excitement. "She said she didn't want to miss out on the chance to visit our little neck of the woods. Isn't that delightful?"

"Delightful," Tye muttered.

"Indeed," Sedge said.

"I'm sure they'll be here any minute. Jack went up to escort her down." A woman waving from across the room caught Lorelie's eye, and she responded with eagerness. "Oh, there's Henrietta. I must tell her all about the countess." She bobbed a nod and flounced off.

Tye and Sedge stared after her.

"She didn't give us a single, solitary detail about the countess, did she?" Sedge said with amusement.

Tye heaved a resigned sigh. "That's one thing you'll have to learn about my aunt, Sedge, you can talk to her for hours on end and come away from the conversation knowing absolutely nothing more than when you started. You're lucky if you can manage to make sense out of anything that comes out of her mouth."

"Charming woman, though."

"That she is." Tye grinned. "It's that wonderful muddleheaded innocence of hers that makes her irresistible. Uncle Jack learned that the hard way.

"They met in St. Louis. It's an odd story having something to do with mislaid ponies and misplaced parasols and mistaken identities and I'm not sure what else." He laughed. "Every time she tells the tale, the yarn changes a little and I've never been able to make sense out of it.

"Anyway, Jack demanded her hand in marriage, telling her father he was the only man alive who could truly take care of her. Probably scared the hell out of the old man. It was her father's money that gave him a start out here, and Jack in turn helped his brother—my dad."

"Not quite on a par with tales of the Tudor dynasty." Sedge raised his glass in a toast. "But an excellent family saga nonetheless."

Tye grinned and saluted him back. "Thanks."

Tye took a sip of his drink. Sedge brought his glass to his lips and froze. Slowly, he dropped his hand and aimed his words at Tye, but his gaze was fixed elsewhere.

"Tye, old man, remember your promise to let me keep the countess if she was young and pretty and rich?"

"Sure." Tye swirled the wine in his glass, wishing it was some of that good Scottish whisky Uncle Jack usually kept around the house.

"You won't change your mind, will you?"

What on earth was Sedge up to now? Tye raised his glass. "She's all yours."

"Excellent." Sedge thrust his glass into Tye's hand and strode across the room. Tye's gaze followed his progress toward where Big Jack descended the massive stairway.

Jack was always an impressive sight. A tall, powerfully built man, he towered over most of his acquaintances. Even at his age, an air of intimidating command hung around him. Tye's mouth widened in an automatic grin. It took less than two minutes to get to know Big Jack Matthews, and then, unless you were a business associate or a natural enemy, the impression of authority and domination dissolved to an image of genial good humor, generosity and charm.

Tye's gaze drifted past his uncle to the woman on his arm, and his breath caught.

This couldn't be the countess. She was too young and far too pretty to be a widow traveling alone. She was taller than any woman had a right to be, and her hair was the deep, lush red of fine mahogany, twisted on top of her head with a careless elegance. Her skin wasn't quite as pale as fashion decreed but instead had a flush of color that hinted at spirited blood and high passion. He couldn't tell the exact hue from here, but her eyes were wide spaced and tilted up at the corners. And her lips, full and ripe and rich with promise.

But the vision wasn't merely lovely. She floated down the stairs with an air of noble grace and perfection that proclaimed to anyone watching that this was a woman of quality.

"Hell." Tye smacked the empty glasses down on a nearby table and headed toward the stairs. A familiar competitive urge surged through his blood. If Sedge thought Tye would keep that ridiculous promise after actually seeing the woman, his old friend was crazy. He and Sedge had always been rivals for the same females, and, through the years, the score was just about even.

Tye strode across the room, pausing to pluck two wine-filled goblets from a convenient tray, and firmly pushed away all the legitimate reasons why he didn't want to be involved with anyone right now. He ignored the endless hours of work still looming before him at the ranch. He disregarded any thought of his pledge to allow Sedge to pursue this creature without interference. Sedge, of all people, would understand. He drew closer to the stairs and a smile grew on his lips.

Damn, she was pretty.

"If you are ready now, darlin'." Big Jack Matthews smiled down at Ophelia with the benevolence of a father. What a nice man he was. Nice people were so delightfully gullible.

"I am quite looking forward to it." Ophelia placed her hand on his arm and allowed him to lead her down the wide stairway. The room below was packed with people, all staring up expectantly, and her stomach knotted. Stage fright, nothing more. She drew a deep breath and concentrated on the proper behavior expected of a countess, the appropriate comments and correct demeanor, whatever that was. My, it was unnerving without a script.

Ophelia glanced at the upturned faces and relaxed a bit. These were indeed simple folk, and she should be able to carry off her deception without much difficulty. Confidence flooded her. If she had fooled Big Jack and Lorelie, the worst was obviously over.

The huge house, as impressive as anything she'd ever seen in Kansas City or Denver, had thrown her initially. Decorated with an odd, yet intriguing, mix of old-world antiques and homespun charm, it showcased fragile porcelain and magnificent paintings under the ferocious glare of a variety of dead animals. They came in the form of enormous skins that passed for rugs in nearly every room and disembodied heads that glowered down on the mortals milling beneath them, as well as a giant stuffed bear posed in a startlingly lifelike stance. But in spite of the grand scale of the house and its equally grand decor, it was very much a home.

Big Jack and Lorelie were as open and friendly as their residence. Ophelia was not at all used to dealing with anyone as candid and downright honest as this couple, and she firmly ignored any twinge of guilt at her deception. After all, she was only taking a bit of room and board from them. If she could arrange some wagering or games of chance in the upcoming days, so much the better. It's not as if anyone was being harmed by her little charade. In fact, if one looked at the situation from an unbiased and completely objective point of view, one might even say she was quite graciously helping them. They'd expected a countess to entertain and fuss over and impress, and she was willing to provide them with one. She lifted her chin and glided down the last few steps to the main floor.

"It looks like the whole county has turned out tonight." The smile of a host well satisfied curved Big Jack's lips.

"It is an impressive gathering." Ophelia gazed around the room. Jenny would have loved it, but the girl was confined to her room with strict orders to stay there. Jenny wasn't happy about it, but she had grudgingly agreed to keep out of sight.

Ophelia and Big Jack were the center of attention, but, as yet, no one had approached them. She leaned toward her host. "I do hope I haven't offended anyone with all the confusion over my arrival."

"Lord, no, darlin'." Big Jack grinned. "They're all just a little shy about having a real live countess here. We're not accustomed to royalty."

"To be specific, Mr. Matthews . . ." A British accent sounded beside her, and Ophelia turned to face an elegantly handsome man with dark hair and sparkling eyes. "While the position of countess is a noble one, it is not technically a royal title."

The man took her hand and lifted it to his lips. "However, even the grandeur of an emperor would pale beside beauty such as this."

"You can say that again, Sedge. You sure do have a way with words." Big Jack's laugh boomed across the room. "Countess, this is our local foreigner and fellow countryman of yours, Sedgewick Montgomery."

She favored him with a gracious smile, but her heart skipped a beat. An Englishman? Here? In the middle of nowhere? For goodness' sake, she was in Dead End, Wyoming. The odds against running into a British gentleman must have been astronomical. Damnation, she'd have to watch every single word she said, and, worse, how she said it. She couldn't let her English accent slip even for a moment. Ophelia squared her shoulders slightly. Surely she was up to yet another challenge. The recent years had been full of them.

"Good evening, Mr. Montgomery."

"I can't tell you how delighted I am to meet you." He held her hand in a firm grip. "It is so rare to run into anyone from England. It is the Countess of Bridgewater, is it not?"

"Yes," she said faintly and tugged at her hand. Why was he staring at her like that?

"It's been months since I was home, and I daresay we know many of the same people." An amused smile played on his lips. "We shall have to have a long chat."

"Of course." Of course not! She had to get away from this man. She tugged again at her hand, but he deftly tucked it into the crook of his arm.

Big Jack chuckled. "Sedge, my boy, she's in your capable hands now. See to it she meets everyone, that's why they're here." He nodded at Ophelia, and she realized he meant to abandon her to her alleged compatriot. "I see somebody I've been meaning to talk to. Countess."

"Mr. Matthews." She smiled.

Big Jack returned her smile and walked away. Desperation seized her. This Sedgewick Montgomery was probably the only person here who could unmask her. She had to escape from him, at least until she was more comfortable with her role. But her hand was firmly tucked in his arm, and for the moment she was trapped.

Montgomery turned and led her away from the stairs. "Now then, my lady—"

"My lady."

She had been too busy worrying about the man beside her to notice the one blocking their path. Until now.

"Champagne?" A smile danced on the handsome face of the man—big and blonde and bronze—holding out a glass of wine with a hand that dwarfed her own.

"Thank you," she said gratefully.

Beside her Montgomery sighed. "You promised, old man."

The other man grinned. "I lied."

Montgomery sighed again and released her hand. "I suppose I had best introduce you, then."

"Excellent idea, Sedge." His words were directed at Montgomery, but his assessing gaze never left her.

"Countess, this is Tyler Matthews." Montgomery shrugged. "Tye, this is the Countess of Bridgewater."

"Countess." Matthews grasped her free hand and quickly brought it to his lips, the light brush of his mouth sending shivers through her blood. "It's a pleasure to finally meet. I've heard so much about you."

"Oh?" Apprehension gripped her, but she kept her voice light. "What have you heard?"

"Nothing really, I suppose." A flirtatious light shone in his eye, and relief washed through her. "Only that you were coming."

"I see." She considered him for a moment. "Matthews? Are you related to my host and hostess?"

"Is he?" Montgomery snorted.

Matthews ignored him. "They're my aunt and uncle."

"Practically raised him," Montgomery added.

Again Matthews paid no attention to the other man. "So, I understand there is no Count of Bridgewater?"

"You knew she was a widow," Montgomery muttered.

"No," she said in a quick, breathless rush. He still grasped one hand; the other held her glass, and she was indeed trapped once again. The warmth of his fingers wrapped around hers was at once exciting and disturbing. She blurted out the words. "The count is dead."

Abruptly, he released her and frowned with sympathy. "I am sorry."

She placed the back of her hand against her forehead and sighed deeply. "The count, my dear, dear Alfred, passed on a year ago. I do miss him so."

"Only a year?" Montgomery frowned. "And you're already out of mourning?"

Ophelia glanced down at the deep sapphire gown she wore. Thankfully, the real countess had a figure only a little fuller than hers, and only a few nips and tucks had been needed to make the dress fit as if it had been made for her.

"Did I say a year?" she said innocently. "I meant two years." She gazed at Matthews through downcast lashes. Overly dramatic perhaps, but effective nonetheless. "It is so difficult at times to carry on alone."

"I can well imagine." Matthews stared down at her with a bemused expression, and triumph trickled through her. Lorelie's nephew was a man well used to dealing with featherheaded women. British accent aside, this was obviously the way to keep him in line. And keep him at a distance. He was far too attractive for her own good. As for the Englishman, she'd better avoid him altogether.

"Tye, aren't you going to introduce us?" A short, stocky woman with the full-blown bearing of an operatic diva bore down on them, a taller, distinguished-looking man a mere step behind. "We've been simply beside ourselves with anticipation."

"Come now, Tye," Montgomery said, "you can't keep the countess all to yourself, you know."

Matthews threw her a glance that said he'd like to do precisely that, and an odd ache stabbed through her. But she had no time to wonder what exactly this new sensation was. The introduction of the eager couple before her seemed to open the floodgates for the rest of the guests. Within moments, they surrounded her with excited greetings and enthusiastic remarks. Ophelia quickly learned she had to actually say very little to this gathering. An occasional comment, astute tilt of the head and polite but sincere laughter were all that was required. It was a surprisingly simple effort and an easy role to play.

The evening progressed in a whirl of conversation, and music and dance with musicians specially sent for from Omaha. The only troubling aspects at all were the nephew and the Englishman. It seemed every time she turned around one or the other of them was staring at her: the dark-headed one with a speculative look that unnerved her, the blond with an equally upsetting gaze that said he was interested in far more from her than she was willing to give.

She laughed with true enjoyment at a comment made by a gentleman who apparently was the town's banker, and wondered briefly if he was also a gambling man. Tonight was not the time to set up anything definite, but it was a good opportunity to gauge the level of possibilities in Dead End.

"We still haven't had our dance." Matthews's voice sounded behind her, and she tensed with a strange mix of anticipation and dread.

"Oh?" She cast him a lofty glance. "I didn't realize I had promised you a dance."

He raised a brow over deep brown eyes the color of fine chocolate. Damnation, she did so love chocolate. "Perhaps I simply failed to ask."

She shrugged. "Perhaps."

He laughed with delight, and the sound seemed to swell inside her. "In that case, Countess"—he swept a low, polished bow—"may I have this dance?"

Refusal was impossible, especially with the crowd around her staring expectantly. But the same natural instinct that had kept her and Jenny alive and well through the years now screamed a warning. This man was dangerous. Still, there was no other choice.

"That would be lovely," she said in as gracious a manner as she could muster. He led her to the floor and took her in his arms, and they moved as one in a surprisingly effortless way.

"So, how are you enjoying Empire City?" His breath

brushed against her ear. His hard body pressed subtly against hers and the intoxicating scent of bay rum and male heat enveloped her.

"Empire City?" What was he talking about?

He smiled, and her stomach fluttered. "We changed the town's name." He lifted his shoulders in a gesture of dismissal. "It was ridiculous, really, but it's what the folks here wanted. They think the new name sounds more respectable and civilized."

"Is it?" She could barely follow his words. The warmth of his body seemed to sear her flesh even through the gown, and she wanted to melt at his feet. What was happening to her? Lord knows, handsome men were nothing new in her life. One could not avoid handsome men while growing up in the theater. But this bronze god stirred her emotions in a distinctly foreign and unexpected way.

He pulled his brows together in confusion. "Is it what?"

Goodness, his eyes were dark. Dark and deep and forever. "What?"

"What what?" His puzzled expression jerked her attention back to the discussion of—what was it again?—oh yes, Empire City.

She drew a deep breath. "I was merely questioning if a minor name change would provide respectability."

"Who knows?" He shook his head. "But to go along with the new name, we've got a new mayor."

"Oh?"

"Yeah." He laughed again, and she steeled herself against its effect on her. "Me."

"You?"

He eyed her thoughtfully. "You sound surprised."

"I am." She shrugged as best she could in his arms.

"You don't seem like the type of man who would be interested in politics."

"This has nothing to do with politics. It's simply a matter of respectability." He adopted a lofty attitude. "A question of civilization, as we know it."

She laughed at the contrived arrogance of his expression. "Is civilization really that important out here?"

He snorted with amazement. "You wouldn't think so, would you? At least, I never did. But now, all of a sudden, good old Dead End wants to attract people and business and growth. So, for some odd reason, it's important to be respectable and civilized."

"I see," she murmured, the tiny seed of an idea taking root within her fertile brain.

"But I guess it's not all bad." A twinkle shone in his dark eyes.

"Civilization?"

"That's still up in the air." He chuckled. "But being mayor has a few interesting benefits I hadn't expected."

"Really? What kind of benefits?"

"Well, for one thing"—he drew his head closer to hers, and the sharpness of his gaze belied the lightness in his tone—"as mayor, I'm pretty much expected to play host to visitors."

"Are you?" she said faintly.

"And that, Countess, would be you."

That annoying twinkle was back. Was it a promise or a threat? She didn't particularly want to find out.

"I plan on spending a great deal of time with you in the next few days." His voice was stern, but his eyes laughed. "It's my official responsibility."

"Well, I wouldn't want to do anything to compromise the duties of your office." She forced a lightness to her tone that belied the emotions churning inside her.

This man twirling her around the dance floor held an attraction she'd never known before. In fact, she'd actively avoided involvement with any male for her own sake and her sister's. And now was not the time to allow newly discovered passions to cloud her mind. She was right when she thought Tyler Matthews was dangerous. But she was far short of the mark on something else.

The Englishman wasn't the only resident of Dead End she'd have to avoid.

SEDGE STUDIED TYE and the countess through the crowd of dancers surrounding them. The countess—Ophelia—laughed lightly and gazed up at Tye with an expression of delight. Sedge had seen that look before.

He and Tye had always been attracted to the same women, and in spite of his friend's promise, Sedge knew full well Tye would leap into the battlefield of seduction without hesitation, given the right enticement. Ophelia was definitely the right enticement.

Sedge watched the couple, and a slow grin grew on his face. There was no bloody way he'd allow success to come too quickly to Tye. No, his old friend would have to work for this victory. Ultimately, though, he'd let Tye win the lovely Ophelia. It would serve him right. Teach him a lesson. Pay him back for all the times Sedge believed himself to be in love only to have the female in question end up in Tye's bed. Sedge conveniently ignored the nearly equal number of incidents in which he came out the victor in the battle for feminine hearts.

Sedge chuckled to himself and sipped his champagne thoughtfully. The coming days would be interesting indeed. He looked forward to the contest to win the favors of the fair Ophelia with a sense of wicked anticipation, even though he already planned on losing.

The couple glided by, and he wondered idly when, or even if, Tye would realize the dead husband of an English countess wasn't a count.

He was an earl.

Chapter 3

". . . and . . ." Ophelia threw herself backwards on the bed and stared at the ceiling. "They're planning a fox hunt."

"A fox hunt?" Jenny's voice raised in concern. "You don't know anything about fox hunts."

Ophelia tossed her a rueful glance. "That, my dear sister, is precisely the problem."

"Didn't Shakespeare write any plays about fox hunts?" Jenny said hopefully.

"Not that I can recall." Ophelia sighed and pulled herself to her feet. She stepped to a large wardrobe in the huge room allotted her and flung open the doors. Jenny had unpacked all the countess's clothes, and Ophelia rifled through the rich fabrics and high-quality workmanship. "Did you find a riding habit in all this?"

"I think so." Jenny crossed the room, studied the hanging garments and selected one. "Here." She thrust the wine-colored outfit at her sister. "But I'm not sure it will do you any good."

"Oh?" Ophelia examined the habit carefully. Like the gown she'd worn tonight, it would take very little to adapt the clothing to her own figure, especially for two girls raised with the constant demands of altering ever-changing costumes. "Why not?"

Jenny plunked down in an overstuffed chair and smirked. "Because you can't ride."

"I realize that," Ophelia said vaguely, still studying the habit. "I don't intend to try."

Jenny narrowed her eyes suspiciously. "And just how do you plan on avoiding it? I mean, it's pretty hard to join in a fox hunt if you're not on a horse."

Ophelia raised her gaze to her sister's. "I know that too. But I can't refuse to take part in this ridiculous excuse for a sport, since the only reason they're holding it in the first place is because of my visit."

"Because of the countess's visit, you mean," Jenny said pointedly.

"Yes, yes, the countess." Ophelia waved off Jenny's words with an impatient gesture. "I think a real countess would insist on a sidesaddle for a fox hunt. And since I'd bet there isn't a sidesaddle within a hundred miles"—she grinned triumphantly—"I'll be perfectly safe and firmly on solid ground."

"I'd like to learn to ride." A longing look crossed Jenny's face, and Ophelia's heart twisted at the sight.

"Someday, darling, someday soon. We'll have a nice home in a pleasant town and a horse for you and a carriage for me." Ophelia threw her a confident smile. "But for now, these nice people in this pleasant town will provide us with everything we need, at least for a while."

Jenny frowned. "Does anyone suspect you're not who you say you are?"

"I don't think so." Ophelia chewed her bottom lip thoughtfully and considered the events of the evening.

"Mr. and Mrs. Matthews strike me as being far too agreeable to distrust anyone without reason, and, so far, I haven't given them one. There is an Englishman here—"

"Goodness." Jenny's face paled.

"No, I don't think he'll give us anything to worry about. Surely, if he'd noted a problem with my performance, he would have exposed me." She shrugged in a nonchalant manner. "He didn't, so I assume we're safe."

"It does seem to be going well so far." Doubt lingered in Jenny's voice.

"So far . . ." Ophelia hesitated to mention the golden-haired, bronzed-skin cowboy-mayor with the chocolate eyes who seemed to be everywhere she looked tonight. She didn't want to pass on her unease about Tyler Matthews to her sister. Fear that had nothing to do with her deception. On that score she had few concerns. Oh, he appeared intelligent enough, but he was still only a mere man and nothing to cause undue alarm. It had been her experience that when it came to women and cards, men rarely saw beyond what they wanted to see or much past what was already firmly in their hands.

Absently, she clutched the riding habit tighter. No, it wasn't the possibility of exposure that kept his teasing eyes and knowing smile on her mind. She could, somehow, cope with having her true identity revealed. Lord knows, they'd escaped from tighter spots. But how would she handle the odd sensations flooding her when he so much as raised a dark brow or laughed with a sound that warmed her blood and caught her breath?

Who ever loved that loved not at first sight?

The immortal words from *As You Like it* thundered through her head.

"Damnation," she said under her breath.

It couldn't be. It was impossible. She'd spent her entire life avoiding just such a fate. Love was nothing more than a convenient excuse for men to use to get what they wanted. Why, she'd watched her father break the hearts of dozens, possibly hundreds, of women through the years, all willing victims sacrificing themselves in the name of that fickle emotion. And he wasn't unique. Throughout her childhood she'd been surrounded by men, mostly actors, all smooth-talking charmers who used and discarded women like so much rubbish. Ophelia Kendrake refused to join their ranks.

Resolve lifted her chin and squared her shoulders. Regardless of Shakespeare's words as to the existence of love at first sight or love at all, she did not believe in it. Not now. Not ever. Not even if it came disguised as a seductive god of the sun. Tyler Matthews might well consider himself irresistible to other women, but as far as she was concerned, he was an obstacle, plain and simple, and nothing more than another player in her little drama. She could handle him. And the emotions he aroused were probably best attributed to an approaching illness, the sniffles, perhaps, or possibly a plague, both preferable to that dire fate called love.

"When is this fox hunt?" Jenny interrupted her wandering thoughts.

"Day after tomorrow." Ophelia tossed the habit on the bed and turned back to peruse the offerings in the wardrobe. "But we have to select clothes for tomorrow. Big Jack is going to show me around his ranch. And his wife is planning a small dinner party." Ophelia smiled with satisfaction. "I believe they said something about a friendly evening of cards."

Jenny groaned. "You're going to try to take their money, aren't you?"

"Of course, darling, that's what we're here for." Ophelia selected a brilliant yellow gown and a second in a deep green. "These two should do quite nicely." She tossed one to her sister. "If you'll take care of the day dress, I'll work on the evening gown."

"I still don't understand why you get to be the countess and I have to be the maid." Jenny rose to her feet and flounced into the tiny room that adjoined her sister's far more spacious quarters, leaving muttered comments strewn behind her like so many feathers from a flustered fowl. "I can act as well as you can. I could play the countess, you know, or better yet a princess. I would be a great princess."

"This scene doesn't call for a princess, dear." Ophelia struggled to hide her amusement. "Just a countess . . . and her maid."

"Hah!" Jenny stomped back into the room, her carpetbag in hand. "Only because you say so."

"Jenny." Ophelia raised a superior brow. "I am, after all, the director of this little farce."

Jenny glared. "I just hope you make that perfectly clear when it's time for someone to play the part of jail inmate."

A delighted laugh bubbled through Ophelia. "No one's going to end up in jail. Besides, we really haven't done anything wrong."

"We haven't?"

"No, indeed." Ophelia shook her head for emphasis. "We didn't come into town claiming to be someone we weren't. Why, it was that charming gentleman at the train station who assumed I was the countess. If you look at it properly, this entire escapade is his fault."

"It is?" Doubt furrowed Jenny's forehead.

"Oh, my, yes." Ophelia folded her arms over her chest and pinned her sister with a steady stare. "And even if I do manage to win enough to finance, at the very least, tickets out of town and hopefully far more than that, it's not as if I were stealing."

"It's not?" The doubt lingered.

"Jenny." Ophelia pulled herself up ramrod straight and stared regally downward, a towering vision of righteous indignation. It was one of her best roles. "I do not plan to cheat."

"Of course not. I just thought . . . I mean you have . . . it isn't as if . . ." Jenny shrugged helplessly and sank down on the bed.

"That you would even think such a thing." Ophelia covered her eyes with her hand and shook her head in a convincing display of mortification.

"Oh, Ophelia, I'm so sorry." Jenny leapt from the bed and threw her arms around her sister. "I didn't mean to upset you, truly I didn't."

"Apology accepted," Ophelia said with a lilt to her voice, and Jenny stepped back abruptly.

"You were acting again, weren't you?" Sparks flew from the younger girl's blue eyes, and she pointed an accusing finger at her sister. "I can't believe you'd do that to me."

Ophelia lifted her shoulders in a gesture of dismissal. "Call it rehearsal."

"I call it rotten." Jenny glared and grabbed her bag, rummaging through its paltry offerings with an irritated air. "Where in the hell is that damn needle and thread."

Ophelia rolled her eyes heavenward. She had to find them a decent, wholesome place to settle down, and soon. It was one thing for Ophelia to use such language, but quite another for Jenny to do so. Jenny had a future and a much better life ahead of her. Ophelia would see to that.

"I know it's in here somewhere." Jenny shook the bag, and a shower of odds and ends tumbled onto the bed, tiny tokens of Jenny's unique childhood. Here rested a yellowed playbill from a long-ago Edwin Kendrake performance in a town since forgotten. There lay a bedraggled hair ribbon, a souvenir of a holiday celebrated when Edwin was alive and Ophelia's role was simply that of daughter and sister, not provider and protector. Ophelia shook off the sense of nostalgia triggered by her sister's mementoes. Now was not the time for sentimentality.

Jenny pawed impatiently through the items scattered on the bed, pushing aside the rag doll she'd carried in one hand when Edwin had found her and the child's storybook she'd clutched with the other. Ophelia glanced at the meager remnants of her sister's real family. Both were worn and tattered with years of loving. The doll bore Jenny's name in fine needlework on its skirt, and the book bore the title *The Emperor's New Clothes*. Ophelia's gaze slid past the display, then jerked back as if pulled by an invisible string.

The Emperor's New Clothes?

"Jenny," Ophelia said slowly, fighting to control the excitement rising inside her. "Hand me your book."

"My book?" Jenny snatched the volume off the bed and held it tightly against her. "Why do you want it?"

"Just an idea." Ophelia gestured impatiently. "I won't hurt it."

"You'd better not." Reluctantly, Jenny passed the worn volume to her sister. Ophelia couldn't fault the girl for her protective nature regarding the book, but, at this moment, it might have a greater significance for the future than the past.

Ophelia paged through it quickly. She used to read the tale to Jenny nearly every night, but their evening routine had fallen off years ago. The story was just as she'd remembered.

"What are you planning?" Jenny's voice rang with suspicion.

"I'm not exactly sure," Ophelia murmured, her gaze darting from one page to the next. "Not yet, anyway."

Jenny shook her head. "I don't see why you're so interested in my book all of a sudden. What are you looking for?"

"I don't know. I wonder . . ." Ophelia widened her eyes, and the thought simmering in the back of her mind blossomed into a full-fledged idea. A brilliant plot. One worthy of Shakespeare himself. She snapped the book shut and stared at her sister. "This is it!"

"What is it?" Jenny's voice rose in confusion.

"The answer to all our problems." Ophelia hugged the book to her chest and twirled around the room, laughing with sheer exhilaration. "Don't you see?"

"No." Jenny shook her head helplessly.

"Think about it, darling sister." Ophelia spun to a stop and held the book out before her. "Tell me the story," she demanded. " 'The Emperor's New Clothes.' What's it about?"

"You know what it's about," Jenny said cautiously.

"No!" Ophelia slapped the book's cover with a re-sounding smack. "*You* tell me."

"Well," Jenny said slowly, "first, there's an emperor who loves fine clothes."

"He wants the very best, doesn't he?"

Jenny nodded.

"Go on."

"All right." Jenny pulled her brows together thoughtfully. "Two tailors come to town claiming to have the most wonderful material in the world. Magnificent fabric, worthy of the emperor himself."

"But not everyone can see it, correct?" Ophelia prompted.

"Correct. Only people who were very clever and—what was it?" Jenny paused for a moment. "Oh, I remember, those who were worthy of their positions."

"And?" Ophelia said eagerly, waiting for Jenny to get to the point of the story.

"And . . ." Jenny shrugged. "No one did see it."

"Because?" Goodness, didn't this child see what was right in front of her?

"Because . . . it didn't really exist. Nobody would admit they couldn't see the cloth because they didn't want to look stupid. The tailors made the whole thing up to get money . . . or no, maybe it was jewels, from the emperor." Jenny's eyes widened, and she stared at her sister with realization. "Oh, no, Ophelia. You can't! You wouldn't!"

"I can and I will." Determination underlay Ophelia's words. "It's a marvelous scheme, a perfect plan."

"We'll go to jail," Jenny wailed.

"Nonsense." Ophelia flicked her hand in the air in a dismissive gesture. "We won't go to jail if we aren't caught. And I have no intention of getting caught.

Besides"—she tapped her fingers on the volume's cover—"there's only one real emperor around here."

"Big Jack Matthews?" Jenny collapsed onto the bed in a heap of disbelief. "But you said he was so nice."

"He is nice and obscenely rich to boot. That's why this will work so wonderfully well. Don't you understand?" Ophelia perched on the bed beside her sister. "First of all, nice people usually believe the best of others. That's why they're so easy to fool. Secondly, nice people who also have money tend not to be quite as upset about losing some of it as unpleasant people who have money or people who have no money at all."

"You're really going to dupe him out of his money?" Jenny cast her a look that fell somewhere between abject wonder and sheer horror.

Ophelia sighed. "How do you think I've been supporting us for the past six years?"

"You've always said you didn't cheat." Jenny glared.

"Well, I don't for the most part," Ophelia said sharply.

Jenny narrowed her eyes. "And do you steal?"

"Not generally," Ophelia hedged.

"Have you ever swindled anyone?"

"I've had my moments." Ophelia clenched her teeth. "But I suppose not in the strictest definition of the word, at least not in any significant way."

"So, right now, you—I mean we—haven't really done anything terribly illegal."

Ophelia thought for a moment. "Not terribly, no."

Jenny threw her sister a pleading look. "Then why start now?"

"Jenny." Ophelia struggled to remain patient. "We need to settle down. We need to have a real home. But that takes money, and we don't have any. This is the perfect opportunity to change our circumstances. A chance that may only come along once. I refuse to pass it up."

"But it's wrong!"

"Wrong is relative." Ophelia waved blithely. "It's not as if I was suggesting something exceptionally vile. For example, I would never steal from orphans."

"It's good to know you'll draw the line somewhere," Jenny snapped.

"I do have my standards." Ophelia's manner was lofty. "And if you look at this properly, we're orphans ourselves. I'm certain Big Jack wouldn't mind contributing to the health and well-being of orphans."

Hope glimmered in Jenny's eye. "Then why don't you just ask him for the money?"

"Jenny!" Ophelia gasped. "That would be charity." She shook her head. "I could never take money given as charity."

"No," Jenny groaned. "You'd rather steal it."

"It's much more fun that way." Ophelia grinned. "But I'm really not talking about actual thievery here. I shall have to work very hard. Why, it's almost a legitimate . . . job. You could even call it good, honest work."

"Work?" Jenny buried her face in her hands and groaned again. She peeked at her sister through her fingers. "Only your convoluted way of thinking would see swindling as a job."

"Thank you," Ophelia said modestly.

Jenny picked the book up off the bed where Ophelia had tossed it, stared for a long moment, then heaved a heavy sigh of resignation. "What exactly are you planning to do?"

Ophelia pulled her brows together in consideration. "I don't know yet." She rose to her feet and paced the room. "It seems to me there is a great deal of potential here, but I can't quite put my finger on it."

"Well, you can't very well try to sell them fabric that doesn't exist," Jenny said in a matter-of-fact manner. "Besides, I doubt in anyone in Dead End, Wyoming, is particularly interested in the latest fashion."

"No, not fashion," Ophelia said thoughtfully. What were these people interested in? The answer seemed to linger just out of reach. What was it Tyler Matthews had said tonight? "That's it." She clapped her hands together with delight.

"Wonderful." Jenny's voice carried all the enthusiasm of a doomed man's waiting his turn for the gallows. "What's it?"

"What the fair residents of Dead End . . . pardon me, I mean Empire City . . . want."

"And what do they want?" Jenny studied her sister with a wary eye.

"Civilization. Respectability. Sophistication!" Ophelia fairly crowed with delight.

"And you're going to try to sell them that?" Jenny raised a skeptical brow. "It's hard to believe anybody, outside of a fairy tale, would be that witless."

Ophelia smiled sweetly. "Don't forget, these are nice people."

Jenny shook her head in disgust. "Just what are you going to do?"

"I haven't the vaguest idea." Ophelia planted her hands on her hips and directed an irritated glare at the younger girl. "And I do wish you would stop asking me. I'll come up with a plan, and it shall be quite brilliant."

"Brilliant?" Jenny scoffed. "It had better be if you're going to sell this town respectability."

"Not me." Ophelia cast her a triumphant glance. "The Countess of Bilgewater."

"Bridgewater." Jenny sighed.

Ophelia barely heard her sister's correction. Far too many plots and schemes flew through her head to allow the acknowledgement of petty details. At any rate, it scarcely seemed to matter what she called herself. It was simply a role in a play that had now taken on the proportions of a command performance.

A command performance that could set the stage for the rest of their lives.

THE STARS SPILLED across the heavens and the blue-black Wyoming sky seemed to stretch forever, the serenity of the night disturbed only by the sounds of nature herself and the muffled, rhythmic clop of his horse's hooves on the hard-packed ground. It was a hell of a night to be alive.

Ever since Tye started back to his place, long after the party ended and way past the point when he thought the countess might yet return downstairs for a breath of fresh air or a late-night snack or to see if he was still around, an insane feeling of buoyant expectation clung to him. He couldn't stop grinning. He wanted to laugh out loud. He wished the evening would never end.

She was something, all right. Pretty, sharp-witted for the most part, with a subtle sense of absurdity that put a sparkle in her eyes and a smile in his. To top it off, she was rich and a widow. Not that he cared about the money, of course, even if it would make his life easier.

In spite of the encouraging looks he received from

his aunt whenever he went near the countess, he had no desire for a wife. He suspected that was next on his aunt's list of what she wanted for his life. It wasn't enough that he'd spent five long years getting what Lorelie referred to as "polish." She hadn't said anything yet, but the speculative look in her eye tonight told him what new, diabolical plan was simmering in that clever little brain of hers. Lorelie Matthews probably couldn't find her way home in the dark, but Tye had long ago learned that in many respects she was not nearly as light-headed as she usually appeared.

But this time, she'd lose. He didn't want a wife. Not now. Not ever. But a widow—his grin widened— that was another matter. Widows were women of the world, experienced and relaxed about the intimacies that naturally developed when mutual attraction was as strong as that between him and the countess. And he was confident, simply by the way her body seemed to fit so perfectly with his, that she was as attracted to him as he was to her.

Funny thing, though. He pulled his brows together with the unsettling thought. The blasted woman almost seemed to be avoiding him tonight. Maybe she was simply a lot more reserved, possible even shyer, than she looked.

"What do you think, Whiskey?"

The blood bay beneath him nickered her assent. Tye chuckled. He could always trust Whiskey to agree with him. After all, if a man couldn't depend on his horse, who could he count on?

Certainly not his closest friend. At least not where women were concerned. He'd seen the way Sedge had pursued the countess when he'd first spotted her, although, as the evening had progressed, the Englishman had seemed to ease up on his attention to her. Strange. It wasn't Sedge's usual technique.

"Maybe he's already given up." Tye patted Whiskey's neck absently. "Maybe he's conceding this one to me."

The mare whinnied, and Tye laughed. "You're right, old girl, Sedge would never admit defeat so easily. Not with a woman like this."

No, not with this woman. She was damn near irresistible, with hair a deep, dark red just a shade lighter than his horse and eyes the intense green of an exotic gem or rich, spring grass. And her voice. Lilting and lush and just a bit husky with an accent that melted something deep inside him. Hell, when it came to women, he loved a foreign accent. Especially when it fell from lips full and ripe and made to be kissed.

He noticed, though, that her inflection was somewhat different from Sedge's. Her pronunciation seemed much more precise than his friend's. In fact, it reminded Tye of the Shakespearean plays he'd enjoyed back East. Oh, well, it didn't much matter. Sedge and the countess apparently weren't from the same part of England, and the difference in their accents was no doubt due to that. There were probably regional speech differences in their country the same way there were in the United States.

Not that he really cared one way or another. Why, he didn't mind if the woman never opened her mouth again. Well, not to talk anyway. As much as he liked her voice, it was neither the only nor the most important thing about her that made his blood race and his temperature rise.

Even her name was taken straight from the plays

of the master. Ophelia. Of all the worthless subjects he was forced to study in college, Shakespeare was damn near the only thing he actually liked. He'd even brought home a collection of the Bard's works, which now sat proudly on a shelf in his parlor. Maybe he'd dust them off when he got home and refresh his memory. Who knows? A few classic phrases just might help in his campaign to win her fancy.

It had been a long time since a woman had triggered this kind of desire. He shifted uncomfortably on the saddle at the very thought. He wanted this woman and wanted her bad. Maybe it was just that she was the first female he'd met since he'd returned home that seemed worth the trouble. Maybe it was just the challenge of another friendly contest with Sedge to win squatting rights to one more female. Or maybe it had just been too damn long since he'd had a beautiful woman in his bed.

Again a wide grin stretched his face. She'd warm his bed, and soon. He'd lost to Sedge before, but he liked to believe his friend had only come out on top in those cases where Tye hadn't tried quite hard enough. There would be no defeat this time. The Countess of Bridgewater—Ophelia—would be his for as long as he wanted her. After that? Tye shrugged to himself; that was one of the beauties of wooing widows, especially rich ones. Rarely were they looking for a lifetime commitment.

He chuckled aloud. "Women of the world, Whiskey." The bay pricked up her ears. "There's nothing like 'em."

He'd be on hand tomorrow, when Jack promised to show her around the ranch. And tomorrow night, for the dinner that was planned. And every day and every night for as long as it took to win the favors of the lovely lady. Even with Sedge doing his level best to distract her, Tye didn't doubt his own success. There wasn't any question about it.

In no time at all, the fair Ophelia would be his.

Chapter 4

OPHELIA stepped onto the broad veranda of the Matthews family home and breathed a sigh of relief. A shining dark green surrey sat just a few feet from the front steps. The dainty two-seater was perfect. Thank goodness she was not expected to tour the ranch on horseback. Not that she could, of course. While her sister knew she couldn't ride, even Jenny didn't suspect Ophelia's abiding dislike of horses. The very thought of being forced to sit on one of those huge, nasty, brutish creatures sent a cascade of shudders through her. Even facing the backside of a horse from the vantage point of a carriage was preferable to being forced to balance precariously on one.

That would not be a problem today. Ophelia nodded with satisfaction, opened her parasol and stepped lightly down the stairs, scanning the grounds for Big Jack. He said he'd meet her out here, but right now he was nowhere to be seen. No matter. She could use a few quiet moments to enjoy what promised to be a delightful day.

She closed her eyes, pulled her hat off and tilted her head toward the morning sun. Warmth kissed her face like a well-loved friend, and she welcomed the restorative rays seeping into her flesh and into her soul. It was terribly unfashionable, but she did so adore the touch of the sun on her skin. With it she was alive and vital and strong, as if she could conquer the whole world. Or just a tiny part of it. She smiled. This tiny part of it preferably. Soon she would have Big Jack and the residents of Dead End in the palm of her hand, ready and willing to give her what she needed in life. If she could only figure out exactly how. . . .

"Countess?"

Ophelia's eyes snapped open at the familiar voice, and her stomach knotted. She slapped her hat back on her head, hoping her cool tone hid the irritation surging through her. "Mr.—or rather, Mayor—Matthews."

"Ma'am." Matthews touched the brim of his hat in what passed for a greeting and smiled down at her from his perch on a massive red horse. Goodness, he certainly was attractive. "My uncle said he was showing you around today."

"That's correct," she said, her manner crisp and no-nonsense. Maybe, if she was cold enough to him, the damned man would simply go away. "He should be here any minute now."

Matthews chuckled. "Probably got sidetracked. That happens a lot. Jack gets awfully busy around here."

"Perhaps I should go inside and see how long he's been delayed." Ophelia nodded sharply in dismissal, turned and stepped up the stairs, eager to escape from the scrutiny of eyes that seemed even darker in the light of day than at night.

"What's your hurry, Countess?" The drawled words shivered through her blood and she stopped short.

There was a challenge in his tone that she couldn't ignore. Even if she wanted to.

She turned slowly back to him. A teasing smile played about his lips, and there was a gleam in his eye. She'd seen that gleam before, always in the eyes of men who didn't seem to realize that just because a girl knew how to play a good hand of poker, it didn't mean she was willing to indulge in other games as well—games with stakes far higher than she'd ever cared to risk. Her spine stiffened, and she stared with as regal an attitude as she could muster.

"You're quite mistaken, Mayor. I am in no particular hurry whatsoever." She lifted a shoulder in a casual shrug. "I would assume, however, that the myriad responsibilities of your office would demand your attention elsewhere."

He raised an amused brow. "But, Countess, you *are* one of my responsibilities. Duty demands I help escort you around the ranch."

"That scarcely seems necessary." She forced a light-hearted note. "I'm quite certain your uncle is more than capable of showing me the sights. So you see, your presence is really not needed at all." She cast him a condescending smile. "Surely, the mayor of a community such as yours would have more pressing demands upon his time than playing the part of . . . tour guide."

His grin didn't waver, but a speculative glint appeared in his eye. Good. She'd rather have him curious than lecherous. His suspicion she could handle. His lust she wasn't quite sure about.

"Well, Countess . . ." He pulled his hat off thoughtfully and slapped it against a firm, muscular thigh. A cloud of dust puffed outward, and she resisted the impulse to sneeze. "When I was on the Continent—"

"Europe?" Her voice jumped with astonishment.

"Um—hum. That's the continent in question." He replaced his hat. "I've surprised you again, haven't I?"

"Oh, no." Her words came out in a rush. "I've always considered Europe to be the Continent too."

Confusion crossed his face, and the tension within her eased slightly. She'd been right last night. The best way to keep this man off guard was to keep him as confused as possible. And the surest method to accomplish that was to imitate the scatterbrained charm of his aunt. She smiled innocently. "You were saying?"

"I was, wasn't I?" He shook his head and cast her a bemused smile that twisted something deep inside her. "Oh, yeah, I was talking about the tour guides. You could spot them a mile off, leading tourists around like a herd of stupid, confused woollies." He chuckled. "Funniest thing I ever saw, especially amidst the ruins in Rome and Pompeii. Don't you agree?"

She laughed lightly. She'd never seen a tour guide in her life. "Oh, indeed. It does seem quite ludicrous at times."

"I guess it's all part of the experience." He shook his head in amused disbelief. "My aunt and uncle insisted on my taking the grand tour. Lorelie said it would be broadening."

"Travel is extremely broadening," Ophelia said in a superior manner, as if she knew what she was talking about. She had indeed traveled her entire life, but only from one theater to another. Her father had been gradually working his way to California when he'd died, and he used to talk about getting to Europe one day. Ophelia hadn't even seen the big cities of the East since she was very young, and she'd never been outside America.

"I imagine people in your kind of social circle do a great deal of traveling."

"Constantly." She sighed as if the topic was too mundane to dwell on, but her mind raced. What the hell did she know about traveling as a countess? When it came right down to it, what did she know about traveling with money in her pocket?

"I have to admit, in spite of my initial reluctance, I rather enjoyed the sights of Europe." He cast her a wry smile.

"Well." She laughed lightly. "Who doesn't?"

He shifted on his horse as if he was settling in for a long dissertation on the joys of Old World tourism. Just what she needed. Unless it was the setting of a play, she knew nothing about Europe. And she hated a production without a script.

"I did enjoy Paris," he said thoughtfully. "Although the French do seem to look down their noses at anyone who isn't French."

Gad, what had happened to the aw shucks, home-on-the-range quality of his voice? All of a sudden he sounded exactly like a well-bred, distinguished gentleman. What happened to the cowboy-mayor? Who was the better actor here: he or she?

"That is always so disagreeable," she said quickly, hoping she was right.

"I suppose you can't blame them, though. Paris is really something."

"Without question." Paris? She searched her mind frantically. Did Shakespeare ever set anything in Paris?

"It's probably old hat for you." He gazed at her curiously. "I imagine you've visited a great many cities just as impressive. Where have you traveled?"

"Oh, here and there." St. Louis, Chicago, Kansas

City. She waved an airy hand. "Around and about. You understand."

He nodded. "Did your husband like to travel as well?"

"My husband?" Who?

He pulled his brows together in a questioning frown. "Your husband? The count?"

Oh, that husband. "My, yes. Dear, dear, dead Albert. He did so enjoy traveling. And he always did like Paris best."

"I think I enjoyed Italy the most," Matthews said. "Do you like Rome?"

Rome? The setting for *Julius Caesar*? "Indeed." She nodded enthusiastically. "The city of the Caesars. It's quite fascinating."

"But Venice was probably my favorite city."

The Merchant of Venice. "Venice is lovely."

"What did you like best?"

"Best?" She racked her brain. "All that glisters is not gold." Great, that one line she could remember. Was there anything in the damned play about the city itself? Absolutely nothing came to mind. She shrugged in a vague gesture. "It's so terribly difficult to pinpoint one particular thing. It's simply an amazing place. What did you like best?"

"The way the city's built on water probably. It's a fascinating feat of engineering."

"Fascinating," she echoed.

"But I think it was the light in Venice that I remember most."

"The light?" What in the hell was he talking about?

"The sunlight. It's different there somehow. It seems almost golden. I believe that's why it's so popular with artists." His gaze pinned hers. "And lovers."

"Lovers?" Even to her own ears, her voice sounded higher than normal.

He nodded. "The light casts something of a magical glow on everything. It serves not merely to illuminate; it almost seems to caress each person it touches."

The intensity in his voice seemed to caress as well. She swallowed hard. "It does?"

"Um-hum." His position on his horse and her spot on the porch put them at eye level. It was a dangerous place to be. She couldn't pull away from the smoldering depths of his gaze. His eyes seemed to draw her inward, and without thinking she stepped closer. "And it's not just by day. Surely you remember the moonlight in Venice?"

"The moonlight?" Her voice was breathless. "Oh . . . my . . . yes."

"The moonlight casts a spell all its own." His voice was as seductive as his eyes, and again she stepped toward him until he was but a few inches away. At once all she wanted was to lose herself in that voice, drown in those eyes, feel the pressure of his lips on hers.

"A spell." She sighed.

"The moonlight in Venice was made for love." He leaned forward, and she wondered if he meant to kiss her.

She'd been kissed before, of course. Grabbed and forced to endure the sloppy smacks of men who had believed she could have been had with a fine phrase. They'd always paid for it. Usually a slap across the face had made her point. Now and then she'd had to brandish the derringer she usually kept conveniently secreted on her person. And occasionally she'd had to resort to a knee planted swiftly in that most vulnerable spot of male pride and lust. But she'd never, ever returned their desire. Had never, ever particularly wanted to be kissed.

Never, ever. Until now.

"Was it, do you think?" she said softly, drawing closer to him. So close the hot, heady scent of bay rum and man drifted around her. "Made for lovers?"

"I'm certain of it." He leaned forward precariously, tipped her chin up with two strong, tan fingers and stared into her eyes. Her breath caught at the blatant desire she saw there and her own shocking yearning. For the first time in her life she wanted what she knew this man was about to offer. He was so close she could feel the warmth of his breath on her face. "And Venice is lovely this time of year."

"Lovely," she whispered. Gad, he was going to kiss her. And Lord help her, she was going to kiss him back.

His lips brushed against hers lightly, and she gasped at the shock of sensation that rushed through her. Maybe it was her sharp intake of breath. Maybe his balance in the saddle was off. Or maybe his horse didn't like her any more than she liked it.

Abruptly, the beast emitted one of those revolting animal noises that sounded like a cross between a snort and a snicker. She jumped back and glared at the animal.

"Hell and damnation," she snapped.

"What?" Matthews's eyes widened with surprise.

"Oh, dear! I mean . . . um . . ." What did she mean? "Bloody hell."

The creature responded with that nasty noise again. It was definitely a snicker. The beast was snickering at her.

Matthews laughed and slid from his saddle. In two

steps he was beside her on the porch, pulling her into his arms. "Now, where were we before Whiskey decided to put her two cents in?"

She stared at him, and for a brief moment she wanted to give in to the still lingering desire that had been so very tempting. But the satisfied look on his handsome face triggered a swift return of her senses. Where were they? Why, she was about to sacrifice herself to this far too confident, far too fast-talking charmer of a cowboy.

She pushed against him roughly and stepped away. "You presume too much, Mayor."

"Do I?" The smug smile remained firmly in place. Matthews crossed his arms and leaned against the porch rail. "You didn't seem to mind a moment ago."

"I was merely being . . . polite."

"Polite?" He scoffed. "If that's what you call polite, I'd love to see you being downright friendly."

"Mr. Matthews!"

"It seems to me we were simply having a pleasant conversation about Venice . . . and moonlight."

"Yes, well." She struggled to regain her composure. "We are not in Venice, and it's broad daylight. There's no moonlight whatsoever."

"You're right about that." A slow, easy smile spread across his face, and a wicked twinkle danced in his eye. "But next to Venice, Wyoming moonlight is a close second. The moon here is so big you can practically reach out and touch it. I'd expect artists would appreciate it here, and lovers."

"Well," she said haughtily, adjusting her parasol. "I have no intention of finding out. I am not of an artistic nature."

"I said . . ." His voice was low and seductive. "Artists would appreciate it and—"

"Don't say it again!" Annoyance surged through her. "Do your duties as mayor also include seducing female visitors?"

He shrugged idly. "I don't know. I'm new at this mayor stuff." He tossed her a challenging grin. "But I'm certainly willing to find out."

"Mr. Matthews!" Gad, this man was infuriating. Her hand itched to slap the self-satisfied expression off his face. Better yet, she could shoot him. What an excellent idea! Now, where did she leave her gun?

"Countess. Tye." Big Jack strode out the door and approached the couple. He nodded at his nephew. "Glad to see you could make it today."

"I wouldn't miss it for the world," Matthews said casually.

"I hope you and the countess here have been getting along without me." Jack turned to Ophelia. "Has he been filling you in on our little corner of the world?"

"He's been filling me in, all right," she said in a deceptively mild manner. "Mostly on the duties of being mayor. They're far more involved than I suspected."

Matthews grinned. "It seems the countess and I share a lot in common."

"Not exactly," she said under her breath.

"Oh?" Jack raised a bushy brow. "What do you two have in common?"

"Travel and the like," Ophelia said, forcing a pleasant smile.

Matthews nodded. "Yep. We were just discussing the relative merits and the attraction of cities like Venice for artists and—"

"Tourists," she said quickly.

Matthews grinned. "Tourists."

"I knew it." Jack slapped his nephew on the back in

a good-natured, if forceful, gesture. "I knew sending you back East and on to Europe was a good idea. See what the rest of the world is like. Give you . . . what is it your aunt calls it?"

"Polish?" Ophelia said innocently.

Matthews laughed. "I've been polished, all right." His words were directed at his uncle, but his gaze remained fixed on her. "I just never thought it would do me any good. Until now."

"One never knows when experiences in life will come in handy," she said loftily. "Still, it's probably best to note that even with the thickest coat of polish, some things can't be disguised."

"Or denied," he said with a look that would have melted her knees if given half a chance.

Jack's considering gaze darted from Ophelia to his nephew and back, and he smiled, as if he was all too aware of the undercurrents in the conversation. "Now, Tye, your aunt was right on that score. I'd bet she's right on others as well."

Abruptly, Matthews's smug expression took on a shade of warning. "That's a bet I wouldn't make, Jack."

"You never know," Jack said thoughtfully. "You just never know."

Obviously, there was more than one topic up for grabs here. Ophelia had no idea what it was and couldn't care less. All she wanted right now was to put a fair amount of distance between herself and Tyler Matthews.

She turned to Jack. "Mr. Matthews? Perhaps we should be on our way."

"Of course, darlin'." Jack offered her his arm, and she took it gratefully. "But I've got to tell you. We're not real big on formality out here. And since I think we're all going to be great friends, I'd be pleased if you'd call me Jack."

"I'd love to," she said. Relief surged through her. It wasn't easy responding to "Countess" all the time. Staying in character constantly was proving to be much more difficult than she'd expected. Answering to her own name would eliminate at least one possibility for error. Still, a real countess no doubt wouldn't offer to drop her title. But even a real countess would be gracious enough to accede to local etiquette or lack of it. At least, her version of a countess would. "And you're absolutely right. We will be friends, and you must call me Ophelia."

"Ophelia it is, then." Jack grinned and led her down the steps to the carriage, his nephew trailing in their wake.

"Ophelia," Matthews said reflectively. "It's an unusual name, isn't it?"

"Not at all." She turned toward him. "It's from Shakespeare. My father was a Shakespearean act—scholar. He studied the Bard most of his life. He named me Ophelia."

"*Hamlet*?" Matthews said.

"That's right." Surprise colored her voice. Lord, was there anything this man didn't know?

Matthews smiled with satisfaction. "It seems I just keep amazing you."

"Amazing is the word all right," she muttered.

Again Jack looked at the couple with a speculative eye. What was the man thinking? He helped her into the carriage and strode around the vehicle to the other side. Matthews was there before him.

"You go ahead and ride, Jack," Matthews said, leaping into the surrey and taking up the reins. "I know how much you hate this rig."

Jack tossed him a relieved grin. "Thanks, Tye." He nodded toward Ophelia. "Lorelie talked me into buying this fancy little toy. It's pretty, all right, but it's damn near worthless for anything beyond a social call." He shook his head with the tolerant exasperation of a man long married who still cherishes his wife. "She thought it was high time we brought some of the trappings of city living out here. Make life a little more civilized."

"I see," Ophelia said thoughtfully. There it was again. The desire for civilization. "It is quite a respectable, sophisticated vehicle."

"What it is is a waste of money," Jack snorted. "But if it's what Lorelie wants . . ." He shrugged, as if further explanation wasn't necessary. "If you'll excuse me, Ophelia, I'll get my horse and be back in a minute." Jack turned and strode off toward the stables.

"Are you ready . . . Ophelia?"

Startled, she turned to find Matthews's smiling face a scant few inches away. She'd been so busy concentrating on Jack's comments that she'd barely noticed the younger man settling in beside her.

"Ophelia?" He said her name as if it was an intimate suggestion or a wicked promise. His hip was snugly fit to hers, his leg touching her own. Heat seemed to generate between them, penetrating her clothes and bringing the insane desire to press closer. Or run.

She stiffened and glared. "Would it be possible for you to move over, Mr. Matthews?"

"Tye," he said firmly and shook his head in an obviously feigned display of remorse. "Nope. Can't do it. This carriage is just too tiny. There's nowhere to go."

She narrowed her eyes. "I'm certain we can think of somewhere you could go."

Laughter glittered in his chocolate eyes. "Where?"

She pulled a deep, steadying breath. He was impossible. The desire to shoot him grew stronger. He had no idea how lucky he was she wasn't armed.

Jack rode up on an enormous, gold-colored horse with a white mane and tail. It would have been an extremely pretty animal if it hadn't been a horse. The beast would have made an absolutely charming dog, or even better, a rug. "If you two are ready, we'll head off. I thought we'd head south a ways, to the back range."

Tye snapped the reins, and the black creature pulling their carriage started off with an easy gait. Jack rode beside them, keeping up a steady stream of commentary about the country and the cattle and Lord only knew what else. Every now and then she'd nod or smile or emit an occasional "you don't say" or "how interesting" or "I never would have suspected," but for the most part her mind wandered, returning again and again to the annoying presence of the man beside her.

She shifted uncomfortably on the seat in a futile effort to put a modicum of distance between them. Tye glanced at her, grinned and settled even closer than before, if closer was even remotely possible. Her hand tightened on the handle of her parasol and she clenched her teeth. Had there ever been a more irritating man in the history of the world?

She stared at his strong, handsome profile. No. She was wrong. He wasn't attractive at all. Why, his nose was too aristocratic, his jaw too firmly chiseled, his eyes too darkly mysterious and those dimples—well, she shrugged to herself and turned away. Add to that the man's impressive height, the hard, powerful body she couldn't help noticing when he'd taken her in his arms and the revolting way he seemed to put out heat like a furnace, and what did you come up with? Nothing. Absolutely nothing. Why, she'd known dozens of actors, maybe even hundreds, who had been far more handsome than he.

No, he wasn't at all attractive, and she was not at all attracted. She nodded firmly. "All's well that ends well."

"What?" Tye cocked a questioning brow. "Did you say something?"

Had she said something? She cast him an innocent smile. "No, nothing at all."

"Funny, I thought I heard—"

"Mr. Matthews." She gazed at him innocently. "I believe your uncle is trying to explain a pertinent detail." She pointed at Jack, who rambled on without apparent notice that his audience was paying no notice whatsoever.

"Tye," he said, his voice heavy with some unstated meaning. "You're supposed to call me Tye."

"Yes, of course. At any rate, *Tye*"—she fairly spit the word—"I think we should be listening to your uncle."

"Why?" Insolence colored his tone. "You haven't paid any attention up to now."

"I most certainly have," she said with indignation. She glanced at Jack, who continued his stream of commentary without pause.

"Nope." Tye shook his head. "You certainly have not."

Sarcasm dripped from her words. "And exactly what have I been doing?"

"You've been thinking about our kiss," he said softly.

"What kiss?" she hissed in a quiet tone. "We didn't kiss."

"I know. And that's exactly what you've been thinking about." His smug smile was back. What she wouldn't give right now for her gun. No. Shooting was too good for him. She'd rather torture him. Yeah, that was it. Stake him out in the burning sun and force him to listen to Shakespearean tragedies performed by incredibly bad actors over and over again until even death began to look good and his—

"So what do you think, Ophelia?" Jack waved at the vista confronting them, and her mind jerked back to reality.

They were on a slight rise. The land stretched before them endlessly, dotted here and there with herds of cattle that looked like children's playthings in the distance. Far off, mountains reached heavenward under skies so blue it took her breath away.

"It is beautiful, Jack," she said with a quiet reverence that fit their surroundings.

Jack nodded with satisfaction and tipped his hat back on his head. "This is why I don't understand all the talk in town, and from Lorelie, about respectability and civilization. To me, this is perfection." He gestured at the panoramic view. "This is paradise. I own every acre, every foot of it. Once, it was nobody's. Now, men like me put it to good use. Raising cattle, feeding the rest of the country. It doesn't have all the trappings of a city, but it's perfect nonetheless. And civilized enough for me."

Tye gazed at the scene before them. "You're right, Jack. Land, and the use of it, really is what sets us apart from other creatures on this earth."

Jack chuckled. "I bet you've never seen anything quite like this."

"No." Ophelia drank in the beauty of the scene. "Never."

"It's true everywhere, I'd imagine. The taming of the land is man's way of civilizing the earth. What could be more civilized, and respectable even, than using the land the way God intended it." Jack glanced at her. "Of course, we're fairly new at it here. In your country, the land's been tamed for a long time."

"Oh my, yes." What did she know about land in England?

"Sedge says for centuries the worth of a man and his title depended on his ownership of land," Tye said.

"Indeed." She nodded. "Alford used to say that all the time."

"Alford?" Tye raised a brow.

"My husband," she said with a touch of hauteur. Confusion washed across his face, and she hurried to continue. "Alford firmly felt it was the estate that kept him and his title from becoming a mere shadow of what the nobility once was."

"It's that title business that makes the difference between your county and mine. Why, I've got enough property here for my own country." Jack released a long-suffering sigh of disbelief. "But my darlin' Lorelie still doesn't think it's good enough. Why, if titles came along with land here in Wyoming the way they do in England, she'd be as happy as a cow in clover."

"Titles are terribly civilized." Ophelia gazed at the land, and the group fell into a companionable silence.

Titles are terribly civilized.

What kind of an idiot was she? Had she taken leave of her senses altogether? This was it! This was the answer she'd been searching for! How could she have missed it before now? It was so obvious.

"It is so awfully sad, though." She heaved a heartfelt sigh.

"What is?" Tye said.

"Oh, dear." She sighed again. "One does so hate to inflict one's problems on others."

"What is it, darlin'?" Jack threw her a sympathetic gaze. Goodness, the man really was nice.

"Well." She started to sigh again, then checked herself. It would not do to be overly dramatic. "Times are extremely trying in England right now for the old families. What with taxes and . . . other difficulties. Especially for a widow. Alone."

"What other difficulties?" Tye said.

Jack slanted him a quelling glance, then returned his attention to Ophelia. "Go on."

"I fear the time has come . . . oh, my, I'm not sure how to say this." She gazed down at her lap as if composing herself, then stared at Jack bravely. "This trip is my last fling, so to speak. I have a certain measure of funds in trust, but they are minimal. I fear, when I return home, I shall be forced to sell my land, and the title that goes with it." A tiny tear trickled out of the corner of her eye, and she sniffed delicately. Gad, she was good.

Silently, Tye handed her a handkerchief, and she nodded her thanks.

"Lordy, that's a shame." Jack shook his head. "I hate to see anybody lose their land."

"It's a shame, all right." Tye studied her with an uncomfortable intensity and she ignored him.

"But what can I do?" She fluttered her free hand. "I must sell if only to get the financing I need to survive. I have no other choice." Ophelia shook her head mournfully. "If only I knew the man I sold it to was of good, honest stock. A man worthy of the ancient, extremely respectable and highly civilized title of Count of Brick-water."

Tye frowned in confusion. "I thought it was Bridge-water?"

Damn. She nodded. "Of course."

He shook his head in a puzzled gesture. "Didn't you just say Brickwater?"

"Surely not, but"—she sniffed again and dabbed at her eyes—"I might have. This whole topic is so dread-fully upsetting to even think about. I tend to get ter-ribly, terribly confused. Why, sometimes I forget my own name."

"There, there, darlin'." Jack gazed at her with the lost expression of a man who is helpless in the face of a woman's tears. "I'm sure everything will work out."

"Nothing will work out. It's hopeless." She covered her face with the handkerchief and sobbed.

For a long moment her weeping was the only sound. Silence from the two men stretched on until she won-dered how many more tears she could squeeze out. Honestly, how long would it take Jack to recognize the answer to her alleged dilemma and his own?

"Ophelia?" Jack's voice broke through her sobs.

"Yes?" She gazed at him with all the pathos in her arsenal.

"Would you consider selling . . ." Jack paused as if considering his words. "To an American?"

Triumph speared through her, and it was all she could do to keep it from showing on her face.

"What American?" she said, as if she didn't already know the answer.

A grin spread across Jack's face. "Me."

"Jack!" Shock rang in Tye's voice.

"You!" Ophelia gasped. "Why, I couldn't possibly."

Tye heaved a sigh of relief. "Damn right."

Jack threw him a stern look. "Keep out of this, Tye. I'm serious, Ophelia. I'd like the chance to buy your property."

"You are a dear, dear man, but I can't imagine an American as the next count." Ophelia shook her head. "Why, the scandal alone would be extraordinary."

Jack set his lips in a firm line, the sure sign of a man who had his mind made up. "Think about it, Ophelia. I'd pay you a good price."

"Jack, this is the stupidest thing I've ever heard." Disbelief sounded in Tye's voice. "You can't be serious. Why would you even consider leaving Wyoming for England?"

"What makes you think I'd leave?" Jack gazed at his nephew as if he had taken leave of his senses.

"Wouldn't you?" Confusion once more colored Tye's face, and Ophelia smiled to herself. She did so love it when this arrogant male didn't know what was going on.

"Of course not." Jack laughed. "I'd get one of them English lawyers and a good manager to handle things for me. Lorelie and I would go over maybe once a year." He leaned toward Ophelia. "She's never been abroad, and I've always promised to take her. And she'd be going as a countess." He pulled his brows together. "She would be a countess, wouldn't she?"

Ophelia nodded. "Naturally."

Jack grinned his satisfaction. "She'd have all the respectability and civilization any one woman could handle, and I'd hardly have to do much of anything except part with a bit of money."

"I don't know, Jack." She stared at him helplessly. "I'm not sure what to say. Or what to think, for that matter."

"I think it's ridiculous," Tye snapped.

"Why?" She gazed at him, wide-eyed.

He clenched his teeth. "It just is, that's all."

"I think it's a great idea," Jack said with enthusiasm. "So, Ophelia, what do you say?"

"It's a very big decision. I'm really not . . ." She shrugged and gazed around as if the answer could be found somewhere out there in the Wyoming countryside. Abruptly, she squared her shoulders and stared Jack straight in the eye. "Very well. I'll sell."

"I'll be damned." Jack shook his head and laughed. "I'm going to be an English count."

"More like a Wyoming jackass," Tye muttered.

Ophelia turned to Tye and smiled sweetly, her voice meant for him alone. "One could say it's better to be a Wyoming jackass"—she dropped his sodden handkerchief in his lap—"than a lover in Venice. At least the animal doesn't have to depend on the fickle whims of moonlight to get what he wants."

Tye stared as if he couldn't quite believe her words. Lovely self-satisfaction flooded her. Then a wicked smile quirked the corners of his lips and her heart sank. What was he up to now?

"I've never considered moonlight fickle." His eyes simmered with a challenge or a threat or a promise, and she shivered with unwanted anticipation. "And I always get what I want."

She drew a deep breath and matched his gaze with hers. "I shouldn't wager the ranch on it if I were you. Not this time."

He laughed, and she tossed her head and turned to

Jack. This was going far too well to waste time worrying about Tye Matthews. Besides, once she and Jack set a price for her imaginary title and estate and she collected the money, she and Jenny would get out of Dead End so fast Tye wouldn't know what happened. Then she could firmly put behind her all his talk about lovers and moonlight and the crazy idea that she actually wanted to kiss him. She sighed to herself.

She might have to shoot him after all.

TYE IGNORED MUCH of the conversation between Ophelia and Jack on the drive back to the house. He had far too much to think about to pay attention to their enthusiastic discussions. He had a bad feeling about this. A real bad feeling.

He couldn't quite put his finger on it. Yet. But something was wrong. It wasn't simply Jack's determination to buy Ophelia's land and title, although the idea was probably one of the most asinine things he'd ever heard.

It wasn't Ophelia's denial of their mutual attraction. Hell, she was only a woman and couldn't be expected to know her own mind. Even with her reluctance this morning, his confidence hadn't wavered as to his eventual conquest. She'd be in his bed before she knew it. And she'd love every minute of it.

He shook his head as if to jar odd, unsettling pieces of an unfamiliar puzzle into some kind of rational order. The answer seemed to beckon just beyond his reach. But his bad feeling was never wrong. And this was the strongest it had ever been.

Abruptly, one tiny piece snapped into place. He threw her a quick glance, then stared straight ahead. Lord, she was lovely. He was certain the body hidden beneath that prim yellow dress was made for loving. And he'd already had a tempting glimpse of the passionate nature simmering just beneath that cool, English exterior.

Could it be that her mind was really as convoluted as his aunt's? Or could there be another reason altogether? He clenched his jaw and thought long and hard. Did it mean anything at all? Or did it mean everything?

What the hell was her dead husband's name, anyway?

Chapter 5

Jenny sighed with disgust and threw the riding habit on the bed. If she had to sew one more stitch, she'd go stark, raving mad. Besides, it wasn't fair, none of it. Ophelia was out having a good time touring the countryside with Big Jack while Jenny was stuck here, ordered to stay in their rooms, no less, and forced to do menial, slave labor. All right, she conceded to herself, maybe it wasn't exactly slave labor, but the effect was the same nonetheless.

She glanced around Ophelia's room and sighed again. Jenny had already finished altering the riding habit and had two more dresses to tackle, one for herself. She'd give her sister that much: at least Ophelia was sharing some of the countess's clothes. And she had to admit there were probably a lot worse things one could be doing than stitching on the kind of luxurious fabrics with their fine workmanship that comprised the countess's wardrobe. Even if she was bored to tears.

She pulled herself to her feet, folded her arms over her chest and glared at the innocent habit. There was no reason in the world why Ophelia got to be the countess and Jenny was stuck with the part of the maid. Certainly her sister was older and far more experienced with clever deceptions than she, but Jenny considered herself every bit the expert actress her sister was.

Impulsively, she gathered up the habit and stepped to a full-length mirror on an oak stand. She held the dress up before her and stared at the image. See? She glared at the Jenny facing her. She'd be just as good a countess, maybe even better. Of course, she couldn't ride any more than her sister could. She didn't know the first thing about socializing. And she had absolutely no experience with men. It seemed Ophelia was determined to keep her away from those interesting creatures. Jenny heaved another sigh. She might consider herself as good an actress as Ophelia, but she wasn't nearly as expert an out-and-out liar as her sister. She tossed the garment back on the bed. Maybe Ophelia was the best choice for this role after all.

Still, surely even maids had a bit of freedom once in a while. She grinned at the girl in the mirror. Ophelia wouldn't be back for hours. It would be a simple matter to slip out and explore this impressive house. Maybe even get outdoors and look around. What would be the harm in that? The reflected Jenny smiled in innocent agreement. Why, no harm at all.

Jenny's glance fell on a breakfast tray that had been left outside her door this morning. What a perfect excuse to go down to the kitchen. Besides, returning the breakfast dishes would be the polite thing to do, as well as what would be expected of a maid. Doing it herself would give her the opportunity to thank the cook in person. Jenny picked up the tray with one hand, pulled open the door with the other and stepped into the hall. She ignored the tiny twinge of guilt at disobeying her sister's specific orders to stay in her room, but Ophelia had to learn she could be trusted. After all, she was nearly seventeen, practically a grown woman.

Jenny tossed her long hair over her shoulder and strode down the corridor to a back stairway she had noted on their arrival. She stepped lightly down the darkened stairwell until it opened up into a sunlight-filled kitchen. Jenny blinked at the brightness and hesitated in the doorway.

"Come on in, child." A cheery, buxom, silver-haired woman bustled up and took the tray from her hands. "Sit right down over here and let me have a look at you."

Jenny stepped to a big wooden table and plunked down in the first available chair. The older woman placed the tray on a sideboard and gave her a welcoming grin.

"Well, just look at you. You are a pretty little thing." The woman's gray eyes studied her with an intensity that would have made Jenny uncomfortable had it not been for the warmth radiating from them. "You must be the countess's maid."

"My name's Jenny." She returned the friendly smile.

"I'm Alma." The woman's voice was as robust as she was. "I'm the cook, housekeeper and just about everything else around here."

"Really," Jenny said in surprise. "I would think a house this big would need a whole staff of servants."

"I am a whole staff." Alma laughed, a big, booming sound that echoed in the room. "We have girls from town who come in now and then when needed, but it's just Mr. Jack and Miz Lorelie here, and they're pretty easy to take care of. It's not like there's a whole house full of folks." A shadow passed over the housekeeper's face so swiftly that Jenny thought she must be mistaken. "Course, with you and the countess staying here now, and all the entertaining that's planned, I'll be getting some help in this afternoon, but right now it's just me."

She cocked a curious brow. "I hear you're what they call a 'lady's maid'?"

"Yes, indeed," Jenny said with barely disguised regret that lingered in her words. She should have been the countess. "That's me, all right."

Alma studied her. "How come you don't have one of those fancy accents like that employer of yours or Mr. Sedge?"

"Who's Mr. Sedge?"

"Mr. Sedge is from England too and a good friend of Mr. Tye's—Mr. Jack's and Miz Lorelie's nephew. Tye grew up right here in this house after his folks died. They treat him just like a son. He took the place of their own baby."

"Oh, I'm so sorry." Sympathy washed through Jenny. "Their child died?"

Alma's voice was grim. "They lost her when she was two years old." The shadow Jenny had noticed before flickered once again. Alma shook her head slightly as if to throw off sorrowful memories and her smile returned. "But enough of that. You didn't answer my question."

"Oh, about accents?" Jenny groaned to herself. Why hadn't she thought about that before she'd come downstairs? Her mind struggled to come up with a reasonable explanation. "I . . . um . . . I'm not from England, originally," she said with relief.

"Where are you from, then?" Amusement twinkled in Alma's eyes. "Originally."

"Oh, here and there."

A frown creased Alma's forehead. "Where are your parents from?"

"Parents?" Jenny shook her head. A half-truth was better than nothing at all. "I don't have parents." She thought for a moment. "They died. Quite tragically, when I was very young."

"So you're an orphan." Alma nodded, as if she'd expected such an answer, and clucked in sympathy. "That's a shame."

"Isn't that the truth," Jenny said mournfully, hiding her satisfaction at how well her charade was going. She was just as good an actress as Ophelia, and nearly as good a liar. And she could prove it too. "I was raised in an orphanage, but when they tried to send me to the sweatshop, I ran away." Jenny cast Alma a heartfelt glance. "Now I have to make my own way in the world any way I can. I'm all alone. It's so hard sometimes."

"So how'd you hook up with the countess?"

"How?" How indeed? She groped for an answer. "Well, I can sew . . . and I found work with a seamstress . . . and met up with the countess and . . . her maid . . . um . . . died and she hired me." She finished with a sense of relief and a fair amount of pleasure. Maybe she was as good a liar as her sister, after all. And just maybe she was better.

"Does that woman treat you all right?" Suspicion underlay Alma's words.

Goodness, she'd probably given this nice lady the idea Ophelia was some kind of maid-killing ogre. And in fact, she could be quite beastly at times, even while claiming it was all with Jenny's interests at heart. Still, Jenny never doubted that Ophelia did the best she could for both of them. Jenny nodded. "She's really very nice."

"Good." Alma beamed. "Now, I just finished baking some nice fresh apple pies. How would you like a piece?"

Jenny's stomach rumbled in assent and her mouth watered. It had been a while since breakfast. She grinned. "I love apple pie."

"Of course you do, child," Alma said, as if there was no doubt whatsoever. She turned to a counter where a row of pies sat cooling, sliced a large piece, slid it on a plate and presented it to Jenny. "I make the best pie in Wyoming."

Jenny stared at the huge portion before her. "I'll bet you do."

Alma laughed, and Jenny dug in. The pastry was as good as it looked. Jenny reveled in the succulent flavors, and Alma kept up a running stream of conversation. Before long, Jenny thought she knew all there was to know about Jack and Lorelie Matthews and their nephew and the town and just about everything else. She was well into her second helping of pie when a tiny blonde woman fluttered into the room.

"Alma, we must discuss dinner tonight. We'll be having a dozen or so—oh." The woman stopped short and stared at Jenny with a perplexed expression. "Who are you?"

Jenny struggled to get a word out around the pie stuffed in her mouth, but Alma leapt ahead. "This is Jenny, Miz Lorelie. She's the countess's maid."

"Oh, I see." Miz Lorelie smiled a greeting. "I do hope her rooms are satisfactory. I don't mind telling you we don't have many countesses here." A thoughtful frown furrowed her forehead. "In fact, I don't believe we've ever had any at all. Have we, Alma?"

Alma shook her head. "Nope, this is the first."

"I should like to think we'd get more, though. Dead End, or rather it's Empire City now, is such a lovely place." Miz Lorelie raised a pale brow. "Don't you think so?"

"It's very nice," Jenny choked out before swallowing a mouthful of pie.

"I am sorry." Miz Lorelie shook her head. "How terribly thoughtless of me."

Jenny glanced at Alma, who rolled her eyes at the ceiling. Jenny's words were cautious. "What are you sorry about?"

Miz Lorelie's eyes widened with surprise. "Why, I asked you a question when your mouth was full. It was quite rude of me. Not at all civilized, and hardly proper." She leaned toward Jenny in a confidential manner. "We are working very hard right now to become civilized and respectable."

"So I hear," Jenny said, stifling a giggle.

"It's quite important, you know," Miz Lorelie said. "Civilization. Although, just between us, I've always rather liked the rugged ways we have out here. Still, it's no doubt time for a change. I was born in St. Louis. It's extremely civilized there."

"I was in St. Louis once," Jenny said.

"How lovely." Miz Lorelie's voice was bright, as if she'd just found a long lost friend. "Then we have something in common. Did you like it?"

Jenny shrugged. "I don't remember much. I was just a baby."

"I see." Miz Lorelie hesitated, a sad look in her eyes, as if remembering something she'd just as soon forget.

"I don't see why everyone wants all this respectability, anyway," Alma grumbled.

"Why, Alma. You know as well as I do it's all part

of progress." Miz Lorelie's voice held a chastising note. "We're going to be a state someday soon, and we'd hate to have the rest of the states looking down their noses at us."

"Well, I think it's silly. Especially changing the town's name. Empire City." Alma snorted her disdain. "It will always be Dead End to me."

Miz Lorelie sighed. "Yes, well, I agree with you there. It is so difficult to get used to new ideas. But I suppose it's the price one pays for progress."

The kitchen door opened and a tall, lanky cowboy strode into the room. "Alma, I hear you've got some fresh pie and I—" He stopped short at the sight of Lorelie and snatched his hat from his head. "Beg pardon, Miz Lorelie, I didn't know you were in here."

Miz Lorelie waved off his apology. "Not at all, Zach. I was just having a pleasant talk with this nice young lady. Jenny, have you met Zach?"

"No," Jenny said a bit breathlessly and stared into eyes the color of the Wyoming sky, endless and bewitching, beneath an unruly shock of thick, black hair. She met his gaze, and an easy smile spread across his face. Heat crept up her cheeks and she jerked her gaze away.

"Jenny," Miz Lorelie said. "This is Zachary Weston, one of our hands and quite a scamp. We've known him all his life, and he's still as ornery as when he was just a little tyke."

"Miz Lorelie." Zach groaned in obvious embarrassment and stalked over to the table. He cut a huge piece of pie, jammed half of it into his mouth, chewed and swallowed. "I'm a grown man now. High time you stopped telling people what a cute kid I was."

Alma chuckled. "He was a cute kid, though."

He still was, as far as Jenny could see. Of course, he wasn't a kid anymore. This was definitely a man. Why, he was at least eighteen. Tall and lean, as if he'd grown too fast, with a smile that promised a quick laugh and something else she couldn't quite put her finger on but intrigued her nonetheless.

"Zach," Miz Lorelie said, "why don't you take Jenny out and show her around the ranch. Unless the countess needs you, Jenny."

"I doubt it." Jenny was not about to pass up this opportunity to taste a bit of freedom. Especially not with the interesting Mr. Weston by her side. "She's not even here right now."

"That's right," Alma said. "She's out with Mr. Jack and Mr. Tye."

"Tyler's with them?" Miz Lorelie said. Alma nodded, and Miz Lorelie smiled with delight. "I see. Isn't that interesting?"

Alma cast her a warning glare. "Now, don't you go getting any big ideas about Mr. Tye and that foreigner. I know you're used to running his life, but settling down with a woman ain't something a family should be meddling with."

"Pshaw." Miz Lorelie waved off the objection and her eyes sparkled. "Settling down is the very sort of thing a family should meddle with. Why, it's what families are for." A frown flittered across her face. "Although I daresay I'm not at all fond of the term 'meddling.'"

"Well, how about 'interfering' or 'butting in'?" Sarcasm dripped off the housekeeper's words. "Or just plain sticking your nose in other people's business where it don't belong?"

"No, no, I don't like those at all either." Miz Lorelie

drew her brows together, as if searching for just the right word. "I know, guidance. That's it exactly. All Tyler needs is a little bit of helpful guidance and he'll do exactly what he should."

Zach popped the last bite of pie in his mouth and shook his head. "You can call it meddling or guidance or whatever you want, but Tye ain't gonna like it."

"Now, Zach." An admonishing note sounded in Miz Lorelie's voice. "You were just a boy when Tyler left to go away to school. His attitude about such things could be quite a bit different now than it used to be."

Zach cast her a disbelieving glance. "Miz Lorelie, I was thirteen when Tye left. Old enough to remember the yelling and screaming around here when you tried to make him go back East." He crossed his arms over his chest. "It takes more than a high-flown education to change a man who's as pigheaded as Tye."

Miz Lorelie heaved an exasperated sigh. "I suppose you could be right. Still, I had hoped he'd mellowed a bit."

Goodness, this woman's mind was nearly as clever as Ophelia's. Jenny watched with fascination. Zach and Alma studied Miz Lorelie with the careful concentration of gamblers waiting for the next card to be played, all the while knowing their opponent wouldn't hesitate to cheat.

"I have it." Miz Lorelie grinned with satisfaction. "We just won't tell him."

Zach and Alma exchanged glances as if to say they'd seen this kind of scheme before. Tye had obviously lost the battle over going to school. Jenny wondered if he'd lose this one to his aunt as well. She hadn't met him yet, but it already seemed to her that if this tiny, bird-like creature could get him to leave his home for years, marrying him off to Ophelia would be like rolling off a log in comparison. Ophelia, on the other hand . . .

Jenny gasped. "Oh, no!"

"No, my dear," Miz Lorelie said. "I think it's much better not to tell him. Otherwise, he's bound to put his foot down and refuse even to go near the countess, and if that—"

"That's not what I meant," Jenny said quickly. "I mean, you're probably right not to tell him, but Oph—the countess—well, she might not be at all interested, and she can be every bit as stubborn, and . . ."

And why not? Maybe the idea of settling Ophelia down with Tye Matthews wasn't so bad after all. In fact, it had definite possibilities. Why, if Ophelia married Tye, she and Jenny would never have to move again. They could stay in one place, have a real home, complete with a real family, and put down roots. Ophelia wouldn't have to worry over where their next meal would come from. Better yet, she'd have to give up gambling, and they'd never have to crawl out a hotel window again. Of course, Ophelia would have to pretend to be a countess for the rest of her life, but that was a minor problem—at least for Jenny.

"I think," Jenny said, each word slow and measured, "I think it's a wonderful idea."

"Tye won't go for it." Zach's voice rang with warning.

Miz Lorelie ignored him and cast Jenny a confident smile. "It is, isn't it?"

"And I'll do everything I can to help." Jenny grinned, basking in the warm glow of a newly formed conspiracy.

"This ain't gonna work." Alma glared her disapproval. "And the two of you should know better." She aimed a chastising finger at Jenny. "You're scheming against the lady who pays your salary, and you"—Alma directed a scathing glance at Lorelie—"you're doing what you've always done with that boy, trying to run his life again." She planted her hands on her hips and shook her head. "I don't know about the two of you. It must be the hair."

Jenny and Lorelie exchanged puzzled glances.

Alma sighed with forbearance. "You two both have almost that same shade of wheat-white hair."

Miz Lorelie's eyes widened with surprise. "Why, I hadn't noticed, so we do." She pushed an errant strand away from her face and smiled at Jenny. "Do you know what they say about hair like ours?"

Jenny stared in rapt captivation. "No."

"They say hair like ours is a gift from heaven." Miz Lorelie lowered her voice as if her words were a secret shared only by fair-haired women. "It means you were kissed by an angel at the moment you were born, and the moment you die, they'll welcome you back to heaven."

"That's good to know." Jenny smiled. Good and comforting, given the paths their lives had taken in recent years.

"Hogwash." Alma snorted.

Zach laughed. "Well, it sure is pretty enough for an angel."

Jenny's gaze met his, and again heat flushed up her face. Her stomach fluttered, and an odd ache filled her.

Alma and Miz Lorelie exchanged knowing glances.

"Ready?" he said.

"Oh my, yes." Jenny jumped to her feet.

He grinned down at her. "We'll saddle a couple of horses—"

"No." She stopped in her tracks and grimaced with disappointment. "We can't. I mean I can't. Ride, that is."

"No problem." Zach shrugged. "I can teach you."

"Can you really?" She stared at him with sheer admiration.

"Sure." He tossed her a confident smile. "Nothing to it. Of course, I may have to put off showing you around until you get a feel for the saddle."

"Then let's not waste any more time." She smiled back. "Let's get going." Jenny started toward the door, then turned back and nodded at Alma. "Thank you for the pie." She turned to Miz Lorelie. "And thank you."

"You're quite welcome, I'm sure." Miz Lorelie's smile faded to a look of confusion. "Whatever for?"

"For the story. About the hair." Jenny grinned. "And for not treating me like a maid."

"Think nothing of it, my dear." Amusement danced in Miz Lorelie's eyes. "It seems to me, at one time or another in our lives, we're all maids of some sort."

Alma snorted. "Ain't that the truth."

"If you three are going to gab all day, Jenny'll have to learn to ride by moonlight." Zach's voice held a masculine note of forbearance with feminine peculiarities.

"Don't use that high-and-mighty superior male tone with me, young man," Alma said. "Not if you want to stay welcome in this kitchen for that pie you're so fond of."

Jenny laughed. "We'd better get out of here before you're banished altogether."

"And that'd be rough." Zach wiped the few remaining pie crumbs off his lips, pushed the back door open and grinned. "Alma makes the best pie in the county."

"I'll bet," Jenny murmured, only half of her attention on the young man. Behind her, Alma and Miz

Lorelie had returned to the topic of playing match-maker for Ophelia and Tye. She strained to make out the words.

Miz Lorelie's eager voice trailed after them. "A countess in the family would be so very nice."

Alma muttered something Jenny couldn't quite make out. The girl smiled to herself. Miz Lorelie might well like a countess for the family . . .

But a family for the countess would be even better.

JENNY WAS BACK in her room a good half hour, and already at work on yet another one of the countess's dresses, before her sister finally sauntered in. Ophelia's eyes snapped with anticipation, and a self-satisfied smile danced on her lips. She paused by the doorway and expertly sailed her hat across the room to land precisely in the middle of her bed.

"I have it," Ophelia announced.

"Do you?" Jenny said.

"Indeed, I do." Ophelia closed the door behind her and leaned against it. "What is more civilized than an English title and estate?"

Jenny shrugged. "I don't know. What?"

Ophelia laughed. "No, no, darling, it's not a joke." She grinned wickedly. "Well, perhaps it is, but not on us."

"What are you talking about?"

"I'm talking about my brilliant plan." Ophelia perched on the edge of the bed beside Jenny and fairly bubbled with excitement. "I've decided to sell my title and land in England to Big Jack."

"You don't have land in England."

"Dearest, I don't have a title either. That's what's so brilliant about it." Ophelia beamed smugly. "And he fell for it without a second thought." Her eyes widened in disbelief. "It was so easy. Almost too easy."

"I don't think we should do this." Jenny shook her head. "These are very nice people."

"Of course they're nice people." Ophelia released an exasperated sigh. "We've already established that. That's part of the brilliance of it all."

Jenny studied her sister for a moment. It would do no good to endeavor to dissuade Ophelia from her objective. Once she set her mind toward something, she pursued it with a singular purpose that defied any attempt at rational argument. Still, Jenny was compelled to try. Perhaps a different approach . . .

"Why didn't you tell me about Tye Matthews?"

"Why, there's nothing to tell." Ophelia narrowed her eyes. "How did you know about Tye Matthews?"

"The housekeeper told me." Jenny steeled herself against Ophelia's inevitable outburst. "When I was in the kitchen."

"You left the room?" Ophelia groaned. "How could you? I specifically told you to stay right here. Did you say anything?"

"I said quite a bit, actually. But nothing that would give us away."

"Thank goodness for that. I can't believe you'd completely ignore my instructions and run the risk of exposure. You could ruin everything. Honestly, Jenny, I can't leave you alone for a moment. You can be such a child."

"I am not a child." Jenny resisted the impulse to stamp her foot. "I'm practically a grown woman."

"You're only sixteen."

"I'm almost seventeen." Jenny crossed her arms over her chest. "You were seventeen when Papa died and left us on our own."

"Yes, and I was not nearly as clever at seventeen as I thought I was."

"I am." Jenny tossed her a self-righteous smile. "And I've discovered I'm just as good a liar as you are."

"Congratulations. That's quite an accomplishment."

"It's a skill that seems to have served you well!"

"I don't want to see you make the same mistakes I have."

"What mistakes?"

"None that I can recall offhand, but the possibility is always there. Besides," Ophelia said loftily, "I do not lie. I act."

"Oh, really?" Jenny cast her gaze to one side of the room, then the other. "I don't see a stage. I don't see an audience. It seems to me that without a stage and an audience"—she threw her sister a pointed look—"a paying audience . . ."

"The world is my stage." Ophelia drew herself up and glared righteously. "All the world's a stage, and all the men and women merely players."

"You can quote Shakespeare all you want, but even he would agree with me on this. What you're doing here, pretending to be this countess and selling her land and title, isn't acting at all. It's a big old ordinary lie. A falsehood. A prevarication. A whopper."

"Call it whatever you wish." Ophelia shrugged. "It's going to get us what we want."

Jenny gritted her teeth. "I don't like it. It's not right."

"Right is all in your point of view." Ophelia's brow furrowed in annoyance. "Was it right for Papa to die and leave us all alone? Is it right for us to keep moving from town to town, barely making ends meet? Is it right for me to have to fend off the advances of every man who sits down for a game of cards just because they assume I'm willing to play for something other than money?"

"No!" Jenny glared. "But this isn't right either, and I don't think we should go through with it."

"Well, we are going through with it." Ophelia narrowed her eyes in a menacing manner. "Whether you like it or not."

"I don't like it." This time Jenny did stamp her foot. "And I refuse to be any part of it."

"You don't have to be any part of it. You just have to do what you're told!"

Anger and frustration colored Ophelia's face. The sisters stared at each other for a long, tense moment. Finally Ophelia's expression softened, and she sank down on the bed. "Jenny, I don't know what else to do. I'm so very tired of the life we've been living. You're growing up so fast, and I don't want you to have to go on like this."

At once Jenny regretted her words. Ophelia was only trying to make things better for them both. She sat down beside her sister. "I'm sorry. I just wish there was another way."

"Me too." Ophelia sighed.

"Couldn't you find some kind of job?"

Ophelia smiled grimly. "Do you have any idea how few respectable jobs there are out here for single women? And aside from gambling, I don't have many skills."

"You can act."

Ophelia pulled a deep breath. "Didn't you ever wonder why we didn't stay in the theater after Papa died?"

"I just thought you weren't particularly interested in going on the stage."

"Not exactly." Ophelia chewed her bottom lip. "I can quote Shakespeare accurately until the end of time. I can remember every card played in every hand. But I have never, ever been able to remember"—she winced—"my own lines."

Jenny stared in disbelief. "You can't remember your own lines?"

Ophelia shook her head. "Never."

Abruptly tiny discrepancies that had long nagged at Jenny made sense. She studied her sister. "What's the countess's name?"

Ophelia glanced around the room, as if looking for the answer. "Brightwater?

Jenny groaned. "Bridgewater."

Ophelia grimaced. "Oh, dear."

"I never even suspected. I just thought you had so many other things going on in that head of yours that minor details escaped you. That's another reason why we need to stop this charade right now. How on earth are you going to pull it off if you can't remember your lines?"

Ophelia brightened. "Well, I did tell Big Jack and Tye that I was still so distraught over my late husband's death that—"

"What's *his* name?"

Ophelia furrowed her brow. "It begins with an *A*."

Jenny rolled her eyes heavenward. "You can't do this."

"Oh, yes, I can." Ophelia rose to her feet, her manner firm and decisive. "True, I have this tiny memory flaw—"

"Tiny?"

"—but overall, I am quite quick witted and intelligent. I've proved that time and again in these past few years. And I will prove it once more with this deception. I am confident no one will ever discover I am not really the Countess of . . ."

"Bridgewater," Jenny said with a sigh.

"Thank you." Ophelia cast her a tentative smile. "I can do it, you know. If you'll stand by me."

Jenny shook her head in resignation. "I don't see that I have a whole lot of choice."

"Excellent." Ophelia grinned. "You'll see. This is a brilliant plan. It can't fail. You won't be sorry."

"I hope not." Jenny smiled weakly. "I'd hate to see everything blow up in your face."

"It won't." Ophelia radiated confidence Jenny tried hard to share. "You'll see, darling, everything will work out. My little plot will be terribly successful, and we shall live happily ever after. Just like in your storybook."

"The only ones living happily ever after in my book were the swindlers," Jenny muttered.

"Of course." Ophelia's eyes twinkled. "But that's us. Now . . ." She turned and started toward the wardrobe. "There is a dinner planned for this evening. What are the options for appropriate attire?"

Jenny shrugged to herself and joined her sister. The two discarded the gowns already altered and instead selected a charming, emerald-colored confection. Jenny picked up her needle and thread and started to work. Ophelia busied herself with her own preparations for the evening, keeping up a running stream of conversation all the while. Ophelia only chattered when she was nervous. It did not bode well for success.

Jenny paid enough attention to her sister to allow herself to make the appropriate comments when needed, but her thoughts were elsewhere. The revelation of Ophelia's difficulties remembering lines only solidified Jenny's earlier decision. Yes indeed, marrying Ophelia off to Tye Matthews would solve everything. They'd get a home and escape from this ridiculous masquerade in the process. No matter how clever Ophelia was, she was bound to trip up sooner or later. Imagine, not remembering your own name! Why, someone would surely notice. This match had to be made, and made as soon as possible.

Determination flooded Jenny. Ophelia was basically a very good person. She would make Tye Matthews a wonderful wife.

If, of course, she could only remember his name.

Chapter 6

AVOIDING Tye Matthews and Sedge Montgomery was next to impossible. For some horrible reason, Lorelie had seen fit to seat Ophelia between the two men for dinner. Obviously, the dear woman had assumed she'd have much in common with Montgomery. And as for Tye, well, Lorelie probably thought since they'd been together this morning, Ophelia would feel more comfortable sitting beside someone she already knew. The older woman was decidedly wrong. Dinner was anything but comfortable.

For one thing, both men were outrageous flirts. And even when Ophelia directed her comments to Big Jack, or that pleasant banker, or that interesting woman who ran the general store, somehow Tye or that annoying Montgomery would manage to insert himself into the conversation. Honestly, men were all alike. Whether in a saloon at a gaming table, or in a proper home in an elegant dinner setting, they only seemed to have one thing on their minds. Tye studied her with a look that suggested the meal before him wasn't the only thing whetting his appetite. And Sedge continued to eye her with an amused gleam that seemed to indicate he knew far more about her than he let on. No, there was nothing comfortable about this meal.

Ophelia greeted the gathering's move into the massive parlor with a great deal of relief. At least there she could mingle with the others. Still, it was far harder to keep up her pretense than she had expected.

Lorelie pulled her aside as they entered the room, and she gestured at a number of tables set and ready with decks of cards. "I know it's doubtless not the kind of entertainment you're used to, but we thought an evening of cards would be quite pleasant." Lorelie frowned anxiously. "Unless, of course, you would prefer something else?"

"Not at all." Ophelia's polite smile hid her surge of delight. "It sounds extremely enjoyable."

"Thank goodness." Lorelie released a sigh of relief. "I know in certain circles cards are sometimes considered to be reserved for men, but at parties here we play whist and a few other inconsequential games deemed suitable for both men and women." She studied Ophelia in a considering manner. "May I tell you a little secret?"

"Please do." How very curious. What kind of a secret could this nice little woman have, anyway?

"Some years ago, the women of Dead End grew tired of quilting bees and baking and all the other activities regarded as proper for women."

"I can certainly understand that." Ophelia struggled to keep the amusement from her voice.

"So we began the Every Other Tuesday and Thursday Afternoon Ladies Cultural Society." Lorelie lowered her voice confidentially. "It was for the express purpose of innocent amusement, you understand."

Ophelia shrugged in agreement. "What else?"

"Indeed." Lorelie hooked her arm through Ophelia's and led her along the edge of the room. "We began with the very best intentions. At first we confined our meetings to poetry readings and discussion of literature and that sort of thing, but we found it dreadfully boring after a while."

"I can see how that can happen."

"And then at one session, someone, I forget exactly who now, suggested cards." Lorelie frowned thoughtfully. "I believe we started with cribbage and"—she wrinkled her nose with distaste—"whist."

"Whist is pleasant." Ophelia tried not to choke on the words. What on earth had these women been up to?

"Pleasant, but not terribly exciting." Lorelie sighed. "So we went on to euchre and faro. Anna Rose Simmons has a faro box. She and her husband run the saloon, and she's quite disgusting when she's around the obnoxious man, but when she's away from him, she's much more likeable. A little pathetic, perhaps, and not at all helped by that mustache. She really should do something . . ."

"The games?"

"Oh, yes, well." Lorelie tapped her chin with her forefinger. "We also play twenty-one. I do enjoy a rousing game of twenty-one. And then there's poker and—"

"Poker?" Ophelia gasped. "The ladies of Dead End play poker?"

"Of course, my dear." Lorelie smiled innocently. "It's quite stimulating."

"Poker." Ophelia shook her head in amazement. "And do you wager as well?"

Lorelie cast her gaze around the room as if to make sure they weren't overheard. "Oh, most certainly.

What on earth would be the point of playing without a friendly wager on the line?"

"What, indeed?" Ophelia said faintly.

"Dear me. Now I've shocked you, haven't I?"

"I'm not shocked exactly, just somewhat surprised." What kind of odd community had she stumbled into, anyway? She lifted a shoulder in casual dismissal. "But this is America, and life is extremely surprising here."

"Isn't it, though? Still, I suppose it's not entirely respectable. For women to play poker, that is, especially for money."

"Not entirely, no."

Lorelie heaved a sigh of regret. "I suppose we shall have to dissolve the Every Other Tuesday and Thursday Afternoon Ladies Cultural Society if we're going to be respectable. After all, what one would condone in Dead End would not be at all acceptable in Empire City."

"Does everyone know about the Cultural Society?"

"Well, certainly everyone knows of its existence. My dear, you can't spend every other Tuesday or Thursday afternoon at a meeting without people, particularly husbands, noticing your absence. But surely you, as a widow, understand that. I can't believe men in England are substantially different in that respect from the way they are here."

Ophelia's gaze fell on Tye across the room. He noted her attention and raised his glass in a jaunty salute. She jerked her gaze back to Lorelie. "No, I'd say men are much the same the world over."

"That's precisely why the activities of the Cultural Society are kept secret." Lorelie leaned toward her in a conspiratorial manner. "Men always seem to get so upset when they discover women are doing the same things they do to have fun. Besides, some of us have built up quite a tidy little nest egg that we'd just as soon not share."

"Will you be playing poker tonight?" Ophelia said in a strangled voice.

"Goodness gracious, no." Lorelie's eyes widened with shock. "It wouldn't be at all proper. Besides"—she cast Ophelia a wicked grin—"we'd probably beat the pants off them." Lorelie laughed, and Ophelia joined her. "Have you ever played poker, my dear?"

Ophelia shrugged nonchalantly. "A hand or two."

Lorelie's face lit with enthusiasm. "Then you shall simply have to play tonight."

"Didn't you just say it wouldn't be proper?" Gad, this woman made no sense at all.

"It wouldn't be proper for me, but for you . . ."

"It would be acceptable for me to play?"

"Of course. You are, after all, the Countess of Bridgewater, and by far the most respectable and civilized thing to ever happen to Dead End." Lorelie beamed with pleasure.

"Empire City," Ophelia murmured.

The older woman shrugged. "There too. At any rate, if you play poker, why, it would most certainly open the way for us, and then—"

"And then . . . you could beat the pants off them."

"Not on a regular basis, mind you. Only now and then, and just when they really needed it. There is something wonderfully delightful about beating a man at his own game, particularly when the game in question is as inconsequential as cards."

Again, Ophelia's gaze caught Tye's, and she wondered just what kind of game this man was playing. Was it as insignificant as a hand of cards, or was it far,

far more important? Delightful fear and unwanted anticipation shivered down her spine.

"Jack, gentlemen." Lorelie nodded at the gathering around one table. "The countess has expressed an interest in playing poker."

Big Jack drew his bushy brows together. "Now, then, Lorelie, honey, I'm not at all sure that the countess—"

"Nonsense, Jack." Lorelie waved off his objections. "Poker really is the game of choice in this part of the world, even if it isn't generally considered acceptable for women. If the countess is going to be able to truly experience American life while she's in this country, I think she should play America's favorite game with genuine Americans."

Jack shook his head. "Lorelie, I don't—"

"I think it's a great idea, Jack." Tye stepped up to the table with an insolent grin. "I think the countess should get a taste of a game enjoyed by Americans."

Jack glared at his nephew, tossed an annoyed glance at his wife, then heaved a sigh of resignation, as if realizing all protest was futile. "Countess, if you'd like, you're welcome to join us."

"Well, if you're sure." Ophelia's polite murmur hid the excitement racing through her. Let's see, she still had thirty-two dollars and seventeen cents hidden in her room in a stocking, stuffed inside a glove, packed firmly in the toe of a slipper. One could never be too certain of safety when traveling. With a bit of luck, coupled with her considerable skill, she could turn the meager amount into a nice, comfortable sum in, oh, say, just an hour or two. By the end of the evening she'd be financially solvent again.

Montgomery stepped behind her to pull out her chair, and she sank into it in a graceful manner, casting her gaze around the table. Big Jack would play, of course, and so would that pleasant banker. It also appeared the sheriff was joining them—not especially someone Ophelia would like to get to know, but manageable nonetheless—along with another rancher she'd been introduced to but whose name escaped her. And, of course, Tye.

"Well, gentlemen." She smiled sweetly at the group. "This is not a game I am terribly accomplished at, but I am willing to try."

"You just do your best, darlin'," Big Jack said and settled in the seat next to her. The other men sat down, with Tye taking a spot across the table from her. Good. She preferred not to have the annoying man too close.

"I am afraid, though, that I did not bring any funds to dinner with me, so I assume you will all be willing to take my marker?" She glanced around the table for confirmation.

"I'm afraid not, Ophelia." Big Jack shook his head. "You see, we're not used to playing poker with ladies, so"—he drew a deep breath—"we'll just be playing for chips." A chorus of groans broke out around the table. "This is only a friendly game."

"Of course." The tone of her voice belied her disappointment. Damnation. There went the possibility of a little ready cash.

"If that meets with your approval?" Tye said.

She laughed lightly. "I enjoy any kind of game that's friendly."

"I bet," Tye said under his breath. What on earth did he mean by that? Abruptly, unease swept through her. His gaze met hers, and she wondered if it might not be better to have him at her side rather than to have to look into his eyes all evening.

"Friendly or not, let's get this game going," the sheriff said, picking up the cards and dealing the first hand.

The next hour passed in a flurry of pasteboards and wooden chips. Ophelia did her best to play evenly, losing as often as she won. It would not do to have these men suspect her skill with cards. Far better for them to think she had beginner's luck on her side. And aside from Tye, they were no real match for her if she put her mind to it.

Still, it was scant comfort to know that if they hadn't been so determined not to take advantage of a mere woman, she could have taken them for a bundle.

SHE WAS GOOD. She was very good. Tye studied Ophelia's playing as much as he watched the woman herself. Oh, she was subtle, all right. Never winning too often, never losing too much. The others at the table were, no doubt, taken in by what Tye realized was nothing more than an act. A very good act. This was no beginner. The Countess of Bridgewater was nothing short of a cardsharp.

Why did she obviously feel she had to hide her skill? Surely a woman as confident as a countess would revel putting men, American men no less, in their place, especially when it came to their own game. More and more about this woman simply did not add up.

The list grew longer each time he was in her presence: her odd forgetfulness about her husband's name, the accent that was a little too perfect—at least given the Englishmen he'd encountered back East and abroad—and now a knowing hand with cards that went far beyond the boundaries of typical female behavior. No, there was definitely more to this woman than met the eye. Tye suspected she hid much more than proficiency at poker. But what?

Abruptly an answer hit him, and he swore to himself. There were too many inconsistencies here. Contradictions that apparently only he had noticed. Only one explanation accounted for the discrepancies. Ophelia, the lovely Countess of Bridgewater, was not at all what she appeared. She probably wasn't even a real countess.

And if she wasn't, just what, and who, was she?

OPHELIA GLANCED UP and again met Tye's gaze. It was positively unnerving the way the man always seemed to be scrutinizing her as if she'd been some sort of scientific specimen to be studied or, worse, as if he meant to catch her in a mistake.

Unease with his examination distracted her, and absently she won three hands in a row. She raked in her winnings, disgusting, worthless chips, and Big Jack laughed. "You are having a run of luck, little lady."

"Is she?" Tye said quietly.

Ophelia ignored him and cast Big Jack a pleasant smile. "I am, aren't I? And I have always believed one should take advantage of luck when it appears. Shakespeare said—"

" 'So we profess ourselves to be the slaves of chance and flies of every wind that blows.' From *The Winter's Tale*." Tye threw her an arrogant smile.

"No." She stared at him with a mix of irritation and surprise. "I was thinking of 'Who seeks and will not take when once 'tis offered, shall never find it more.' *Antony and Cleopatra*."

Tye narrowed his eyes. " 'They laugh that win.' *Othello*."

"Hell, Tye." Big Jack chuckled. "I'm impressed. Did you pick up that Shakespeare lingo in school?"

"Some of it." Tye shrugged. "I liked what I learned then. But"—his gaze never left hers—"I've found a new interest in it lately. I actually sat down with a book last night and did a bit of catching up."

"How nice," she muttered to herself. Just what she needed. A cowboy who quoted Shakespeare.

"Personally, I have no idea what some old English writer might have said." The sheriff tossed down his cards. "But I say a game of poker without something on the line is like watered-down whiskey. It looks good, but it just ain't the same."

"It is a shame we can't play for some kind of stakes." Ophelia's manner was casual, but hope surged within her.

"Absolutely not." Big Jack shook his head firmly. "Why, Lorelie would . . . wait a minute." He cast her a speculative look. "I have an idea for a little wager."

"What kind of wager?" the banker asked.

"Well, now's as good a time as any to announce it, I guess." Big Jack leaned back in his chair and surveyed the room. "Lorelie, come over here for a minute."

The little blonde bustled to his side. "Jack?"

"Lorelie, darlin', you and the rest of this here town are so dad-burned determined to become civilized and respectable that the countess and I came up with a way, a relatively painless way, to do just that."

"Oh?" Lorelie's gaze flitted from Jack to Ophelia and back.

"It seems the countess is having a few money problems—"

Ophelia smiled sadly in her best down-on-her-luck manner.

"—and she's agreed to sell me her estate and her title." Big Jack's grin could have stretched across the entire territory of Wyoming. "I'm going to be the Count of Bridgewater."

Behind her, Montgomery emitted something that sounded like a cross between a choke and a laugh.

"And you, darlin' Lorelie, are going to be a countess." Could Jack's grin get any bigger?

"Oh, my." Lorelie's eyes widened with delight. "A countess?"

"Yep."

"My goodness." Lorelie stared with astonishment. "A countess? Me?"

"Hard to believe, isn't it?" Tye said through gritted teeth.

"You'll make a lovely countess," Ophelia said, hoping Tye would resist putting his two cents in. Gad, the man could ruin the whole deal if he didn't keep his obvious reservations to himself. The thought of simply shooting him and taking care of the problem of his vexing presence once and for all again flittered through her mind.

"Do you really think so?" Lorelie turned excited eyes toward Ophelia. "But, oh, my dear, what will you do?"

Ophelia shrugged in a gesture of noble resignation. "I shall carry on with my life as best I can. As much as I hate to admit it publicly, my financial straits are such right now that if I do not sell my beloved home, I shall surely lose it to creditors in the near future anyway."

"If you're certain of your decision . . ." Doubt colored Lorelie's words.

"Oh, I'm certain. I'm very certain," Ophelia said quickly. Goodness, between Lorelie's sympathy and

Tye's suspicions, this deal could turn sour if she didn't move fast. Her words came out in a rush. "You will love it. The countryside is beautiful."

"We won't be going over there but once a year," Big Jack said with a quelling glance at his wife. She nodded absently, intent on Ophelia's description.

"Rolling hills, lush green grass . . ." What did England look like, anyway? Surely it must be lovely, but never having been there . . . Still, in her mind's eye she could see. "Fields of spring flowers that seem to go on forever. And the castle—"

"Castle?" Big Jack's eyes widened with surprise.

"You didn't tell me there was a castle," Lorelie said, enthralled.

Big Jack shrugged. "I didn't know."

"Oh, didn't I mention the castle?" Ophelia said. "How could that have slipped my mind?"

"One wonders," Tye said dryly.

"Yes, the castle." A dreamy note sounded in Ophelia's voice. She could practically see it, and she could make these people see it too. "It was built, oh, three hundred or so years ago. Blackwater Castle—"

"I thought it was Bridgewater," Montgomery said.

"It is." A grim note rang in Tye's voice.

"Grief, boys." Big Jack tossed them a pointed look. "It does terrible things to the mind. Now, Countess, darlin', go on."

"Thank you." Ophelia released a heartfelt sigh. "Bridgewater Castle has been the ancestral home of my husband's family for generation after generation . . ." The remaining guests had all gathered around Ophelia. Her audience listened, spellbound, to each detail about the imaginary castle on the make-believe estate. She held them mesmerized, in the palm of her hand. Even Tye seemed interested in spite of his evident doubts. Maybe she should have gone on the stage after all. Why, if she could command attention like this with so little effort, think what she could do with a bit of rehearsal and a theater packed with an eager audience. Perhaps she could even overcome that disagreeable memory flaw of hers. ". . . and dear, dear, dead Alphonse always said—"

"Alphonse?" Montgomery said.

Tye sighed. "The count."

Montgomery cast him a puzzled look. "The husband?"

Tye nodded. "The dead husband."

Montgomery raised a brow. "Grief?"

Tye narrowed his eyes. "What else?"

Why couldn't she remember that blasted man's name? This made-up dead man was causing her just as many problems as the living, breathing ones gathered around the table. Thankfully, Big Jack seemed to chalk all her memory discrepancies to a continuing mourning for her dead husband, whatever his name was.

"At any rate"—she sighed dramatically—"my late husband felt the castle, his home, our home, was the heart and soul of the family. Now that he's gone and I have no family of my own, this is perhaps all for the best." She directed a brave smile at Lorelie. "It will do me a world of good to know that people like you and Jack will now be the custodians of . . ."

"Bridgewater Castle?" Montgomery supplied helpfully.

"I was going to say that," she said under her breath. She gazed at Lorelie. "Bridgewater Castle and the accompanying title."

"So you're going to be a count." The sheriff chuckled. "Count Big Jack Matthews. It has an interesting ring to it. Lord knows, you can certainly afford it. What's this little slice of respectability setting you back anyway, Jack?"

"We haven't decided yet." Big Jack toyed with the cards on the table. "That's what I was getting around to. Everyone here seems to think playing for mere chips isn't much fun, so I propose we wind up our negotiations on the price of my new holdings right here and now." He nodded at Ophelia. "If that's to your liking, Countess?"

His gaze meshed with hers, and abruptly she realized Big Jack Matthews was by no means an ignorant cowboy. In spite of his relaxed, casual attitude and ready laugh, this was obviously an astute businessman.

She studied him for a long moment. In affairs like this, he was no doubt more than a match for her. Ophelia hadn't the faintest idea what an English estate, complete with title and castle, was worth, but she'd bet Big Jack did. At least he'd have a definite idea of how much he was willing to pay. In this case, his business savvy, coupled with his obvious honesty and apparent sense of honor and fair play, could well work to her advantage. This was one bet she simply couldn't pass up.

"What did you have in mind, Jack?" Her words were calm, but her heart thudded in her chest. She drew a deep breath.

Jack's eyes gleamed with enjoyment, the look of a man with a quarry in sight or a goal within reach. Uncertainty flashed through her. Perhaps this was not the kind of man to swindle after all. "I thought you could give me your asking price and I could give you my offer, and we could play a hand for it."

"I'm far too much a beginner for that." She laughed softly. "Why don't we just cut the cards for it?"

Jack nodded. "Fine by me."

"This is ridiculous." Tye got to his feet and stared as if he couldn't believe his ears. "You have no idea what this property is worth or even what it looks like."

"I don't need to know, Tye." Jack studied Ophelia thoughtfully. "I have Ophelia's description, and her word's as good as gold in my book. She is, after all, a countess."

Ophelia's smile belied an annoying stab of guilt.

"But shouldn't you talk to a lawyer before you go making any deals? Shouldn't she?" Tye glared at his uncle.

"I shall write to my solicitor immediately," Ophelia said.

"Randolph." Jack turned to the banker. "What do you think?"

"It's not how I'd do business, Jack." The banker shrugged. "But Lord knows, you've been a lot more successful than I have. I suppose even if you end up losing money on the deal . . . say the title's tainted and the castle is in ruins—"

"It is not!" Ophelia glared with indignation. Imagine anyone thinking her castle would be less than wonderful.

"You've certainly got the money to sustain a loss. Even a big one. What the hell, Jack." Randolph grinned. "It's your bet."

"Jack, listen to me for a minute." Tye stepped around the table and leaned toward his uncle, close enough to Ophelia for her to catch the words, but just barely. "I have a lot of reservations about this deal and that

woman. I don't think she's who she says she is. I think
you should hold off until—"

"Nonsense, Tye." Jack shook his head. "Even with
all that education of yours, you've had no experience
with wheeling and dealing in the business world. I'm
afraid, son, you're just not, well, sophisticated enough
to grasp the little intricacies of this venture."

Anger flushed Tye's face, and he stared, speechless.
Ophelia almost pitied him. Almost.

"If, however, you insist on negotiating over a cut
of the cards," Randolph said, "I would not advise
announcing your bids out loud. Rather, each of you
should write down a figure on a piece of paper."

"Good enough." Jack grinned. "And whoever wins
the cut wins the deal."

Jack stretched his hand out to hers, and she grasped
it with a firm grip. "Agreed."

Within minutes someone handed her a slip of paper
and a pencil. She stared at the blank page for a long
moment. What did she know about the worth of property in England? Or the going price for a title? Or the
cost of a castle? The white of the paper glared omi-
nously. This was her big chance. The opportunity of a
lifetime. She and Jenny could live for the rest of their
lives on the money from this deal. The only question
was: just how much could she get?

She searched her mind for an answer. There was
only one thing to do. She had no idea what to ask for in
terms of her nonexistent property. Ten thousand dollars, perhaps? No, no, way too little. It was simply not
a believable figure. Twenty thousand? No. Twenty-five
thousand had a much better ring to it. She and Jenny
could live quite well on twenty-five thousand dollars.

Still, if twenty-five thousand was good, twice that was better. With a decisive stroke of the pencil, she wrote out the sum that would ensure her future: fifty thousand dollars.

She folded the slip of paper, placed it in the center of the table and met Big Jack's gaze. He slapped down his own offer beside hers.

"Well, now." Randolph laughed nervously. "Who goes first?"

Jack nodded at Ophelia. "It's always ladies first. Countess?"

"I can't believe you're doing this," Tye muttered.

Montgomery grinned. "Although you've got to admit, old man, it does liven up the game."

Ophelia swallowed hard and stared at the deck of cards. There was no skill in cutting a deck. It was luck plain and simple. Chance and nothing more. The fortunes of fate. She drew a deep breath and noted the slight tremble of her hands. With a deliberate, methodical movement she cut the cards near the center of the deck and pulled the top card up slowly, for her sight alone.

The queen of hearts.

She glanced up, straight into Tye's dark eyes, and a current of electricity arced between them. Her breath caught, and she wrenched her gaze away to mesh with Jack's. It was a good pick. Would it be good enough? Years of bluffing had taught her well, and she kept her face expressionless. His turn.

He cut the deck, and a rueful smile grew on his face. Gently he placed the top card faceup on the table.

The ace of clubs.

Her heart fell. She knew she should have gone last. She always did better when she went last.

Ophelia placed her card beside his and shrugged. "You win, Jack. The bid, please?"

Randolph picked up Jack's offer and handed it to her. She opened the folded paper and sucked in a sharp breath, stifling the need to gasp aloud.

She'd never seen so many zeros in her life. The amount was far beyond what she'd ever dreamed of asking or hoped of getting.

Goodness, she was rich! Fabulously, wonderfully wealthy! She and Jenny could go anywhere they wanted, live any way they wanted. Now all she needed to do was get her money and get out of town, and just like the tailors who swindled the emperor, they'd live happily ever after.

"Randolph," Jack said, "I'll come into town tomorrow and stop by the bank. You can probably just set up a new account for the countess and transfer the funds—"

"Actually," Ophelia said quickly, "I'd much prefer a simple bank draft for the bulk of the money and the rest in cash. I really won't be taking advantage of your generous hospitality much longer. I should be on my way as soon as possible. I do need to catch up with the others in my party."

"It will take some time to arrange everything," Randolph said.

"And you will want to stay for the ceremony," Big Jack added.

Ophelia stared. "What ceremony?"

"Why, the ceremony making me a count, that's what ceremony." Big Jack frowned. "Isn't there some kind of official ceremony?"

Montgomery nodded, amusement glimmering in his eye. "I should think there would be something on that order."

Big Jack shook his head. "I'm afraid without a ceremony I sure won't feel much like a count."

"And we would hate for you not to feel like a count," Tye said.

They wanted a ceremony now? One would think a title, let alone a castle, would be more than enough. She clenched her jaw. Fine. She could whip up something, anything, to make them happy. It would only delay her for a few days.

"Shouldn't the queen be the one to make Jack a count?" A worried expression crossed Lorelie's face, and she tilted her head at Montgomery. "Isn't that the way these things are done?"

Montgomery shrugged. "I would imagine it would depend on the circumstances. But certainly it would be well within the purview of Her Majesty to bestow a title." He smiled a wicked smile. "And from what I've heard, she has always enjoyed creating new lords. Especially counts."

Ophelia groaned to herself. "I don't think the queen—"

"Would we have to go to London?" Lorelie said. "Or would we have the queen come here?"

"Oh, by all means," Tye said wryly, "let's have the queen of England come to Dead End."

"Empire City," Randolph said.

Ophelia tried again. "I don't think the queen—"

"How does one entertain a queen?" Lorelie said. "I shouldn't think cards would be quite in order."

"She doesn't travel much outside England, you know," Montgomery said in an aside to the banker and the sheriff.

"Can't say I blame her," the sheriff said, the banker

nodding his assent. "If I had my own country, I'd be hard pressed to go anywhere else either."

"Indeed." Montgomery nodded. "What would be the point?"

"Still," Lorelie said, her brows pulled together thoughtfully, "travel is so broadening and terribly educational. Why, look at everything Tyler learned when he traveled. And I'm sure Ophelia has learned a great deal as well."

"Yes, Countess." Tye pinned her with a firm stare. "Just what have you learned in your travels?"

"What have I learned?" Ophelia's gaze skimmed over the expectant faces surrounding her. Her fist clenched on the precious slip of paper in her hand. "Well, I suppose I've learned not to judge a town by its name."

"We told you." The banker nudged a disgruntled-looking Tye and grinned.

"And I've learned how very helpful beginner's luck can be."

The men at her table chuckled.

"But most importantly, I suppose . . ." She shrugged and smiled weakly. "I've learned never, ever lose your . . . luggage."

Silence fell for a moment, then the gathering burst into laughter, with the notable exception of Tye, whose face resembled nothing short of a threatening thunderstorm. She shivered at the sight. He'd surely discover everything if she stayed in this town much longer.

"However." She held up her hand. "I do not believe it's even remotely possible to get the queen to come to America, let alone Wyoming. Perhaps a prince or a duke or"—she shrugged—"someone else, but definitely not the queen."

"Oh, dear," Lorelie sighed. "Are you quite certain?"

"Quite," Ophelia said firmly.

"Well, in that case . . ." Disappointment washed over Lorelie's face.

"I would like to have some kind of ceremony, though," Big Jack said. "It's not every day you become a real count."

"No," Tye said, "it's not."

"What about an ambassador or another emissary of the Crown?" An innocent light shone in Montgomery's eye.

Ophelia gritted her teeth. "I really doubt that—"

"That's a great idea, Sedge. What about it, Countess?" Tye said, a hint of triumph in his voice. "Can *you* get some kind of representative of Her Majesty here?"

She struggled to keep her annoyance in check. "I wouldn't think—"

"I have met various members of the British delegation to this country on occasion," Montgomery said. "I could write to them and—"

"No," Ophelia said sharply. "I'll do it. I mean"—she smiled at Lorelie and Big Jack—"it would certainly be my pleasure to request the presence of the queen's spokesman at the . . . official ceremony."

"Now, that's respectable." Big Jack grinned. "An official ceremony."

"And civilized." Lorelie beamed.

"I think this calls for some of that champagne." Big Jack gestured to one of the servers hired for the evening.

The room buzzed with eager anticipation. Here and there Ophelia heard excited comments about "sprucing up the town" and "getting ready for this shindig" and "the biggest thing to happen since the railroad." Oh well, how long could this nonsense take, anyway?

A few weeks at best. Surely she could continue her masquerade that long, at least as long as she could keep her distance from Tye Matthews and that Montgomery person.

Especially Tye Matthews.

She rose to her feet and cast a gracious smile around the table. "If you will all excuse me, I believe I need a breath of fresh air."

"Please." Montgomery offered his arm. "Allow me to accompany you."

Ophelia started to decline, but the look of annoyance on Tye's face changed her mind. She took Montgomery's arm. "Very well."

He led her out the doors, onto the wide front porch. Self-satisfaction at leaving Tye's simmering anger behind brought a smile to her lips. There was no doubt at all that Tyler Matthews didn't trust her, but his suspicions hardly mattered now. She had her money, and she'd be out of Dead End long before Tye managed to prove anything. She and Jenny would be far, far away with more than enough to pay for a fresh start and a new life.

As for his wanting her . . . that too was obvious, and he'd fail on that count as well.

Montgomery escorted her to the edge of the veranda, and she noted the moon shone full and golden, casting a glow on the night. It was a beautiful moon, bursting and bright. No doubt as splendid as any moon ever seen in Venice. A moon worthy of artists or . . . lovers.

She gazed at the orb hanging in the endless sky and pushed away a vague pang of disappointment that brought an odd realization.

For some obscure reason, she hated to see Tye Matthews fail.

Chapter 7

"You can't do this, Jack!"

"I do believe, Tye," Jack said with a grin, "I already have."

The two men were alone at the table; the other players had drifted off to refill empty glasses or mingle with guests and thoroughly discuss and dissect the impact of Dead End's having its very own count.

Tye racked a hand through his hair and expelled a frustrated sigh. "I've never seen you go into a business deal as shaky as this thing is. You're buying a pig in a poke, Jack."

"You think so, Tye?"

Tye struggled to keep his irritation in check. "You don't know anything about this woman or her land or her title."

Jack shrugged. "I know all I need to know."

Tye glared. "Well, I'd sure like to hear what you know that I'm missing."

Jack studied his nephew for a long, thoughtful moment. "Tye, I was doing business long before you were even a spark in your dear daddy's eye. Back when folks were saying cattle was the way of the future, I knew it'd take more than beef on the hoof to build the kind of life I wanted for my family. I took a hell of a lot of risks back then with long-shot investments and risky gambles, and damn near every one of them paid off. I know what I'm doing, son."

"Jack." Tye leaned closer. Surely it wasn't too late for his uncle to get out of this. He had to convince the man how foolish this deal with that woman was. "Just take a good, hard look at this so-called countess."

"Awfully pretty, I'd say, with that red hair and that spark of fire in those green eyes. And aside from Lorelie, of course, I've always liked 'em tall. Tall women mean long legs." Jack cast him a wicked smile. "What about you, Tye? Do you like 'em tall?"

"Well, sure, I appreciate . . ." Tye pulled his brows together in annoyance. "Don't change the subject, Jack. We were talking about the countess."

Jack pulled a cigar from the pocket of his vest and rolled it between his fingers. "That's who I was talking about, all right."

"Not about her looks—"

"Damn fine-looking woman."

"—but about her character." Tye gritted his teeth. When had Jack become so thickheaded? "I don't think she's who she says she is. I don't think she's a countess. I don't think she has a dead husband—"

Jack's eyes narrowed. "You think he's alive?"

"No, I don't think he's alive, I don't think he exists!" Exasperation washed through Tye. How on earth could he get through to this stubborn old mule? "I don't think she has an estate or a castle or anything else. I think she's a fraud, Jack, plain and simple. And she's taking you for all you're worth."

Jack struck a match on the underside of the table and lit the cigar, his manner unconcerned and casual. He puffed once, twice, three times, blowing a plume of blue smoke into the air. Finally, he gazed at his nephew. "If I didn't know better, Tye, I'd think you were accusing me of being some kind of idiot."

Tye blew a long breath. "I'm not saying that, Jack. I admit, she's clever, she's very clever—"

"I always liked 'em smart too."

"—but she's a fake. I'd bet everything I own on it."

"So . . ." Jack drew another puff on the cigar. "Prove it."

"What do you mean, 'prove it'?" Tye cast him a suspicious look.

"I mean, I'll take that bet." Jack aimed the cigar at him. "If you can prove she's a fake, I'll stop this deal dead in its tracks."

"I'll prove it," Tye said grimly.

"Maybe, maybe not. But I'll give you fair warning, son." Jack's gaze pinned his nephew's, and for the first time in his life Tye glimpsed the businessman behind the loving, fun-filled uncle. "I've never been wrong about a horse, a steer or a woman."

"You're wrong about this one."

Jack reached out and picked up Ophelia's bid, still lying on the table. He unfolded the paper and eyed the figure. A satisfied smile lifted the corners of his lips. "Don't count on winning too soon, Tye."

"I'll win." Tye rose to his feet. "Mark my words, I'll get the truth out of her sooner or later."

"You do that, son." A twinkle danced in Jack's eyes. "And I'd start right now if I were you. She's out on the porch with Sedge. In fact, you might need to spend quite a bit of time with the woman to wring the truth from those lovely lips of hers."

"I'll do what I have to." Determination colored Tye's voice.

"And here, take these." Jack pushed the deck of cards across the table. "Beginner's luck or not, she's a damned fine player. But even good players have bad nights. And many a man's been known to confess all kinds of things better kept secret after a losing hand. Who knows? You might just need that kind of help."

"I doubt it," Tye muttered. Still . . . he picked up the deck, shoved it in a pocket and started toward the door, his uncle chuckling behind him. What did Jack think was so funny about all this? He was about to lose a considerable amount of money.

Jack was right about a few things, though. Her lips were lovely and meant for kissing or, more likely, pillaging. Her hair was the color of a Wyoming sunset and, if freed from the pins that held it in place, would surely sweep across shoulders soft and ivory and delicious. And her legs, no doubt, went on forever. The kind of legs a man wanted wrapped around his waist.

He shook his head in a futile attempt to clear the delightful vision from his mind, reached for the doorknob and pulled up short, halted by an intriguing realization.

It had been his experience that the best way to get the truth from a woman, the one sure method to get her to talk, the only place a woman ever seemed to speak freely and without reservation, was in bed. His bed. He rarely failed with women, especially when he'd managed to get Sedge out of the picture. How could Ophelia be any different? He turned, strode to a serving table and selected two glasses and a bottle of champagne. Once again he headed toward the door, grinning all the while. She didn't have a chance.

And his bet wasn't the only thing he'd win.

THE COUNTESS STARED off in the distance, apparently lost in her own thoughts. Sedge studied her silently. Lord, she was lovely, even in the moonlight. Perhaps, he chuckled to himself, especially in the moonlight. But she was not a countess. He doubted if she was even English. She was, however, extremely clever.

Sedge drew his brows together in a thoughtful frown. When the only issue to consider was seduction, he had no qualms about keeping his suspicions about the fair Ophelia to himself. Now, however, there were Big Jack and Lorelie to keep in mind. The couple had been welcoming and gracious to him since his arrival in this new, and completely foreign, western land. They had, in fact, been quite like family—not his family, of course, but a real family. The kind one reads about in storybooks as a child. Sedge did not want to see them hurt in any way.

"Did you wish to say something to me, Mr. Montgomery, or were you simply planning on staring for the remainder of the evening?" Ophelia's words were aimed at him, but her gaze was still fixed on the open countryside, shimmering in the moonlight.

"Sedge," he said with a laugh. "Call me Sedge. We are in America, after all."

"I suspect that would be ill advised, Mr. Montgomery, in America or anywhere else."

"You don't trust me?"

She turned to face him, answering his question with one of her own. "Is there something you wish to ask me?"

He laughed again. She was brazen and delightful. "I was merely curious as to whether we had any acquaintances in common."

"Somehow, I rather doubt that."

"One never knows. British aristocracy tends to be quite close knit."

She raised a curious brow. "Do I detect a note of sarcasm, Mr. Montgomery?"

"Sarcasm?" Sedge chuckled softly. "I daresay, any number of things about the land of my birth would engender that type of derision these days. But no, at the moment I was merely stating a fact, nothing more."

"Very well, then." She sighed, as if resigned to his intrusion on her thoughts. "The count, my late husband—"

"Alphonse?"

For a moment, a puzzled frown creased her forehead; then her expression cleared. "Yes, of course, dear, dear dead Alphonse. At any rate, he was not particularly given to social activities."

"Quite a bit older than you, perhaps?"

"Indeed." She nodded, as if pleased with his insight. "He much preferred the quiet life of the country to the excitement of society."

"I can certainly understand that—in an older man, of course."

"It's not as if he were in his dotage, mind you," she said quickly.

He shrugged. "I would not presume to suggest such a thing." My, she was good. One would almost think her indignation was legitimate. But just how far would she, could she, continue? "Since the moment we met, I've been wondering about something."

Ophelia stilled. Her expression was guarded, and a cautious note rang in her voice. "Yes?"

"I have been searching my memory, but for the life of me, I simply could not place the location of your estate and Bridgewater Castle."

"Oh?"

Tension seemed to pulse from her, and he was hard pressed to keep his amusement under control. Lord, this game of cat and mouse was stimulating.

"Indeed." He nodded vigorously, enjoying the tiny gleam of apprehension in her eye. "And then it came to me."

"It did?"

"Most certainly." He kept his voice deliberately casual, as if he'd been stating a simple fact instead of a complete fabrication. "It's in Leicester, isn't it?"

"Leicester?" she said weakly.

"I knew it." He cast her a triumphant grin. "Wait, hold on now." He clapped his hand to his forehead. "How could I have made such a mistake?"

"A mistake?" Did the lovely Ophelia look just a shade green around the edges?

"Of course. I didn't mean Leicester, I meant Warwick." Sedge held his palms up and shrugged. "I always have gotten those two counties confused. Surely you can see how that could happen?"

"One does make mistakes now and then." A subtle note of relief sounded in her voice. No doubt Ophelia thought that if he wasn't sure where her castle was located, she was safe.

"I mean with both counties so similar. Still, I do apologize."

She waved away his comment. "Nothing to apologize for. A simple error. Let's leave it at that, shall we."

"You must miss it a great deal." He stared thoughtfully. "The country here is completely different from what you're used to."

"That is why one travels, you know." Her tone was light. "To experience the unfamiliar."

"Indeed, but Wyoming is so very far from the sea."

Confusion played across her lovely face. "Yes . . . well, I daresay that's part of its charm."

"Do you miss the sea?"

"The sea?" Her words were measured and controlled, but the woman was obviously trying to grasp his meaning. Sedge could barely keep a straight face. "It's always hard not to miss the sea. The, um, waves and salt and such . . ."

He nodded in solemn agreement. "I have always thought the waves crashing against the cliffs of Warwick to be one of the most impressive sights in the world."

Her expression cleared as though she abruptly understood, and Sedge imagined he could see the workings of her mind like the gears and wheels of a fine Swiss timepiece. "It is magnificent."

"I wonder, Countess, if you—"

"Mr. Montgomery—"

"Sedge."

"Mr. Montgomery." Annoyance simmered in her voice. Had Ophelia finally reached the limits of her patience? "What are you doing here, anyway?"

"Well, that's something of a long story." He leaned against the porch rail. "When I returned to England, after completing my education, I—"

"I didn't mean—"

"I shot my brother."

"Your brother?" Her eyes widened with surprise. "How? Why?"

"Why does one usually shoot one's brother?" He lifted a shoulder in a nonchalant manner. "Treachery. Betrayal. Deceit."

"Deceit?"

"Especially deceit." He paused. "I'm certain you'd find it a fascinating story. Shall I continue?"

Uncertainty flitted across her face, then she squared her shoulders in a gesture so slight that he might have missed it altogether. "Go on."

"Very well." He paused for a moment to gather his thoughts. It wasn't as if the tale hadn't been retold over and over again in his head, like a discordant melody that haunts one's nights and fills the silent moments of the day. It wasn't the action itself that brought the taste of bile to his mouth. It was the aftermath.

"My father is the sixteenth Earl of Russelford, my older brother his heir naturally. I am the second son and have always been something of a trial to my parents. You know I went to school in this country with Tye. Surely you must have wondered why, given that England boasts some of the finest universities in the world?"

"It was rather curious."

"My family insisted I pursue my education as far away as possible. Even as a boy I possessed something of a penchant for mischief."

"Hard to believe," she said under her breath.

He pretended not to hear. "Following the completion of our schooling, Tye was sent on a Grand Tour—"

"I have already heard about his travels." Was there a note of irritation in her voice?

"—and I returned home. In the ensuing months, I found myself betrothed to a young woman who, while not of my choosing, was still quite acceptable as a wife."

"An arranged marriage? How antiquated." Ophelia stared with disbelief.

Sedge shrugged. "Surely you realize the practice is

not at all uncommon among the rarified strata of British society we inhabit?"

"Of course not," she said quickly. "It's merely that it is 1888 and I would hope such arrangements were becoming less and less acceptable."

"Yes, well, as recently as a few months ago it was still quite permissible. At least in my family. As I was saying, marriage plans were progressing when I discovered my brother and my betrothed in a, shall we say, compromising position."

"A compromising position?" Discomfort mingled with curiosity in her voice.

"Yes, my dear." His gaze trapped hers. "They were naked, they were wrapped in each other's arms and they were quite definitely unaware of my presence. You see, they had taken advantage of an abandoned crofters cabin on the estate. To add insult to injury, it was one of my favorite places as a child."

"Oh dear." A becoming blush swept up her face. "Is that when you shot him?"

He chuckled to himself. Apparently the lure of scandal could overcome even the embarrassment of blatantly intimate details. "No. I allowed them to dress first."

"Thank goodness." She bit her bottom lip, curiosity victorious over distaste. "Did you . . . ?"

"Kill him?" Sedge shook his head. "To my everlasting regret I did not." Ophelia released a breath, relief clear on her face. "I merely wounded him. However, it was enough for my family to insist I leave the country, tantamount to banishment, actually. Tye arrived in England in time to witness these unfortunate events and offered to help me purchase land here." He bowed and swept out his arm in a gesture fitting the drama of his story. "And that, my dear lady, answers the question of why I am here."

"Not really."

"No?"

"No." Ophelia crossed her arms over her chest. "I was merely asking why you were here on the porch."

He stared for a moment, then burst into laughter. The corners of her mouth twitched as if she too saw the humor in the moment.

"Now if you would be so kind as to answer another question for me."

"I could do no less for a fellow countryman."

"Excellent." She paused. "Exactly what is involved in this fox hunt planned for tomorrow? Somehow, I suspect it's not at all what one would expect at home, in England."

Sedge grinned. "From what I've heard so far, they're having a devil of a time coming up with a fox."

She pulled her brows together in a puzzled frown. "How on earth can you have a fox hunt without a fox?"

He leaned forward in a confidential manner. "Coyotes."

"Coyotes?"

"Coyotes."

"Would horses then still be part of the procedure, if we are to hunt coyotes instead of fox?" A hopeful note sounded in her voice.

He laughed. "I doubt you could hunt coyotes on foot."

"Oh." She struggled to hide it, but there was a slight edge of disappointment in her tone. Why would the woman care about the exact details of hunting coyote?

"It should be quite an interesting experience. I know I am looking forward to it."

"As am I," she said with a smile that did not quite reach her eyes.

"You know, Countess." Now that he had dispelled any vague doubts about her legitimacy, he was compelled to offer her a subtle warning. "I dislike pretense and deceit, be they in a fox hunt or other activities."

"I know." She snorted in a most unladylike manner. "You shot your brother."

"Indeed. And I was rather fond of him." He heaved an exaggerated sigh of regret. "It was unfortunate, but it was also a question of my honor and my family's honor."

"But your family threw you out of your own country." She tilted her head in a provocative manner and studied him. "It scarcely seems they were particularly concerned with your dedication to their honor."

"Nonetheless, it concerned me." His gaze caught hers, and he stared for a long, silent moment. "Regardless of how they felt, I believed my brother and my fiancée disgraced my family as well as myself. Given enough time, I am also certain they would have brought public humiliation down upon us all. Made us look like fools, as it were. I did what I needed to do to prevent that."

"How very noble of you."

"Be advised, my dear." He lowered his voice and gazed into her lovely green eyes. "I consider Tye's aunt and uncle to be family."

Her gaze didn't flinch from his, and in spite of himself, admiration swept through him. Whatever else she might be, Ophelia was no coward. "How wonderful for you all."

"Do you have family, Countess?" he said softly.

"No." Her voice was sharp, as if she'd had enough of

their game. "But what I do have right now is an agreement for a great deal of money to relinquish my ancestral home to new owners. I also have a number of plans to make. So if you would not think it impolite of me, I would much prefer to be alone."

"By all means." He grasped her hand and pulled it to his lips. "I shall look forward to seeing you tomorrow, then."

"Excellent," she muttered and yanked her hand from his.

He turned and strode toward the door, meeting Tye on his way out. As much as he'd initially thought it served Tye right to be taken in by this imposter, his loyalty to the Matthews family now demanded that he tell his old friend everything.

"Tye, I must talk to you."

Tye's brow creased with annoyance. "Is Ophelia out here?"

"Ophelia is exactly what I need to discuss."

Tye grinned and held up a bottle of champagne and two glasses. "I have better things to do right now than talk."

"I can see that," Sedge said wryly. "Still, I think there are a few things about the countess you should know."

Tye's expression hardened. "I know all I need to know."

"I know you suspect she isn't who she says she is." Tye raised a brow. Sedge shrugged. "It was obvious, old man, the way you baited her at every turn tonight. Tsk, tsk. Not exactly the way to earn her trust."

"I know what I'm doing."

"Indeed. Well, perhaps I could lend a bit of assistance on that score."

Tye's gaze narrowed. "I don't need any help. And I don't need any competition. What I need is for you to stay away from her."

Sedge laughed. "It's not at all what you think."

"What I think—what I know—is that you and I have always pursued the same women. But this is different. There's more at stake here than an evening with a beautiful woman."

Sedge gritted his teeth, fighting off a growing sense of irritation. "I realize that. What I'm trying—"

"I'm warning you right now, old friend. I have plans for the countess, and I don't want your amorous intentions to mess them up."

"I'm not—"

"You bet you're not."

"I merely wanted to—"

"I know what you want."

"Very well." Sedge glared. "You're so bloody stubborn and so damned smart. Do what you want. I wash my hands of the whole blasted thing."

Tye cast him a self-satisfied smile. "Thank you."

"No, *thank you*. It will do me a world of good to see you make a fool of yourself." Sedge turned and threw open the door.

He should have known better than to try to help. Through all the years they'd known each other, Tye had always believed he'd known best. Fine. He was on his own. Bloody fool. He wasn't nearly as smart as he thought he was. If he had listened to Sedge, he would have had the proof he needed to unmask the fraudulent countess.

There was no possibility Sedge would share that proof with him now. On his own, Tye would never realize that an English countess's husband was not a count. And he couldn't possibly know the waves never crashed below the cliffs of the county of Warwick. Warwick was as landlocked as Wyoming. Ophelia didn't know it either. There wasn't a doubt in Sedge's mind she was not English and not a countess. He wondered about her claim of widowhood as well.

He'd like to be around when Tye made that discovery. Abruptly, good humor washed away his anger. It would be great fun to let Tye try to ferret out the obvious discrepancies in Ophelia's story. Right now, all the man had were suspicions based on the relatively minor problem of poor memory, easily explained by lingering grief. Only Sedge's unique background gave him the knowledge to see through Ophelia's masquerade. Surely the woman had never expected to run into an Englishman in this part of the world.

No, let Tye work, and work hard, to learn the truth. Sedge suspected the coming duel of wits between Tye and Ophelia would be quite impressive. From the little he'd seen so far he was confident she was a fitting match for his friend.

This was one contest he'd almost enjoy more as an observer than a competitor. He chuckled to himself. The odds here appeared even, and only a fool would wager on the outcome. Sedgewick Montgomery was no fool. Still, the temptation was strong to make a small bet.

If only with himself.

Chapter 8

"CHAMPAGNE?" With a flourish, Tye presented the wine.

Ophelia released an exasperated sigh. "Does this porch attract everyone in Dead End? What are you doing here?"

"I just—"

She thrust out a hand to ward off his answer. "No, no, don't tell me. The last time I asked that question I ended up listening to Mr. Montgomery's life story."

"It's quite a story." Tye grinned and offered her a glass. Ophelia eyed the vessel as if about to refuse, then accepted it with a resigned shrug. He popped the cork and filled her glass. "What did you think?"

She took a sip of the wine and gazed off in the distance, a note of amazement in her voice. "He shot his brother."

Tye poured a glass for himself and set the bottle on the wide porch rail. "With good reason, I'd say."

"Would you?"

"Yep." He pulled a healthy swallow of the wine. "He was betrayed, Ophelia, and lied to."

"Still, to shoot your own brother . . ." She shuddered

and fell silent, staring out at the endless Wyoming night.

What was going on in that clever brain of hers? What was she thinking, with that faraway look on her face? A look not quite of reminiscence but more like longing. An odd thought shot through him. How would he feel if she had that look for him?

"Do you have a brother?"

"Me?" The abrupt question took him by surprise. "No, I was an only child."

"And your aunt and uncle raised you?"

"My folks died of influenza when I was ten."

"That must have been very difficult," she said quietly.

"I guess it was." His gaze followed hers into the moonlit night. "It's been a long time since I thought much about it."

"I am sorry." She turned toward him, the pale light reflecting a genuine sympathy in her eyes. "I shouldn't have brought it up."

"No, it's all right." He smiled. "I don't mind. They were good people, and I still miss them. Especially now that I'm back home, on the ranch they built." Tye shook his head, abruptly self-conscious. "You don't want to hear about this."

"I'd very much like to hear."

He studied her for a long moment until convinced of her sincerity. "Their ranch, the Triple M—"

"Triple M?"

"Yep." He laughed softly. "My dad's name was Mitchell, my mom's Megan—"

"And the third *M* is for Matthews?"

"It sounds kind of silly and sentimental."

"I think it sounds very nice." Her voice was as

gentle as the night, and it warmed his blood. "It has a wonderful ring of family to it. You must have been very close."

"I guess we were." He leaned forward, rested his forearms on the porch rails and stared into the night. Memories washed through him. As though it was yesterday, he could see the tall, fair-haired cowboy with the laughing eyes. "My dad taught me to sit a horse and chase calves and fish in the creek that runs through the west range. It flows down straight from the mountains, and the water's fresh and clear and icy cold. It's damn near the prettiest spot in the territory, maybe the country."

"It sounds lovely."

He flashed her a quick, surprised look. "Would you like to see it some time?"

"I believe I would . . . some time." She smiled. "Tell me about your mother."

"Megan Matthews was pretty and young. I recall her hair was the color of sunshine."

"Like yours?"

"Like mine." He laughed and remembered the mother who kissed away the hurts of the day and the bad dreams of the night. With a start, he saw vividly as an adult what he couldn't recognize as a child: the happiness the three of them shared had as much to do with the secret, teasing looks he'd catch his father giving his mother and the desire returned in her gaze as it did the love of a family, one for another.

Would he ever find the kind of woman who could share a love of children and family, as well as a passion for him and him alone? The surprising question struck him with an unexpected sharpness. He hadn't looked for such a woman, hadn't especially wanted to share his life with anyone, hadn't really considered it one way or the other. Why on earth did the thought even occur to him? And why now? Perhaps it was simply the keen edge of poignant memories of happy days. Perhaps it was merely that he was finally home again after so long away. He raised his gaze to hers, to eyes that gleamed with an understanding he didn't expect and never suspected. Perhaps . . . it was something altogether different.

"I'm living their dream, you know," he said as much to himself as to her.

"Are you?"

"My dad started his ranch with help from Uncle Jack, and it was all going great. And then they got sick." He paused, and the fears and confusion and anger that he'd thought long forgotten flooded him, and he was once again a little boy watching the people he loved lose the battle for their lives. He drew a shaky breath and firmly pushed the memories away. He was an adult now, and the best homage he could pay Mitchell and Megan was to finish what they'd started and make their dream of life out here a reality.

"And you came to live with Jack and Lorelie?"

"Yep." He straightened and settled his back against a post, crossing his arms over his chest. He stared at her lovely features, illuminated and shadowed by the moon with every breath she took. What on earth had she done to him to get him to spill his guts like this? Lord, he hadn't talked about his parents in years. And wasn't he supposed to be getting the truth out of her? "So, Countess, it's your turn. Tell me about your family."

She laughed, a light, lyrical sound that drifted on the breeze. "There really isn't much to tell. My husband—"

"Albert?"

"Um-hum. He's dead, of course."

"Of course."

She shrugged. "And I really have no other family."

He raised a brow. "No brothers? No sisters?"

"No." She hesitated, then sighed with dramatic regret. "No, I am very much alone."

"But surely you had parents?"

"Well, certainly, everyone has parents." A slight note of indignation colored her words. "Mine are both dead."

"Tell me about them."

"I don't think—"

"You listened to me. The least I can do is return the favor." Besides, the more he made her talk—whether she told the truth or pure fiction—the more likely she would be to make a mistake. And then he would have his proof. Odd, though, for a fleeting instant there, it no longer seemed quite as important to unmask her as it had earlier. He brushed away the disquieting thought. "Go on, Countess."

"Very well." She pulled a deep breath. "If you insist . . ." Ophelia stood silently for several seconds, as if gathering her thoughts or concocting a story. A tiny touch of guilt pricked his conscience. What if her memories were as real and as bittersweet as his? No matter who she said she was today, she'd still once had parents and a family. Was his quest for the truth reason enough to force her to dredge up remembrances that could be as gripping as his own?

"I never knew my mother." Her voice was calm and controlled, as if she struggled to maintain a sense of distance. Instinctively he knew that if nothing else she said was the truth, this was. "She died when I was an infant. My father—"

"The Shakespearean scholar?"

She laughed ruefully. "Indeed. Shakespeare was very much his life. To the point that we never had a real home but simply moved from thea—university to university. The life of a gypsy, really."

His own love for his family home washed through him, and he wondered how anyone could grow up without knowing there was one place in the world where you'd be safe and warm and welcome. "I see."

Something in his tone must have struck a nerve. Her spine stiffened, and she straightened her shoulders. Her eyes glittered in the moonlight. "No, Mr. Matthews, you do not see. My father had a great many faults, prime among them his lack of desire to settle in one location and his failure to commit to any single woman long enough to provide a mother for his offspring. However, those shortcomings pale in comparison to his virtues."

"I didn't mean—"

"Let me tell you something, Mr. Matthews." Anger emanated from her like a physical force. "No matter what else he was, he was a good father. No child could have asked for a more caring and loving parent. He left very little when he died. His legacy was barely more than an innate mastery of the works of Shakespeare, arguably the most beautiful words in the English language, quite a heritage really, and the unquestioned knowledge of his love. And then, Mr. Matthews, I married Alvin—"

"Alfred."

"Whomever," she snapped with a dismissive wave of her hand.

Lord, the woman was furious. And absolutely magnificent. Whatever else she was, her loyalty to her father was impressive. Tye watched with fascination. Ophelia was far too riled to even notice that poor, dead Albert-Alfred-Alford-Alphonse's name had changed once again. Oh, this was delightful. She was delightful. And wringing the truth from her would be delightful, in whatever way he could.

"Then he died, and any thought I had of a real family and a real home died with him."

"What about the castle?"

"The castle?" She shook her head impatiently. "It was always his really, not mine. But now your uncle has given me what I've always wanted. The means to provide a home just like his and yours. A place to put down roots and call my own. Where I don't have to worry about who might be at the door or how I'm going to pay the rent or whether or not I'll break my neck climbing out windows—"

"Alvin made you climb out windows?"

"No, of course not. At least not often." Even in the dim light he could see her brow furrow in a desperate attempt to explain away her words. While the deceased count was obviously a fabrication, he had no doubt her fears were real. "He was quite a . . . um . . . joker. Very fond of pranks, that's all." She downed the remaining champagne in her glass and held it toward him for more.

He raised a questioning brow. "Do you really think you should?"

"My dear Mr. Matthews." Her haughty, royal tone had returned, and he struggled to check a smile at the transformation from passionate defender of father and family to regal countess. "I never have more than two, and I have only had one glass as yet."

Tye shrugged, picked up the bottle and filled her

goblet. Her hand holding the glass shook slightly. She lifted it to her lips and swallowed quickly. As if the wine had renewed her courage, she turned to him. "Now then, if you don't mind, Mr. Matthews—"

"I thought you agreed to call me Tye."

"I don't like calling you Tye."

"You have before."

"Yes, well, here and now it implies a relationship I would prefer to avoid."

"Oh?" Her continued annoyance suited him. She said far more in this mood than she did otherwise. What was that nonsense about climbing out of windows anyway? He considered her carefully and noted how the moonlight caught the fire flashing in her eyes. Abruptly, he wanted that fire to flash for him in the throes of an emotion far more satisfying than anger. "What kind of relationship?"

She cast him a startled glance, then pulled her gaze away, ignoring his question. "Very well, *Tye*, I have a great deal of thinking to do, and I would prefer to do it alone."

He studied her in the dark. She was an enigma. What was real and what was false? He wanted the answer almost as much as he wanted her. His determination to get both strengthened. "But it's a beautiful evening, Countess. Far too beautiful to waste alone. Why, the moon is—"

"I know all about the moon," she said through clenched teeth.

"Then I needn't remind you of Venice?"

"No, thank you."

He set his glass on the railing and stepped closer. Her scent teased, intriguing and warm, like an exotic flower or an undiscovered spice. She moved back.

"In that case, perhaps I'll simply remind you of Wyoming."

"Wyoming? I've never been to Wyoming before." Suspicion underlay her words.

He chuckled and took another step. So did she. A few mere inches separated them. "But earlier today, right on this very porch, I believe we were about to—"

"We were about to do absolutely nothing," she said sharply.

"Why, Ophelia, I'm shocked." He leveled his best indignant gaze at her.

"Shocked?" The word was cautious.

"That you would lie to me." His gaze drifted lower to the intriguing cleavage revealed by his proximity and framed by the low-cut emerald concoction she wore like a second skin.

"Lie? What on earth do you mean?" she said slowly.

He stifled a chuckle. "How can you deny that you and I were all set to share a kiss?"

"I wouldn't call it share," she said in a lofty manner. "I believe *steal* is a more appropriate word."

"Ophelia." He sighed in an exaggerated manner and shook his head, stepping forward once again. A bare inch now separated them. The heat of her body permeated his shirt. And if she smelled this wonderful, how delicious would she taste? "It's a simple matter of perspective. I was certain you wished to kiss me every bit as much as I wished to kiss you, although—"

"You were wrong." Her back was against the post, and he noted with satisfaction she had nowhere left to go.

"I can well imagine why a woman, even a widow, would prefer to believe she was coerced into a kiss than to admit she gave her favors freely."

"That's not it at all!"

"Methinks thou dost protest too much." He rested his hand on the post just above her head and stared down at her. She was only a few inches shorter than he, and it would take very little effort to meet her lips with his.

"Don't you dare quote Shakespeare to me!"

"And why not, oh fair Ophelia?"

Lips that pouted and swelled with a promise of passion.

"Because I don't like it." A slight breathlessness in her voice belied the force of her objection.

"Well, I do."

Lips that would deny the unquestionable glow of desire in her eyes. Desire evident even in the moonlight. Desire she probably didn't recognize . . . yet. He brushed an errant strand of hair, silky and sensual, from her face.

She slapped his hand away. "Well, I don't. Besides, you don't do it at all well."

"Really?" He was so close he could see the pulse throb in her throat. He could easily press his lips to the inviting beat. "What's wrong with the way I do it?"

"Well . . ." She stared up at him, her eyes wide, her breath fast. "The actual phrase is . . . um . . ."

"Yes?" He lowered his lips to that tempting point in the hollow of her throat, and she gasped.

" 'The lady doth protest too much, methinks.' " There was an edge of apprehension and misgiving and need in her voice. "That's . . . um . . . the proper quote . . ."

"Is it?" Her flesh was warm beneath his touch, and his tongue teased and tasted and slowly traveled up her neck to the line of her jaw. "And does she?"

"She does," she whispered.

"I stand corrected." He straightened and stared into eyes glazed with awakening passion.

"Tye?" The word was little more than a breathless sigh.

A sense of victory surged through him. She'd used his name. She would soon be in his bed. "Yes, Ophelia."

"You were right."

He raised a brow. "Oh?"

She swallowed and shook her head. "I did want to kiss you."

"I know." He struggled to keep a smug smile from his lips.

"And"—she shuddered, as if losing a battle with herself—"I want to kiss you now."

"I know."

"So . . ." Her tongue flicked over her lip, and his stomach tightened at the sight of it. The satisfaction he'd noted a moment before flew in the face of that simple, nervous, almost innocent gesture. He dismissed the thought at once. While Alvin-Alphonse-Alfred etcetera probably never existed, there wasn't a doubt in his mind that Ophelia was an experienced woman of the world. "So . . . kiss me."

He cupped her chin with his hand. "I'd be delighted, Countess."

He brought his lips to hers gently, with a restraint that had always driven women to distraction. He brushed his mouth across hers with a light touch, and she sighed against him. His lips teased hers, and his tongue traced the inner rim of her mouth. Dimly he heard the shatter of a wineglass hitting the porch floorboards.

She wrapped her arms around his neck with a charming hesitation, as if she'd never really embraced a man before. He gathered her to him in an easy, fluid motion designed to prolong the slow, steady pace of his building seduction and her growing desire. Her breasts crushed against his chest, and he could feel the beat of her heart against his. He pulled her tighter and deepened his kiss, his tongue exploring her mouth and meeting her own oddly halting response until she moaned and sagged against him.

She tasted of wine and honey. Hot and savory and sweet. Abruptly, all thought of restrained technique vanished under the onslaught of his own insistent need, and his lips plundered hers with a fierce ache that demanded to be fed. One hand splayed across the small of her back; the other cradled the nape of her neck and held her defenseless against his conquering mouth. He lost himself in her touch and her taste, and he wanted her naked and hot and throbbing beneath him. She affected him more than he'd expected, more than he'd dreamed. And desire swept away all concern for any truth beyond the prospect of the ecstasy to be found in her embrace.

A peal of laughter sounded from inside the house, and he jerked his head up to check the door. No one was there and he relaxed, turning his gaze back to her.

Her eyes were wide with wanting and something he couldn't quite define, and her breath came in short gasps. She was as affected by their encounter as he, and no doubt wanted him as much as he wanted her. A yearning fire coursed through him, and he bent to claim her lips once more.

"No." She pushed her hands hard against his chest, and he pulled back in surprise.

"No?"

"That's what I said." She squirmed out of his grasp and stood facing him, her breasts heaving with an obvious attempt to quell frustrated desire with deep, soothing breaths of night air.

He stepped toward her. "But why?"

She thrust a hand out in front of her to stop his forward progress. "Mr. Matthews—Tye—this is neither the time nor the place for any kind of assignation. Your family, your friends are just inside the door. This is certainly not acceptable or proper behavior for . . . for a mayor."

He laughed and grabbed her hand; pulling it to his lips, he placed a kiss in the palm. His gaze meshed with hers. "I never wanted to be mayor."

She stared, and her voice was strained, as if she too was struggling with unrequited passion. "Regardless of what you want, you are the mayor."

"Do you know what I want now?"

Her hand trembled in his. "I imagine I do."

He pulled her back into his arms, noting in the recesses of his mind how perfectly her body fit with his. "I have wanted you since the moment we met."

Something that might have been fear mingled with longing in her eyes. "Have you?"

"Surely that doesn't surprise you." He bent to nibble the tender flesh just below her ear. "You're a beautiful woman, Ophelia. And a widow. You're no stranger to the passion between men and women."

Lord, she tasted as good as she smelled.

"What does that mean?"

"What does what mean?" he murmured. He could spend forever with the flavor of her on his lips.

"That I am no stranger to passion?"

"Only that you're a woman of experience. You've been married, and you've known the intimacies that entails." He nuzzled her neck. "I want to share that intimacy with you. I want to show you the heights a man and woman can reach. I want to make love to you until you swoon from the sheer sensation and cry my name into the night."

She stilled beneath his exploring lips, and her skin seemed to cool. He raised his head and studied her. A heavy knot formed in his gut. The desire that had lingered in her eyes was gone, replaced by a vague look of shock and a not-so-subtle anger.

"Release me, Mr. Matthews." Her tone was cold and firm.

He stepped back and stared. "What did I do?"

"I'm afraid you have jumped to conclusions that are in error. I may well be a widow, but I'm not willing to leap into every bed presented me at the beckoning of a gentleman's little finger."

He pulled his brows together in annoyance. "See here, Ophelia, I didn't mean to offend you. I assumed the attraction between us was mutual."

"Be that as it may, I am not used to being grappled."

"Grappled? What kind of an insult is that? I've never grappled in my life." He glared, her verbal slap at his seduction wiping away all thoughts of restraint. "I'll have you know, women have thrown themselves at my feet for a chance to be in my arms and in my bed. Grappled, my ass!"

"Harlots. Tarts." She cast him a look of sheer disdain. "Loose women, no doubt."

"Not at all. Most of them were"—he stared with a triumphant glare—"widows."

Even in the night he could see the sparks fly from

her eyes. "Well, this is one widow who would rather see you rot than in her bed!"

"Hah! Once again, Ophelia, you're protesting too much."

"I detest you with every fiber of my being." She turned on her heel and started toward the door.

"You're lying, and you don't do it nearly as well as you think you do." He grabbed her and pulled her, struggling, into his arms. "But this, fair Ophelia, is not a lie."

His lips claimed hers with a fury and a vengeance. And she battled against him with a rage of her own, which changed, in an instant of mutual insight and acceptance, to a fierce passion that took his breath away and stole his soul. For a moment or a lifetime they clung to each other, and he fought against a tide of emotion and sensation that threatened to bring him to his knees. He wanted to take her right here, and regardless of what she might say or what she might deny, he knew, as he had never known anything before or since, that she wanted him too.

At long last, they pulled apart and he gazed into her eyes, her expression reflecting his own feelings: bemused and dazed and confused.

She stared up at him, and her voice was little more than a whisper. "I despise you."

"I know." He grinned and brushed his lips against her forehead. "Now, kiss me again."

"I will not." She pulled away from him, and this time he let her. She brought her hand up to her throat and stared at him as if she wasn't quite sure of what she said or even where she was. His satisfaction was tempered only by the realization that his confusion matched her own. "So . . . good evening."

" 'Parting is such sweet sorrow'—"

She gasped at his words, turned and fled. The door banged shut behind her.

" '—that I shall say good night till it be morrow.' " He grinned and leaned against the railing. That was one quote she couldn't argue with. And she couldn't very well complain about his kiss again either.

The grin slowly faded from his face. What happened here tonight? He'd come out to get the truth from her, and admittedly seduction had seemed the most enjoyable way to do that, but who was seducing whom? And why did he abruptly want so much more from her than a mere night of pleasure? And what exactly was "so much more"? Was there another truth here that he didn't seek but existed nonetheless?

Regardless of the unexpected emotions she aroused, emotions so far beyond lust he was hard pressed to identify them, he still needed proof. Perhaps that maid of hers could be helpful? Alma said the pretty little thing had spent much of the day with Zach. He'd ask the boy to see what he could learn from the girl.

Tye had learned quite a bit about his quarry tonight, though. If nothing else, the woman had a strong sense of loyalty. Her diatribe about her father proved that. And surprisingly, she cared about the same things in life that he did: home and family.

As intriguing as that information was, it didn't help in his quest for the truth, even though he now knew that when Ophelia was caught up in turbulent emotion, anger or—he smiled—passion, her British accent seemed to disappear. But, damnation, she was lovely when aroused. The high color in her face, the heat of her skin, the expression in her eyes like that of a frightened doe or a trusting child or an innocent girl.

Abruptly the look in those eyes registered in his mind, and he jerked upright like a puppet on a string.

Ophelia's eyes were deep green pools of molten gems filled with fire and flame.

But they were not the eyes of a widow.

IT WAS THAT damnable moon again. The blasted orb shone through her window and lit her room as if it had been day. Ophelia tossed and turned, and still could not avoid the light and the images it conjured. Images of a golden-haired cowboy with a gleam in his eye and the lilt of Shakespeare on his lips. She threw the blankets off and slid out of bed to stalk back and forth across the room.

She was just grateful that Jenny was already fast asleep when she had finally slipped back into her room tonight. Ophelia would tell her all that had happened tonight in the morning. Right now, she was in no mood for idle chat. Besides, she was certain her sister would know what had happened. Surely the heat Tye had triggered within her would show up on her face. It was bad enough to walk back into the house and encounter his aunt and uncle and their guests. She was fairly confident most didn't notice anything, but Big Jack did cast his speculative gaze first at her, and then at the door and back to her. If anyone suspected her activities on the porch, Jack would. The man was obviously both crafty and smart.

As for his nephew . . . Ophelia shuddered and wrapped her arms around herself. How was she going to handle Tyler Matthews? All he had to do was kiss her and she melted like a schoolgirl. Her entire life, she'd avoided men exactly like him. Men who were arrogantly confident of their own considerable charms.

Men who used women for their pleasure and their pleasure alone. Men who freely bandied about words like "love" without a second thought as to their effect on their adoring victims. Men just like her father.

Edwin Kendrake was a good father and, judging by the women eager to share his company, an expert in the art of love as well. But when it came to that curious emotion, her dear father was no different from any of the other actors she'd grown up around. She often wondered if, even with her mother, Edwin had ever really known the genuine love of a man for a woman. If so, his children had never observed it. Men were, no doubt, all the same.

Even Tye.

Ophelia brushed her hair out of her eyes and gazed out the window, glaring at the moon that filled the Wyoming night. His words, his touch, his kiss, everything about him screamed the truth: he, too, was an expert in seduction, an accomplished competitor in the sport of bedding, a master of the art of lust.

It was his skill and nothing more that she'd nearly succumbed to. She nodded firmly to the moon. Indeed, his prowess with the finer points of ravishment explained everything. It was no doubt the reason why any coherent thought she might have had faded with a mere touch of his hand. Why his face, his laugh, his eyes filled her mind and kept her body taut and restless. And why she was almost ready to sacrifice her well-guarded virtue for a night of pleasure in his arms.

"I won't become one of those sniveling, weeping women who lose their hearts and minds and very souls to a man." She folded her arms over her chest. "I refuse to let any male use me and toss me aside like a bad card in a worse hand. And I don't care if his eyes do remind me of chocolate and his skin is as warm as the sun in midsummer and his kiss is as intoxicating as a third glass of champagne . . ."

She glared at the silent moon. "And I don't care . . ." Her voice faltered. "I don't care one whit about the desire in his eyes when he talks about his home and his family. And when he looks at me.

"He is the most infuriating, maddening man in the world. I hate him." The moon stared down at her, mute and accusing. "Very well, perhaps I don't hate him. But I don't love him. I could never love him. And I don't especially like him. Not even a little."

Why hadn't she ever paid much attention to the shadows on the moon? Shapes and shades that looked very much like a face. A smugly smiling face. A male face. "All right, maybe a little." She leaned her forearms on the windowsill. "Maybe a lot."

Did the moon's grin widen? "But it doesn't matter. Not at all. I know all about the Tyler Matthewses of the world. And I won't let him break my heart." She sighed. "No matter how exciting the breaking might be.

"Besides—" She shrugged. "He thinks shooting your brother is an appropriate response to a little deception. Lord knows what he'd think about selling land one doesn't own. The man may well be a scoundrel when it comes to women, but I'd wager he has a horribly honest streak a mile wide.

"No." Resolve pulled her upright. "There is no place in my life for Mayor Matthews. Especially not in the life his uncle's money will so comfortably provide." She threw a final, firm glare at the moon. "So you can go cast your magic somewhere else. Venice, perhaps. I have no use for you here."

She nodded and strode from the window, throwing herself into her bed and yanking the coverlet up around her ears. First thing in the morning she had that horrible fox hunt to avoid; then she could try to figure out how to get her money out of that nice banker's vault and come up with a way to circumvent Big Jack's insistence on an official ceremony complete with Her Majesty's representative. How did the tailors in Jenny's book ever manage to juggle all the annoying details of selling something that didn't exist? Gad, this was actually work. Hard, exhausting work.

Still, she smiled and snuggled deeper, it was satisfying. And she was so very close to success. So very close to Jenny's heart's desire and her own. She'd tell her sister everything in the morning. Well, everything regarding the money and how well their act was progressing. She shut her eyes tight and willed for sleep to come. Once again her treacherous body betrayed her, and through much of the long night, slumber lingered just out of reach. And when, exhausted, she finally escaped her earthbound bonds, even then oblivion eluded her.

And she dreamed of floating on a Venetian canal under a laughing moon and a supper of chocolate and wine.

Chapter 9

THE day dawned bright and beautiful, with scarcely a cloud in sight. Damn. She could use a cloud, or preferably a cloudburst, perhaps a downpour, even a flood. At this point the end of the world was far more inviting than the sight unfolding before Ophelia.

A crowd of about thirty or so residents of Dead End mingled just off the steps of the Matthews's porch. Most of the women wore skirts split in the middle, looking very much like oversized pants with a bit of feminine style. The men more or less wore what they always seemed to wear out here: denim pants, cowhide vests, boots and hats. Ophelia, of course, was attired in a fashionable English riding habit, complete with boots just a shade too big. It seemed everything about the real countess, from her waist to her feet, was a tad larger than Ophelia. Ophelia was, perhaps, a bit overdressed for the rest of the company, but she was a countess, if a bogus one, and did have to keep up appearances.

She hesitated at the top of the steps and studied the scene. Here and there, those she'd been introduced to smiled and waved, and Ophelia responded. They were such very nice people, after all. But they were not alone.

Dispersed among the crowd were—she shuddered—horses. She realized there was probably only one horse per person, yet it seemed the crowd of four-legged creatures was far greater than the gathering of two-legged ones. Perhaps it was just that they were so incredibly huge. She stared at the beasts and, one by one, they seemed to stare back. Gad, even their eyes were big. They inclined their heads toward one another, nodding like gossiping biddies, and she could have sworn they were talking about her.

Not that she cared. No, indeed. Regardless of their size, they were still just ignorant animals. She cast the one nearest, that nasty brute of Tye's, a glare of defiance. The horse stared for a long moment, then pulled its lips back and snickered. Again. Just like it had when Tye had nearly kissed her. The creature snickered once more, and the sound seemed to wash around the other horses like a wave. In seconds, they were all snickering. Every single one of those beastly, terrifying creatures was laughing at her. And not one other single human being here seemed to notice.

"Morning, Countess." Tye strode into view at the bottom of the steps. "Sleep well?"

She stared. He couldn't possibly know how very little she'd slept and how her slumber had been fraught with dreams of him. She squared her shoulders and smiled sweetly. "Quite well, and you?"

"Like a baby." Something flickered through his eyes, and she knew with a sure and certain instinct that he hadn't slept any better than she had. Good. If he was going to invade her nights, the least she could do was create havoc with his slumber as well. Still . . .

had she filled his dreams the way he had filled hers? Odd, how very much she hoped she didn't like him. Not even a little.

"Are you ready for Dead End's version of a fox hunt?"

She raised a brow. "I had heard all attempts to find a fox had failed, so I assumed this particular event would be canceled."

"Canceled? Countess, this is the most interesting thing to hit Dead End in a long time. Why, folks are downright delighted at the chance to chase a fox, or anything else they come up with, through the county."

"But without a fox . . ." Hope sounded in her voice.

Tye grinned. "We'll just have to go after coyote."

"That's what Mr. Montgomery said, but it sounded so . . . so . . ."

"Insane? Ridiculous? Stupid?"

"Well . . ." She shrugged weakly. "Yes."

"That's Dead End for you." Tye laughed, and the sound shivered through her and weakened her knees. "Of course, we'll all be a lot smarter when we get used to calling this place by its new name."

"Empire City?"

"Right. Still and all, when it comes down to it"— his eyes sparked, dark and dangerous with a secret promise—" 'What's in a name—' "

"Stop it, Mr. Matthews, stop it right now." She crossed her arms over her chest and tapped her foot on the porch floor.

His eyes widened with innocence. "What? It's just a little Shakespeare, that's all."

She clenched her teeth. "I know what it is, and I know what you're doing."

"And am I doing it well?"

She heaved an exasperated sigh. "Yes, you irritating man, you do it extremely well."

"And are we still talking about Shakespeare?"

"Well, what on earth would we be talking about if . . ." Ophelia stared at his knowing grin. Lord, she had to get out of this town and away from those eyes and those lips and that strong, solid body before she threw any sense of self-preservation to the winds and leapt into his bed. She struggled to get her rampaging senses back under control and tossed him a pleasant smile. "Shakespeare aside, I suggest we get this little performance underway."

He nodded in the midst of an obvious battle to keep a straight face. She wanted nothing more than to smack him. Or shoot him. But once again she'd left her gun in her room, within handy reach in the top drawer of a washstand by the side of her bed in the case of midnight intruders. Damned inconvenient, though, when it came to the ever-present need to shoot Tyler Matthews.

Shooting him would regretfully have to wait. Right now she had to escape from the ersatz fox hunt. But that was easy.

Ophelia took a single step toward the porch stairs, stopped and gasped, as if she'd just remembered something crucial. She clapped her hand to her cheek in dramatic dismay. "Oh, dear."

"What's wrong?" Concern flashed across Tye's face.

"I'm afraid I won't be joining the rest of you after all." She heaved a deep sigh of regret. Lord, she was good. Sarah Bernhardt had nothing on her. "I had completely forgotten where I was. I simply can't ride on one of those." She gestured at a saddle. "I'm afraid I'm accustomed to an English sidesaddle. And I'm certain you don't—"

"Oh, I have one." Montgomery sauntered up to stand beside Tye.

"Mr. Montgomery." Her heart sank to the pit of her stomach, but she forced a tight smile. "I didn't see you arrive."

Montgomery shrugged. "No matter. I am indeed present and, anticipating the needs of a noble Englishwoman, have brought along a sidesaddle. English, of course."

"Of course," she murmured.

"I'll be damned." Tye grinned in admiration. "Where did you come up with a sidesaddle?"

"I've had it for years. It's a souvenir of sorts. I, um"—amusement gleamed in Montgomery's eye—"shall we say won it? Its previous owner, due to a series of unforeseen events, found herself in a rather remarkable situation, and I simply offered, after a unique and completely memorable evening of previously unknown—"

"Never mind, Mr. Montgomery," Ophelia said quickly. "I scarcely think it's necessary to go into extreme detail over how you acquired the saddle."

"Oh, I don't know." Tye's drawl was slow and sultry, and she wondered if everything he said always had a double meaning. "Sometimes the details are the best part."

"Well, I for one don't wish to hear them," she snapped.

Montgomery leaned toward Tye. "Later, old man."

Later, she'd be on a vile horse, all because of that annoying foreigner, unless she could figure a way out of this mess and fast. There was no way in this world or any other she was going to climb on one of those creatures. Not now. Not ever. And definitely not with an instrument so obviously designed for sheer torture as a sidesaddle. But how? She drew her brows together and groped for an idea, any idea that would keep her firmly on solid ground.

"Ophelia?" Tye said. "Are you ready?"

"Certainly." She clenched her fists by her side and stepped forward, her boots slipping with her walk. Hell. She thought they'd fit well enough to handle this. She would likely kill herself right here on the ground and save the blasted horses the trouble. She'd trip and fall flat on her face if she didn't watch out, no doubt cracking her skull or breaking a limb or twisting an ankle . . .

Twisting an ankle?

She winced at the very idea of pain and hesitated, but one glance at the snickering beasts, obviously prepared to damage far more than a mere ankle, convinced her. While there might well be another method of escape, she had absolutely no idea what it was.

"As ready as I'll ever be." She smiled brightly, drew a deep breath and took a broad step off the first stair and into . . . nothing.

It should have been so easy. A simple little step off the porch. A tiny stumble. A mild, moderate drop and success. But Ophelia misjudged the exact width of the stairs and the tendency of just about anything to bounce. She tumbled down the stairs hitting the wooden planks once-twice-three times. Panic and pain surged through her. Finally she came to rest in a bruising heap of ripped fabric, disheveled hair and sheer humiliation. There had to be a better way.

"Ophelia!" Tye was at her side in a flash, genuine concern in his eyes. Eyes that seemed to see right into her soul. For a moment the world receded, and even her aches disappeared. "Ophelia? Are you hurt?"

"I . . . don't know." It was, for once, the truth. Her plan had worked far too well.

"Is she all right?" Montgomery crouched down beside Tye.

Lorelie and Big Jack ran toward her, followed by the others.

"Countess, darlin', can you move?" Big Jack cast his gaze over her with the practiced eye of a man experienced in the injuries of ranch hands or livestock.

"Oh, dear." Lorelie eyed her with an anxious look. "I very much doubt if she'll be able to ride after this."

Triumph filled Ophelia. Thank goodness. Any minor pain was well worth it to avoid the horses from hell.

"Pity," Montgomery said, "you'll have to cancel the hunt."

"Nobody much wanted to hunt coyote anyway." Jack shrugged. "Once we couldn't find a damned fox, it seemed kind of pointless and—"

"Stupid?" Tye said.

Lorelie planted her hands on her hips and glared down at him. "There was nothing stupid about it, Tye. It was our way of making the countess feel at home. And it sounded like a great deal of fun when the idea came up." She cast an accusing glare around the crowd. "If those of you who had volunteered to find a fox in the first place had done your job, we wouldn't—"

"Wait just one minute there, Lorelie. It ain't easy to find a fox when you want one," an indignant voice rang out from the crowd.

Ophelia craned her neck to see who was talking. Not an easy task. Only Tye and Montgomery were beside her on the ground. Everyone else stood towering over them. And everyone else seemed, more or less, to have forgotten all about the injured countess at their feet.

"Tye's right, anyway," another man called. "This was stupid. Trying to be something we're not."

At once the air above her filled with flying comments and accusations and charges, with everyone throwing in their own opinions and doing so at the top of their lungs.

"This whole Empire City thing is ridiculous and—"

"It is not! It's a great—"

"—needs civilization and respectability any—"

"—my opinion, it's all a load of—"

"—the price you pay for progress! I think—"

"—and I think *you're* a load of—"

Tye and Montgomery exchanged knowing grins.

"What on earth is going on?" Ophelia stared at the two men.

Laughter glittered in Tye's eye. "Town meeting."

Ophelia stared with disbelief. "Shouldn't somebody do something? It sounds like they're about to kill each other."

"She's right." Montgomery nodded. "Somebody should do something."

"What about you?" Tye said.

"Me? I'm not the mayor." Montgomery shook his head in an overstated gesture of regret. "I hardly think I should get involved. I'm practically a stranger. You grew up with these people."

"No, he's right." Ophelia glared at Tye. "You're the mayor. Do something."

"You think I should?" Tye glanced at his friend.

"Good question," Montgomery said thoughtfully. "But I daresay you can't let it go on. Sooner or later the good citizens of Dead End—"

"Empire City," Ophelia murmured.

"—will come to blows. Possibly even gunfire, and

before you know it"—Montgomery choked in an obvious effort to restrain a full-fledged laugh—"any possibility of respectability and civilized behavior will be gone."

"Dead in its tracks," Tye said solemnly.

"Along with one or two of its citizens, I expect," Montgomery added.

Ophelia gasped. "Mr. Matthews! Tye!"

Tye heaved a long-suffering sigh. "Well, we can't have that."

"No, indeed." Montgomery nodded.

Tye sighed again. "I guess I'll have to do something."

He rose to his feet, and the crowd parted around him but ignored his presence, their scathing comments still littering the air. With a swift, sure move, he bent and swept her into his arms.

"Ow!" Pain shot through her. "Hell and damnation."

Montgomery leaned forward and whispered into her ear. "I believe you mean 'bloody hell.' 'Hell and damnation' are far too American for a countess."

"Thanks," she muttered and glared at Tye. "And just what do you think you're doing?"

He grinned down at her. "Something. Just like you told me."

"I didn't tell you to pick me up like a sack of flour."

"Can you walk?"

"Well, of course . . ." What was she about to admit? ". . . not." She shook her head vigorously. "No, no, I think I've hurt something. Possibly my ankle. Very likely my ankle. Twisted, no doubt."

"Put your arms around me," he said softly.

"Mr. Matthews, I really don't think—"

"Do you want me to drop you?"

"Very well." She wrapped her arms around his neck. "Where are you taking me?"

"To your bed." His voice was firm, and he started up the steps leaving the squabbling citizens of the fair community of Whatever behind him.

"Aren't you going to stop them?"

"Nope."

"Do you think they'll kill each other?"

"Nope."

She thought for a moment. "Do you think taking me to my room is really such a good idea?"

"Yep."

"I don't," she said as firmly as she could manage.

"We'll see."

She swallowed a lump, probably her heart, lodged in her throat. What was he up to? And more to the point, what did she want him to be up to? The man had her so confused. At any given moment she either wished to kiss him or kill him. She sighed, and he pulled her tighter against his chest. Gad, he was solid. His warm, male scent enveloped her, and she was hard pressed to keep her thoughts from running to all kinds of curious ideas about touching him and being touched by him and—

"Ophelia?"

She raised her head. When had they reached her room? She stared at him.

"I'm going to put you on the bed now." His eyes were tender, his voice considerate.

Her blood pounded in her veins. He carefully laid her on the bed. Terror battled with excitement and anticipation. This was surely it. One kiss and she'd melt into a puddle in his arms. She sucked in a deep breath. And oh, what a glorious melting it would be.

"I'm going to take your boot off," he said gently.

"My boot?" she said without thinking. "Don't you want to kiss me first?"

His brows pulled together in a puzzled frown. "Well, sure, I'd love to kiss you, but first let's get the boot off."

Certainly Ophelia had never been with a man, but one didn't grow up backstage among actors and actresses without picking up at least the rudimentary mechanics of love and lovemaking. She had heard about unusual acts of intimacy, and this boot business of his sounded odd to say the least.

"Wait just a minute." She struggled to sit up.

"It will be easier if you lay down," he said impatiently and gently pushed her back, flat on the bed.

"Well, then, let's make it a challenge, shall we?" She sat up again and glared.

"What is wrong with you, Ophelia?"

"Me? There's nothing wrong with me. What's wrong with you?"

He stared at her as if she was a complete idiot. "I'm fine. I didn't fall off the porch."

"Well, I did, and if you could just control your lust long enough—"

"My lust? What are you talking about, woman?"

"My boot." She shook her foot. "Why do you want to start with my boot?"

"I thought you twisted your ankle?"

"My ankle?" Gad, she *was* a complete idiot. "Yes, of course . . . my ankle."

"What did you think?" Tye stared at her. Awareness dawned on his face, and his eyes widened. "I'll be damned, Ophelia, you thought—"

"No, Tye, really." She clasped her hands together

and shook her head. How mortifying. Had she ever been so embarrassed? "I didn't think anything. Nothing at all."

He threw his head back and laughed. Unrestrained mirth filled the room. She released a breath she didn't know she held; at least he wasn't mad. He laughed, and tears glimmered in his eyes. Her chagrin faded. Honestly, it wasn't that humorous. How was she to know he wasn't that kind of man?

"Good Lord, Ophelia." He wiped the tears from his eyes and sat down beside her. "I haven't heard anything so funny in years."

"I'm delighted to have provided so much entertainment." She crossed her arms over her chest. "Now if you would kindly leave my room?"

"I don't think so." He chuckled again. Could any man's laugh be quite so annoying?

"And why not?" she said coldly.

"Because, my love." He leaned forward abruptly and kissed the tip of her nose. She jerked back and glared. "We have yet to check on that ankle of yours."

"I'm certain my ankle is fine." She clenched her jaw and nodded at the door. "Now get out."

"No." He stared her straight in the eye. Determination glimmered there and a subtle challenge. "I'm taking your boot off."

She lifted her chin in defiance. "You're not taking my boot, or anything else, off."

A wicked smile lifted the corners of his lips. "Oh, no?"

The realization of exactly what she'd said flashed through her, and heat rushed to her face. Still, he would not get the better of her this time. And she was keeping those blasted boots on.

"Get out, Mr. Matthews."

"I'll make you a little deal, Countess." Tye got to his feet and with a leisurely gesture pulled a deck of cards from his back pocket.

She narrowed her eyes. "What are those for?"

"You seemed to have had such a good time last night settling your negotiations with my uncle with a mere draw of the cards that perhaps we can settle our little dispute the same way."

"We don't have a dispute. I have a boot. I want it on. You want it off." She shrugged. "My boot. My foot. My choice."

"Oh, come now, Ophelia." He sat down on the bed beside her and shuffled the cards methodically from one hand to the other. "You seem to me like a woman who enjoys a bit of chance. What if, say, we draw. Winner decides if the boot stays on or comes off."

She stared at him for a long, considering moment. When it came right down to it, what harm would it do, anyway? If she lost, he would take off her boot and she'd pretend pain in her ankle. Not that it was all that far-fetched. Her little tumble had left her whole body aching, but with her luck lately, her ankle would be completely unscathed. And if she won, he'd get out of her room and leave her alone. Exactly what she wanted, wasn't it?

"Very well." She heaved a sigh of resignation. "But you go first."

He raised a brow. "Ladies first."

"My boot. My foot. My choice." She gritted her teeth. It was superstition on her part, but she always seemed to do better when she went last. She'd ignored that with Big Jack and had lost the draw, even if ultimately she'd won the contest. "Go ahead."

He shuffled the cards in a manner slow and almost

seductive. His long, tanned fingers seemed to caress each pasteboard like a teasing lover. Ophelia stared, mesmerized. She'd seen a lot of men deal a lot of cards in a lot of different ways, but she'd never yet seen anyone make the process look, well, suggestive. Her gaze rose to meet his, and he lifted a brow. He couldn't possibly know what she was thinking, could he? His hands never halted. His arrogant smile never faltered. His gaze never left hers.

"Cut." His voice, just like his actions, was provocative and personal and thrilling.

She glanced at the deck, picked it up and expertly split it with one hand alone. It was a trick she'd learned as a child. One she rarely used. It was never good to let other gamblers know just how skilled you really were. But somehow, with Tye, at least for a moment, she wanted very much for him to realize he was not dealing with a mere pretty face. She doubted she was like any other woman he'd ever met. And right now, she wanted him to know it.

He raised a brow in grudging admiration. "Very nice."

"Thank you." Her gaze met his. "I believe it's your turn, Mr. Matthews."

He picked a card from the deck, his gaze locked on hers. "Now you."

"But you haven't looked at your card."

He shrugged. "I can wait."

"Can you?" she said softly. "For how long?"

"As long as it takes."

She couldn't seem to pull her gaze from his. His eyes, deep and endless and dark as eternity, held her captive, and an ache she'd never known before shuddered through her. She drew a deep, steadying breath and pulled a card. Without looking, she flipped it faceup on the bed.

She glanced down, and her stomach knotted with disappointment or . . . anticipation.

The two of clubs lay on the coverlet.

"It looks like I've won." His voice was heavy with a meaning she didn't dare explore.

"Not yet, Mr. Matthews. Your card?"

He tossed it toward hers. The pasteboard fluttered through the air with an insolent indifference, as if the card and the man had been partners in this curious contest where, she suspected, the stakes were much higher than the removal of a mere boot.

The card settled next to hers.

The king of hearts.

She could have laughed at the irony, but any amusement died in her throat. She stared into his eyes and read a promise of desire that stole her breath and her will.

"Like I said, I won. Now, lay down."

"Very well." Her stomach fluttered and she sank back onto the pillow. Why was it so warm in here all of a sudden? "You may remove"—she swallowed hard and stared at the ceiling—"my boot."

He slipped one hand beneath her left heel, his other reaching under her skirts to grip the top of the boot that stretched nearly to her knee. Why on earth were these boots so high, anyway? Slowly, he pulled the leather footwear downward, gently sliding it off her foot with a surprising ease.

Tye frowned. "Well, there's your problem, Ophelia, it's no wonder you fell. These boots are definitely too big for you."

"Really?" She widened her eyes in feigned surprise.

"I shall have to chastise my bootmaker the moment I return to London. He has my measurements. I can't imagine why he'd make such a—oh, my goodness!"

Tye's clever fingers carefully probed and explored and massaged her silk-covered ankles. What a unique sensation. How personal. How exciting. How intimate. He shook his head. "I don't see any swelling. There doesn't seem to be any bruising either."

"Well . . ." She sighed. "Now that I think about it, the problem could be with . . . the other ankle."

"The other ankle?"

She cast him a look of innocence. "I may have gotten confused."

A spark of sin gleamed in his eye, and her heart thudded against her ribs. "May I check that ankle, or do I have to draw for the honor first?"

"Why, Mr. Matthews, I admit, you won. I scarcely think it would be in the proper spirit to make you select another card." She nodded firmly. "Please, proceed."

The corners of his mouth twitched as if he was hard pressed to contain a smile. She squeezed her eyes shut. At this particular moment, she didn't really care about the flicker of triumph in his eyes. She'd never known the touch of a man's hand on her leg, or anywhere else, before. A touch that was quite remarkable in the delightfully terrifying sensations it aroused. A touch she wanted to experience again.

He repeated his actions with her other boot, his movements even slower and more deliberate than before. Again, he pulled the boot off with no difficulty and checked her ankle with fingers warm and clever and knowing. His hands circled her leg, his touch a mere whisper of intoxicating sensation that climbed upward from her limbs through her body and her soul. His fingers traveled higher to her calf and then the back of her knee, and she lost herself in the sheer bliss of his caress.

How had he gone so far? Her breath came faster. She really had to stop him. Soon. A tiny moan escaped her lips. Definitely, she must put an end to this. Any moment now.

Abruptly, his touch vanished and she snapped her eyes open. His face filled her vision.

"I believe"—he'd settled himself on the side of the bed and sat leaning over her—"your ankles are uninjured. In fact, I'd say they're really quite lovely ankles. In damn near perfect shape."

"Thank you," she said breathlessly.

"But I am still concerned. You took a nasty fall."

"Oh, I'm quite certain I'm fine."

"You can never be too sure." His voice was low and deep with meaning she feared and wanted. "For example, it would be a real shame if, say, that lovely neck of yours was damaged in any way." He bent his mouth to a surprisingly sensitive point just below the lobe of her ear and kissed the spot gently.

She gasped. "I didn't fall on my neck."

"Still . . ." His mouth traveled lower to meet the top of her buttoned jacket at the base of her throat. "One can never be too careful about injuries incurred in a fall."

Gad, if she thought his touch on her ankle was exquisite, it was nothing compared to his lips on her neck. She struggled to get the words out. "I suppose not."

Dimly she heard the pop of her buttons and the jacket loosened around her. His mouth nudged the collar of her blouse, and at once cooling air and warm breath sent chills scampering across her exposed skin. Heavens, when did he unbutton her blouse?

"Tye, I don't think—"

"Ophelia." His voice was firm. "We have to make sure you're all right."

"I'm . . . all . . . right," she said in a voice weak with arousal. What was he doing to her?

"No, no." His voice was muffled against her skin. "I'm not completely confident of that yet."

His lips drifted lower, pushing aside the flimsy protection of her chemise to breasts supported by a corset she hadn't realized was far too confining.

"Tye! I don't—"

"It's your lungs, Ophelia." Tye murmured against skin that burned with the merest graze of his lips. "You could have damaged your lungs."

"My lungs?" she whispered in a haze of desire that scrambled her senses and dazed her mind. His mouth fastened on her breast, the nipple tightening at his touch. She arched upward with an involuntary jerk of sheer pleasure at the shocking feel of his tongue on her sensitive flesh. She clutched at his shoulders and marveled at the overwhelming rush of elation and need and heat that surged through her.

So this was what women found in the arms of a man. This was what they sacrificed their honor and virtue and very souls for. What they willingly offered with no thought of what tomorrow might bring or what might be stolen forever today. At once she understood the glory and the wonder and the sheer joy that was worth whatever sacrifice it asked, whatever price had to be paid. Whatever the cost, it was nothing compared to what was to be shared with this one man at this one moment.

No!

The word screamed through her head in a final effort to affirm all she'd ever been or wanted to be or refused to become. She would not be like those women who hung on her father's every move or the pathetic creatures who waited at clandestine late-night suppers for actors who swore undying love and fealty. She would not be the plaything of any man. Not even a man who made her body ache and her heart sing.

Not even for Tyler Matthews.

"Tye." She gasped, and her arms flailed out at her sides in a desperate attempt to sit up. He seemed not to notice or not to care, and she realized with a newly sharpened instinct that he was as overcome as she was, or at least, as she had been a moment ago. Her hand hit the washstand beside the bed, and she fumbled with the drawer until it slid open.

"Tye," she said again. "Stop! Now!"

"You don't mean that, Ophelia," he murmured.

"Oh, but I do."

Tye raised his head and his eyes widened, passion fleeing in the wake of surprise and possibly amusement. She aimed her derringer at a point right above, and a few mere inches away from, the bridge of his nose, smack dab between his eyes. His delicious chocolate eyes.

"I suspect this means you're feeling better." A wry note colored his words.

"Why, yes, thank you." There was an annoying breathless quality to her voice, and she fought for control.

"Your hands are trembling," he said calmly. "Perhaps if you'd point that a bit to one side or the other, it won't discharge accidently and shoot my head off."

"I assure you, Mr. Matthews, it will be no accident."

"Ophelia, I told you last night you were a bad liar." He heaved a sigh of regret and straightened up. "The way you're shaking, that gun could easily go off at any minute. And even as small as it is, it would probably kill me, and I can't believe you really want that."

She pulled herself up to a sitting position, all the while keeping the barrel leveled in his direction. "You don't know anything about what I want."

"Oh, but Ophelia, I do." His gaze trapped hers, his eyes simmered with a need she shared, his voice low with a truth she could deny to him but not to herself. "I know exactly what you want."

"And what do I want?"

He reached forward and gently clasped her shoulders, ignoring the gun now pointed straight at his chest. Did he really believe she wouldn't shoot? Or was he the biggest fool she'd ever met?

"You want to lose your senses and your mind in my arms. You want to feel sensations and emotions you've only begun to explore. You want to surrender to the ache crying inside you for release."

She stared. "Do I?"

"You do."

"And what do you want?"

"I want you, Ophelia." He pulled her to him, the gun in her hand pressed against his heart. He ignored it and crushed his lips to hers. How could he trust that she wouldn't shoot him right here? Right now? The answer sank into her like a stone. He was right. She did want him and everything he offered. But heaven help her, she wanted more.

"Ophelia!" Jenny's indignant voice sounded from the doorway.

Instinctively, Ophelia and Tye sprang apart. The derringer jerked and fired. Ophelia stared in horror.

"You shot me!" Tye's voice rose with disbelief.

Blood oozed from the top of his shoulder.

"Damnation, Ophelia, did you kill him?" Jenny cried.

"Don't curse," Ophelia said without thinking and winced at the red stain spreading across his shirt. "Of course I didn't kill him. If I killed him, he wouldn't be sitting up."

"You almost killed me!" He glared accusingly.

"I did not. Honestly, it's not even serious. If it was serious, it would be spurting. It's just sort of"—she wrinkled her nose in disgust—"flowing. A trickle, really."

"A trickle? It doesn't feel like a trickle. It feels"—he paused dramatically—"fatal."

"Well, it's not. It's a trickle. And it appears to be stopping, at any rate." Now that the initial shock had passed, she realized he was scarcely hurt at all. "Here." She snatched up a towel from the washstand and tossed it at him.

It slapped across his face and he glared, clamping it on his wounded shoulder.

"And look." She pointed to a small nick in the wall near the ceiling. "See? Right there? That's where the bullet hit. It just grazed you."

His mouth dropped open, as if he couldn't believe her apparent disregard for his injury. "It hurts!"

"Are you sure you didn't seriously injure him?" Jenny said anxiously.

"Of course she seriously injured me. She shot me. That's serious." Tye stared at Jenny. "Who in the hell are you?"

"Who am I? Who are you? Who *is* he?" Jenny planted her hands on her hips and glared.

"This is my sis—my maid, Jenny." Ophelia gestured at Jenny.

"Oh." Tye brightened. "You're the one Zach was talking about."

"Who is *he*?" Ophelia frowned.

"He's one of the hands," Tye said. "Actually, he's lived here at the ranch since he was about fourteen, when his dad died."

Ophelia stared in confusion. "I thought Big Jack and Lorelie raised *you*."

"They really are nice people, you know," Jenny said to Ophelia.

"We've established that. It's the best part," Ophelia said under her breath. "Do Big Jack and Lorelie take in all the homeless waifs in Wyoming?"

"Not really. Just me and then Zach." Tye cringed. "Ouch. I'm really in a great deal of pain. Are you going to do something about this?"

"You must be Tye." Jenny smiled shyly. "I've heard a lot about you."

"How do you know this Zach?" Ophelia scrambled off the bed.

"I think I'm bleeding to death," Tye said, craning his neck to peer at his shoulder.

Jenny shrugged. "He's teaching me to ride."

"Yep." Tye heaved a heavy sigh. "I'm dying, all right."

"A horse?" Ophelia gasped.

"My life is flashing before my eyes," Tye said.

"Of course a horse. What else?" Defiance colored Jenny's voice.

"I'm getting weak." Tye groaned.

"But horses, Jenny." Ophelia shook her head. "They're vile, nasty creatures. Big and huge and always laughing."

Tye stared. "I've never heard them laugh."

"Well, they do," Ophelia snapped.

"I really don't think they laugh," Jenny said.

"Nope. They definitely don't laugh. They're good and loyal beasts. For example." He stood and clasped his hand to his shoulder. "Your horse would never shoot you."

"She would if you were trying to seduce her." Ophelia glared.

Jenny gasped. "He tried to seduce his horse?"

"Not his horse." Ophelia released an irritated sigh. "Me."

"But I don't understand. Then why was the horse laughing?" Jenny shook her head as if to clear it.

"Horses do not laugh!" Tye's voice boomed through the room. "And I was not seducing you!"

"What would you call it?"

"Well . . ." Tye's gaze darted around the room as if looking for an answer. "All right, I was seducing you. But you weren't resisting."

"I shot you." Ophelia squared her shoulders. "I'd say that's resistance."

He narrowed his eyes. "You said it was an accident."

"My goodness! What's going on here?"

Lorelie stood in the doorway, eyes wide, hand clasped to her cheek, shock coloring her face. At once, Ophelia realized how very odd the scene must have looked. She and Tye screaming at each other about laughing horses and seduction and—

"Countess, I would suggest . . ." Lorelie nodded discreetly at the front of Ophelia's riding habit.

"Ophelia!" Jenny rolled her eyes toward the ceiling.

"Good Lord!" Ophelia grabbed the edges of her blouse, pulled them together and frantically tried to get the buttons in their tiny little holes. Damn. She had completely forgotten how horribly exposed she had been when the gun had gone off. She glanced up to meet Tye's gaze. Surely the man was not amused by all this? "You must accept my apologies, Lorelie, I was—"

"Don't give it a second thought, my dear." A weak smile touched Lorelie's lips, as if she really wanted to mean what she said but couldn't quite manage. "These things happen."

Tye cast Ophelia a smug smile. "I'm glad to see you can walk."

"I'm glad to see you're not dead!" Ophelia said sharply.

He snorted in disdain. "No thanks to you."

Ophelia gritted her teeth. "It was an accident. However, given further consideration—"

"Countess . . . Ophelia! Tyler!" Lorelie's voice snapped with the uncompromising tone of a mother chastising bickering children. "That is quite enough. Ophelia, you can continue to disrobe and get in bed. Whether you can walk or not, you took quite a tumble. I daresay you'll be stiff and in pain by evening. And as for you." She stepped in front of Ophelia and turned her glare on Tye. "I can't imagine what you were thinking, forcing your attentions on a guest in my home. Such behavior, indeed!"

"She shot me." His voice rang with indignation.

"I probably would have shot you too," Lorelie said.

"It was an accident," Ophelia said. Why wouldn't the irritating man accept that?

"Hah! Some accident."

"If I did it on purpose"—Ophelia grinned at him from behind Lorelie—"you'd be dead."

"Ophelia!" Jenny clapped her hand over her mouth.

Tye's gaze slid from Ophelia to Jenny and back. "So this is your maid?"

"Yes," Ophelia said cautiously.

"So why does she call you . . . Ophelia?" Triumph flickered in his eyes.

"It's her name?" Jenny said helpfully.

Ophelia groaned to herself. Why was it every time she turned around there was some annoying little detail that had completely slipped by her? She didn't recall the tailors having this much problem with the emperor. She glared at Tye, a conceited smile plastered on his face. It was a good thing he hadn't worn that look when she'd still had her gun in her hand.

"Well?" he prompted smugly.

She should have killed him. "Well . . . she calls me Ophelia because . . ." *Why? Why? Why?* Of course! Gad, she was good. "Because she has a speech difficulty and she can't pronounce *countess*."

"Poor little thing," Lorelie murmured.

Tye laughed. "Oh, come now. Do you really expect me to believe that?"

"It's true." Ophelia turned to Jenny. "Say 'countess.'"

Panic flashed through Jenny's eyes, then she pulled herself up to her full, if tiny, stature and said, "C-c-c-c-c-."

"Very well." Tye clenched his teeth. "What about 'my lady'?"

Ophelia shrugged. "Jenny?"

Jenny lifted her chin defiantly. "M-m-m-m-"

"This is ridiculous." Tye snorted in disbelief. "You're

telling me the only words this child can't say are *count-ess* and *my lady*?"

"I have a problem with *Bridgewater* too," Jenny said sweetly.

"Ah-hah!" Tye pointed at Jenny. "Caught you! You just said—"

"That's quite enough." Lorelie glared at her nephew. "You have thoroughly embarrassed this child, and I refuse to let you continue—"

"But—"

"No buts, Tyler Matthews. You get right down to the kitchen and let Alma take a look at that little scrape of yours." Lorelie hustled him out of the room. "And, Countess, you get some rest."

He stopped in the doorway and glared at Ophelia over his shoulder. "You're lying to me again. And I still say you don't do it well."

"Come along now, Tyler." Lorelie nudged him down the hall.

"I do not lie," Ophelia said in a haughty manner, adding under her breath, "I act."

"She shot me, you know." Tye's voice trailed behind him down the hall.

"I know, dear," Lorelie replied faintly. "You'll live."

Jenny turned wide eyes to her sister. "I can't say *countess*? You are good."

"Thank you." Ophelia bit back a smile. "I rather liked your addition of Bridgewater. Did you see his face when you pronounced the word you said you couldn't?"

Jenny grinned. "I've never seen anyone look quite so—"

"Shocked? Confused? Victorious?"

"Actually, I was going to say silly."

The sisters stared at each other for a moment, then burst into laughter. They tumbled onto the bed in the throes of hysteria until tears ran down their cheeks and their sides ached.

"Goodness." Ophelia wiped her eyes, propped her head on her hand and stared at her sister. "That was funny. I really didn't mean to shoot him."

"He'll no doubt realize that." Jenny grinned. "When he heals."

"It won't take him long. It's not much of a wound." Ophelia chuckled. "I could have done some real damage, but this was, of course, an accident."

The sisters fell into a companionable silence. What would have happened if Jenny hadn't come in when she had? Would Ophelia now be a fallen woman? Regret battled with relief. Not that it really mattered. She was past the point when most women married. Goodness, she was already twenty-three and well on her way to becoming a genuine spinster. Why, when it came right down to it, what was she saving herself for?

The feelings Tye aroused in her were at once wonderful and frightening. A sudden thought struck with a surprising clarity: why couldn't she relinquish her virtue, give in to her own desires and still remain true to herself? There was no reason why she had to sacrifice her soul in order to experience the bliss Tye so eloquently offered her body. Still, could she really separate one from the other?

"He knows, doesn't he?" Jenny plucked at the coverlet on the bed. "About us? About you?"

Ophelia sighed. "Probably. But he has no real proof, and until he does—" she shrugged—"I doubt Big Jack will believe him."

"So, what do we do now?"

Ophelia rolled over on her back and stared at the ceiling. "I don't know exactly. I have to figure out some way to get our money."

"You mean Big Jack's money?"

"Not anymore." Ophelia couldn't resist a slight note of satisfaction. "It's our money now. And we need to get to it and get out of town."

"How are you going to get around this official ceremony they're planning?"

"I don't know that either," Ophelia said, her tone sharper than expected. "I'm hoping to avoid it altogether. I said I'd write and determine if a British representative can come to Dead End, but perhaps the letter will get lost. It will all work out."

Jenny was silent for a long moment. "How do you feel about Tye Matthews?"

"He's annoying. He's irritating. He's arrogant. He's smug. He's—"

"You like him, don't you?"

"Most certainly not!" Ophelia sighed. "I'm afraid I do."

Jenny's voice was soft. "Do you love him?"

"I don't know." Ophelia tried to put her thoughts into words. "I'm not sure I know what love is. I know when he touches me I feel like rare crystal that could shatter with the barest pressure of his fingers or his lips. I know he seems to linger always in the back of my mind and I want to avoid him and be with him at the same time. I know at any given moment he makes me long to be in his arms or shoot his head off. And I very much fear"—her voice softened—"when we leave here, I shall miss him quite a bit."

Jenny nodded sagely. "It's love, all right."

Ophelia groaned. "I certainly hope not."

•

"He's awfully handsome, isn't he?" Jenny grinned. "So tall and strong, with all that blonde hair and those brown eyes."

"Chocolate."

"What?"

"Chocolate." Ophelia sighed. "His eyes are like chocolate."

"Oh dear," Jenny murmured.

"I know." Regret and resignation sounded in Ophelia's voice. "I've never been able to say no to chocolate."

Chapter 10

"**I** REALLY think I'm quite recovered." A hopeful note sounded in Ophelia's voice.

"Well, perhaps today, dear, you may get up." Lorelie perched on the side of the bed and smiled.

It had been two full days since Ophelia's fall, and Lorelie had insisted—no, commanded—that Ophelia stay in bed every minute of them. Whoever would have thought this tiny, sweet little woman had a will of iron, strong enough to rule not merely her home but probably the entire world? Queen Victoria herself would likely meet her match in Lorelie Matthews.

"Actually, I had been thinking of an outing you might enjoy." Lorelie's eyes twinkled with excitement. "The Every Other Tuesday and Thursday Afternoon Ladies Cultural Society meets today."

Ophelia sat up straighter. "For cards?"

"Cards and . . . other things."

"What kinds of other things?"

"You really have missed a great deal, dear, by staying in bed," Lorelie said with a shake of her head.

"But you insisted I stay in bed."

Lorelie cast her a knowing smile. "And don't you feel much better because of it?"

Ophelia nodded in surrender. She did have to admit that her fall had left her bruised where she'd never imagined she'd have bruises, She'd been too stiff to move and too sore to really care. Today, at least, she seemed nearly normal.

"So tell me, Lorelie, what did I miss?"

Lorelie's expression brightened. "To begin with, the Every Other Tuesday and Thursday Afternoon Ladies Cultural Society has decided we really must improve ourselves if we are going to have a representative of the queen visit. Goodness, if Jack is to be a count, we would hate to do anything that would disgrace him."

"Of course not."

"So, we'd like you to teach us proper deportment."

"Proper deportment?" What on earth did that mean?

"Yes, indeed." Lorelie nodded enthusiastically. "None of us have the faintest idea how to act with an ambassador or a count, even though that will be Jack and I daresay being a count probably won't change him a great deal, at least I hope not, but one never knows what a man might get into his head. Admittedly, only a few of us have spent any time with you, but we've decided you're an exception. You're so pleasant and terribly—" Lorelie shrugged in an apologetic manner—"normal. The ladies have discussed it, and we all agree. You're not much different than an American, except for the accent, of course. Why, you're not at all the way we expected an English countess would be."

"I'm not?" Ophelia said faintly. Mild disappointment and curiosity trickled through her. "Exactly how am I not what you expected?"

"Well, I don't know that I can put my finger on it. You simply seem to be so much more on one hand and on the other . . ." She winced. "Somewhat less."

Ophelia stared, resisting the urge to shake her head in a futile effort to understand Lorelie's convoluted comment. "What?"

"Gracious, I'm not explaining this at all well, am I? Well then, never mind. And you mustn't let it worry you, my dear." Lorelie waved her hand in a vague gesture of unconcern. "We mean it as, well, a compliment."

"Thank you. I think."

"Not at all. Now then . . ." A brisk businesslike tone colored the older woman's words. "We feel if we are to be ready in time, we haven't a moment to lose. So the Every Other Tuesday and Thursday Afternoon Ladies Cultural Society will meet every day until further notice. Except for Sundays, of course, and perhaps Saturdays. One must draw the line somewhere, I should think."

"Why must you meet every day except Sundays and perhaps Saturdays?"

"Why? Well, we all need to learn to curtsy, I suspect, and anything else you wish to teach us."

Ophelia could handle teaching them to curtsy, although it could end up a bit more like a stage bow. But who would know? As to anything else . . . "I'm not sure you need much more than a curtsy."

"Really?" Lorelie drew her brows together thoughtfully. "In that case, I suppose we shall simply have to resort to cards."

"That would be nice," Ophelia said. Perhaps here

was her opportunity for a little ready cash. Especially since she had yet to determine how to get her money out from under the watchful eye of Dead End's banker.

"It would, wouldn't it?" Lorelie beamed. "Of course we will have to forgo our meeting on those days when we're involved in construction of the opera house."

Ophelia stared. "The Every Other Tuesday and Thursday Afternoon Ladies Cultural Society is going to build an opera house?"

"Don't be absurd, Ophelia. We won't be doing the actual work. We shall allow the men to do that. We will simply add moral support." Lorelie narrowed her eyes thoughtfully. "I rather suspect it takes a great deal of moral support to build a proper opera house."

"Why are you building an opera house?"

"Honestly, Ophelia." Lorelie sighed. "If we're going to have a respectable town with our very own genuine count, we need an opera house. Why, where else would we watch performances of the classics of the civilized world?"

A nasty, sinking sensation settled in the pit of Ophelia's stomach. "Which classics?"

"Oh, the usual." Lorelie ticked them off on her fingers. "Opera, naturally, and the Greek tragedies. Melodramas—"

"I would scarcely consider melodramas classics," Ophelia said wryly.

"—and, of course, Shakespeare."

"Shakespeare?"

"Certainly, my dear. And Tyler mentioned you're practically an expert on Shakespeare."

Ophelia bit back a caustic response. "He mentioned that, did he?"

"Indeed he did. He felt with your expertise you'd be

the perfect person to advise us on the construction of the theater."

"He's really very helpful, isn't he?"

Lorelie nodded in agreement. "Tyler has always been willing to help."

"I'll bet," Ophelia said under her breath. The man had a lot of nerve, volunteering her without the slightest thought as to whether or not she'd be willing to engage in such an activity. Although it really wasn't a bad idea. In fact, it might be fun. Enthusiasm built within her. Why, this was her opportunity to assist in the creation of a theater that would keep in mind that the heart and soul of any performance was the actor. Besides, she wasn't ready to leave Dead End quite yet, anyway. And these were such nice people. Assisting with their opera house was the least she could do.

She cast Lorelie a gracious, countess-like smile. "I would be delighted to help."

"I knew you would." Lorelie nodded with satisfaction. "Now, we don't have much time. There's only three weeks left until the ceremony."

That unpleasant sinking feeling returned. "What ceremony?"

"Ophelia, dear, are you certain you're all right?" Concern shadowed Lorelie's face. "What I mean is, you didn't damage your head when you fell, did you?"

"My head is fine. What ceremony?"

"Why, the ceremony to make Jack a count, of course."

"Perhaps I did injure my head after all." Ophelia raised a hand to her forehead and winced. "I have absolutely no recollection of writing to the ambassador."

"You didn't."

"I didn't?" Ophelia frowned. "But wasn't I supposed to?"

"Well, yes, but after your fall . . ." Lorelie leaned forward in a confiding manner. "And you took a dreadful spill. Why, the sight of you tumbling end over end . . ." She shuddered. "It was a very unpleasant thing to witness, you know."

Ophelia snorted. "I know."

"We were concerned about your recovery, and Sedge—"

"Mr. Montgomery?"

"Um-hum, Sedge thought he should go ahead and telegraph the British embassy in New York Ci—"

"He wired the embassy?" Ophelia fairly choked on the words.

"Indeed. And he received a telegram back yesterday." Lorelie glowed with excitement.

Ophelia bit her lip. "And what exactly did the telegram say?"

"Unfortunately, the ambassador can't make it."

Ophelia breathed a sigh of relief.

"But there is an Englishman, some kind of lord, a duke, I think, or maybe an earl, no, no, it was something else—"

"Never mind, Lorelie, it doesn't really matter."

"I suppose not. Still, it is annoying not to remember." She sighed. "At any rate, this gentleman, a genuine representative of the queen herself, mind you, wired Sedge and said he'd be delighted to officiate at the ceremony and award Jack his title."

"How . . . wonderful." Ophelia managed a weak smile. "And this happens in three weeks?"

"So we really do have a great deal to do and a very short time in which to do it."

"Don't we, though," Ophelia murmured.

"I have a hundred tiny details to attend to before

this afternoon's meeting." Lorelie rose from the bed. "I rather suspect we'll start right in on the fundamentals of proper behavior today. Although that shouldn't take more than a half an hour or so."

"And then what?"

Lorelie's eyes widened. "Why then, my dear, we'll play cards, of course."

"Lorelie, I'm afraid I have a bit of difficulty in that regard." Ophelia drew her brows together and chewed on her bottom lip. "I don't have a significant amount of cash on me. I wonder if the other ladies would accept my marker?"

"Oh, goodness no, dear." Lorelie shook her head emphatically. "We decided long ago that anything written down could be read by the wrong people, husbands and such. But it should be no problem for you to withdraw funds from your new account at the bank."

"But won't the banker be suspicious?"

Lorelie laughed. "Gracious, Ophelia, you don't want to go through Randolph. That would never do. His wife, Henrietta, lovely woman, a bit of a bluffer, though, you can always tell, her right eye twitches a bit when she hasn't a decent card in her hand, and sometimes—"

"The money?"

"Oh, yes. Henrietta will arrange to procure some of it for you and Randolph will never know."

"How much do you think I'll need?"

"Let me think." A thoughtful frown creased Lorelie's forehead. "We have fourteen regular players, fifteen with you, we shall be playing most of the afternoon, I should think five or six hundred should do it."

Ophelia gasped. "Dollars?"

Lorelie's eyes widened. "Well, my dear, we certainly don't use pounds."

"No, I meant isn't that a lot of money to squander on poker?" Ophelia stared with disbelief. "Aren't these incredibly high stakes?"

"Perhaps, although it doesn't seem terribly significant." Lorelie paused as if considering the question. "We've been playing for years, and at first we started with pennies. But that got rather boring, and the stakes just kept getting higher.

"You must understand, Ophelia, in spite of its appearance, there is a great deal of money in Dead End. Jack isn't the only area rancher to have made a fortune here. And as for businesses, well, we're the only real town for a fairly good distance, and there is the influence of the railroad as well. Altogether, our merchants have become quite prosperous. As wives we see nothing wrong with using some of that prosperity for our own entertainment. Do you?"

"Not at all." Ophelia shook her head. The activities of the Every Other Tuesday and Thursday Afternoon Ladies Cultural Society could well provide her with the means to get her money out of the bank and a little extra besides. Of course, it would take some time. But the ladies planned on playing nearly every day, and as long as she could get out of town before this Englishman arrived, she was safe. "In fact, I think it's more than reasonable for wives to share in the profits made by husbands."

"So do I." Lorelie smiled and headed to the door. "By the way, Tyler left that for you yesterday." She pointed to a tiny package on the washstand. "He said he didn't want to disturb you, so he didn't come up."

Ophelia picked up the small, awkwardly shaped, tissue-wrapped item. "How is his shoulder?"

"Practically perfect." Lorelie chuckled. "My goodness, the way the man carried on about that tiny little scratch, you'd think he was seriously injured."

Ophelia cast her a look of surprise. "Well, I did shoot him, after all. I can't believe that was an entirely pleasant experience."

"No, but it was an accident. I imagine if you'd really wanted to shoot him you would have killed him." She smiled sweetly. "Wouldn't you?"

"Without question." Ophelia pulled off the tissue and studied a delicate piece of glass that resembled a fish with two tails. "Lorelie, do you know what this is?"

"Haven't you seen one of those before?"

Ophelia turned it over in her hand. The tails were clear, and inside the round body, droplets of yellow color met and meshed with a swirl of blue-green. "I don't think so. It looks something like a piece of candy."

"Exactly, it's supposed to look like candy. Tyler brought home a handful of them. He thought they'd be a nice remembrance. He got them in Europe. Venice, I believe." Lorelie nodded and swept out the door.

"I see." Ophelia couldn't hold back a satisfied smile. She hadn't seen Tye since the shooting, but she was obviously on his mind, just as he was on hers. These past days of enforced rest had given her time to think. Too much time. And most of those thoughts had centered on Tyler Matthews.

Would she take what he offered? How had he put it? Oh, yes. *"I want to show you the heights a man and woman can reach. I want to make love to you until you swoon from the sheer sensation and cry my name into the night."*

Ophelia could admit, at least to herself, she wanted

that too. But did she want the risks that went along with it? Not that she cared especially about losing her virtue. She just didn't want to lose her heart.

A sudden thought struck her with the crystal clarity of the glass in her hand. Perhaps it was already too late? Perhaps her heart was already lost?

She stared at the bauble and faced the truth. Regardless of her feelings for him, she was a liar and a cheat and a fraud. And he could never love her the way Shakespeare's heroes loved his heroines. Not that she wanted his love anyway. Love only crippled women and made them objects to be pitied and discarded. Lust, on the other hand . . .

Perhaps, with this particular man, it was time to sample the pleasures of the flesh. It would be something of an appropriate farewell to the life she'd led since her father died. And once she and Jenny had a respectable home, there would be no opportunity for such goings-on. Yes, indeed.

Tyler Matthews would be a memory to keep captive in her heart for the rest of her life, just as the color was held captive in the tiny ornament in her hand. She stared into the glass and smiled. Did he pick this piece deliberately, or was it just a coincidence? Did the glassmaker know what he did when he mixed these particular colors?

Or was she the only one who stared at the piece and saw the yellow of the full moon teasing the blue waters of Venice?

"ARE YOU QUITE certain you wish to go through with this farce?" Frederick Hunt, the Marquis of Charleton, dropped into an elegant wingchair and propped his feet on a conveniently placed footstool.

"That will be all for today." Eloise Dunstall nodded to the troupe of seamstresses she'd had working nonstop ever since her arrival in Chicago. The young women left the extravagant hotel room in a flurry of quickly gathered silks and satins and giggles and promises. Eloise sighed and settled on a nearby chaise lounge. "Honestly, Freddy, I never knew commissioning a completely new wardrobe would be so exhausting."

Freddy raised a jaded brow. "You could have waited until we returned to London and civilization."

"You obviously know far less about women than you think you do, my dear."

"I obviously know far less about you than I thought I did." Freddy heaved a long-suffering sigh. "Explain to me again why you've changed your mind about letting the authorities handle this whole matter."

"I will admit that when you first received the telegram, I was quite upset. However, my curiosity overcame my annoyance, and I decided it would be far more interesting to deal with this myself."

Freddy groaned. "I don't see why you have to drag me along to this godforsaken spot. What's the name of it again?"

"Dead End."

"Sounds bloody awful," Freddy grumbled.

"It sounds like an adventure." Eloise cast him an impish glance. "Just think of it, Freddy. Out there, practically in the middle of nowhere, some woman is using my name and selling my title."

"It's fraud is what it is."

"No doubt, but don't you find it amusing?"

Freddy glared silently.

"Well, I do. Besides, it's just the kind of thing I might have done in my younger days."

"Well, you most certainly wouldn't do it now."

"Of course not," she said in a chastising manner. "I have no need for such adventures these days. Now I'm the dowager Countess of Bridgewater—"

"You could be the Marchioness of Charleton if you'd just give in and marry me."

"—and my poor, dear husband left me extremely well off. Still, when I met my late love I was simply another young, pretty American actress struggling to survive on the London stage."

"I don't know why we left London in the first place," Freddy muttered.

Eloise released an exasperated sigh. "Goodness, Freddy, I haven't been home in more than twenty years. I wanted very much to see the land of my birth. And I especially wanted to see the West before I re-marry."

Freddy brightened. "Me?"

"Well, naturally you. Who else would I marry?"

Freddy narrowed his eyes. "When?"

"Soon, dearest, very soon," she said vaguely. "But first, as soon as my wardrobe is completed, it's off to Wyoming and Dead End."

"And what happens then?"

She drew her brows together and thought for a moment. "I'm not entirely certain. We shall simply have to wait and see."

Freddy rolled his eyes heavenward. "Dead End, Wyoming. What a horrible name."

"But weren't we supposed to visit there originally? I thought it was on our initial itinerary, and we even had train tickets before my luggage went astray and we had to return to Chicago."

"It was." Freddy winced as if anticipating her response. "But it was a joke, and I gave the tickets away. At first I thought the name sounded quite in the spirit of the Wild West, but, tickets or not, I never intended for us to actually go there."

"Well, now we shall. And right now, the joke, my love, is on us." She shrugged and smiled. "But when I am face-to-face with the other Countess of Bridgewater, we'll see who has the last laugh. I suspect this will be the most fun I've had in ages. I do wonder, though"—Eloise picked up a length of sky blue satin and held it up to the light—"if, in addition to my name, the woman has my clothes as well.

"I don't mind sharing the name so much." She sighed. "But I would like my blasted clothes back."

"HELL AND DAMNATION."

Tye threw the book across the room and rubbed his hand over his eyes. He couldn't work, he couldn't sleep, he couldn't concentrate. All because of that woman. That infuriating, annoying, desirable woman.

It wasn't enough that she hadn't an honest bone in her beautiful body, or that she was trying to steal from Jack but she had to go ahead and shoot him as well. His shoulder still ached where the bullet had grazed it.

He pulled himself to his feet and stalked across the room to pick up the volume of Shakespeare. He had a list of things as long as his arm he should be doing in the middle of the day, and reading the work of dead British playwrights wasn't on it. But the book had lured him this morning, as it had yesterday and the day before. No matter how hard he tried, he couldn't get away from the words of the Bard. Or thoughts of her.

Ophelia.

Every word he read reminded him of her. Every quote had a double meaning. Every line of dialogue brought his mind back to thoughts of her.

Ophelia.

He'd stayed away since she'd shot him. At first he was just too damned mad. It was still hard to believe even his aunt didn't seem to take the shooting seriously. Why, Ophelia could have killed him. And that maid of hers, or whatever she was, was apparently just as big a liar as Ophelia. Who on earth couldn't pronounce *countess* or *my lady* or *Bridgewater*?

"Hah! She must think I'm a complete fool," he muttered.

Lord, now she had him talking to himself. Maybe he *was* a complete fool. Yesterday, he'd even brought her a gift, the little glass bauble he'd picked up in Venice. It reminded him of moonlight and water and—he groaned—her. He raked a hand through his hair. What had she done to him?

Ophelia.

He wanted her in his bed. Hell, he'd wanted that from the moment he'd first seen her. But he'd wanted women before and he'd had them—those he hadn't lost to Sedge, anyway. And he wanted proof of her deception. Proof that would save Jack a great deal of money and more than a little embarrassment. But now it seemed he wanted more.

What did he want, anyway?

He sank back into the chair, the answer hitting him like a blow to the gut. He wanted mahogany-haired children he could teach to ride a horse and chase calves and fish in the creek. He wanted long winter nights around a crackling fire with the sonnets of Shakespeare read aloud in a voice lilting and lush and just a bit husky, with an accent that melted something deep inside him. And he wanted the first thing that he saw every morning and the last thing he saw every night to be eyes the color of emeralds and lips full and lush and made to be kissed and hair like a Wyoming sunset.

He wanted Ophelia, and he wanted her forever.

He sighed and leaned his head back against the chair. It must be love. What else could it be? What a mess. What a disaster. She was a liar and a thief and who knew what else. But she was also smart and loyal, and there was a look in her eye when she talked about home and family that tugged at his heart.

A sudden thought struck him, and he straightened in the chair. She didn't have to be a thief and a liar and who knew what else. She didn't have to take Big Jack's money. She could reform. He could reform her. Of course, she'd never admit anything to him, so he'd still have to get his proof first. But then—he grinned— she'd be his.

He leapt from the chair and paced across the room. He only had three weeks until some British lord Sedge had wired showed up for the bogus ceremony making his uncle a count. Ophelia was far too clever to stay for that and risk being exposed. He'd have to get to the truth before she tried to leave town. And then he'd have her.

She was smart, all right, but he was smarter. He laughed out loud. Oh, certainly, some people could say his plan smacked of blackmail. But it took a bit of a scoundrel to catch a scoundrel. And who would appreciate the irony of that better than the fair Ophelia?

Lorelie had said Ophelia would be at the meeting of that silly women's society today, but tomorrow he'd start putting his plan into effect. Ophelia would never leave Dead End without getting her money from the bank. And she couldn't possibly do that before the ceremony without arousing suspicion. But just to make sure, he'd have Randolph keep him informed as to her banking activities. Why not? He was the mayor, after all. And just maybe there were some benefits to the job.

He flipped open the book and settled back in the chair. Once he had Ophelia reformed, he had to win her heart. Lord knows, she already wanted him. But he'd never before set out to make a woman fall in love, and, with Ophelia, Shakespeare was undoubtedly the best place to start.

He glanced down at the open book and grinned. A line from *The Merchant of Venice* stared up at him. How appropriate. How prophetic. How perfect.

To do a great right, do a little wrong.

Chapter 11

"**W**HO ever would have imagined a simple little building like an opera house would be so incredibly complicated?" Ophelia said under her breath. She stared at drawings and plans and ill-formed ideas spread before her on the makeshift table smack dab in the middle of Dead End's main and, for the most part, only street.

"The way I see it, the facade of the building should . . ." The banker spread his arms in a wide, dramatic gesture that would put even the most experienced actor to shame.

"No, no, no Randolph." The woman from the general store interrupted. "The front of the opera house . . ."

"Just think of it, Ophelia." Lorelie sighed. "The Dead End opera house."

"The Empire City opera house," someone else said firmly.

Was every single resident of Dead End involved in this project? Obviously, the town's people had gotten past their ambivalence over the name change and direction for the future. Now they worked together for the same goal. At least today. Ophelia glanced around the gathering with a sense of sheer helplessness. This project had the feel of a community event or a barn raising. And she had no idea how to raise a barn.

But these people, these very nice people, were looking to her, or rather to a sophisticated countess, to direct them in the construction of their shining symbol of civilization. Certainly, from an actor's point of view, she could guide them here and there. But a great deal of the ongoing discussion had to do with things like "joists" and "load-bearing walls," and it was all she could do to keep a perplexed, if not downright stupid, expression from her face. She took a deep breath and squared her shoulders. Fine. If a countess confident in construction was what they wanted, they were in for a rude awakening. She was all they had, and they'd better learn to accept that.

"Gentlemen, ladies." Even Ophelia's best stage voice couldn't penetrate the din for more than a ten-foot radius, but those within range turned toward her expectantly. "I have been in a great number of opera houses and theaters in my life. I have even been backstage in a few. I am more than willing to give you my thoughts and advice on decor and design and various other details, but I simply cannot tell you how to build the thing."

The crowd stared at her as if she was insane, then traded looks among themselves.

"Countess." The sheriff—what was his name?—stepped forward. "We don't expect you to tell us how to build it."

"No, indeed," Randolph said. "We know how to put up a building."

"What we need from you is just what you said." The shopkeeper ticked the list off on her fingers. "Decor, design, details."

The sheriff chuckled. "We didn't figure you could tell us how to build the damn thing."

Relief flooded through her. "I simply thought with all this . . ." Ophelia swept her hand toward the papers and plans littering the table and shrugged. "Well, I must say I am relieved."

"And rather, what we need from you now, ma'am, is this here part." A big, hulking, sweaty man she believed was the town's blacksmith selected a large paper from the debris on the table and spread it before her. A rudimentary sketch of what the building would allegedly look like was drawn in pencil. He traced a line with his finger. "We ain't sure if this is . . ."

Was this all they wanted? Ophelia listened to the blacksmith's questions with a surging sense of excitement. She'd been just plain silly to think they wanted her to tell them how to build anything. They simply wanted her to make certain their opera house was as civilized and respectable as it could be. This might even be fun.

Helping with this project was, after all, the least she could do for the town. Or rather, for the ladies of the town. Ophelia realized she couldn't possibly get Big Jack's money out of the bank until after the ceremony. And if she hung around until then, she'd surely be exposed and wouldn't be allowed to claim the money anyway. But the ladies of Dead End offered her salvation.

She'd played with them yesterday and the day before and both times had left considerably richer than when she'd started. They'd wagered shocking sums on every hand, almost as if their money had no real worth. Ophelia had seen such disregard for money before, among the very rich, the very bored or the very good. And there was no doubt about it; the publicly proper, apparently upright, staunchly moral ladies of Dead End were sharps.

Plainly and simply, every single one of them was a better player than most men she'd met. Ophelia could put just about any of them in any saloon from here to St. Louis and they'd break the house. Playing with these women was more than enjoyable; it was something of a challenge. They were good, but, thankfully, Ophelia was better.

The blacksmith smiled and nodded his approval, then strode off shouting orders right and left. Ophelia glanced up and down the street. The opera house was under construction at the north end of Main Street, and from here Ophelia could see clear down to the train station that bordered the town on the south.

It wasn't a bad little town. In fact, it was almost charming in a rustic sort of way. The buildings had all been recently painted, no doubt part of the effort to achieve respectability. The streets were fairly clean. Even the horses tied up here and there along the rails were relatively well behaved.

Beyond the flurry of the construction area, there was still quite a bit of activity in town. Some centered on the saloon, but most seemed to be the typical ebb and flow of life in a small but vital community. A community to be proud of, with nice people who worked together. Exactly the type of town she wanted for Jenny and herself. A pang of regret twinged through her, and she pushed it firmly aside.

This would never be their home. No matter how nice the people, or how respectable the opera house or how handsome the mayor.

"Countess." The banker's wife, Henrietta, hurried

toward her with a sheaf of papers in her hand and a query in her eye. "Countess, we were wondering if the . . ."

Ophelia gratefully turned her attention to the myriad of questions Henrietta threw at her. Anything to get her mind off the one subject her thoughts were always on these days. Damn, where was the man, anyway? She still hadn't seen Tye since the day she'd shot him, and she did hope he wouldn't hold that minor accident against her.

No, he had sent her that charming piece of glass, after all. But time was fleeting. She only had three weeks before she had to get out of Dead End. Three weeks to win as much as she could from the Every Other Tuesday and Thursday Afternoon Ladies Cultural Society. And three weeks in which to seduce Tyler Matthews.

The very thought sent delicious shivers of fear and anticipation up her spine. Now that she'd made her decision, she really did want to get on with it. Of all the things she planned to accomplish in the time she had left here, seducing Tye would probably be the easiest. There was no question the man wanted her. No doubt the tiniest hint of her willingness to submit would be enough to attract him to her bed. Any man who sent baubles to a woman who'd shot him was obviously deep in the throes of mindless lust. And wasn't lust what this was all about? On both sides?

An odd thought picked at the back of her mind, and the more she tried to ignore it, the more it nagged and badgered and refused to go away. Ophelia believed she knew a great deal about lust simply from backstage observation, and she freely admitted she knew nothing at all about love and had probably never seen that emotion displayed. But there was one tiny aspect of Tye's behavior that didn't quite seem to fit under the heading of lust. Not that it could possibly be love, of course. Love was a far cry from lust. No, it was probably a gesture of insignificant affection. That was it. Tye might very well like her.

The man had kissed her on the tip of her nose.

He definitely liked her. A kiss on the tip of the nose was something one bestowed on a beloved sister or a dear child or a close friend. It was completely innocent with no meaning to it whatsoever and easily explained away. Still . . .

Why had he called her "my love"?

THERE SHE WAS. His lovely liar. His beautiful thief. His future. Ophelia stood in the midst of a crowd of people waving her arms in gestures of drama and grace, obviously telling them how to build this new folly. Lord, she looked like a genuine countess in that group. Who was she really? He'd find out eventually. Wives didn't keep secrets from husbands, and women didn't keep secrets from lovers. He grinned and strode toward her. Ophelia would soon be both. He'd make an honest woman out of her, in more ways than one.

The crowd scampered off to do her bidding, and he stepped up beside her. "Morning, Countess. How's your opera house today?"

Warmth flashed in her eyes, as if she was glad to see him. "Very well, I think. I can't believe how fast it's going up. Of course, we've got everyone in town working on it." She narrowed her eyes and planted her hands on her hips. "Everyone but the mayor, that is. Wherever have you been for the last two days?"

He'd meant to be here yesterday for the start of this

nonsense, but mooning over Ophelia with a book in hand and nursing his shoulder had put him off schedule. "Here and there. Trying to catch up on work at the ranch. But it hasn't been easy."

"Oh. Why not?"

He rubbed his shoulder and grimaced. "I'm still not quite healed. You know, it's not easy to recover from a bullet wound."

"Mr. Matthews. Tye." She favored him with a tolerant smile. "I am truly sorry. But it really wasn't much of a wound. And it was an accident. I didn't mean to shoot you."

"I realize that." He released a long-suffering sigh. "If you'd meant to shoot me, you probably would have killed me."

"That goes without saying." Confidence and conviction rang in her voice. Was she really a good shot? What else was she good at? And what else didn't he know about the fair Ophelia?

She grinned and turned, casting an assessing gaze over the construction site. "The shell will be up in a day or two, and I should think the whole thing will be completed by the end of next week."

The building was progressing with astonishing speed. Grudging respect for the people of the town, his town, seeped through him. He'd obviously been away far too long. How could he forget what they could do when they put their collective minds to it? Maybe he hadn't given them enough credit. Maybe their goal of civilization wasn't so ridiculous after all. And maybe, just maybe, Dead End was a community with a real future. Or rather, Empire City was. "It looks like it'll be done in plenty of time for the big celebration."

"Indeed." She nodded, and an awkward silence fell between them. Ridiculous, of course; he had a great deal to say to her. Odd that he wasn't quite sure where to start.

"Tye."

"Ophelia."

They stared, then laughed in that uncomfortable manner that marked two people struggling to choose their words with care. He pulled a steadying breath and tried again. "I would consider it—"

"I was wondering if—"

Once more silence settled between them. Hell. What was wrong with him? He'd never had a problem talking to a woman, any woman, before. Of course, he'd never planned to marry one before either.

"I was just going to say"—she straightened her shoulders, as if gathering courage, and smiled—"how much I've missed you."

"You have?"

"I certainly have." She seemed distinctly encouraged. What was she up to now? "I was wondering, hoping, actually, that we could spend some time together."

"You want to spend time with me?" He narrowed his eyes and stared at her. There was no doubt about it. She was definitely up to something.

"Um-hum. I think it's important." Her eyes widened with a candor that was at once difficult to believe and impossible to resist. Had he ever seen eyes so green before? "I very much fear you have some reservations about my dealings with your uncle."

"I have a number of concerns." Eyes so deep and intense they were endless and inviting, calling to something buried inside him, capturing his soul.

"And I believe you also have questions about whether I am who I say I am?" Her voice was breathless, a shade huskier than he'd remembered, with that accent that tensed his stomach and curled his toes.

"Well . . . yes." Why was his mouth so dry?

"It's been quite obvious. I'd very much like to answer those questions and alleviate those concerns." Lord, he could listen to that accent, so sweet, so sultry, forever. She reached out and trailed her finger along the line of his jaw. "I'd hate for you to distrust me."

"Would you?" He swallowed an odd lump caught in his throat. What was she doing to him?

"I would." The words were little more than a seductive sigh.

"Perhaps I should spend more time at Jack and Lorelie's?"

"Perhaps you should." Her voice was ripe with an unspoken promise.

"Well . . . I suppose . . ." He couldn't seem to get his words out or his mind straight. He couldn't seem to get anything past the thought of those lush lips pressed against his, that lovely body crushed beneath him, that captivating accent murmuring words of passion and surrender and love in his ear. "I mean . . . I guess . . ." He laughed self-consciously. He really had to pull himself together. He blew a long breath. "I should go help? Shouldn't I? With the building?"

"By all means."

How could he tear himself away? All he wanted was to take her right here, right now, right in the middle of Main Street.

"Perhaps I'll see you this evening?"

"Sure." He nodded, turned and took a few steps. Oh, what the hell. Without a second thought, he swiveled back to her side, pulled her into his arms and planted his lips firmly on hers in a kiss of urgency and desire and warning.

Her body stiffened with surprise, then relaxed, and her arms wrapped around his neck, her response eager and without reservation.

Abruptly he pulled back and grinned. "I'm going to go build your opera house now."

"Wonderful." A blush shaded her cheeks, bemusement tinted the emerald of her eyes.

This time when he turned away he couldn't keep the satisfied grin from his face. Damn, this was going well. And lust, for a woman, just might be the first step to love. Of course she'd made it easy for him.

His step faltered. Too easy. Obviously, this was a woman skilled in the art of enticing men. She did it extremely well. He didn't quite believe that widow nonsense, but he was certain she was an experienced woman. He drew his brows together in a troubled frown. Just how experienced was she? He didn't like the question or the possibilities.

Did it really matter?

No, of course not. Ophelia was the woman he loved regardless of how many men had come before him. After all, it wasn't as if she was the first woman to have fallen. And he himself was scarcely virginal, although he had rather expected that quality in a wife.

No, he could be noble about this. He could forgive her transgressions.

This was just one more thing about her he'd have to reform.

THROUGHOUT THE LONG morning, she tried not to stare at him. But it seemed everywhere Ophelia's gaze fell, there was Tye. He'd catch her eye and smile, a secret, private smile that fluttered her stomach.

Well, this was what she wanted, wasn't it? Confidential glances and mysterious smiles. She'd brought it on herself, of course, and quite well too. Whoever would have thought flirting would require that much effort? The actresses and other women she'd watched in her youth had always made it seem so easy and natural. Perhaps it was for women with experience. She shrugged to herself. She would never know.

Tye was the only man who would ever share her bed. She knew it with a certainty that shocked her in its steadfastness and strengthened her resolve. It was obviously fate that drew her to this one man in a tiny town in the middle of nowhere. Odd, how strangely life worked. Ever since her father had died she'd wanted to come to Wyoming, not for her sake but for Jenny's. Ophelia had suspected Jenny might have family in the territory somewhere, but she'd never managed to get here before now. And here and now there was Tye.

She couldn't seem to tear her gaze away from his strong, tall figure. His shirt was open nearly to the waist, and she caught glimpses of hard, bronzed chest. The fabric strained across his back in a caress of broad muscle and taut strength. The hot Wyoming sun gilded his hair into a golden halo. He worked on the open framework of the building, looking for all the world like the master of everything he surveyed, like a king or a god. He was magnificent, and if her determination to have him was wrong in the scheme of her life or her future, well, it was, very likely, worth it.

" 'Think you there was, or might be, such a man as this I dream'd of?' " she said under her breath.

"Pardon me, my dear?"

"*Antony and Cleopatra*." Her manner was absent, her thoughts intent on the golden figure in the sun.

"He is a handsome man, isn't he?"

"Um-hum."

"He'll make someone an excellent husband."

The words and the voice finally penetrated Ophelia's thoughts and snapped her attention from Tye to the woman beside her.

"No doubt he will." Ophelia paused for a moment. "Just out of idle curiosity, mind you, Lorelie, tell me, why isn't Tye married?"

"Oh, I don't know." Lorelie studied her nephew. "I've wondered that myself on occasion. Lord knows, he's had plenty of opportunity. Women have always thrown themselves at Tyler."

"My goodness." Ophelia struggled to hide her sarcasm. "What a surprise."

"Do you think so?" Lorelie raised a curious brow. "I don't. Tyler's just the type of man I would have found attractive in my younger days. Why, just look at him." She nodded toward her nephew, and Ophelia's gaze followed hers.

"He's tall and nicely shaped, quite dashing, really, with all that blonde hair and those brown eyes, dark as—"

"Chocolate," Ophelia murmured.

"Chocolate! What a delightful comparison."

"I love chocolate."

"Most of us do, dear. It's no wonder he's always had his pick of women." Lorelie leaned toward her in a confidential manner. "He's always been something of a rogue when it comes to the fairer sex."

"But he never found someone to marry?"

"Not yet, but I'm certain he will some day. He just needs to find the right woman."

"What kind of woman do you think would be right for him?" Ophelia said with a casual air.

"Idle curiosity again?" Innocence rang in Lorelie's voice, and Ophelia slanted her a quick glance. The older woman still studied her nephew.

Ophelia shrugged. "Just wondering."

"I suspect if you asked Tyler, you'd get a completely different answer, but I think, and Jack agrees with me, my nephew needs a woman who's as intelligent as he is." Lorelie shook her head in resignation. "But you know how men are. They are more than likely to prefer a pretty face and a fair figure to attributes that are more lasting. And then there are those moral qualities men seem to insist on in women—well, women they marry, at any rate—that they don't feel at all compelled to abide by themselves."

"Moral qualities?" A weight settled in the pit of Ophelia's stomach.

"Yes, indeed. Let me see." A thoughtful frown creased Lorelie's forehead, and she counted the items on her fingers. "There's loyalty. Men do seem to insist on that in their horses and their dogs and their wives. There's fidelity. A man can sow his wild oats when and where he pleases, but women are expected to confine their amorous activities to just one man. Not that I mind, not at all, but it does seem dreadfully unfair that what's good for the gander isn't allowed for the goose. And there's honesty—"

"Honesty?" The weight grew heavier.

"Men are real sticklers for honesty." Lorelie paused. "Although there are ways to skirt the issue."

"What kind of ways?"

"First and foremost, never volunteer information. Take the Every Other Tuesday and Thursday Afternoon Ladies Cultural Society, for example. There would be, well, quite frankly, hell to pay if Jack or any other man in this town knew we were playing poker. And my gracious, if they had any idea of the stakes"— Lorelie clucked her tongue—"I wouldn't even want to imagine how the scandal would rock this community. There would be weeping and wailing and gnashing of teeth." A wicked twinkle sparked in her eye. "And the women would get upset too."

Ophelia laughed. "So, you're saying—"

"What I'm saying is extremely simple. No one ever said, 'Lorelie, my love, have you and the other ladies of Dead End been playing poker with stakes that would have a riverboat gambler shaking in his boots?' And if the question isn't asked, you can't answer with a falsehood, thereby avoiding an outright lie. And there you have it." Lorelie spread her hands out in a gesture akin to a magician showing nothing up his sleeve. "Honesty."

Ophelia stared in complete admiration. That was perhaps the most convoluted piece of logic she'd ever heard. Yet somehow, it made perfect sense. "That's amazing."

"Thank you," Lorelie said modestly.

"But let me ask you something else." Ophelia narrowed her eyes thoughtfully. "What if, say, just as a for instance, a person wasn't actually lying? That is she— or he—hasn't told a fib to a direct question. But what if that same person—"

"She or he?"

"Right. Was, say, hiding something important about themselves. Maybe, even, pretending to be something or someone they weren't?" Ophelia's light tone belied the anxiety within her. For some unknown reason, this fascinating little woman's answer was important to her.

"My dear." Lorelie leaned toward her and placed a hand gently on her arm. "We are all pretending to be something or someone we aren't. It's human nature."

"I see." Again, Lorelie's explanation was positively frightening in its twisted rationale. And yet it was also so sensible and practical and liberating.

"I can't believe you haven't considered any of this before. I can't imagine your own husband—what was his name?"

"Aloysius."

"Yes, well, I should think Aloysius would have inspired much the same philosophy in you that Jack has in me." Lorelie tapped her bottom lip in a considering manner. "Unless, of course, life really is that much different in England than it is here."

"That's it," Ophelia said gratefully. "Life is ever so much different in England."

"Dear me." Lorelie heaved a mournful sigh. "In that case, I'm not at all certain I'll like being a countess."

"Oh, you'll like it." Ophelia threw her a confident smile. "And everyone will like you. I have no doubt you'll be a wonderful Countess of Bluewater."

"Thank you." Relief brightened Lorelie's face. "And what of you, my dear? You're a young woman. Why haven't you remarried?"

"Me?" Ophelia cast around for an answer and a name. "Why, I haven't even considered it. I . . . um . . . my marriage to—"

"Adolf?" Lorelie suggested innocently.

"Yes, Adolf. Was so very—"

"Happy?" Lorelie nodded as if she already knew the answer.

"Brief, actually, I was going to say brief. We didn't have much time together." A sorrowful note sounded in Ophelia's voice.

"You and Austin."

"Austin?" Who?

"Your husband?"

"Of course, Austin, dear, dear, dead Austin." Ophelia shook her head sadly.

"I'm certain he'd want you to carry on." Lorelie's voice held a note of encouragement.

Ophelia sighed. Gad, this dead husband was a lot of work. "I do try, but sometimes it's so difficult."

"He'd probably want you to go on with your life, find someone else. Remarry."

"Possibly."

"You would want to find the right person."

"Naturally."

"Now that I think about it," Lorelie said, "we have a significant number of eligible men in this area."

"How very interesting." Ophelia's offhand manner matched the other woman's.

"Several area ranchers are looking for wives, most of them quite wealthy."

"Wealth is always a nice touch."

"Yes, indeed. We have ranchers and merchants and even"— Lorelie's tone was nonchalant—"an occasional mayor."

"A mayor?" Ophelia shot a startled look at Lorelie. "You mean Tye?"

"He is the only mayor we have."

"I don't think . . . I mean I haven't . . . it's simply not . . ."

Marriage? To Tye?

The very idea was absurd, ridiculous. She had no intention of marrying this man or any man. Seduction, yes; marriage, absolutely not. Why, she didn't know the first thing about being a wife. And while Tye was obviously more than willing to share her bed, she had no doubt sharing the rest of her life was the last thing he'd want. The realization brought an odd stab of pain.

"Never mind, dear." Lorelie's voice was bright. "It was just a random suggestion. Don't give it a second thought."

"Consider it forgotten." Ophelia forced a light-hearted laugh and turned the subject back to the opera house and the planned afternoon with the Cultural Society. But the idea of marrying Tye refused to go away. It would mean pretending to be a countess for the rest of her life. Not an insurmountable problem.

But sooner or later, Tye was sure to learn the truth about her. For good or ill, the man was not stupid. He had a college education, no less. And once that happened, wife or not, he'd be certain to cast her aside—the low card in a bad hand. She'd be just like all the other women she'd ever seen who'd sold their souls for love and ended with nothing but misery. And there was no question about it: it would take very little for her to love him.

No, seduction was definitely less of a gamble with Tye than marriage. The most she'd lose with lust was her virtue. With love, the stakes were much higher.

With love, she'd lose her heart.

OPHELIA STOOD LAUGHING with Tyler, and Lorelie smiled with satisfaction. She and the countess would have a bite to eat at the cafe down the street, and then proceed to the Every Other Tuesday and Thursday Afternoon Ladies Cultural Society meeting. It should be an excellent afternoon. Why, look at how well the morning had gone.

Tyler had actually kissed Ophelia right here in public for anyone and everyone to see. It seemed as if Lorelie's matchmaking plan was working without any effort on her part at all. At least up til now.

She'd been greatly encouraged by that little incident in Ophelia's room after the ill-fated fox hunt, although it was a shame Ophelia had to shoot him. Men didn't usually take kindly to being shot. But Tyler seemed to handle it well—it was such a very minor wound, after all—and he was still in obvious pursuit of the lovely countess.

It was apparent he wanted her, and equally apparent she wanted him. Perhaps neither realized it yet, but they were perfect for each other. And there was something in his eyes when he looked at her, something reflected back in Ophelia's gaze, something very special. If Lorelie could see it, why couldn't they?

Honestly, people rarely saw what was right in front of them. They were always too busy looking for what they should see or, worse, what they expected to see. Love was definitely in the air in Empire City, even if Lorelie was the only one who knew it.

She frowned to herself and studied the couple. They made such a nice-looking pair. But now that the sparks of desire had smoldered, it would not do to let them burst into flame. At least not yet. No, she must do all she could to throw Tyler and Ophelia together without letting them be, well, too together. What was it they said about the horse and the barn door? Lorelie had always believed lust denied, or at least delayed, was a sure and certain path to marriage and love. It was such a very small step from lust to something far more lasting and certain. Especially with someone willing to give a push in the right direction.

There wasn't even the tiniest doubt in Lorelie's mind that there would soon be a countess in the Matthews family. And as pleasant as that thought was, the title was only the icing on the cake. This woman would make Tyler's life rich and happy and probably extremely chaotic. Exactly what he needed. Men should always be kept a bit off balance.

Ophelia would be the perfect wife for Tyler.

And perhaps, with this husband, she'd even manage to remember his name.

Chapter 12

"You ride like you were born to the saddle."

Heat flushed Jenny's cheeks at the admiration in Zach's voice. She leaned forward to pat her horse and hide her face. "Thank you. It seems to come naturally for me."

"I've never seen anybody pick it up so fast." Zach shook his head in disbelief. "Especially not somebody who's never ridden before."

"Well, I love it," Jenny said firmly. She and Zach walked their horses at a leisurely pace alongside a bubbling creek. "I feel like I'm on top of the world when I sit up here. And when we gallop, it's like flying. It's exhilarating and frightening and absolutely marvelous."

Zach laughed. "It's old hat to somebody like me. I've been on a horse all my life."

"Ophelia doesn't like them."

"Your countess?"

"No, indeed." Jenny shook her head. "Ophelia hates horses."

"Why?"

"It sounds a little silly."

"Oh, come on. I won't tell." Zach grinned. "I promise."

Jenny eyed him for a moment. He did seem sincere. "Very well. She thinks they're big and ill behaved, but most of all"—Jenny drew a deep breath—"she thinks they laugh at her."

"I've never heard them laugh." His voice was solemn, but a twinkle glimmered in his eyes.

"I don't think they do." She leaned toward him. "But Ophelia would never believe that. She's convinced that she's the laughingstock of every horse that ever came her way."

Zach frowned in confusion. "How does she hunt foxes if she doesn't like horses?"

"Carefully." Jenny grinned and reined her horse to a stop. She really had to watch exactly what she said to Zach, but so far she'd made few mistakes. Any time she slipped, she always managed to cover it up. They'd spent a great deal of time together, what with Ophelia occupied by the opera house and the Cultural Society. And with every minute spent in his company, Jenny thought he was just a little more wonderful. "Why don't we walk a bit?"

"All right." Zach slid to the ground and strode around his animal to help her dismount. He caught her waist, and she slid against him in a manner slow and interesting and exciting. She wore an old pair of pants Alma had dug up from somewhere, and the unusual attire gave her a sense of illicit freedom she reveled in. He held her a moment longer than was necessary, and his gaze meshed with hers. Goodness, was he going to kiss her? "Here we are."

He released her, and disappointment mingled with

relief. Why didn't he kiss her? Didn't he want to? Didn't she want him to?

"This is one of my favorite places." Zach nodded at the vista spread before them in a gently rolling valley. The creek gurgled by their side. Far off in the distance, mountains rose like sleeping giants. Here and there, gnarled trees held their own against the wind and weather. "Tye's too. He showed it to me when I was just a kid."

"It's very pretty." She leaned back against the rough bark of an oak, and longing surged through her. What a lovely place this was. What a perfect place to live. "I'd love to stay here forever."

Zach's voice was casual, as if her answer didn't matter. "Why don't you?"

"I can't. Not without Ophelia."

Zach was quiet for a moment. "How's Miz Lorelie coming with that plan of hers?"

"Plan?"

"You know. To get Tye married off to your countess?"

"Oh, yes, that plan." Jenny smiled. "I'd forgotten about that for a minute. Sometimes it's impossible to tell what Ophelia is thinking, but I believe it's going pretty well. They're spending every morning together in town at the opera house. And he's come to the house every evening. It's funny, though."

"What is?"

"Miss Lorelie. She was so determined to get the two of them together, yet every time Tye tries to get Ophelia alone, Lorelie is right there coming between them. At least that's what Ophelia says. It seems to be driving her quite mad.

"Still, I'm positive she likes him. A lot." Jenny widened her smile to a satisfied grin. "She shot him, you know."

Zach grimaced. "Didn't know that was a sign of affection."

"It certainly is. If she didn't like him"—Jenny shrugged— "she would have killed him."

Zach leaned against the tree. "So, do you like me enough to shoot me?"

Her heart fluttered in her throat. He was flirting with her. Like a man flirted with a woman. She'd never flirted before. Still, she could act. How much harder could flirting be? She drew a steadying breath and smiled innocently. "I don't think that's really the question."

"It's not?" His voice was a lazy drawl.

"No, indeed. The question is"—she angled her head in a teasing manner and glanced up at him—"if I shot you, would I kill you?"

His blue eyes simmered and her stomach somersaulted. He tilted her chin up with a tanned finger. "And would you?"

Goodness, he *was* going to kiss her! How could she possibly kiss him back? At this moment, she could barely breathe. Or talk. Or sigh. "No."

He touched his lips to hers gently, more a whisper than a kiss. Her heart thudded against her ribs so hard that she marveled it didn't burst through her skin. He gathered her closer and she went willingly, far too caught up in truly delightful and completely unique sensations to protest. Not that she wanted to.

No, indeed. What she wanted . . . was more.

He deepened his kiss. Her eyes fluttered closed and her knees weakened. Tentatively, she snaked her arms around his neck. He pulled her tighter against him, and she could feel the long, taut length of his body against hers.

A man's body.

She'd never been this close to a man before, a hard, solid man. She'd never been kissed by lips so warm they seemed to melt something deep inside her. She'd never been held by arms that were at once strong and yielding. Goodness, this was confusing and odd and more exciting than she ever would have imagined. If kissing was this exhilarating . . . She tightened her arms around his neck.

Zach pulled back and stared down at her. She'd never seen desire before, but surely that was the look in his eyes. "Jenny, I—"

"Kiss me again, Zach." She angled her lips toward his and closed her eyes. She waited for a long moment, but nothing happened. She opened one eye. "Well?"

"Well what?" A slight smile raised the corners of his mouth.

She opened her other eye. "Well, aren't you going to kiss me?"

"I did kiss you."

"I mean again."

A shudder ran though him, as if he was struggling for control. "I don't think so."

"Why not?"

"I don't think it would be a good idea." Gently, he unwrapped her arms from around his neck.

She planted her fists on her hips and glared. "Why not?"

"Because." He clasped her shoulders and stared into her eyes. "You are as luscious as one of Alma's pies and as pretty as an angel, and if I start kissing you I'm afraid I'll never stop."

"Good!" She threw her arms back around his neck, closed her eyes and waited. And waited. She sighed and opened one eye. "Well?"

"Well . . . um . . ." A kind of queasy embarrassment shone on his face.

"Well what?"

"You've never done this before, have you?"

"Is that all?" Relief washed through her. "I thought it was something of importance. No, never, but I am willing to learn." Once again she closed her eyes. Once again she waited. And once again she opened one eye. "What now?"

He heaved a regretful sigh. "I've never done this before either."

Her eyes widened with surprise, and she released him. "You've never kissed a girl before?"

"Well, sure, oh yeah, I've kissed a girl, plenty of girls, I . . ." His shoulders slumped, and he looked like nothing so much as a chastised puppy. Jenny had always wanted a puppy. "Once. I kissed a girl once."

"But you know how, don't you?"

"Sure." He shrugged. "Everybody knows how to kiss. It just kind of comes naturally."

"Excellent. Then I don't think there's a problem." She threw her arms around him and closed her eyes. This time she refused to open them. "You're not going to kiss me, are you?"

"No," he said softly.

"We could learn together?" There was a hopeful note in her voice.

"Jenny." He groaned with some emotion she couldn't quite define.

She sighed, opened her eyes and stepped back. "I don't understand why you won't even try."

"I like you, Jenny, I really like you a lot."

"And I like you," she said eagerly. "A lot."

"But, well . . ." He ran his fingers through the thick black of his hair. "It's like this." He took her hand and sat on the hard-packed ground beneath the tree, pulling her down beside him. "Miz Lorelie says there are two kinds of girls in the world. The kind that are free with their favors—"

"You mean like kissing." She leaned forward and nuzzled his neck. My, he smelled wonderful. Just like horses and leather and warm, spicy man.

Zach swallowed. "Yeah."

"And what's the other kind?" Could she reach his lips from this angle? And even if he wouldn't kiss her, why couldn't she kiss him?

"The kind you marry."

She froze. "Which kind am I?"

"I'd kind of hoped you were the first." He stared into her eyes. "But I'm afraid you're the second."

"The kind you marry?"

"The kind I want to marry."

"You want to marry me?" Her voice rang with a strange, tense squeak.

Zach nodded solemnly. "Yep. I sure do."

"Nobody's ever asked me to marry them before." She shook her head in astonishment.

"I'm asking now." Earnest sincerity rang in his voice. He clasped her hands in his. "Jenny, I've known from the moment I saw you in Alma's kitchen, and that was nearly two weeks ago, that we were meant for each other. We've been together nearly every day, whenever you could get away from the countess, and

I haven't changed my mind yet. You sit a horse like no woman I've ever seen. And you're pretty and you're kind of smart and I love you."

"Damnation," she breathed.

"What did you say?" His brow furrowed.

"Um . . . I said . . ." She smiled with sheer joy. "I love you too."

"Then?"

She nodded eagerly. "I'll marry you."

"Well then, now that we're officially betrothed, I guess"— a wicked twinkle sparked in his eye—"I can kiss you."

She shook her head. "I don't think so." His expression fell, and she grinned. "*I* can kiss *you*."

She threw herself in his arms, and the two of them tumbled backwards onto the welcoming grass. Her lips met his with the eagerness of newly discovered passion. Her spirit soared, and all she wanted was more of the sheer intoxication of his touch. She'd never dreamed love could be like this. No one ever told her. Why, Ophelia—

The thought of her sister sobered her like a splash of icy water, and she pulled away from Zach and scrambled to her feet.

"What?" Confusion and interrupted passion dazed his eyes. "What happened?"

"Ophelia."

"Where?" He staggered to his feet and cast a frantic gaze around the area.

Jenny stared. The dear boy really did look rather amusing, with his hair all disheveled and bits of grass clinging to his clothes. And that look in his eyes like a sleeper roused out of a deep slumber. "She's not here."

"Good." He paused. "Then why did you call her name?"

"Well, I can't possibly marry you until Ophelia is firmly settled with Tye."

"Why not?"

"Goodness, Zach, if Ophelia isn't matched with Tye and matched soon, she'll insist on leaving Dead End and taking me with her."

"Why would she want to take you with her? You're just her maid."

"It's kind of hard to explain exactly. Just take my word for it. When Ophelia leaves Dead End she'll want me to go with her."

He narrowed his gaze suspiciously and pointed an accusing finger. "You're hiding something from me."

"Nonsense." She tossed her long hair over her shoulder. She couldn't possibly tell him everything. At least not now. "What would I be hiding?"

"I don't know, but you are." He crossed his arms over his chest. "Wives do not keep secrets from their husbands."

"Really?" Jenny knew absolutely nothing about the rules that governed relations between a husband and wife, but Zach's pronouncement struck her as totally and completely wrong. Besides, she wasn't his wife yet. "We simply have to make sure Ophelia never wants to leave."

"But you haven't told me—"

"For goodness' sake, Zach, we have to get back. Now. We need to help Lorelie get her nephew and my sis—countess together." She turned to go, but Zach grabbed her arm and twirled her to face him.

"But it doesn't matter, does it?" His anxious gaze

searched her face. "You'll stay with me regardless of what she does, won't you?"

Stay with him regardless? Choose between the man she loved and the sister who'd sacrificed her own life for her. It was a choice she didn't want to make. And a choice she didn't have to make right now. But he didn't have to know that. "Of course."

Relief washed across his face and he pulled her into his arms for a quick kiss. He released her, and she drew a deep breath. "I suspect we shall do a great deal of that when we're married."

"I suspect we will." He grinned. "And I know I'm looking forward to it."

They strode toward the horses, and Zack helped her into her saddle. He wasn't the only one looking forward to marriage. Kissing and marriage and settling down in one place forever. Everything Jenny had ever longed for was within her grasp.

Determination raised her chin. Regardless of what Ophelia said, Jenny would not be leaving Dead End. This would be her home now. She dug her heels into her horse's side and headed toward the Matthews place. The best solution to her dilemma was to make certain Ophelia didn't want to leave either.

And Tyler Matthews was the only sure way to do just that.

"I THINK IT's a lovely stage." Ophelia perched on the edge of the high platform that, with a few finishing touches, would be the center of performance for the Empire City opera house.

"I think you're right." Tye gave a jutting nail a single whack with his hammer and nodded in satisfaction. "I think the whole thing has turned out surprisingly well."

"It's not completed yet," she said quickly.

"No, but it'll serve for Jack's ceremony next week."

"Indeed it will." Ophelia stared out into the area that would be fitted with seats for the anticipated audience that would soon fill the Empire City opera house. Tye studied her silently. What was she thinking? What were her plans?

The damned town had once again surprised him. He'd never dreamed this building would go up so fast. Aside from getting her money out of the bank—Randolph said he hadn't seen her make any withdrawals—there wasn't much to keep Ophelia in Dead End. And he would do whatever necessary to keep her here. But the longer she stayed, the more she risked exposure. Now that the building was more or less finished she could disappear from his life at any minute. Funny about that, though. She'd seemed to revel in the frenzy of activity surrounding the construction. She apparently liked the now daily meetings of Lorelie's Cultural Society. And he knew she enjoyed their evenings spent together on the porch at Jack and Lorelie's, even though whenever he made any kind of definite progress toward getting her in his bed, his aunt seemed to magically appear.

Still, he'd learned a great deal about her. About her thoughts and feelings and dreams. She continued to hide the truth behind her masquerade, and while he would have to determine that at some point, she revealed so much more that he no longer cared quite as much about what she continued to conceal. And with every day spent together, his admiration grew, and so did his love.

"What are you thinking?" he said softly.

"Nothing of importance. Nonsense, really. Can you hear them?"

"Hear who?"

"Why, the audience, of course." She laughed lightly and gestured at the nonexistent assembly.

"Oh, the audience." He clapped his hand to his forehead with feigned chagrin. "How could I have possibly overlooked them?"

"How indeed." Ophelia scrambled to her feet and strode to the center of the stage. "Why, just look at them, Tye." He stepped to her side.

"Over here"—she covered her mouth with her hand as if imparting a secret—"these are the terribly expensive seats, you know, reserved for only the very best people."

"I see."

"It's opening night. The men are all charming and handsome and dressed in their finest. The women, mostly wives, of course, but here and there is an occasional—"

"Mistress?" He grinned.

She lifted an indignant brow. "I was going to say companion."

"A companion." He nodded somberly. "Of course."

"At any rate," she continued in a lofty manner, "their gowns are from Paris. Their manners impeccable. And their noses kept firmly in the air."

He laughed. "I don't think you'll find a gown from Paris anywhere in Dead End."

"Probably not." An impish twinkle shone in her eye. "But you might in Empire City."

"Maybe someday, but right now in Empire City, here's what you'll see on opening night at the opera house." He took her hand, tucked it in the crook of his arm and escorted her to the left side of the stage. "Over here"—he nodded at the space directly below them—

"you'll find the town's banker, Randolph Watson, and his wife—"

"Henrietta," she murmured.

He nodded. "Henrietta. She'll be all atwitter with excitement. And he'll be ready to burst with pride at this shining symbol of civilization."

"And rightfully so," she said with a firm nod.

"In this area, as far from Randolph as you can get and still be in the good seats"—he led her to the other side of the stage—"Joe Simmons."

"The saloon keeper?"

"Yep. Joe and his wife, Anna Rose, will be seated right there. There'll be the barest spark of anticipation in her eye that for just a moment will distract you from notice of her rather impressive mustache—"

"Tye!"

He ignored her. "—and Joe will be reluctantly admitting to himself that maybe civilization isn't such a bad thing after all."

"Only to himself?"

Tye chuckled. "Joe doesn't much see the need for anything that smacks of respectability."

"I see."

"And here." He walked her to the center of the stage. "Just to one side of the middle will be the town's leading citizens."

"Big Jack and Lorelie?"

"Other area ranchers will be here, of course. But Jack's the one who's always run things around here and run them well. And people like him."

"He's a very nice man," she said quietly.

"Yes, he is." He placed his hand over hers and nodded at a point beside the Matthews family's imaginary seats. "And do you see who's sitting right over there?"

She laughed. "No. Who?"

He gasped in mock surprise. "Don't tell me you don't recognize him?"

She clapped her hand over her mouth. "What a horrible breach of social etiquette. Can you ever forgive me?"

He heaved a long-suffering sigh. "I'll try."

"Thank you." Her eyes sparked with humor. "Now tell me, who's in that seat?"

"Why, Ophelia, that's where the mayor sits."

"Of course." She leaned toward him confidentially. "He has excellent seats."

Tye shrugged casually. "Well, he's the mayor." He paused and considered his words, then plunged ahead. "Do you see who's in the seat right beside him?"

Ophelia squinted and shook her head, laughter in her voice. "I can't quite make it out."

"That's the mayor's wife."

She stilled beside him. "His wife?"

"Yep. I don't how you can miss her." Damn, this was hard. His heart was in his throat. He hadn't planned on saying anything like this, hadn't planned on declaring himself at all until he'd wrung the truth out of her, but the moment seemed so natural, so right. "With that hair that reminds you of a summer sunset, and eyes like deep green pools, and the way he looks at her . . ."

"The way he looks at her?" she whispered.

"Why, only a fool would fail to see that he's—"

"There you are." Lorelie's voice rang from the back of the room, and they broke apart like children with their hands caught in the cookie jar.

"I have been looking all over for you two."

"We were just discussing . . . opening night." Ophelia smiled. Surely only he could hear the slight tremble in her voice?

"Opening night?" Lorelie wrinkled her nose. "But aside from Jack's ceremony, and of course a town party, we have no opening night. Frankly, beyond that, no one has really considered exactly what we'll do with an opera house."

"Eventually, you can get troupes of actors to come and perform. You can even present an opera or a play yourselves," Ophelia said.

"Ourselves?" Lorelie's eyes widened with delight. "What a charming idea."

"But keep in mind," Ophelia said, "it takes a great deal of time for, well, amateurs to put together any kind of real performance."

"Except for readings," Tye said slowly, the glimmer of an idea in the back of his mind.

Lorelie tilted her head with interest. "What kind of readings?"

"Well, poetry, for one," Tye said, the idea growing. "Doesn't your Cultural Society read poetry? Couldn't you do something with, oh, say, Keats's 'Ode on a Grecian Urn'? I can see you ladies playing the parts of Grecian urns."

Lorelie paled, as if upset by his simple question. How odd. Why should reference to the Every Other Tuesday and Thursday Afternoon Ladies Cultural Society distress her? No doubt he was mistaken.

Lorelie shook her head. "We're not all that fond of poetry, dear. And we especially dislike urns."

"Well, then." The idea snapped into a form so sharp and clear he could have crowed with delight. An idea that would keep Ophelia firmly planted in Dead End for that much longer. "What about Shakespeare?"

"Shakespeare?" Ophelia gasped.

"Shakespeare," Lorelie said thoughtfully.

"Shakespeare." Tye's voice was firm. "Ophelia is almost an expert on Shakespeare, aren't you?"

"Well, yes, but . . . ," she stammered, obviously not as intrigued by the idea as he was.

"What a wonderful idea." Excitement rang in Lorelie's voice. "You could direct us. Why, we could do readings from *Romeo and Juliet* and *Much Ado About Nothing* and—what else, Ophelia?"

Ophelia sighed in resignation. "Oh, I don't know, *A Midsummer Night's Dream*?"

"*The Taming of the Shrew*?" Tye said, innocence in his voice.

Ophelia cast him an irritated glance.

"Or . . . why not . . ." He grinned. "*Twelfth Night*?"

TWELFTH NIGHT? THE play about Viola? A woman posing as a man? A woman pretending to be someone she wasn't?

He knew!

There wasn't a doubt in her mind. It explained everything. She'd known of his suspicions, of course. She'd have to have been a complete fool, given his snide comments to Big Jack and his interrogation of Jenny, not to have known that. But it had all been so terribly subtle, a quiet backroom type of game between the two of them. Until now. His suggestion and the wicked look in his eye was blatant. A challenge, if you would.

The man was calling her bluff.

Blind panic seized her, and she wanted to run. Now. Get out of Dead End and never look back. But she'd been in tight spots before, and natural instinct took hold. As quickly as fear had struck, calm descended.

He still didn't have any real proof. What kind of

game was he playing now? With that talk of the mayor's wife? And what was Lorelie up to? She'd brought up the subject of marriage as well.

"Ophelia?" Concern laced Lorelie's voice. "Are you quite all right, dear? For a moment you looked as if you might swoon."

"Thank you, Lorelie, I fear it was just a momentary twinge of"—she slanted Tye a pointed glare—"indigestion."

"Then you will help us put on a reading of Shakespeare?"

"I don't see how I could possibly refuse." She smiled graciously but seethed inside. He tricked her. She wasn't sure how exactly, but he did.

Very well. She still had a week in which she could safely stay in Dead End. And she grudgingly admitted she liked the members of the Every Other Tuesday and Thursday Afternoon Ladies Cultural Society, and she liked the town and, well, now and then, she even liked the mayor. This might be fun. Besides, she wasn't planning on leaving yet anyway.

While she'd won a tidy sum from the Cultural Society initially, she'd since had less success. She wasn't sure how it happened; on any given day, she'd win just a little more than she'd lose. At this rate it would take next to forever to get even a paltry amount together. Still, she could afford to stretch her stay here as long as possible. It would be cutting it close, but she could easily leave the day before the arrival of the queen's representative and be long gone before anyone noticed.

And as for Tye, why on earth was he looking like a cat sated with cream? What would she do about him? Certainly, seduction was still in her plans if she could avoid Lorelie long enough. An idea simmered in the corners of her mind.

She cast Tye a sweet smile and his grin faltered, as if he feared what she might be up to now. She was right about him. He was smart. But he had greatly underestimated her.

She was smarter.

Chapter 13

"No, no, no, Anna Rose, you're supposed to be the queen of the fairies. It requires a very light touch." Ophelia smiled her encouragement and sighed to herself.

Perhaps it wasn't such a good idea to allow the ladies to select their own readings. But who would have ever dreamed the very sturdy Anna Rose Simmons had a secret longing to play Titania? Right now, Anna Rose and the other ladies made even Keats look appealing. No doubt these women would make far better Grecian urns than wood nymphs or fairies or virgins.

"So doth the woodbine the sweet honeysuckle gently entwist the female ivy so . . ." Anna Rose's voice rang out with all the authority, and much of the charm, of a barkeep breaking up a free-for-all.

It was all Ophelia could do to keep a supportive smile on her face. No doubt Shakespeare could probably overlook the rather fascinating facial hair of this Titania. After all, most of his female roles were played by men. But that voice—Ophelia shuddered. He must surely be rolling over in his grave at the enthusiastic desecration of his words. It wouldn't surprise Ophelia one bit if the Bard's ghost showed up any minute in eerie, indignant protest.

It was all Tye's fault, of course. The day after he'd suggested this farce he'd shown up with a stack of volumes of Shakespeare's plays. The Every Other Tuesday and Thursday Afternoon Ladies Cultural Society had descended upon them like a biblical plague of locusts. Before Ophelia could utter a word of protest, she had a matronly rancher's wife declaring herself to be Cleopatra, an elderly spinster memorizing Juliet's lines and the quiet, retiring sister of a shopkeeper spewing the speeches of Lady Macbeth with a vengeance that widened even Lorelie's eyes in surprise. There was no casting according to type in this little performance.

Ophelia had to admit that there might not have been a lot of talent, but there was a great deal of fervor and unrestrained eagerness. It was, in fact, quite a lot of fun. The women had even changed their name. From now on they were the Every Other Tuesday and Thursday Afternoon Ladies Cultural Society and Theater Troupe. Every morning they rehearsed. Every afternoon they won and lost tremendous wagers in a continuing game of high-stakes poker.

"Do you think we're ready, dear?" Lorelie settled in the seat beside Ophelia.

"As ready as we're ever going to be."

Even the opera house was ready, the finishing touches essentially complete, the seats installed, the curtains hung. It wasn't a huge building, no match for the theaters of Denver or Kansas City, but it was a nice opera house nonetheless.

"I do hope so." A nervous note sounded in Lorelie's voice. "Why, Jack's ceremony is the day after tomorrow."

"It will certainly be something to remember." Ophelia cast the older woman a confident smile belying the pang of regret shooting through her. She wouldn't be around to see Lorelie take the stage for her reading of Kate's "husband" speech from *The Taming of the Shrew*. Lorelie was one of the better actors in the group.

Lorelie leaned closer as if to impart a secret. "I do believe I'm experiencing a good deal of stage fright."

"You'll be fine."

There was every possibility Lorelie wouldn't perform anyway. Ophelia planned to sneak herself and Jenny on the afternoon train tomorrow. Word of her disappearance probably wouldn't get around town until the queen's man arrived for Big Jack's celebration.

Then the truth would come out.

Lorelie sighed. "I would so hate for Jack to be disappointed in my performance."

"You needn't worry. I'm certain he'll love it."

It was bad enough that they'd all know she wasn't a real countess, but they'd realize she wasn't even a very good thief. She'd only managed to get a minimal amount of her money out of Randolph's bank, and she hadn't won nearly as much from the Cultural Society as she'd expected. All in all, she'd leave Dead End with barely more than eight hundred dollars—a pathetic amount compared to what she should have gotten. Of course, it was considerably better than thirty-two dollars and seventeen cents, and she'd never had this much money in her life, but it didn't come close to what she wanted or needed. And it scarcely seemed worth the effort.

Lorelie brightened. "Well, he does love *me*, and I suppose that will make a bit of a difference."

"I suspect love might make a difference," Ophelia murmured.

She'd even failed at her plan to seduce Tye. Certainly, the man was around every evening, but she could never seem to get him alone. She still wasn't sure exactly what to do with him or about him. Thank goodness he hadn't brought up that marriage nonsense again. Marriage, and or love, was not in her future. No matter what Tye knew, suspected or believed, the complete truth in all its deceitful glory was certain to destroy any feelings he had for her. It would be bad enough if that happened before they wed, but after would be disastrous. No, the only person Ophelia could count on was herself. She was not interested in marriage, and regardless of the suspiciously sentimental thoughts she had about Tye, she was not interested in love.

"I do have a confession to make to you, Ophelia."

Ophelia smiled. "What kind of confession could you possibly have, Lorelie?"

"I shall very much miss you when you leave."

"What?" Ophelia widened her eyes in surprise and forced herself to remain calm. "What do you mean?"

A puzzled frown drew Lorelie's brows together. "Why, nothing at all. Except you've extended your visit much longer than you originally intended." She studied Ophelia thoughtfully. "Have you ever considered staying here permanently?"

"Living in Dead End?"

"No, dear, living in Empire City."

"No, Lorelie." Ophelia laughed, a slight, unexpected shade of bitterness in the sound that echoed the odd pang inside her. "I'm afraid that wouldn't be possible."

"Why not? You have nothing left to return to England for. This would be the perfect place to start a new life."

"It is a nice town," Ophelia said softly.

"With very nice people." Lorelie nodded firmly. "And many of those nice people are men who need wives."

"I believe you mentioned that before." A wry note sounded in Ophelia's voice.

"Did I?" Lorelie's eyes were innocent, her manner vague. "Well, then, obviously if I'm bringing it up again, there must be a great deal of merit to the idea."

Ophelia chuckled in spite of herself. "I have no intention of remarrying."

Lorelie rolled her eyes heavenward. "My dear, you simply must cease your mourning for Alcazar—"

"Ambrose," Ophelia said without thinking.

"Addison?"

Ophelia drew a deep breath and glanced up into Tye's amused gaze. "No," she said firmly, "Ambrose."

"My mistake." He grinned.

"Tyler." Lorelie raised a brow. "What are you doing here? Surely you've not come to offer your services? Although I daresay we could use a male presence. Anna Rose's mustache is the most virile thing in this presentation. Still, we are sadly lacking for someone to play . . . oh, say, Romeo."

"Romeo?" He sank down in the seat next to Ophelia. "Sounds perfect for me."

"Perfect is not precisely the word I'd use," Ophelia said.

"Ouch." Tyler winced and clasped his hand over his heart in a theatrical manner. "You wound me, fair lady. Why dost thou cast such aspersions upon my innocent person?"

"Innocent?" A laugh slipped through Ophelia's restraint. "Romeo was an innocent, a mere child. I scarcely think anyone in their right mind would cast you in that role."

"Hah! I'd be wonderful! Magnificent! None better." He leapt from his seat and vaulted onto the stage, halting Anna Rose in midword. "If the charming Titania will forgive me."

He caught her hand in his, brushed his lips across it, then swept a dramatic bow. "I need your enchanted land, my Queen, for the barest of moments if that is indeed your pleasure."

Anna Rose stared, stunned, then an odd giggle squeaked out like a rusty hinge stiff from lack of use. She bobbed a stilted curtsy, too-black curls bouncing around her head. "Be my guest . . . my lord."

"Now, let's see." Tye's eyes gleamed with a teasing light that made Ophelia's teeth clench. What was he up to now? "It was Romeo you asked for, I believe."

"I didn't ask for anything." Ophelia rose from her seat.

"Romeo would be wonderful, Tyler," Lorelie said. Ophelia cast her an exasperated glance. "Well, it would."

"Tyler Matthews." Ophelia glared. "Get down here right now."

He shook his head. "Alas, dear lady, you asked for Romeo, and you shall have him."

"I didn't ask—"

"'A grave? Oh, no! A lantern, slaughtered youth, for here lies Juliet, and her beauty makes this vault a feasting presence full of light.'"

Astonishment widened her eyes. She'd expected Tye to go for the obvious, the balcony scene with its sweet, yearning romance. Instead, the man was reciting Romeo's speech when he finds Juliet dead.

His voice rang through the theater with a resonance she hadn't expected. " 'Oh my love, my wife. Death, that hath sucked the honey of thy breath, hath had no power yet upon thy beauty . . .' "

This was quite enough. She should have known he'd get the word *wife* in there somehow. Her patience snapped. "Tye!"

"Hush," Lorelie said under her breath.

Ophelia stared at the older woman. Lorelie's gaze was fixed on Tyler with a rapt attention as if she'd never seen him before.

Ophelia's gaze skimmed over the dozen or so women gathered in the opera house. Each and every one was caught in the heart-stopping sorrow of young love foiled by death.

" '. . . and, lips, O you the doors of breath, seal with a righteous kiss a dateless bargain to engrossing death . . .' "

Reluctantly, she had to admit he was good. Very good. He would have made an excellent actor. The stage door would have been jammed with women seeking his notice. He was certainly handsome enough. Indeed, some women might very well find the combination of a tall, hard body, golden hair and chocolate eyes appealing for something beyond a simple night of passion. Ophelia was not, however, one of those women.

" '. . . here's to my love. O true apothecary, thy drugs are quick. Thus with a kiss, I die.' "

Silence hung in the theater for a long moment. Then, applause and excited chatter erupted.

"Why, Tyler Matthews, I never dreamed—"

"—you could have gone on the stage, I do—"

"—even in Denver I never saw—"

He leapt from the stage to land in front of her and grinned. "Well?"

She favored him with a benevolent smile. "Satisfactory, nothing more."

"You were wonderful," Lorelie said stoutly.

Ophelia shrugged. "Adequate, really quite adequate."

Tye heaved a heartfelt sigh. "Critics."

"What are you doing here anyway, dear?" Lorelie said.

Ophelia crossed her arms over her chest. "We do need to get back to work, so if you don't mind . . ."

"Oh, but I do, Countess." Humor and desire shone in his eyes. Was she the only one who noticed? "I've come to take you away from all this."

Ophelia narrowed her eyes. "Take me away . . . where?"

"I had Alma pack us a basket. I thought we'd ride to a favorite spot of mine and enjoy the rest of this beautiful day."

"Ride?" Dear Lord, not on horses.

"I have that silly little carriage of Lorelie's outside." Tye leaned closer and whispered in her ear. "I just thought after spending every day for a week with the dear ladies of Dead End doing their best to slaughter Shakespeare every morning, and doing whatever silly, female thing they do every afternoon, you needed a break. What do you say?"

She stared at him, then nodded abruptly, her decision made. This was her chance, possibly her only chance, to be alone with him. Excitement and fear shivered through her.

"Good." He exhaled as if relieved at her agreement. "Aunt Lorelie, I'm kidnapping the countess for the afternoon."

"Rescuing would be a more appropriate term," Lorelie murmured.

"Did you say something?" Tye frowned at his aunt.

"No, no, dear, you two run along." Lorelie waved her hands as if to shoo them away.

"If you're sure you don't need me?" Ophelia cast her an uncertain glance.

"We'll manage to muddle along without you. I suspect what we need most of right now is simply practice." Lorelie leaned toward Ophelia and lowered her voice. "I do believe you've done all you can, and we're very grateful." Lorelie studied her for a moment, then clasped Ophelia's hand in her own. "I have become quite fond of you, you know. We all have. We very much feel as if you are one of us."

"Thank you." Ophelia tried to swallow past the aching knot in her throat. Why hadn't she noticed before now? She liked these women a great deal. They'd welcomed her as one of their own. It would be far harder than she imagined to leave. They were, after all, such very nice people. She made a silent vow never, ever to take advantage of very nice people again. One way or another, the price one paid was apparently much too high.

"Shall we go?" Tye offered his arm.

She hooked her hand through his elbow. "Lead on."

He escorted her toward the door and said under his breath, "I was excellent, you know."

"You were awful," she said softly.

"I would have made a magnificent Romeo." A smug note sounded in his voice.

She laughed. "You would have made a passable Bottom."

"Bottom?" He furrowed his forehead and opened the door for her.

Satisfaction surged through her. Finally, she'd stumbled across a reference he didn't pick up on at once. "Surely you remember Bottom? From *A Midsummer Night's Dream*?"

Tye's expression cleared, and a warning growled in his voice. "Ophelia."

She tossed him an innocent smile. "He was the one dressed like an ass."

"THIS IS IT," Lorelie murmured.

"Are you sure?" Henrietta perched on the seat beside her, the rest of the ladies gathering around them.

"Oh, you can always tell."

Two more women nodded sagely to each other.

"I couldn't tell." Anna Rose drew her thick black brows together until they paralleled the ridge of hair above her lips. "How can you tell?"

"Even you can't be that oblivious to your surroundings, Anna Rose," a rancher's wife chided.

Maize sighed. "I think it's romantic."

"How can you tell?" Frustration colored Anna Rose's voice.

"Terribly romantic." The women exchanged dreamy glances.

"He's so wonderfully handsome and she's so very pretty, why it's—"

"—it's like a fairy tale come to—"

"—to life. The Countess and the Mayor." A wave of sentimental sighs washed around the room.

"How can you tell!" Anna Rose stomped her sturdy foot and glared.

"You can tell by the look in their eyes." Lorelie's voice was patient. "She's excited and apprehensive at the same time."

The married women in the gathering nodded wisely.

"And he is more than a touch nervous and just a smidge uncertain."

Again the ladies nodded their understanding.

"And you all know what that means?" Lorelie cast her gaze over the gathering.

"No," Anna Rose said helplessly.

"It means," Henrietta grinned, "Lorelie will soon have a countess in the family."

"Well, of course she will," Anna Rose said sharply. "When Jack becomes a count, Lorelie will . . ." Understanding dawned on her face. "Oh, I see. Tyler and the countess."

"I knew you'd catch on sooner or later, dear." Lorelie smiled.

"But are you certain about all this?"

Lorelie laughed. "Have you ever seen two people as, well, ready to burst as these two? I've thrown them together and kept them from doing anything about it. And when a man can't satisfy his baser urges, he starts thinking about more civilized methods of getting what he wants."

"Marriage." Henrietta grinned.

"And knowing my nephew as I do, I'm confident his thoughts have turned to matrimony. Aside from that"—Lorelie shrugged— "they're in love."

Anna Rose rolled her eyes heavenward as if already regretting what she was about to say. "How can you tell?"

The gathering heaved a collective sigh and burst into a flurry of explanation.

"It's the way he stares at her, as if she's—"

"—dessert and he's a hungry man or—"

"—the way she wants to be stern with him but—"

"—can't seem to keep the smile from her face or—"

"—how he talks to you but his eyes are trained on her or—"

"—the way everything about her seems to soften when he's in the room and—"

"—how he's exactly the same when she's around."

"The truly amazing part about all of this, ladies," Lorelie said with an incredulous look around the gathering, "is that their feelings for each other are so obvious."

"We can certainly see it." The merchant's sister nodded.

Lorelie shook her head. "But they can't see what's right in front of their eyes."

"Where are we going?"

This was it. Ophelia struggled to keep her voice unconcerned, but her stomach fluttered uncontrollably. She could well sympathize with Lorelie right now. Ophelia, too, had something suspiciously like stage fright.

"I think it's about time you saw the prettiest spot in the territory, maybe in the world." The casual tone in Tye's voice matched her own. "There's a creek that runs through—"

"Where your father taught you to fish?"

He grinned. "You remember."

"I remember." How could she forget that night? How the moon spread a touch of magic with its beams. Or the look on his face when he talked about family and land and home. Or the way he'd kissed her for the first time.

"I promised to take you there." He paused as if selecting his words carefully. "With Jack's ceremony the day after tomorrow, I thought this would be the only opportunity. I hope you don't mind."

"Mind?" Of course she didn't mind. The moment she'd agreed to come she'd realized this was her last chance to finally be in his arms. To know what it was to be with a man completely and fully. To be with this man. "Not at all."

"Great." He smiled, and silence settled between them.

Gad, she was nervous. Of course she'd never seduced a man before and wasn't quite certain how to go about it. No doubt all she'd have to do was set it all in motion and Tye would take his cue from her. But what if he didn't? What if she had to carry the flirtatious act she'd practiced on him before to a greater extreme? And the man thought she was a widow. A woman of experience. What would he expect from such a woman? And, dear Lord, what if she did it wrong?

With every turn of the carriage wheel, her apprehension grew. Goodness, if this was what every woman went through prior to sacrificing her virtue, well, it was astonishing the virgin population wasn't far greater than it was.

She cast him a surreptitious glance. What if he brought up the topic of marriage again? And his vision of the mayor's wife? She'd just have to distract him, that's all. Divert him away from any noble intentions regarding marriage and appeal to the lustier side of his character. A side she had already sampled in the most intriguing manner. A side she was fully prepared to explore in a thorough and satisfying way.

No, she was determined to enjoy this afternoon in the arms of the man she loved—no—wanted. Tomorrow at this time she'd be on the train out of town. Leaving Dead End and Tyler Matthews forever. It was a good plan. Damn near a perfect plan. And she really had no other logical choice.

So why did the very thought hurt so much?

THIS WAS IT.

Why was his throat so damn dry? He couldn't even seem to swallow. He slanted her a quick glance.

Ophelia sat looking straight forward, her manner as relaxed as if she had the world at her feet. What he wouldn't do to give her just that.

Odd how life worked. When he first met her, it was her fiery beauty that attracted him. Now, there was much more that pulled him to her. So many little things that added up to love. Why, look at the way she'd helped with their opera house. Or the way she'd been so friendly to the ladies of Dead End. And Lord knows, only a saint would put up with the torture of their versions of Shakespeare day after day.

He chuckled to himself. Ophelia was no saint. Good. He didn't want a saint. He wanted a flesh-and-blood woman. This flesh-and-blood woman. He wanted her naked body, hot and demanding, next to his. He wanted her to gaze at him as if he were the only man in the world. And he wanted her forever as his wife.

But first, he'd get the truth out of her. Not that he cared any longer about the details of whatever it was she was up to. It was more to satisfy his own curiosity than anything else, because who she was or what she wanted no longer really mattered. But once he had the truth she'd have to marry him.

It wasn't as if she didn't want to. She obviously loved him, whether she wanted to admit it or not. No doubt it was the simple matter of her fraudulent masquerade that prevented her from giving into feelings he was confident were as intense as his own. Well, he had all afternoon to break down her defenses and win her hand and her heart.

He laughed softly under his breath, and she tossed him a curious glance. Yes, indeed. First he'd get her confession, and then he'd offer her his own admission of love and proposal of marriage. He grinned. No doubt about it.

This was definitely it.

Chapter 14

"You were right. It's beautiful here." Ophelia extended her hand, and Tye helped her out of the buggy, holding on a moment longer than necessary. Her gaze locked with his and her breath caught at the emotion she saw in his eyes. Was it simple desire that smoldered there or something more?

"Beautiful." His gaze raked over her. He smiled and released her, turning back to the carriage for the basket Alma had prepared. Ophelia stepped away, as much to avoid his glance as to admire the scenery.

He hadn't exaggerated.

The scene spread before them was as much a banquet for the eyes as Alma's provisions were for the body. They stood on a slight rise. A long, low valley fell away so gently that it was almost impossible to discern any drop at all. The plains stretched on and on until they faded to mountains in the distance, so far off they were little more than a suggestion. Tye's creek danced and laughed through a stand of trees—oak, she thought, and the only real shelter to be seen anywhere. Trees were apparently few and far between in this country. But their lack only added to the stark beauty. There was an air of serenity here that seemed to seep inside her soul. She drew a steadying breath. She could certainly use all the serenity she could get.

"Would you help me with this?" Tye held out a scarlet blanket.

A blanket?

"And what are you planning to do with that?" Her voice rang a shade higher than normal.

"I'm planning on laying it on the ground—"

"Just as I suspected." She glared indignantly.

"—so that we have something to sit on when we eat."

"Exactly! And . . . and . . ." A sinking feeling settled in her stomach. Had a woman actually ever died from embarrassment? "And a fine idea it is too." She grabbed the edges of the blanket and stretched it out over the grass.

"What did you think I was going to do?"

She busied herself with smoothing wrinkles from the coverlet to avoid his gaze, but she couldn't miss the smile in his voice.

"Why, sit on it, of course." Ophelia struggled to keep her tone light and innocent, but she wanted to rage out loud. At herself. How could she forget that *she*, not *he*, was the one whose plans included seduction. And even if his intentions did match hers, well, so much the better. It would, no doubt, be far easier to accomplish if he was as willing as she. It was just that she was so damned nervous.

"You look like you're about to bolt at any minute." Tye lounged on the blanket, a smug smile on his face. "Sit down, Ophelia, I won't bite."

Perhaps it was the smile that did it. Perhaps it was the indulgent tone in his voice. Perhaps it was simply the total picture of confidence the man presented, as if he had the world and everyone in it firmly under his control. His arrogant expression abruptly quieted her overwrought nerves like a brisk wind snuffing out a flickering candle. This was her seduction, her performance, and damn it, this man was not going to upstage her!

She was Ophelia Kendrake, daughter of the theater.

She was the Countess of . . . of . . . of wherever with a lovely castle and a charming estate, imaginary though they may be.

And above all else, whether she could recall her lines or not, she was an actress. If her sojourn in Dead End had taught her nothing else, she'd learned she was a better actress without a script than with one. How difficult could seduction be, anyway? Why, men did it all the time.

"Do you promise you won't bite?" She smiled in what she assumed was a provocative manner and sank down on the blanket.

"Of course." He raised a brow as if curious about her abrupt change of attitude, then lifted the cloth covering the basket and rummaged through the contents. His words were muffled but unmistakable. "For now."

She pretended not to hear.

"There's a feast in here, Ophelia." Tye pulled out a napkin-wrapped plate. "There's chicken and biscuits and one of Alma's pies . . ."

"Goodness, we'll never eat all that."

". . . and"—he held up a bottle of champagne and grinned—"a bottle of Jack's champagne."

She tilted her head in feigned surprise. "Imagine. That Alma. She certainly did think of everything."

"Didn't she, though?" It was his turn to look innocent. He popped the cork and fished around in the bottom of the basket until he found two crystal goblets. He poured the wine like an expert and presented one to her with a flourish. "Countess?"

"Thank you," she said primly and took a long sip. While she had a firm grip on her outward appearance, inside she remained as taut as a violin bow. With any luck, the champagne would relax her. She took another sip and noted with surprise the glass was already nearly empty. "I do so love champagne."

"Do you?"

"I do." She held the crystal up to eye level and studied the sparkling wine. "It's the bubbles, I think."

He nodded with the wisdom of an experienced man. "Tickles your nose, doesn't it?"

"Why, I hadn't really considered that, but I suppose it does. No, I like the way it feels going down my throat. So delicate and pleasant." She tossed him a dreamy look. "Like a smile or a laugh. That's it, a laugh. A very light laugh turned to liquid."

"A laugh?" He chuckled.

"A laugh." She nodded firmly. "It definitely feels like a laugh going down and then, right here"—she placed a hand over her stomach—"it turns to a delightful warmth that spreads straight through you from your head to your toes." She drained the rest of her drink and held her glass out to him.

He obligingly refilled it, and she took another sip.

"Is that what women usually say about champagne?"

"Is what what women usually say?" Confusion sounded in his voice.

"About it tickling their nose?"

"Oh, that. Well, in my experience—"

"Have you had a great deal of experience?"

He shrugged. "I imagine that depends on how you define experience."

"For goodness' sake, Tye, you know exactly what I mean." She stared in exasperation and took another swallow of the wine. "Experience with women and champagne. Together and or separately."

He laughed, a full-bodied, male sound that reverberated in her soul. "Why do you want to know?"

"I like to know exactly who I'm dealing with, that's all." She raised her chin in a lofty manner.

He stared at the wine and his voice was soft. "Do you?"

"Indeed I do."

"Is that important? To know who you're dealing with, I mean?" There was an odd undercurrent to his voice, as if his words had a deeper meaning she couldn't quite comprehend.

"Of course it is." She glanced down at her glass, surprised to find it empty. Odd, she didn't remember drinking it all. Perhaps she had spilled it. Of course that's what had happened. After all, Ophelia never had more than two glasses of champagne. She held her goblet out to him. "Who am I dealing with, Tyler Matthews?"

He refilled her wine and smiled. "I thought you knew."

"Refresh my memory." She hiccupped and pressed her fingers to her lips. "Pardon me."

Amusement curved his lips. "Well, let me see. I'm the mayor."

She raised her champagne in a jaunty toast. "And I'm the countess."

"Are you?" His voice was casual.

"No, no, no. None of that." She wagged her finger under his nose. "I most certainly am."

He laughed again and shook his head. "Very well, where was I?"

She sipped her wine. "You were the mayor and I was the countess."

"Of course. I went to school back East—"

"Where you met that terribly attractive but horribly annoying Englishman—"

"Sedge?"

"What kind of a name is that anyway? Sedge." She snorted. "Rhymes with hedge or wedge or bedge—"

"Bedge?"

"Bedge." She drained her glass. "It's a silly name. Not like Addicus—"

"One of your husbands?" Was he laughing at her?

"Yes indeed." She sighed. "Dear, dear, dead Addicus. So sweet, so young—"

"I thought you told Sedge he was an older man?"

"Well, of course he was older eventually." She rolled her eyes heavenward. Why was the man having such a difficult time understanding the slightest detail? "But he was young first."

"I see."

"Now, go on." There was a drop left in the bottom of her glass. If she stretched her tongue just so, she could probably reach it. An odd, strangled sound came from Tye. She glanced up at him. Why did he look so strained? She waved her free hand. "Tell me more."

He swallowed and drew a deep breath. "After school, I toured Europe—"

"And Venice." She held out her goblet. "Tell me again about the moon in Venice and the artists and the . . . lovers." She cast him an alluring gaze. At least she hoped it was alluring. This business of seduction was definitely easier than she'd expected. Maybe it was time for a kiss? Certainly she was more relaxed about the entire endeavor now than she'd been when they'd arrived. Or perhaps it was the champagne? It really didn't matter. She just wished she wouldn't keep spilling it.

"Didn't you tell me you never have more than two glasses of champagne?" He refilled her glass with a hand that didn't seem quite as steady as before.

She shook her head. "Nope. Never."

"But this is your fourth."

She leaned toward him and whispered, "I don't drink them, I just spill them."

He whispered back. "The only place you've spilled it is right down your throat."

"That's silly." She bent closer and kissed him on the nose. "In fact, right now you look rather silly."

"Do I?"

"Yes, indeed." She sipped the wine and gazed at him thoughtfully. Perhaps a kiss on the nose wasn't quite enticing enough to launch a seduction. "You look confused—"

"Hard to believe," he said wryly.

"—and you look . . ." She narrowed her eyes. "Somewhat determined. Yes, that's it, determined."

"I am." His eyes echoed the warning in his voice. She ignored it.

"And you look, oh, I don't know." She chewed on her bottom lip and his gaze drifted to her mouth, and even a woman as inexperienced as she knew with an unerring instinct that he wanted her. How perfect. Her voice softened. "Like a starving man contemplating his first real meal."

His gaze shot to hers and locked. "Is it that obvious?"

"It is to me."

"Ophelia, I—"

"Kiss me, Tye."

"My pleasure."

He leaned forward, across the blanket, and touched his lips to hers, carefully, as if she'd been a delicate flower or a piece of Venetian glass. She sighed beneath his touch and her mouth opened, her breath mingling with his. Gad, she would surely melt with the sheer sensation of his lips on hers. She strained forward to press her lips harder against his. Her heart raced. Her blood pounded. Her breath stilled.

She hiccupped, and a giggle escaped her.

"Oh, dear." She pulled back and clapped her hand over her mouth.

Tye's deep eyes simmered, and he heaved a heavy sigh. "Excellent timing, my dear."

"Thank you." Lord, she had certainly shattered that moment. Well, it was perhaps all for the best. Now that his lips, his wonderful, warm, intoxicating lips were no longer against hers, sanity returned. And so did her anxiety. Any effect from the champagne vanished. Maybe seduction was more difficult than she thought after all.

She scrambled to her feet. "So, is this the creek where your father taught you to fish?"

He stared at her for a moment, as if wondering whether to pull her back down beside him or to join her. With obvious reluctance, he plastered a smile of resignation on his face, unfolded his long body, and pulled himself to his feet. "Yep, this is it."

She walked toward the creek and stared at the rushing water. "Would you teach me to fish?"

His brows pulled together. "You want to learn to fish?"

"Not really." She drew a calming breath and caught his gaze with hers. "I'd just like for you to teach me."

He stepped closer and cupped her chin in his hand. His eyes drew her deeper and deeper until she thought surely she could see his very soul. "Would you?"

"I would," she whispered.

He stared silently and she wondered . . . no, she wanted him to kiss her again. And more. Perhaps he would ravish her right here and she needn't bother seducing him at all. What a glorious idea. She leaned toward him in blissful surrender.

"Excellent." He released her chin and she nearly staggered forward. "First . . ." He stepped away, his gaze skimming the ground beneath the trees. "You have to find a nice, straight stick."

"A stick?" She could barely choke out the words. "What do you need a stick for?"

He cast her an innocent glance. "For a fishing pole, of course."

"A fishing pole?" She glared in frustrated indignation. "What about a kiss?"

"Ophelia." Condescension rang in his voice. "You can't catch a fish with a kiss. Won't work." He turned and continued his search. "I suspect it's been tried, fishermen will try damn near anything. But I think a stick for a pole and a nice, fat, juicy worm would work better."

She stared in disbelief. Here she was all prepared to seduce him or, better yet, allow him to ravish her, and all he could do was talk about fish and worms. *Worms!*

"This will do nicely." Tye held up a stick and grinned like a little boy.

Didn't he understand when she gazed into his eyes and whispered for him to teach her that the very last thing she wanted to learn was how to fish?

"Now." He walked toward her, pulling a jackknife from his back pocket. "I think it works best if you shave the bark off and shape it up a little . . ."

Perhaps she'd been too subtle.

She stalked back to the blanket, found her glass and filled it again. This time, she wouldn't spill it.

"What are you doing?"

"Nothing. Not one little thing. You just go ahead and make your stick and I'll be right back." She waved gaily, turned and scanned the stand of trees. Oh, she'd be back all right. And he'd better be ready.

There was a spot just to the left of the blanket that looked fairly protected. She cast an assessing gaze first at Tye and then at the trees. Yes indeed, she could do what she needed to over there. She stepped toward the sheltered area. She didn't know a great deal about love-making, but she did have a grasp of the basics. And one thing she was certain of was that clothes simply got in the way. Well, she'd take care of that right now. And then she'd see if he was still interested in the fine art of fishing.

Or an altogether different sport.

IT WAS ALL he could do to keep the grin from his face or stifle his laughter. Tye sat beside the stream, paring long strips of wood from his stick. Lord, her expression when he'd removed his hand from her chin had been priceless. The woman had practically fallen flat on her face.

He glanced up toward the blanket to see her disappear behind a knot of trees. What was she up to now?

It didn't really matter. He had the upper hand and would not hesitate to use it to his advantage.

He'd probably need to use that second bottle of champagne as well.

DAMN. THIS WOULD never, ever do.

Ophelia took a thoughtful sip of her champagne and sighed. She simply wasn't a good enough actress to carry this off; besides, it was a bit breezier than she'd thought. Perhaps the fault wasn't in her acting but in her character. She brightened at the realization. Only a true tart could walk out from behind the trees stark naked. Although she was confident her nudity would attract his attention, she was definitely not a tart. Still . . . he did think she was a widow.

Why couldn't she compromise? After all, she didn't have to be completely nude. What a brilliant idea. What a clever solution.

What a relief.

WHERE ON EARTH was she? He'd have this stick whittled down to nothing if she didn't reappear soon.

Still, he supposed a few more minutes or so made little difference. They had the entire afternoon and no Aunt Lorelie anywhere in sight to spoil it. He had all the time in the world—or at least all the time he needed.

NOW SHE PROBABLY looked ridiculous.

It was a compromise, all right, but it definitely lacked something—aside from clothes, that is. And she felt nearly as awkward as she had without anything whatsoever on. She sipped her wine and considered her options. No, indeed.

Shoes alone simply wouldn't do it.

ALL THINGS CONSIDERED, the afternoon was progressing quite well.

Another glass or two of wine and Ophelia would, no doubt, spill all of her secrets. He could see it clearly in his mind's eye.

First, he'd forgive her, after extracting a promise that she would reform her questionable ways. Next, he'd tell her of his love. And finally, he'd ask her to marry him, sealing the proposal with, at the very least, a kiss and, hopefully, much, much more.

He grinned. And then maybe he'd even teach her to fish.

SHE SCRAMBLED BACK into her dress, leaving her shoes and corset and all the other articles respectable women wore under their clothing these days lying in a lacy heap. She cast a regretful glance at the pile of unmentionables. The real countess did have such lovely underpinnings, but they wouldn't do her a bit of good right now.

The obvious answer, although why she didn't think of it earlier escaped her, was to discard everything but her dress. That way, once the seduction was in full swing, when the point came for him to rip her clothes off her body in a frenzy of passion—and she did hope there would be a frenzy of passion—he would find no need to battle his way through garment after garment. Goodness, seduction took a great deal of planning.

She lapped the last drop of champagne from her glass. Normally, spirits of any kind affected her senses a great deal, but today she barely noticed it at all. What she noticed quite distinctly was the sensual feel of the bare whisper of her summer frock against her unprotected flesh and the wonderfully sinful sensation of freedom from the lack of undergarments.

Determination squared her shoulders. The curtain was rising on act two, and her big scene lay directly ahead. The scene where the virgin actress pretending to be a widowed countess entices the cowboy mayor into an amorous adventure.

She could hear the applause now.

OPHELIA SAILED INTO his view with all the grace of a milkweed dancing in the wind. The breeze molded her dress against her. Lucky breeze. He caught his breath. It must have been a trick of the light. For a moment, it looked like she had nothing on beneath the frock.

"Are you ready for my lesson?" She cast him a flirtatious smile, and it was all he could do to keep from pulling her into his arms.

"Lesson?" What was she talking about?

"Fishing?" She nodded at the forgotten stick in his hand.

"Oh, yeah." He shrugged. Fishing was the last thing on his mind. Was there anything beneath that dress? "But I don't have a string. You really need a string for a fishing pole."

"Does that mean you can't teach me . . . to fish?" She gazed at him, her eyes wide, a slight pout on her lips. Lips that were too tempting to resist and made to be tasted and crushed—

"Tye?"

"I . . ." Why was his mouth so dry again? "I guess not."

"Oh, dear." She heaved a sigh of disappointment and glanced at the stream. At once her expression lightened. "I have it. We can still have our lesson."

"Can we?" The lesson he wanted to teach her had nothing to do with fishing and everything to do with the curve of her breast straining against the confines of her dress and the—

"We'll just . . . um . . . act."

"Act?" Oh, he wanted to act all right. He longed to play the role of the charming rogue to her version of the merry widow.

"Yes, indeed." Her eyes sparked deep emerald fire. "I'll be the fish." She gathered her skirt up above her knees. Lord, she'd taken off her shoes and her stockings. What else didn't she have on? "And you can try and catch me."

She laughed and ran toward the stream. Tye stared for a moment as if frozen to the spot. He knew exactly what would happen if he followed her. Ophelia splashed into the creek with all the abandon of a water sprite. Damn. It wasn't supposed to happen this way. First, he had to get the truth; next he'd declare his love; then, he'd . . . what the hell.

Tye hopped on one foot, then the other, struggling to get off boots that were abruptly far more stubborn to remove than they'd ever been. Lord, what if she changed her mind before he got there? He started to unbutton his shirt, then stopped. What if he misunderstood her intentions? Hah. Only a dead man could misunderstand Ophelia's intentions. Still, it'd be better to let her take off his shirt. That was it. An experienced woman like Ophelia would probably prefer that.

He hooked his thumbs on his belt loops and strode casually toward the creek. With every step, he forced himself to remain cool and in control. Women liked men who were in control. Besides, it wouldn't do to let Ophelia know she had him right where she wanted him. He stopped by the edge of the water and studied her. "And what do you think you're doing?"

"I'm a fish, Tye." Ophelia laughed and waded in farther. She had reached the middle of the creek. Not that it was very big. Maybe twenty feet wide at best, and for the most part fairly shallow. "And I thought you were a fisherman?"

"I love fishing," he murmured. His gaze traveled along her exposed legs, and he remembered how those limbs had felt beneath his touch. Even though she held it up, the bottom of her skirt was wet and clung to shapely calves.

"Aren't fishermen supposed to catch fish?" She grinned and twirled around in the water.

He returned her grin and bent down to roll up his pant legs, her carefree laughter and the sound of the creek ringing in his ears. He wanted this woman in the worst way. He'd just have to revise his plans, that's all. First, seduction, then confession, then—

A scream and a splash cut through the air. Tye jerked upright, his heart in his throat.

Ophelia had disappeared.

Without hesitation he jumped into the creek, promptly slipped on a rock and fell. He pulled himself up, spitting and choking, and staggered blindly toward the spot where he'd last seen her and crashed straight into a sputtering, coughing body. He clutched at her, and they both tumbled back beneath the water with a cry and a curse and a splash. Again he struggled to the surface and shook the water from his eyes. Before him stood a wet, shimmering vision. A water fairy, a nymph, a goddess.

A quivering, seething goddess.

"What in the hell were you trying to do?" Fury

flashed in her eyes. Anger rang in her voice. And where was her accent? "You almost drowned me."

"Wait just a minute, Ophelia." He glared with irritation. "It isn't deep. Besides, I was trying to save you."

"Save me? Hah! I'm soaked to the skin. My dress is ruined." She spread her arms out and glared. "Why, just look at me, Tyler Matthews, I'm a mess."

"Well, Countess, you're the one"—he glanced at her sodden dress—"who went in the stream"—clinging to every curve and valley—"in the . . . um . . . first"—molding so tightly to breasts that heaved with every angry breath that he could clearly see the points of her nipples hardened by the cold water —"um . . . place and"—the fabric plastered against her midsection to reveal the cleft of her navel—"I . . . um . . . only thought . . . um"—the material adhering to her thighs and the point at which they met, leaving nothing to the imagination. "Damnation, Ophelia, you don't have anything on beneath that dress!"

"Oh, dear!" She glanced down in surprise and crossed her arms over her chest. A charming but pointless gesture. A becoming blush washed up her face. "I forgot."

"You forgot?"

"I forgot." She sighed. "It was supposed to be a surprise."

He pulled a shaky breath. "It's a surprise, all right. Why?"

"I wanted to make it a little easier for you."

"Did you?"

"Yes, indeed." She nodded, and droplets of water flew off her hair like glistening crystals caught in midair. "When I seduced you."

"When you seduced me?"

She laid a hand on his chest and gazed up into his eyes. "Do you want to be seduced?"

"Do I . . ." His heart caught in his throat and his blood pulsed, and he stared down at her into eyes so green and intense he wanted to lose himself in their depths. Desire surged through him, and he hardened with the need to make this woman his. This woman he loved. He pulled her hand from his chest and kissed her palm, never taking his gaze from hers. "Only by you."

"Well, then." She sighed up at him. "Kiss me, Tye."

He gathered her into his arms and met her lips with his. The heat of her body permeated his through the layers of wet clothing between them, the thin, sodden fabric nearly nonexistent. He could feel every delicious curve, every delightful inch of her. Her body melted into his, and he wondered how long he could keep from ravishing her right here in the middle of the creek.

Her arms wrapped around his neck and she pulled him tighter against her. Her mouth opened and his tongue swept inside to pillage and plunder and claim her forever. His breath joined with hers, and he wondered if she was simply the most magnificent woman he'd ever known or if love heightened all sensation. Or both.

His mouth explored hers, then slipped away to taste the line of her jaw and lower to the curve of her neck. She moaned and her head fell back. Beads of water pooled in the hollow of her throat, and he lapped them up as if they'd been the nectar of life itself. She clutched his shoulders, and he marveled at the sweet taste of her and the urgency that rose between them.

He bent his head and cupped her breast, pulling the

taut, cloth-covered nipple into his mouth. She gasped, and her nails bit into his shoulder. He moved one hand to the nape of her neck and stared into eyes stormy and dazed with a need that throbbed though every inch of him. His other hand splayed the small of her back and drifted lower to caress her buttocks and stroke the firm flesh beneath the clinging material.

Impatiently, he pulled the fabric higher until he reached the heated flesh of her leg. Slowly, he pulled his hand up the long length of her leg until he cupped her bare bottom in his hand. He embraced her softness, and his hand skimmed lightly around her hip to the top of her leg and the silken hair that guarded her womanhood. Gently, his fingers pushed farther until he touched the velvet folds of flesh and more, and she gasped. She was slick with wanting, and he stroked her until she sagged against him with a hunger that matched his own.

Ophelia shuddered at his very touch. His hand was so skilled, his lips so knowing, his body so firm and taut against her own. She could happily die under his caress, or stay in his embrace for all eternity. His lips ripped from hers and again her head dropped back. One hand fumbled with the buttons at the bodice of her dress, and she thought to help him, but even breathing seemed a battle. It took forever or only a moment and he peeled the wet garment down her arms and over her hips until she stood before him covered only by aching need and yearning desire.

He stared at her for a long moment, and she stared back, not knowing what to say, not caring about words. She pushed her wet hair away from her face and waited. He caressed her with a look that shivered through her body and into her heart. Without a word, without taking his gaze from hers, he slipped his clothes off and faced her like a proud warrior or a Greek statue or a flesh-and-blood man.

She should have been embarrassed. She should have been nervous. She should have been scared. Instead, with a knowledge culled from somewhere deep inside, she knew this was the moment she'd waited for all her life. Here, under the blue sky of Wyoming, with a stream dancing around her legs and nothing but the vast expanse of this land—his land—as witness, she faced everything that would make her whole and real and live in her soul forever.

The look in his eyes reflected her own feelings. This was more than a mere seduction. She knew it and knew as well, so did he.

"Ophelia?" His voice was strained, as if he couldn't bear not to have his flesh next to hers. Neither could she. He opened his arms, and she stepped into his embrace.

His body pressed against hers, the rough hair on his chest arousing and tantalizing the sensitive skin of her breasts. His lips met hers with a fierce demand she recognized and returned. His erection, solid and strong and not to be denied, pushed against her. His body molded to hers as if made for this purpose and this purpose alone. As if made for her.

Slowly, he pulled her into the water until he sat on the pebbled bottom and she just above him. He pulled her closer and she settled on his lap, the hard, throbbing length of him insistent between them, the water lapping around their waists. Tye cupped her breasts in his hands and bent his head to lavish attention first on one, then the other. Hot delight shot through her and she ran her fingers through the gold of his hair. As if he knew when she could bear no more he pulled his head up and locked his gaze to hers.

"Ophelia?"

She nodded and bit her lower lip, and he sighed as if he had feared her answer. With a gentleness she should have expected, the long length of him slid into her with a surprising ease, then stopped as if halted by an unforeseen obstacle.

Damnation, she hadn't thought of that annoying virginity of hers. She clutched his shoulder and thrust herself forward, a keen pain stabbing her. She gasped, and he looked at her sharply. She closed her eyes and threw her head back and rocked and the minor pain faded, replaced by an increasing delight. With every move her pleasure grew, shocking and intense. She urged him to a rhythm she'd never known, but a rhythm as familiar as the breath coursing through her lungs or the blood surging through her body or the very beat of her heart.

They moved together in a play without words, a performance without end, a drama that evoked the essence of life and death and everlasting existence. Two actors in perfect harmony, their roles so entwined neither knew where one left off and the other began. Higher and higher they danced, until their purpose was lost in the sensation and ecstasy and sheer bliss of their joining. And when she feared she couldn't bear the sweet coil of yearning tension within her another moment without madness or death or joy that transcended anything she'd ever known or ever dreamed, he groaned and clutched her tighter as if he too was dying and she alone could save his life or his soul. She cried out and shuddered with an explosion of a thousand footlights or a million stars in a stunning release that sacrificed her will and her strength and her spirit.

They collapsed together into the shallow stream. The creek where Tye's father taught him to fish bubbled around them, cooling bodies too heated by desire and too spent by passion to move.

And applause thundered in her ears.

Chapter 15

SHE sacrificed her virtue to him twice more.

Ophelia and Tye lay on the blanket finishing up the last of Alma's tasty supplies. Ophelia never would have suspected seduction worked up such a hunger. And such a lack of concern for propriety. They didn't have a stitch on, and it didn't bother her in the least. It simply didn't seem necessary when this golden glow of heady satisfaction and blissful exhaustion surrounded them. Gad, sin was delightful.

"Bite?" Tye propped his head with one hand and held a piece of chicken over her mouth with the other.

"Thank you." Ophelia's manner was as polite as if she'd been at a ladies' tea party instead of lying naked on a scarlet blanket in the middle of Wyoming. She took the bit of fowl as well as the fingers that held it, sucking the last drop of juice from them.

Tye's eyes narrowed with desire. The man was truly insatiable. She liked that about him. Liked as well how he looked stretched out long and powerful by her side like an untamed beast. Her gaze ran lazily down the strong, magnificent lines of his body and back to his eyes. His delicious chocolate eyes.

"Dessert," she murmured.

"What did you say?"

"I said dessert." She lifted up on her elbow and leaned forward as if to kiss him. Instead, she licked a pie crumb from near the corner of his mouth and slowly drew it between her lips.

His eyes smoldered, and she flicked a quick glance lower at the rest of him and trembled with her own rising need. "I love dessert."

"Me too."

"And I doubt if our clothes are quite dry yet."

"Probably not."

She giggled. "I will never forget the sight of you trying to rescue our clothes from the stream."

He shook his head. "Well, your dress hung up on some rocks and the buckle on my pants pretty much weighted them down, so those were easy, but that damn shirt." He laughed. "The current moved it pretty fast, and I was starting to think I'd have to chase it clear into Colorado in my birthday suit."

"I would have liked to have seen the reaction of the Community Betterment Committee to that. I can hear them now. Isn't that the mayor? Surely he's not bare-bottomed, is he?"

He grinned. "I doubt if even Dead End would see the humor in that, and it definitely wouldn't be funny in Empire City."

She laughed. She could lie next to him like this forever. Just the two of them, with no obligations or responsibilities or demands save those of one body for another. Idly, she ran her hand along the firm, solid planes of his chest. His muscles tightened beneath her touch.

"Ophelia." There was a growl of warning in his voice.

"What?" She widened her eyes in an innocent manner and bent to flick his nipple with her tongue.

He gasped and grabbed her wrists. "Ophelia."

She stared straight into his deep eyes. "Tye, you said yourself our clothes aren't dry yet." She inched closer, her breasts brushing against his chest, and a now familiar ache shivered through her. "And didn't somebody say something about dessert?"

"Ophelia." He groaned in surrender and crushed her against him, his body hot and urgent next to hers. She responded with the enthusiastic eagerness of a newly discovered passion, and before she lost herself to the sheer sensation of his touch a thought fluttered through her mind.

One must always be willing to sacrifice.

DAMN, IF HE thought she was pretty naked, the look of her right now, halfway clothed with only those frilly underthings on, was enough to spur him to rip them off her with his teeth and take her yet again. He shifted uncomfortably at the thought. His Levi's were still damp and fit a bit snugger than they did this morning. It wouldn't do at all to allow images of Ophelia's soft, rosy body writhing beneath him to make his jeans even more uncomfortable than they were.

Not that it seemed he was actually the one doing the taking. No, indeed. Ophelia made love with all the enthusiasm and energy of a teetotaler taken to drink or a heathen taken to God. Odd, something he couldn't quite put his finger on nagged at the back of his mind. Something he'd noted earlier but now seemed to have slipped away. No doubt it was just one more truth he had to wring out of her. And he might as well get to it.

"Ophelia?"

She wore some kind of pantelet and was lacing up a frilly wisp of a chemise. "Um-hum?"

"We need to talk."

Her hands stilled and she stared at him. "Do we?"

He drew a deep breath. "Yes, we do." He stepped to her, grasped her shoulders and trapped her gaze with his. "It's time, Ophelia. I want the truth."

Her gaze slid from his. "What truth?"

Annoyance surged through him, and he wanted to shake the answers out of her. He clenched his teeth. "You know what truth, Ophelia. Who you are and what you want."

She shuddered beneath his hands, and for a moment he wanted nothing more than to pull her back into his arms and tell her to ignore his demand. To tell her he didn't care and the truth didn't matter. To tell her all he really wanted was for her to trust him enough to confide in him. Like a wife in a husband.

"I am . . ." She met his gaze with hers, defiance flickering in the lush depths of her eyes. "I am the Countess of . . . of . . ."

"Bladewater?" he suggested.

"Indeed." She wrenched free of his grasp, drew herself up and glared. "I am the Countess of Bladewater."

"And your deceased husband, the count, his name is?"

She furrowed her brows in thought; then her expression brightened. "Adrian."

"Are you certain?"

"Of course I'm certain." Contempt at his question rang in her voice. "His name was definitely Adrian."

"Hah! Since you've been in Dead End, you've yet to call that dead count of yours, who probably never existed in the first place, by the same name twice. Let's see, there's been"—he ticked the names off on his fingers—"Alfred, Albert, Alford, Alphonse—"

"I've always been rather fond of the name Alphonse," she murmured.

"—Aloysius, Adolph, Austin, Addison—"

"I never called him Addison!"

"My mistake." He glared and continued. "Alcazar—"

"I like Alcazar too, it has a nice ring to it."

"—Ambrose, Alvin and finally," he finished with an angry flourish, "Addicus."

She gave him a cool look. "And is there a point to your ravings, Mr. Matthews?"

"A point? A point?" Hell! Was he sputtering? The damn woman had him sputtering! "Of course there's a point. You can't seem to remember the name of your own husband. And do you know why?"

"Of course I know why. Do you?"

"I most certainly do. You can't remember the name of your dead husband, or your own name for that matter—"

"Ophelia?"

"No, not Ophelia." He clenched his fists by his sides in an effort to keep from strangling the infuriating woman. "Bridgewater! You can't remember Bridgewater!"

"Oh, that."

"And do you know why you can't remember your make-believe name or that of your fictitious husband?"

She pulled her brows together in a thoughtful manner and tilted her head as if grasping for an answer that lay just beyond her reach. "Grief?"

"No! No, it's not grief!" Why was he yelling? He couldn't remember the last time he'd lost control like this. What had she done to him?

"Grief does terrible things to a person's mind, you know." She cast him a smile of pity, as if he was too insensitive, or just too plain stupid, to know that basic fact of life, and turned her attention back to her chemise.

"Yes, I know! I also know one can't grieve for someone who never existed."

"And you claim my dear, dear, dead Avery never existed?" Ophelia finished with the undergarment, plucked her corset off the ground and studied it. "Can you prove it?"

"Prove it?"

"Prove it." She dropped the corset on the blanket as if deciding it wasn't worth the trouble, picked up her stocking and settled her back against the tree. "You have no proof, Tye."

"I don't need proof!" Damnation, he'd tried to get proof. But every time he'd gotten near her, she'd distracted him with those feminine wiles of hers. "I have your own words as proof."

"What words?" She pulled one stocking up a long, shapely leg.

"For one thing, every time you talk about your dead husband—"

"Abraham." A spark snapped in her eyes. Was she toying with him now?

He heaved an exasperated sigh. "Fine, Abraham, he's either young or old—"

"Most people are." She tied the garter, pulled the pantalet over the top, and turned her attention to her other leg. He struggled to ignore the innocently seductive scene she presented.

"—and he's been dead one year or two—"

She rolled up a stocking and held it poised over the

toe of a nude limb. For a fleeting second, he wished to be a stocking. She cast him a pleasant smile. "Confusion, brought on by grief."

"Confusion perhaps, but grief has nothing to do with it. You simply can't remember which lie you've told from one minute to the next. And I've said it before, Ophelia, you're a bad liar."

And the most seductive woman he'd ever met. Here he was, more annoyed than he'd ever been in his life, determined to get the truth from her, and all he could concentrate on was the slow, sensual way she unrolled the stocking up her leg and the silk that caressed every curve of her long and lovely limb. Was she even aware of how she appeared? Her every move was enticing, yet natural and almost innocent. . . . That was it. Innocent.

Ophelia made love with all the enthusiasm and energy of a teetotaler taken to drink . . .

This very experienced woman was . . .

. . . or a heathen taken to God . . .

"Good Lord!"

Or a virgin!

"What now?" She tied the last garter and glanced up at him. Her gaze met his, and her expression froze. "Tye?"

He couldn't seem to get the words out. At once everything snapped into place. What a fool he'd been not to have noticed before now. Everything else about her was a fraud. It only made sense she'd lie about this too. He'd realized right away there was no dead count, but he'd just assumed she was an experienced woman. He'd noticed that brief moment in the water, of course, how could he not, but the passion and the intensity and the sheer frenzy of their joining had wiped away all rational thought. Until now.

She'd given herself to him and there was no way in hell he was going to let her out of his life now.

"Tye?"

His gaze narrowed. His voice was hard. "I have proof, Ophelia."

A LIGHT OF quiet triumph glittered in his eyes, and her heart caught in her throat. What proof could he possibly have? Short of producing the real countess, there was no way to prove or disprove her act. "I hope you're not planning on using anything I've said against me. I've told you, any discrepancies can be explained by grief."

"I don't have any need to use what you've said."

"Then what are you talking about?" Gad, she didn't like the look in his eye.

"I'm talking about this." In one long step he reached her side and hauled her into his embrace. Her arms were pinned, his lips crushed hers, and she struggled until the familiar greed for him welled like a relentless thirst within her and warmth spread from hidden parts of her body still aching with the need for his touch. She moaned against his mouth and he pulled back.

An unnamed emotion simmered in his eyes. "I have been with a number of women in my life, Ophelia. The majority of them quite experienced and very good at what they do."

"I know. Widows." She glared, her passion squelched. What kind of a cad was he, anyway? Telling her about his previous conquests? "And what does that have to do with me?"

"You're nothing like them."

Panic fluttered within her and she pushed at him,

but he held her tight. "Of course I am. I'm just like them."

"No, you're not." His gaze burned with an amber fire that glinted somewhere in the depth of his endless brown eyes. "When you touch me, when I touch you, there's a joy that comes from discovery, from the beginning of something fresh and new and never before even dreamed of."

Her heart stilled. "What do you mean?"

"I mean you weren't a widow, you weren't a woman of experience, and before this afternoon, my fair Ophelia, you were a virgin."

"I was not!"

Total disbelief darkened his eyes.

"Very well, then, if you prefer to believe that, fine," she snapped. "I know how men enjoy their little fantasies about innocent vir—"

"Stop it, Ophelia," he said roughly. "And just tell me the truth."

"You have as little proof on this charge, Tye, as all the others."

He stared down at her without a word then released her, combing his fingers through his tousled hair in a gesture of frustration. "You're right. You've got me there." Abruptly a grin stretched across his face. "Except for one little thing."

"And what's that?"

"I have, through the years, built up a rather impressive reputation with the ladies." He crossed his arms over his broad chest in a smug manner that made her long to shoot him again. "If Tyler Matthews says a woman is a virgin, there's not one person in this town, male or female, who's going to dispute it. And virgins are generally not widows."

She gasped. "You wouldn't!"

"I sure would."

He had her there, right where he wanted her. She probably should have killed him when she'd had the chance. Now what would she do? Or more to the point, what would he do? "What do you want from me, Mr. Matthews?"

"I want the truth, Ophelia, that's all. Just the truth."

"Why?" Her voice rose. "Why is it so important to you?"

"Because wives always tell the truth to their husbands!"

Images of countless married actresses and the ebb and flow of their lovers popped to mind, followed in quick succession by the faces of the Every Other Tuesday and Thursday Afternoon Ladies Cultural Society and Theater Troupe. "Where on earth did you ever get such a stupid idea?"

Tye glared. "Big Jack."

"Big Jack? Big Jack Matthews? Lorelie's husband?" Ophelia laughed and couldn't seem to stop. "Lorelie's husband says wives always tell their husbands the truth?"

"Other people say it too."

"Do they?" Tears of mirth pooled in her eyes. She sniffed and wiped them away. "Men, no doubt."

"Well, yeah," Tye said defensively.

"For a man who works around cattle all the time, you certainly can't seem to see manure when it's being thrown around."

"Oh, no?" He raised a brow. "I saw through you, didn't I?"

"That remains to be seen." She flounced over to

the bush where her dress was spread out to dry and snatched it off the branches. Abruptly, something he'd said earlier caught at her mind. She whirled and glared at him. "What does that nonsense about wives telling the truth to their husbands have to do with you and me?"

He stared at her for a long, strained moment. Tension pounded through her veins. She feared the answer. She prayed for it.

"I want you to be my wife." His voice was quiet and steady, and it melted her resolve and her will. "I want to marry you."

Her pulse leapt. And for a moment the thought of being in his arms and by his side forever seemed solid and safe and right. Then reality crashed around her. A man like Tyler Matthews could never be happy with a woman like her. And sooner or later he'd know that, and she'd be left with nothing but bittersweet memories and a broken heart.

She squared her shoulders and lifted her chin. "That's very nice, Mr. Matthews, but I don't want to marry you."

A slow smile lifted the corners of his mouth. "Oh, yes you do."

"Why, you arrogant—"

"Thank you." He shrugged in a modest manner. "Regardless of your assessment of my character, you do want to marry me."

"I most certainly do not. And furthermore, you don't really wish to marry *me*."

"I don't?"

"No." She shook her head. Tye seemed to actually be listening to her. Good. Exactly what she wanted. She ignored a niggling twinge of regret. "You don't even know me."

"I know all I need to."

"Just what do you know?"

"I know you believe in home and family. I know you're intensely loyal. I know what makes you laugh, and I've watched you not laugh when it might hurt someone's feelings—"

"Anna Rose," she said under her breath.

"And just about every other member of the Cultural Society. I know you're willing to extend your help with something as ridiculous as an opera house. I've watched you be patient and kind and thoughtful." He paused and pinned her with an intense glance. "You see, I do know you."

"No, no, no." She paced before him, her dress waving in one hand like a flag of truce or surrender. "You don't know me at all. Tye." She stopped and took a deep breath. "I am a gambler and a liar—although admittedly there's a fine line between acting and lying—and a thief."

"And those are your good qualities." A twinkle danced in his eye, but, whether he wanted to admit it or not, he was right. "I can forgive you and you can reform."

"Thank you."

"Don't you see, Ophelia." His voice was soft and fraught with meaning. "I don't care about your past—only your future. A future with me."

She shook her head. "But why, Tye? I don't understand."

"Why?" Confusion crossed his face as if she spoke another language. Then his expression cleared and he grinned. "Don't tell me I didn't mention it?"

"Mention what?"

He stared at her with a look that seemed to reach inside and shake her soul. "I love you, Ophelia."

I love you, Ophelia.

The words rang in her mind and panic flooded her. "Oh, no you don't. I'm not falling for that."

"Falling for what?" Tye's brows pulled together in confusion.

"Falling for that . . . that . . . line of dialogue. For goodness' sake, Tye, you underestimate me."

"What are you talking about?"

"You're no different from any other handsome man—"

"You think I'm handsome?" He grinned.

"—who thinks a few flowery phrases will turn a woman's head, leaving him free to lead her astray—"

He snorted. "*You're* accusing *me* of leading *you* astray?"

"—and when he's had his way with her, will leave her crying and brokenhearted."

"Now, wait just a minute, Ophelia." Tye glared with righteous indignation. "I've already had my way with you, as you so charmingly put it, although, it seems to me, you were pretty much having your way with me as well—"

"It scarcely matters." She sniffed.

"—but given that, why would I only now, after the fact and not before, declare my love?" He cast her a triumphant smirk. "Explain that if you will."

"You didn't think of it before!"

"I did think of it, I just didn't say it." He shook his head as if to clear it. "I don't understand any of this. My intentions here are completely honorable."

"Honorable. Hah!" She threw him a scathing look. "You want to marry me!"

"Because I love you!"

"No! No! No!" She pulled on her dress, a frantic need to escape pushing her faster.

"Ophelia!"

"No, Tye, you're just like every man who thinks a few overused words to a woman will give him not just her body but her soul. Well, not me, Mr. Mayor." She struggled to fasten the buttons on her dress. "You've had my body, and it was quite delightful, thank you, but my soul is my own. I refuse to be left alone and pathetic at a stage door waiting for someone who never comes, who never planned on coming in the first place. No, not me. There are far too many Edwin Kendrakes in the world to take a chance that you're the exception."

"Who's Edwin Kendrake?" Tye stared in confusion.

She gritted her teeth and glared. "My father."

"The Shakespearean scholar?"

She shrugged. "All right."

"I see," Tye said slowly. "Your father treated women—"

"I don't want to talk about my father's behavior toward women. He was a wonderful father. That's all that really matters."

"But—"

"It's not just my father. It's every man I ever saw growing up. Not any of them knew what love meant. Yet every single one freely and sincerely declared his devotion to achieve his ends, and women were the sorry victims. I will not be one of those women. I will not be a victim of you or any man."

She trapped his gaze with hers. "You've taught me a great deal today about passion and lust, and for that I'm grateful. But I do not believe there is such a thing as love, and if that emotion exists at all, it does so only in the special bond between parent and child or siblings for each other, but never, ever truly among men and women."

"I'm not giving up, Ophelia. I love you."

She clapped her hands over her ears. "Stop saying that! I don't want to hear it. I'm getting the hell out of this town, and I'm getting as far away from you as I can!"

He stared at her with eyes grim and determined. "There's no possible way I'm letting you leave."

She planted her hands on her hips. "And just how do you intend to stop me?"

"I'll have you thrown in jail." The line of his jaw clenched, tight and unyielding.

She gasped. "How could you?"

"It's easy."

"Wait just a minute here. I haven't done anything, not really. I mean, Big Jack's money is still in the bank. You can't put me in jail."

"Sure I can."

"How?"

He shrugged. "I'm the mayor."

A sudden thought struck her, and her stomach clenched. "Are you going to tell Big Jack and Lorelie about your so-called proof?"

"I don't know."

"Don't. Don't tell them." She bit her bottom lip and cast him a pleading glance. A glance that said what she couldn't say aloud. The words that stuck in her throat. *If you really love me . . .* "Let me tell them."

"Why?"

"I suppose I feel in their debt. They're very nice people. If you could just give me some time?" If he'd give her enough time, she'd be on the afternoon train tomorrow.

"How much time?"

"Until the morning of Jack's ceremony."

His expression was impassive. "Why should I?"

"Because you say you love me." She studied him for a moment. "If there's one thing I learned from watching all those pathetic women fall in love with men like my father, only to be abandoned, it's that in spite of the pain that comes with it, loving and offering love is very often enough. That love, real love, demands nothing in return. That's what I'm asking from you.

"Whether or not this declaration of yours is genuine, Tye, you should know I do . . . well . . . appreciate it. I never expected to hear those words, and I never suspected they'd sound so . . . well . . . wonderful—"

"Ophelia—"

"No, Tye." She thrust out a hand to stop him. "Let me finish. Please."

She drew a deep breath and stared straight into his eyes. If ever she needed to be a good actress, to prove in some way she was indeed her father's daughter, this was it. For Tye's sake and her own.

"Tye, I don't love you." She clenched her fists to calm her trembling hands. "I enjoyed today for what it was, an afternoon of pleasure, nothing more. I'm sorry if this is painful, that was not my intent—"

"Ophelia, I—" Disbelief creased his forehead.

"—but the fact is, I care nothing for you. So don't delude yourself into thinking we are star-crossed lovers in some Shakespearean tragedy. We're not. We are"—she shrugged— "nothing."

Silence fell between them. She longed to pull her gaze from his bottomless brown eyes simmering with pain and shock, but she couldn't. She couldn't so much as flinch if she wanted him to truly believe she didn't love him. And he had to believe.

His expression hardened. He released a long, pent-up breath. "You'll tell Jack before the ceremony?"

Relief rushed through her. "Of course."

She stared at him, and at once she knew that he knew it was a lie. She'd be on the next train out of Dead End, and he probably knew that as well.

"You're still a bad liar, Ophelia," he said softly.

"I don't lie." She turned away to gather their things together and added under her breath, "I act."

Silently, Ophelia and Tye picked up the remains of their afternoon. Every time she stole a glance at him, his expression was granite, his eyes cold and hard. There was no doubt she'd hurt him. Maybe he really did love her, and maybe it was the kind of happily-ever-after love that she'd read about in fairy tales. But this was real life, and she'd seen too many men use those magic words without a moment's thought as to the consequences to believe in anything as elusive as love.

They drove back to Big Jack and Lorelie's house without exchanging a word. Even the horse pulling the carriage seemed to sense their mood, and Ophelia didn't hear a single laugh. The quiet was a shame, really. She had far too much time to think. And far too much time to face the truth.

It might have been the moment he first talked about the moon in Venice, or it might have been the moment he first took her in his arms, or it might even have been the moment he kissed her right in the middle of Dead End, but whenever it had happened, she had to admit, if only to herself, she loved him. She loved him with an intensity that buckled her knees and stole her breath. And she loved him far too much to risk losing him.

And lose him she would. Even if he meant all his talk about forgiveness and reforming her, even if he could overlook the questionable nature of her past, he could never love her forever. It wasn't really his fault. As far as she had seen, it wasn't in a man's nature to love a woman forever. And if she couldn't have him forever, she didn't want him at all.

It was best if he thought she didn't love him. If he even suspected the truth, he'd never let her leave. Eventually she'd give in and admit to loving him, or worse yet, marry him, and inevitably, one day, he wouldn't love her or want her anymore. And she'd be no different from the women she'd vowed her whole life not to become.

No, it was better this way. She'd leave Dead End and never look back. At a town full of very nice people. At a creek where a child once fished and a woman discovered joy. And at a tall, bronzed, golden-haired man with a laugh like sunlight and eyes as dark and delicious as chocolate.

And she would never want chocolate again.

Chapter 16

SEDGE stared, unseeing, at the dark amber liquid in the small glass on the bar at Simmons's Saloon. The words of the telegram crammed in his pocket repeated over and over in his mind like the lingering memory of a nightmare or the rantings of a lunatic. He laughed to himself and slugged down the whiskey. The wire came from his family's solicitor. His beloved mother didn't even have the decency to notify him herself of the untimely demise of his father and brother. Something akin to pain flashed through him at the thought of how very little her second son meant to her.

The telegram called it a boating accident. The solicitor urged his return to England at once. One could well appreciate the wonderful irony of it all. The black sheep being asked—no, urged—to come home when just a few months ago they couldn't get rid of him fast enough. Bloody hell.

He was the Earl of Russelford.

And his first decision as an earl would be to choose between his new life in Wyoming and a life, and a home, he'd thought lost to him forever.

Sedge held up his glass. "Joe, my good man, my glass is regrettably empty."

Simmons grabbed a bottle and expertly poured the shot, setting the bottle down on the counter. Shoving the glass across the bar, he leaned forward in a confidential manner. "Hey, Montgomery, listen to me for a minute."

Simmons's oily gaze slid from one side of the saloon to the other as if he didn't want anyone to overhear. "You know, I think this business about becoming respectable and civilized and calling ourselves"—he snorted—"Empire City is just so much bull."

Sedge raised his glass in a toast. "I daresay everyone in the entire territory knows of your feelings."

"Yeah." Simmons bared a yellow-toothed grin. "I ain't too much for keeping my mouth shut."

"Regrettably," Sedge murmured.

"Like I was saying, I don't much care for what's been going on around here, but"—he heaved a resigned sigh—"my Anna Rose does."

"Why, Joe Simmons." Sedge raised a brow. "Concern? About your wife? I am impressed."

Simmons grunted. "Thanks. But what I'm trying to say is, it seems to me the visit of that there countess has had a lot to do with how things are going. You know, how folks feel and act about the town."

"A sense of accomplishment? Perhaps pride?"

"Yeah, yeah, that's it." Simmons nodded. "I'd hate to see anything happen to her. Anna Rose likes her."

The effects of the whiskey vanished. Sedge narrowed his eyes, his senses sharp. "What do you mean?"

"See that man at the end of the bar?" Simmons casually inclined his head in the direction of the only other man seated at the bar.

"Who is he?"

"Says his name's Leeland Stubblefield. Says he's a gambler. And he's looking for a woman."

"Aren't we all?" Sedge said with a casual manner he didn't quite feel.

"Yeah, but he's looking for one particular woman." Joe lowered his voice. "Claims she cheated him in a game, out of money and train tickets and . . . marriage."

"Marriage?"

Simmons nodded. "He says she's the daughter of some dead actor, but he can't remember her name. Only that it starts with *A* or *O*."

Sedge laughed uneasily. "Well, that doesn't—"

"He also says she's tall and a real looker. Red hair, green eyes. Travels with a sister, a little blonde." Simmons cast him a knowing glance. "Sound like anybody we know?"

Sedge clenched his teeth. "It does, indeed. Thanks, Joe, I'll take care of it."

Sedge slid off the stool and started toward the gambler. He paused and snatched up the bottle of whiskey just as Simmons reached for it. The saloon owner scowled his disapproval. Sedge grinned and made his way to the far end of the bar. He settled on the seat beside the newcomer. Greasy was the word that came to mind to best fit the short, squat gambler. And there was a rather distinct odor that lingered about him.

"I hear you're looking for a woman," Sedge said idly.

"Who ain't?" Stubblefield grunted.

"Drink?" Sedge held up the bottle.

The stranger narrowed his eyes suspiciously, his gaze shooting from Sedge to the bottle and back. He shrugged. "Sure."

Sedge filled the gambler's glass and watched him pour it down his throat in one long swallow. "What do you want her for?"

"She owes me." Stubblefield thunked the glass down on the counter and raised a brow at the bottle. Sedge obligingly poured him another drink.

"So Joe said."

"Yep." Stubblefield sipped slowly this time. "And I aim to find her."

"Why?"

"Well, she was sure as hell cheating in that last game. Or somebody was, anyway. I figure it might as well be her."

"I see," Sedge said. "Did you lose a great deal of money?"

"Oh, it ain't the money. The pot wasn't much. It isn't even the train tickets." He nodded at Sedge. "I'm pretty sure she stole those, and I should have won 'em."

"I'm afraid you have me at a disadvantage, old man." Sedge pulled his brows together. "If it's not the money or the tickets, why do you want her?"

"Lord, she was the prettiest little filly I ever seen." An expression of pure rapture passed over the man's face. "Her hair was like a flaming bush, and her eyes just like jewels and her skin"—he shuddered with obvious desire—"I wanted to touch that skin. Real bad."

"But surely you're not looking for this woman just because she was pretty?"

"Hell, no." Stubblefield drew himself up on the barstool to what appeared to be a rather insignificant height. "I offered to marry her. I would have made her respectable. I ain't never offered marriage before." His eyes narrowed in a dangerous manner. "And I ain't never been turned down."

"She turned you down?" Sedge struggled to keep a sympathetic tone.

Stubblefield snorted in disgust. "She disappeared is what she did. Skipped out of the hotel room in the dead of night."

"So . . ." Sedge chose his words carefully. "Why are you looking for her here?"

"This is where the tickets were for. I should have been here sooner, but"—he shrugged—"I had other things to take care of, ya know."

"Indeed," Sedge said thoughtfully. "When did all this occur?"

"About a month ago."

Just about the time Ophelia swept into Dead End. Bloody hell. He'd have to pass this on to Tye. As obstinate as the cowboy was, he was still Sedge's closest, maybe even his only, friend in the world.

"You've been asking all these questions." Stubblefield's beady little eyes glittered. "You seen her?"

"From her description, I daresay I'd remember her, but no." Sedge shook his head in a good show of remorse. "I haven't seen—wait a minute." Sedge snapped his fingers. "Of course? How could I have forgotten?"

The slimy little man perked up. "What? Where?"

"I do believe . . . now, let me think."

"Yeah, yeah?"

"That's it." Sedge cast Stubblefield a triumphant glance. "I did see her. Why, right here in Dead End. Just about a month ago. Had a short blonde girl with her."

"Yeah, that'd be her sister. Didn't ever see her myself, but heard they traveled together."

"I can't imagine how I could have forgotten. That intriguing hair and a well-turned ankle . . ." Sedge elbowed Stubblefield and winked.

"Yeah, yeah?" The vile creature was practically drooling. "Where did you see her? Is she still here?"

"Oh, say, I am sorry." Sedge shook his head in feigned regret. "When I saw her she was getting on the train for Laramie. Sorry, old chap."

"It's all right, mister. I appreciate the help. And I'll find her sooner or later." Stubblefield's eyes gleamed with determination. "Laramie, you say?"

"Laramie."

"That's where I'm headed, then." He picked up his glass, downed the last of the contents, nodded to Sedge and swaggered out the door.

No wonder Ophelia was pretending to be someone she wasn't. He'd no doubt do the same thing to avoid anything quite as distasteful as that revolting little man. He could well see why a woman, any woman, would run from the likes of Stubblefield.

Good Lord, even aside from the leer in his eye and the lack of hygiene on his person, the gambler had the hairiest knuckles he'd ever seen.

"I DID LEAVE her a note, but other than that . . ." Jenny shrugged.

"She's going to be mad." Zach and Jenny rode side by side away from the setting sun. Zach had told her they were headed to Laramie, wherever that was. "Although why you felt we had to run off like this . . ."

"I told you, she'd never understand."

He shook his head. "She'll find another maid, Jenny."

"That's not it exactly." If he was going to be her husband, perhaps she'd better tell him everything. Well, maybe not everything. "Ophelia isn't exactly my employer."

"Oh?"

"We're much closer than that."

Zach reined his horse to a stop and shot her a suspicious stare. "What do you mean? How much closer?"

"Well . . ." Just how much should she tell him? "She's more like . . . like . . . um, a relative than an employer."

He reached out and grabbed her reins, pulling her horse to a halt. "How much more?"

She grimaced. "Kind of like, oh, maybe, a sister."

"I still don't see the problem. So she likes you and thinks of you as . . ." He stared, and comprehension dawned on his face. "She *is* your sister, isn't she?"

Jenny sighed. "Pretty much."

"Holy cow." Zach shook his head in disbelief. "She's going to be a damned sight more than just mad, I'll bet."

"I'd take that bet." Jenny shifted in the saddle. "At least I won't be around when she finds out."

"You want to tell me the truth now?" Zach stared at her sternly. "Seeing as how we're going to get married when we get to Laramie, there's no time like the present to start telling me the truth."

"You're not bringing up that nonsense again about wives not keeping secrets from their husbands, are you?"

"It's not nonsense," he said staunchly. Goodness, he actually seemed to believe it.

"Oh." She raised a brow. "And just who passed on this little secret to marriage?"

"Big Jack Matthews." A smug note sounded in his voice, as if she wouldn't argue with an edict that came straight from Big Jack himself.

"Big Jack, huh?" Jenny bit back a chuckle. Ophelia had told her all about the Every Other Tuesday and Thursday Afternoon Ladies Cultural Society and Theater Troupe. Her sister had also mentioned that the leader of the organization, the coordinator of every undertaking, the virtual mastermind behind the society, was none other than the very feather-headed Lorelie Matthews. Jenny would wager serious money this was one little secret Jack had no inkling of.

"So, are you going to tell me?" Zach glared indignantly.

"There really isn't much more to tell."

"Why don't you start with why the sister of a countess is pretending to be a maid."

"Oh, I'm not . . ." She burst into a grin. "Why, Zach, how sweet. You thought I was a countess's sister?"

"You're not?"

"No, indeed. Actually, I'm not even Ophelia's real sister. Her father found me and adopted me."

"Was that the count?" Zach's brows furrowed in confusion.

"What count?"

"Ophelia's father."

"Oh, no." Jenny shook her head. "Father was an actor. And a very good actor too, I might add. You should have seen his reviews. Why, when he played King Richard or Hamlet . . ."

"But he wasn't a count?"

"Of course not."

"So, who was the count?" Zach raised a dark brow as if he had just narrowed in on the right question.

"What count?"

Zach's eyes widened, and his face turned the most intriguing shade of red. "I don't know what count! But isn't there supposed to be a count if she's a countess?

"I see what you mean." Jenny nodded sagely. "That count. The dead count."

Zach heaved a sigh of relief. "Now you're talking. Tell me about the dead count."

Jenny shrugged. "I can't."

"Why not? Wives aren't supposed—"

"Stop it right there, Zachary Weston." She wagged a finger under his nose. "I don't care what you've heard about husbands and wives, but I will not allow you to accuse me of lying to you this way."

"I wasn't—" Goodness, he certainly did look cute when he was protesting his innocence.

She held up a hand to stop him. "Well, I should hope not. Now, did you have another question?"

Zach stared with a look that reminded Jenny of a man she'd once seen who'd just been kicked in the head by a mule.

"Never mind, Zach, about the dead count. He isn't."

"Dead?"

"That's right. Primarily because he was never alive."

"He wasn't alive." Zach's words were slow and measured. He didn't seem to be understanding this at all. Lord, she hoped he wasn't feebleminded.

"Nope. Ophelia made him up."

"Why?"

"She needed a dead count."

"Why?" There was a plaintive note in his voice.

"So she could be a widow, of course," Jenny said patiently.

"Why?" It was as much a groan as a word.

"You know." Jenny drew her brows together thoughtfully and tapped her chin with her forefinger. "I'm really not quite sure how that part happened. I think someone just assumed she was a widow and she went along with it. It seemed like such a good idea to her at the time, although, personally, I thought we'd both end up in jail. Still, Ophelia saw the entire endeavor as a way to—"

"Hold on!" Zach narrowed his eyes. "I've figured this out."

Jenny smiled sweetly. "It really wasn't all that complicated."

He glared. "Just let me go over this."

She shrugged.

"First of all, the countess, Ophelia, is your sister."

"That's right."

"And there is no count, dead or alive."

"Also right."

"And Ophelia isn't really a countess."

"That's it, Zach, you've got it." Jenny beamed. Thank goodness, he wasn't feebleminded after all. Just male.

"So . . . this means she doesn't have a title or property in England or a castle." He stared at her intently.

"Nope."

"Come on." Zach set his lips in a determined line and turned his horse back toward the ranch. "We have to tell Big Jack."

"Why?" Jenny stared.

"Because she's swindling him, that's why."

"Big Jack is a big boy, a very big boy. He can take care of himself." She shook her head slowly. "I'm not going back."

"Of course you are." He jerked his head toward the direction they'd just come from. "Let's go, woman."

"Let's go, woman? Did you just say, 'Let's go, woman'?" She cast him a look of disbelief.

"Well"—a sheepish expression washed over his face—"yeah."

"Did you learn how to talk to women from Big Jack too?"

"Kind of." A stubborn light glinted in his eye. "Big Jack says you pretty much treat women the same way you treat a good horse or a heifer."

"A heifer? Isn't that some kind of cow?"

"It's a young cow," Zach muttered.

"I don't care if it's a baby cow still in its mother cow's arms. I don't want to be treated like some old cow."

Zach cast her a helpless look. "I'm sorry, Jen, I just don't know what I'm doing when it comes to being around girls. And Big Jack—"

"Let me make a suggestion about Big Jack," Jenny said firmly. "Have you ever seen him treat Lorelie like a cow?"

Zach's eyes widened. "Well, no, Miz Lorelie would—"

"She'd shoot him, wouldn't she?"

"I don't think she'd shoot him, but she wouldn't take kindly to it."

"My point exactly. And neither do I." She cast him a benevolent smile. "Don't pay any attention to what he says but how he acts."

"All right, but"—that annoying stubborn expression of his was back—"we have to go back."

She clenched her jaw. "I have no intention of going back. If I go back, Ophelia will have me on the afternoon train out of town tomorrow." She sidled her horse closer to his, leaned forward and placed two fingers under his chin. "And then I'd never see you again." She widened her eyes and lowered her voice. "I'd hate that, wouldn't you?"

He swallowed. "Well, sure."

"I mean . . ." She paused and ran the tip of her tongue over her upper lip. His eyes focused on the movement, and satisfaction surged through her. "You do still want to marry me, don't you?"

"Oh, yeah," he breathed.

"Well, then, we should get going." She placed her fingers over his lips. "I'll make you a deal, Zach. We go ahead to Laramie and get married, and afterwards, if you still want to, we can come back and tell Big Jack everything." She leaned closer, replaced her fingers with her lips and brushed her mouth softly against his. He groaned beneath her touch. "What do you say, Zach?"

His eyes were dazed, not quite like he'd been kicked in the head by a mule, but close enough. He shook his head as if to clear it, and she smothered a smile.

"All right, Jenny." He nodded in a firm manner, as if this was all his idea. "We'll get married and then we'll tell Big Jack about your sister."

"Whatever you want, Zach," she said demurely.

Once again they turned their horses eastward, and Jenny struggled to keep from laughing out loud. My, that was delightful. It was amazing the impact a few well-acted lines would have on a man. There was certainly a great deal of potential in the relationship between a man and a woman. And Jenny suspected men, or the manipulation of them, might be a great deal of fun.

Probably why Ophelia had kept her away from them in the first place.

"WHAT ON EARTH are you doing?" Sedge slipped off his horse and strode toward Tye. His friend sat slumped on the front steps of his porch, a long stick in one hand, a knife in the other.

"Well, I'll tell you. With this knife"—Tye held up the somewhat feeble-looking excuse for a lethal weapon—"I'm whittling this stick"—he waved the branch in the air—"into a fishing pole."

"You're going fishing?"

"Probably not. It was either use the knife to carve the rod or use it"—he smiled grimly—"to slit my throat. Frankly, that's still an option."

Sedge stared for a long moment. He wasn't sure he'd ever seen Tye look quite so . . . defeated. "Ophelia?"

Tye laughed mirthlessly. "Who else?"

Sedge studied his friend. This was indeed an interesting turn of events. He settled on the step beside Tye and pulled a deep breath. "There are several things I should tell you about Ophelia. I probably should have mentioned them before now."

Tye shaved long slivers off the stick. "Go ahead."

"First of all, the dead husband of an English countess isn't a count, he's an earl. Ophelia's not a countess."

"I'd figured that one out."

"Secondly, she's not British. She hasn't even the most fundamental grasp of the country."

Tye snorted. "I thought her accent was a little too perfect. It's a shame, though."

"What's a shame?"

"I loved that accent."

"You don't seem very surprised."

"Her accent disappears when she's mad or"—a smile struggled to lift the corners of his mouth—"very, very happy."

"I see." Obviously Tye had already had his way with the lady, so why did he seem so beaten? "Did you know all this already?"

"I'd guessed most of it."

"Very well." Sedge studied his friend. "Did you know that maid of hers is her sister?"

Tye paused his whittling for a moment, then shrugged and continued. "Nope."

"And did you know her father was an actor?"

Tye's gaze rose to meet his. Finally, something the man was surprised to hear. "That explains a lot. How did you—"

"And did you further know there's a rather vile gambler looking for her who swears she cheated him?" Sedge finished with a flourish and a strong sense of satisfaction.

Tye's expression hardened slightly. "Where is he?"

"I managed to convince him she'd gone to Laramie."

"Did he believe you?"

Sedge shrugged. "I think so."

Relief flickered over Tye's face, and he nodded. "Good."

"So, old man." Sedge's words were precise and measured. "I'd say you've got all you need. You can expose Ophelia for what she really is to Big Jack and everyone else." Tye didn't say a word, and suspicion planted a moment ago in the back of Sedge's mind blossomed. With just a bit of a push . . ."I daresay they'll run her out of town. Maybe even throw her in jail. Why, folks in Dead End will be so out—"

"I love her, Sedge." Tye sighed in surrender. "I love her and I need her, and damn it all, I want to marry her."

"Marriage?" Sedge nearly choked on the word. "You want to wed someone? Anyone? Let alone Ophelia?"

Tye clenched his teeth. "It sounds pretty far fetched, doesn't it?"

Sedge stared in stark disbelief. "Who would have dreamed that Tyler Matthews, beloved of women on not one but two continents, master of seduction, with the gift of charming women with a single glance, would be felled by an imposter. 'Far fetched' is something of an understatement." Sedge grinned. "It's positively amazing."

"Yeah, that's what I thought." Tye went back to work on the stick, apparently unwilling to say anything more.

"Am I to gather the lovely lady does not return your affection?"

"That about sums it up."

Sedge pulled his brows together thoughtfully. "Are you certain? Very often, women—"

"I'm certain." Tye set his lips in a straight, narrow line. "She told me she doesn't love me. She doesn't care for me. We are not star-crossed lovers. We are nothing."

Sedge winced. "That sounds rather definite."

"Yep." Tye glanced off in the distance. "I feel like a complete and total idiot. I love her and she wants nothing to do with me. And I don't know what to do."

"If you really want her," Sedge said slowly, "it sounds like you're in for a fight."

"I've never had to fight for a woman before."

"Nonsense, old man, you and I have fought over women dozens of times."

"That's different. None of that ever really meant anything. I always knew there'd be another woman, another time, and another more or less friendly competition. But this." Tye narrowed his eyes as if studying something only he could see. "Damn it, this isn't just another conquest, Sedge. I want her by my side forever. Till death do us part and all that. I want her to share my name and my life. But none of it matters, because regardless of what I want, she doesn't want me."

"It sounds like you're giving up."

Tye's gaze dropped to his hands, and his voice was quiet. "Hell, I don't know what I'm doing."

Sedge considered his old friend carefully. "You never gave up when you had to fight me for a woman."

A halfhearted smile touched Tye's lips. "I always knew I could beat you. But Ophelia . . ." He shook his head. "I'd have to fight her for her, if that makes any sense. And I don't know how. I've never even told a woman I loved her before."

"Never?"

"Never."

"Not even as the final strike in a seduction?"

"Never."

"My, I am impressed. I've very often found it necessary to resort to declarations of affection to get to that last—" Tye shot him a sharp glance. "Sorry, perhaps this is not the time." He studied his friend. "In spite of her words, definitive though they may be, do you think there's a chance that she does love you?"

"I don't know." Tye shrugged. "Sometimes I think she does, and other times I think the whole idea of love terrifies her."

"It always used to terrify you."

Sedge shuddered. "That's bloody awful, Tye. We certainly have come a long way from our younger days."

"Yeah, well." Tye blew a long, resigned breath. "I guess it's just not meant to be. She doesn't want me, and that's that."

Was this really Tyler Matthews? Hell-raising, womanizing, hard-drinking Tyler Matthews? Certainly not the Tyler Matthews Sedge knew. Bloody hell, it must be love. And just look what it did to the poor chap. Sitting here, feeling sorry for himself, defeated and depressed. Why, he was almost pathetic. Where was his fortitude, his perseverance, his zest for life? Sedge had never seen Tye give up on anything, especially not something he wanted, and never without a fight.

Perhaps, a thought teased the back of his mind, Tye just needed to get his spirit back. His fighting spirit. Maybe . . . he just needed to get angry.

"You're no doubt better off without her." Sedge slapped Tye's back.

"No doubt," Tye muttered.

"After all, what was she but a liar and a fraud—"

"Don't forget a cheat and a thief."

"Indeed." Sedge nodded. "And those are her good qualities."

"That's what I told her."

Sedge stopped and stared. "Perhaps you need to work on your technique."

Tye narrowed his eyes.

"I don't know what you saw in her anyway, old boy." Sedge eyed Tye. So far, this wasn't working quite as he thought it would. Perhaps he wasn't pushing hard enough. "She is a beauty though, I'd have to give you that much. The thought of having those lovely legs—"

"Sedge." A slight warning underlay Tye's words.

"—wrapped around my neck . . . and those glorious breasts, why, a man could—"

"Sedge." The warning came sharper. Still, how far could he go?

"—sell his very soul for just a taste—"

"Sedge!" Tye stilled and looked at his friend, a dangerous gleam in his eye. "If you say one more word, I'll be forced to shove it down your throat."

"I see," Sedge said quietly. "So it's not over."

Tye glared silently.

"Tell me, why are you willing to fight me and not her?"

"Damn it all, Sedge, I can beat you." Tye pulled his gaze away and stared into the night. Abruptly a grin creased his face. "And I can beat her too."

Relief flooded Sedge. Tye was back. The woman didn't have a prayer. "Excellent. How?"

"I don't know." Tye raked a hand through his hair. "But I do know I haven't got a chance if I let her leave town. So that gives me until tomorrow afternoon."

"Are you sure?"

"Yeah. I threatened to tell Jack what I know and have her thrown in jail, although I didn't have any real proof." A grin stretched across his face. "Well, I do have some proof. But she asked me to let her tell him, and she agreed to do so before that silly ceremony."

"That's the day after tomorrow. Do you think she'll still be around?"

Tye snorted. "No way in hell. I knew it, and I'm sure she knew I knew it. Agreeing to let her tell Jack was tantamount to letting her go."

"So what are you going to do?"

"I'm going to tell Jack."

Sedge chose his words carefully. "Didn't you promise not to tell Jack?"

"Not exactly. What I promised was to let her tell him." Tye grinned. "I never said I wouldn't tell him first."

"I don't think Ophelia will see it that way," Sedge said slowly.

"Perhaps not at first, but she'll come around." Tye's voice was confident.

"And how would telling Jack keep her in Dead End?"

"Think about it, Sedge. Jack told me he would stop his deal with her if I could prove she was a fake.

The information you've given me proves it beyond a doubt—"

"Glad I could help," Sedge murmured.

"Jack will see he's been taken. Then I'll have Sam throw her in jail—"

"And then what?" Sedge shook his head. "Certainly it's an interesting plan, as far as it goes, but Ophelia will not take kindly to being locked up."

"It doesn't matter. She can rot in jail, or, as the mayor, I can pardon her"—his gaze narrowed wickedly—"or marry her."

"It's a big gamble, Tye." Sedge crossed his arms over his chest and leaned back against the stairs. "She might just prefer rotting over marriage."

Tye snorted his disbelief. "You know as well as I do that women always want marriage."

"Apparently not this one."

"Apparently. At least not yet." Tye laughed. "But she's a woman just like any other. And whether she knows it or not, she wants exactly what every other woman wants. She just hasn't faced up to it yet. All I have to do is convince her."

"Oh, well, if that's all." Sarcasm dripped off Sedge's words. "And a few days in jail should soften her up nicely."

"Oh, I doubt it will come to that." Tye jumped to his feet and grinned down at his friend. "Nope, I think just the idea of a damp, dark jail versus marriage to me, well, she'll be in my arms in no time." He turned and strode toward the barn.

"Where are you off to now?" Sedge said.

"I'm going to saddle up Whiskey and go talk to Jack," Tye called over his shoulder. "There might not be a ceremony for a new count the day after tomorrow, but there will damn well be a wedding."

"I wouldn't wager on it," Sedge said under his breath. He'd never seen Tye quite this impulsive before. Or quite this stupid. The man was obviously smitten. Sedge shook his head. It was a sorry fate for a once noble warrior in the never-ending battle between men and women.

Any idiot could see Tye was going about this all wrong. Ophelia would see Tye's telling Jack as betrayal. And Sedge wouldn't be at all surprised if she did indeed choose rotting over marriage.

"Bloody hell." Sedge rose to his feet and started for his horse, noting vaguely that Tye's problems took his mind off his own. He pulled himself up into his saddle and spurred his horse. It would take Tye a few minutes to saddle Whiskey, and with luck, that would be long enough. This was the least he could do for his friend and men in general. He hated to see a good man like Tye brought so low by a woman. It was humiliating. It was pathetic.

And Sedge envied him every agonizing moment.

Chapter 17

"Tye, is that you?" Lorelie called into the night from the brightly lit porch.

"Yeah, sorry to come over so late." Tye slid from his saddle. "Jack around?"

"Right here, son." Jack appeared from the shadows at the far end of the porch.

"I need to talk to you."

Lorelie and Jack exchanged glances.

"What about?" Jack said.

"Why don't we sit down first?" Lorelie led Tye to an old, rustic rocker, then joined Jack on the porch swing. "Now then."

"It's about Ophelia." Tye drew a deep breath. How was he going to say this?

"What about Ophelia?" Jack said.

Tye leaned forward and rested his elbows on his knees. "You remember when you said you'd call off the deal with her if I could prove she was a fake?"

"I remember." Jack's voice was quiet.

"Well, I learned something very interesting today."

"Did you?"

"Yeah, I . . ." Tye's voice faltered.

Don't tell them.

It wasn't what she'd said aloud, but what he'd read in her eyes. She didn't need to say the words. If he loved her, he wouldn't tell. And he did love her. Really love her. But that's exactly what had brought him here in the first place. He loved her and he wanted to keep her right here in his town and his arms. Sure, she probably wouldn't buy his rationalization that he had only promised to let her tell Big Jack and Lorelie and hadn't agreed not to reveal her secrets himself, but surely that was a minor point.

Love, real love, demands nothing in return.

And he was demanding something from her, wasn't he? He demanded her love. He demanded that she share his life. He demanded a future together. Was that wrong? Or was this simply the wrong way to go about it? Didn't his whole scheme smack of coercion and blackmail? Now who was the liar and the cheat and the fraud?

Loving and offering love was enough.

Was it? Was it worth the pain that had nearly crippled him from the moment she'd said she didn't love him until Sedge had fanned the spark of anger he'd been too anguished to notice? Could he really selflessly let her go?

"Tyler?" Concern colored Lorelie's face.

And what of these people and this love? Big Jack and Lorelie had raised him as their own. Didn't he owe them the truth? They'd taught him right from wrong and brought him up to be an honorable man. Was there any integrity in this? In betraying the woman he loved to get what he wanted? Maybe the truth wasn't all he owed them. Maybe he owed them honor as well.

"Tye?" Jack frowned. "What did you learn about Ophelia?"

"She . . . um . . ." He groaned to himself. He couldn't tell them the truth. He couldn't reveal Sedge's proof, let alone divulge what he'd learned in the creek. "Can swim! That's it. She knows how to swim."

"She does?" Jack said slowly.

"Yep." Tye nodded. "You know, there aren't many women who can swim. It can sure come in handy."

"Does it, dear?" Confusion underlay Lorelie's words. "And how did you learn about this skill of Ophelia's?"

A vision of her wet and naked and wanting sprang to his mind, and he struggled to keep a smug smile from his lips. "We were at the creek."

Jack narrowed his eyes. "The creek's not nearly deep enough for swimming."

"No, no, of course not." Tye's mind raced, and he barely noticed his words. What had she done to him? How could he even have considered giving her up without a fight?

"It just came up." No, if he had to drag her kicking and screaming back into his life, so be it. "Swimming, that is." No matter what she said, she loved him. He knew it in the deepest recesses of his soul. Besides, she was a terrible liar. Why hadn't he remembered that sooner? "In the conversation." And now that he knew about her father, so much of what she'd said made sense. No wonder she was scared of any man declaring his love.

"Actors." He fairly spit the word.

"What do actors have to do with swimming?" Lorelie turned to Jack.

"Nothing, darlin'." Jack smiled. "The boy's just a little rattled, that's all. So, Tye, did you come up with the proof you needed about Ophelia's legitimacy to win that little bet of ours?"

Proof? What did he have, really? Sedge's word was pretty damning evidence, of course, but how could you expect an American like Tye to remember such nonsense about the geography of Britain or counts and earls and such? As for his own evidence, in spite of his threat, he would never tell anyone, let alone his uncle, of Ophelia's innocence. Or rather, her loss of innocence.

Tye shook his head slowly. "I hate to admit it, Jack, I don't know much more now than I did when I made that bet. There's really nothing to say. I guess I lose."

Jack's eyes twinkled. "Are you sure? You seemed so certain she was a fake."

Tye shrugged. "My mistake. Whoops. Speaking of Ophelia, have you seen her tonight?"

Lorelie tapped her chin with her forefinger in a thoughtful manner. "I saw her, oh, about fifteen minutes ago, I think. She was heading toward the corral. I believe she muttered something about a ride. Odd, she seemed rather distracted, possibly even upset."

"She talked about a ride?" His heart thudded against his ribs. Surely she hadn't already left? He hadn't even considered the possibility that she'd leave on horseback. Damn.

"Why don't you go find her?" Jack's voice was nonchalant.

"Yeah." Tye stepped toward the barn, stopped and turned back. "And thanks."

"For what, dear?" Lorelie said.

"For teaching me right." He grinned and strode off.

Jack put his arm around his wife's shoulders, and they watched Tye disappear into the night.

"He was right about her, wasn't he?" Lorelie said.

"Um-hum."

She sighed. "You knew it all along, didn't you?"

"Damned near."

"Then why did you give her all that money?"

"Lorelie, darlin'." Jack settled back as if preparing for a long story. "It's only money, and we've got plenty of that. Besides, it was the only way I figured we could get her to hang around here long enough."

"Long enough for what?"

He cast her a loving glance. "You know for what."

"Oh, dear."

"Well, that's what you were planning, wasn't it?"

"More or less." She sighed. "I simply knew from the moment I first met her she was the woman for him. Something in her eyes, I think. It just took him a while to recognize it."

"It's not always easy to see what's right in front of your nose."

"Like in the fairy tale?"

His arm tightened around her. "Just like that."

She reached up and kissed his cheek. "But you knew from the very beginning that she wasn't who she said she was."

He chuckled. "Well, I'm a pretty good judge of character. Women, horses, cattle. I always knew she was a decent person in spite of her little masquerade. And as for that, Sedge filled in all the specific details for me."

"When did you talk to Sedge?"

Jack grinned. "About a minute before Tye showed up. And if I'm not mistaken, he's probably still around here somewhere. Sedge?"

"Yes, sir?" a voice from the bushes rang out.

"He's gone, you can come out now."

"Thank God," the voice muttered. A moment later, Sedge strode into view. "I think that all worked out quite nicely, sir."

Jack studied him for a second and nodded. "I appreciate your telling me about Ophelia."

Lorelie glanced from one man to the other. "I don't understand."

"It's simple, darlin'. Sedge knew that if Tye told me about Ophelia, she'd never forgive him. So he figured he'd tell me, and if I was willing to go along with him, I'd refuse to believe Tye. Tell him he was full of—well, he was mistaken about her." Jack laughed. "Tye had some crazy plan about throwing her into jail until she agreed to marry him."

"Oh, dear," Lorelie murmured. "Ophelia wouldn't like that one little bit. And it's not at all typical of Tye to be so, well, stupid."

Sedge and Jack traded knowing glances.

"He's not stupid, darlin'." A wide grin stretched across Jack's face. "He's in love."

"DAMN YOU, YOU nasty beast, you laugh at me one more time and I'll shoot you." Ophelia glared at the horse in the stall before her, only to get a grin in return. A very smug grin.

Ophelia brushed her hair away from her face with an impatient gesture. It was already late. She'd been so devastated after leaving Tye that she'd collapsed onto her bed the moment she'd walked into her room. Collapsed and cried until she'd fallen into an exhausted sleep. She didn't find Jenny's letter until she woke up.

Jenny's letter.

Tears welled and spilled onto her checks. She sank

down in the straw and swiped at her eyes angrily. She hated weak, whinny women. She'd never cried like this in her life. Of course, she'd never known heartache like this either. First with Tye and now with Jenny.

Damn him, anyway. If she ever had a second chance to shoot him, it certainly wouldn't be a minor scratch. No, this time she'd aim lower than his shoulder. Much, much lower. The nerve of the man. Telling her he loved her. And adding insult to injury by asking her to marry him. Not that the thought hadn't crossed her mind long before their afternoon in the stream.

She plucked at the pieces of straw clinging to her skirt. She'd never imagined how very hard it would be to tell him she didn't love him when all the while she wanted to scream the truth. And she didn't doubt what would happen if she did admit she loved him and agreed to marry him. Oh, they might be happy for a while, but sooner or later, just like every other man she'd ever seen, he'd leave her for the next conquest. No, you couldn't count on a man. Not like you could count on family.

Jenny.

Ophelia scrambled to her feet. She'd noted her sister's unusual quiet when Ophelia had announced they'd leave on tomorrow's train, and she should have paid more attention to the defiant set of her chin, but she'd never dreamed Jenny'd had other plans. When had the child gotten so close to that ranch hand? Ophelia knew someone was teaching her to ride, but apparently she was too distracted by Tye and the Ladies Cultural Society and the opera house and rehearsals to realize what else the boy was teaching her. Well, she'd spent way too many years looking out for Jenny to let her go off and destroy her life now.

"I hope you're ready, you vicious animal." Ophelia clenched her jaw and forced a smile. The horse tilted its head. A saddle hung over the top of the stall wall at about the level of her chest. She glanced from the saddle to the horse and back. How in the hell did you get this thing on that thing?

She squared her shoulders, grabbed the saddle and yanked it off the wall, putting all her strength into the effort. Perhaps too much strength. The saddle nearly flew through the air, the momentum throwing her backwards, and she stumbled and fell, trapped beneath the leather. Ophelia stared up at the overhead beams and heaved a sigh. Then she heard it.

The horse snickered.

"When I get up from here"—she put as much menace into her voice as she could muster—"you're going to be sorry."

Ophelia gritted her teeth and tried to ignore the snickering that verged on the edge of a full-fledged laugh. She sat up, pushed the saddle off and pulled herself to her feet. The contraption was certainly a lot heavier than she'd expected. She glanced at the horse. It bared its teeth in a malicious grin. She narrowed her gaze. No vile, stupid brute was going to get the best of her.

She grasped the knoblike thing at one end of the saddle, hooked her fingers on the other end and lifted, trying to balance some of the rig's weight on her legs. She inched toward the horse.

"Now then, you disgusting creature, stay right there. Don't move. Just stay put . . ." She lunged toward the animal, thrusting the saddle out in front of her like a shield. The horse laughed and stepped out of her path. Ophelia barreled into the wall, bounced and landed, once again, flat on her back, staring upward, trapped by leather.

"Damn." She glared at the rafters. "I can do this. I will not let one of those animals make a fool out of me."

Once more she struggled to her feet, clutched the saddle and stood before the horse. She stared the animal straight in its eyes, or rather, straight in one of its eyes.

"Let's get something clear here. You are the horse. I am the person."

The horse chuckled.

Obviously, reason wasn't going to work. How can you reason with a laughing horse? She'd already tried threats and had ended up on her well-bustled backside. Twice. Perhaps it was time to—she shuddered—be pleasant.

"Why don't we both be reasonable, shall we?" She smiled as sweetly as possible and stepped closer. "I need to put this saddle on you so we can go find my sister. Doesn't that sound like fun?" The horse pricked its ears. She sidled up next to it. "We'll have a nice long ride in the moonlight. Just you and me. It will be great—hah!" She leapt forward and slapped the saddle on the beast's back. The animal didn't move so much as an inch. "Got you! That will teach you to try and make a fool out of me."

She stepped back and grinned. "Man, or in this case woman, has always been more intelligent than creatures like yourself. That's why you can chuckle all you want but I have the last laugh."

"It looked to me like that horse let you win."

She gasped and swiveled at the familiar voice. "Tye!"

"Horses making fun of you, Ophelia?"

Her breath caught in her throat and her heart leapt

with hope and fear. He leaned casually against the stall gate, his arms crossed over his chest, his expression unreadable. She forced an icy calm to her voice. "What do you want?"

"You."

She shook her head. "Why don't you just leave me alone?"

"I can't." Why did he have to stand there looking for all the world like every secret dream and desire she'd ever had?

"We've been all through this, Tye," she said quietly, trying to hide the desperate longing and temptation to surrender that his presence aroused. "I don't love you."

"A few hours ago you accused me of not being able to recognize manure when I saw it. Well, I sure do recognize it now." A dangerous spark flared in his eyes. "You don't lie well, Ophelia."

She sighed in resignation. "I don't lie at all, I act."

He shrugged. "You can call it whatever you damn well please. The point is I love you."

"But I don't even like you." She groaned.

He laughed, and she knew she was lost. It wasn't the laugh of a heartbroken man, or a man ready to give up, or a man who accepted the fact that he was about to fail. No, his was a laugh ringing with success.

"I don't have time for this right now." She tossed her head and turned back to the horse. She'd managed to get the saddle on the beast, but how in the hell did she get into it?

"What are you doing?" His voice sounded beside her ear, and his lips nuzzled her neck.

She jerked and whirled around. "What are *you* doing?"

"Kissing your neck."

"Why?"

"Oh, I don't know." His eyes widened with innocence. "Because it's a lovely neck?"

She glared at him, struck by the certainty that she would fall into his arms with the least provocation and then, no doubt, willingly sacrifice her soul, and eventually become what she'd vowed she never would. Unless . . . she could buy a little more time.

"I can't discuss this right now, Tye. I have other things to do." She pivoted toward the horse, but he caught her arm and pulled her back to face him.

"I'm not letting you leave Dead End." Determination shaded his face. "I love you, and you're staying here."

She frowned. "Well, I don't love you, and this has nothing to do with us. It's my sis—maid. Jenny."

He raised a brow. "The girl with the speech problem?"

"She's disappeared." Ophelia shot him a pointed glare. "With one of Big Jack's ranch hands."

"How do you know that?"

"She left me a note. She said she wanted to stay right here in Dead End forever with this boy Zach. But first they're going to Laramie, to get married. Married!" Fear and panic, forgotten during her battles first with the horse, then with Tye, threatened to overwhelm her. "I've got to find her."

Tye's gaze narrowed thoughtfully. "Why?"

"Because I . . . I care for her. She's my—"

"Sister?"

"Yes, damn it, Tye, she's my sister. The only family I have." Her voice broke. "And I don't want to lose her." She sniffed and turned back to the horse. "I have to find her, so if you could help me get this saddle on this brute, I would appreciate it. I think there's something that hooks under here somewhere." She bent and peered at the animal's belly.

"Ophelia, what are you doing?"

"I told you, Tye." Impatience rang in her voice. "I'm saddling this horse to go after my sister." She straightened upright and glared.

What on earth was wrong with him? He furrowed his brow with the oddest expression and looked from her to the horse and back. Abruptly, his eyes widened and he smiled. "You don't know the first thing about horses, do you?"

"It's not precisely my biggest accomplishment."

"Do you even know how to ride?"

She blew an exasperated breath. "Not exactly. But it doesn't look all that difficult." She shuddered. "Not that I've ever wanted to try. I'm not fond of horses."

"Sure, they laugh at you."

"That's one reason," she snapped. "Other than that they're big and nasty, they smell and you always have to watch your step when you walk around one."

"If you don't know how to ride—"

"I'll figure it out as I go along."

Tye shook his head. "You won't make it as far as the road, and you don't stand a chance in hell of catching up to them. It's a three-day ride under the best conditions for an experienced horseman. Besides, it wouldn't be safe for you alone."

"Fine." She fisted her hands on her hips. "Then you go with me."

He grinned. "I would like nothing better than to ride in the moonlight with you, but you'd just slow me down."

Ophelia narrowed her eyes in suspicion. "What do you mean?"

"I mean, my love—"

"Don't call me that!"

"—that I'll go after your sister and Zach and bring them back here on one condition."

"I don't really have much of a choice, do I?"

He shook his head. "Nope."

"So what's the condition?"

"You stay put until we get back."

Well, that was easy. She certainly wouldn't leave without Jenny anyway. "Agreed."

"And . . ." He cast her an assessing gaze. "You give me the chance to convince you that I love you."

She sighed. "Very well. But I don't love you."

"Hah!" He pulled her into his arms, kissed her hard and fast, and released her. "You're not much of a liar."

Why did he do that? He damned near took her breath away. "I don't lie, I—"

"I know, I know." He laughed and turned to leave. "Whiskey's outside and all ready to go, so you can take the saddle off that horse."

Ophelia groaned. "But it took so long to get it up there."

"It wouldn't have done you any good."

She glared. "Why not?"

"You see the horn, at the end there? It should face the horse's neck, not his rump." He grinned. "You've got it backwards." Tye nodded and stepped out into the night.

The horse cast her an innocent glance and she stared back at it. Lord, she despised these beasts.

Especially when they got the last laugh.

Chapter 18

WHERE in the hell were they? Ophelia paced across her room, trying to fight her growing exhaustion and despair. What if he couldn't find them? What if she never saw Jenny again?

She had barely slept at all last night, and here it was evening again. Tye had been gone nearly twenty-four hours. He'd said it was a three-day ride to Laramie. Surely he should have found them by now.

Ophelia flopped down on her bed and stared at the ceiling. What was she going to do? Today's train was long gone, and with it their easiest chance of escape. Tomorrow's train would bring that British lord Montgomery had invited for Jack's celebration. She groaned and rolled over on her stomach, folding her arms under her chin. Damnation, she didn't want to be around when the Englishman proclaimed her to be a fraud. Maybe she could sneak on the train while he was getting off? The idea lifted her spirits, but only for a moment. She couldn't go anywhere without Jenny.

Hadn't she taught her sister anything at all in the years they'd been on their own? Apparently not. And definitely nothing about men. Ophelia had been too busy trying to protect Jenny to pay notice to that lack in her education. And too busy trying to protect herself. She should have suspected Jenny would fall for the first man to come along. But Ophelia never dreamed *she* would as well.

Right from the beginning, Tyler Matthews had inched his way into her heart. Why, she'd even considered the existence of love at first sight the very night they'd met. Maybe it was fate. Or destiny. Or just plain bad luck. And she'd certainly had her share of that lately. Not exactly a good position for a gambler to be in. But it sure seemed appropriate for a woman stuck in a town called Dead End. She should have run hard and fast in the other direction the moment she'd seen the name.

First, she'd come up with this brilliant idea for getting the money she and Jenny needed, thanks to a silly fairy tale. It had seemed so simple, so easy, so effortless. Hah! How had it become so incredibly complicated? From the something-water title that wouldn't stick in her mind, to the name of her dead husband, dear, dear, dead whoever, the plot had snowballed out of control. Add to that the farce of a fox hunt, building an opera house, gambling the afternoons away with the Every Other Tuesday and Thursday Afternoon Ladies Cultural Society, and, for a finale, readings from Shakespeare and a ceremony to mark the crowning, if that's what you'd call it, of Big Jack Matthews as a count, and you had a disaster that came nowhere close to "happily ever after." She had a grim suspicion the tailors in that damn story probably ended their days in the emperor's dungeon after he sent troops to haul them back by their ears.

What would Lorelie and Big Jack and everyone else

do when they learned the truth? That Ophelia was no countess. That Big Jack would never be a count. And that Lorelie would never have a castle to call home. Ophelia sighed. She hated the thought of how disappointed all the very nice people of Dead End would be tomorrow. She'd always been so proud of the fact that she'd never steal from orphans. Now she'd add very nice people to that list for the future.

Very nice people, very nice town, very nice mayor.

Why can't we stay?

What a treacherous thought. The reasons were too numerous to list. Big Jack and Lorelie and all the other residents of Dead End would never forgive her for deceiving them. And even if they did, she couldn't run the risk of trusting her heart to Tye and believing in that fickle emotion she'd seen destroy women time after time.

But what if he really loves me?

She propped her chin on her hand. She had no way of knowing if his declaration was true and, more to the point, if it would last. This whole love and marriage nonsense called for trust in the emotion, in the future and in the man. And trust was one thing she simply couldn't fake, no matter how good an actress she was.

No. It was better this way. If Tye got back with Jenny in time, she'd take her sister and the two of them would sneak on that train and hide until it pulled out of Dead End, leaving far behind the nice people in the nice town with the very nice mayor.

And leaving behind, as well, her heart.

DAWN CAME AND went, and the late-morning sunshine crept across the kitchen floor. And still no word.

Ophelia jumped up from her chair every few minutes and paced or stalked to the window and peered into the distance, far too restless to sit still. Alma bustled around in a quiet manner. Lorelie sat silently embroidering, her hands busy, her gaze darting to Ophelia with every step the younger woman took. If Lorelie or Alma considered it at all odd that a countess was so concerned with the welfare of a servant, neither showed it. Ophelia gritted her teeth. Why did they all have to be such nice people?

Ophelia stared out the window. "Why aren't they here yet?"

"They'll be here, dear," Lorelie said. "You can count on Tyler."

"Can I?" Ophelia said softly.

"He's a good man, Ophelia." Lorelie dropped the needlework into her lap and leveled her a steady stare. "He's honest and loyal and steadfast—"

"Add housebroken and he'd sound like a puppy," Alma muttered.

Lorelie ignored her. "I've never seen him hurt anyone deliberately."

Ophelia sighed. "It's not deliberately that I'm worried about."

"What are you worried about?" Lorelie's voice was soft.

"About what happens next." Ophelia swiveled to face Tye's aunt. "About what happens when his passion fades and I'm no longer something he wants but simply something he has. I will not give my heart to anyone only to see it discarded like an extra card. I will not become one of those women who have sacrificed their lives and their souls for a man's declaration of love." She squared her shoulders. "And I will not accept, on blind faith alone, a promise of love from a man."

"But my dear"—Lorelie's eyes widened—"blind faith is the very essence of love." She studied Ophelia for a moment. "How do you feel when you're around Tyler?"

"He makes me ill, deep-down-in-the-pit-of-my-stomach sick. And he scares me."

"Excellent." Lorelie beamed.

"I don't love him, if that's what you're thinking," Ophelia said sharply.

Alma snorted in disbelief.

Lorelie smiled knowingly.

"All right." Ophelia sighed. "Perhaps, just perhaps, I might possibly love him. But if I did, it would only be a little."

"If you love him at all," Lorelie said gently, "you have to have trust."

"Then I must not love him." Ophelia's voice rang dangerously high. "Because I certainly don't trust him or any other man."

Lorelie grinned. "And well you shouldn't, dear. Trust any man, that is."

"No, indeed," Alma said. "That would be just plain stupid."

Ophelia stared in confusion. "But you just said—"

"What I said, Ophelia, was that you had to trust, not necessarily trust *him*."

Was this another one of Lorelie's convoluted philosophies on life? "I don't understand. What do you mean?"

"It's really quite simple. You'll never know Tyler, or any other person, for that matter, as well as you know yourself. Ophelia, the Countess of . . . of . . ." Lorelie raised a brow.

Ophelia shrugged. "What difference does it make?"

"Well said." Lorelie rose to her feet and stepped toward her. "Don't trust his words, don't even trust his actions, but trust yourself. Look at your own feelings deep within you. I think you already know the kind of man Tyler is. And you're the only one who'll know, really know, if you can trust your heart to him."

"But what if I'm wrong?" Fear edged Ophelia's words.

"You won't be." Lorelie took Ophelia's hands in hers and stared into her eyes. "I don't know where you came from, Ophelia. I don't know where you've seen these women you're so frightened of becoming but I do know the only one you can trust in this life is yourself. Trust in yourself and in your heart, and you'll know if what you feel for Tyler and what he feels for you is real and true and lasting."

"I don't know if I can." Ophelia stared at the older women helplessly. "I'm scared."

Lorelie laughed lightly. "Why, dear girl, we are all scared. There's no more frightening thing in this world than the relationship between a man and a woman. Goodness, it's the sheer terror of love that makes it so thrilling. And so very wonderful."

A choked, strangled cough came from Alma's direction.

"They're home." Big Jack burst into the kitchen followed closely by a sheepish Zach, a defiant Jenny carrying her old carpetbag and an exhausted Tye.

"Jenny!" Relief flooded Ophelia, and she rushed to throw her arms around her sister. Jenny's rebellious expression stopped Ophelia in her tracks. "Jenny?"

"Why did you have him haul us back here?" The girl slammed the bag down on the table, crossed her arms over her chest and glared.

"She wasn't real pleased to see me." Tye stalked across the room to accept a cup of coffee from Alma's outstretched hand. "And she let me know just how unhappy my presence made her all the way back here."

Jenny narrowed her eyes at Tye but directed her words at Ophelia. "You should have killed him when you had the chance."

Tye took a sip of the steaming liquid and grimaced. He nodded at Ophelia. "She reminds me a lot of you."

"But you did find them before . . ." Ophelia bit her bottom lip.

"They're not married," Tye said. "I caught up to them about halfway to Laramie."

Ophelia sighed in relief. "I can't believe you wanted to get married. Married! Of all things."

Jenny shrugged. "Married sounded like fun." She grinned at Zach. "You know, kissing . . . and such."

Tye groaned.

Big Jack rolled his eyes.

Zach blushed.

Lorelie and Alma exchanged glances.

Ophelia gasped. "And such? What do you mean 'and such'?"

"You know, Ophelia." A wicked gleam sparkled in Jenny's eye. "And such." She nodded at Tye. "I bet he'd be willing to show you 'and such.'"

Tye snorted in an obvious attempt to stifle a laugh.

"There wasn't any 'and such,' Countess . . . um . . . Ophelia." Zach's eyes were wide in frantic defense. "Honest."

Jenny scoffed. "And whose fault was that?"

Tye cleared his throat. "There was no 'and such,' Ophelia."

"Thank goodness." Ophelia ran a weary hand through her tangled hair. "Why, Jenny? Why did you go?"

"Love," Jenny said staunchly. "And I didn't want to leave here."

Ophelia shook her head. "Here? You mean Dead End?"

"Yes, I mean Dead End." Jenny stared up at her. "You've always talked about how we'd find a nice town someday with nice people and we'd stay. Well, look around, Ophelia. This is a nice town." She gestured at the gathering in the kitchen. "And these are nice people. Far too nice for you to do what you've—"

"Jenny!" Ophelia said sharply.

"Honestly, Ophelia, Zach knows everything, and I'll bet Tye does too. Don't you?" Jenny jerked her head at Tye.

"I like to think so," Tye said in a casual manner.

Jenny nodded. "And you like it here too, Ophelia, I know you do."

Ophelia shook her head helplessly. "Jenny, I—"

"And you like him, as annoying as he is." Jenny flicked a disgusted wave in Tye's direction. "In fact, I'd bet you even love him."

"I don't love him." Six faces turned toward her. Six pairs of eyes pinned her. Six expressions of total disbelief. "Well, I don't."

"Well, whether you do or don't, and we all think you do"—Jenny set her lips in a straight, stubborn line—"I'm not leaving Dead End. If you want to go, you have to go without me."

"Jenny!" How could her own sister do this to her?

"You won't make me go, will you?" Jenny turned to Lorelie.

"I'm afraid I'm just a bit too confused to answer that, my dear." Lorelie's brow furrowed. "I need to sort some of this out first, but I suppose you can stay. After all, Ophelia is only your employer."

"Sister," Tye said.

"Sister? Oh, my." Lorelie shook her head. "That makes it a tad different, doesn't it?"

Ophelia reached out and took Jenny's arm. "Come upstairs with me and we'll talk." She rolled her gaze toward the ceiling. "About whether we stay or go."

"Ophelia!" Jenny threw her arms around her sister in a quick hug. "You'll see. You'll love living here." She twirled around the kitchen with sheer delight.

"I only said we'd talk about it." Ophelia heaved a resigned sigh. Maybe it would be best if she confessed everything right now. And took her chances that these very nice people would forgive her. And then accepted Tye's offer of marriage and profession of love. And wrapped up the day by becoming a permanent, card-carrying member of the Every Other Tuesday and Thursday Afternoon Ladies Cultural Society and Theater Troupe. Or maybe she could pick up the tattered threads of her deception and try to sneak out of town. Or maybe she could simply hide under a bed and hope everything and everyone would go away and leave her in peace.

Jenny's arm swept her bag off the table and it clattered to the floor, spilling out the possessions of her lifetime.

"Damn," Jenny said.

"Jenny," Ophelia snapped.

"Oh, my goodness," Alma gasped.

"No, really," Ophelia said quickly, "she's trying not to curse."

"Jack?" Lorelie clutched her husband's arm and stared at the scattered contents of Jenny's bag.

Crumpled clothes lay under a yellowed playbill. A frayed hair ribbon curled between a rag doll and a child's storybook: *The Emperor's New Clothes.*

Jack knelt and gently picked up the doll and the book. His hand trembled, and his voice was gruff. "Where did you get these?"

"They're mine," Jenny said, a defensive note in her voice. "Give them to me."

Jack handed Lorelie the doll, and she stared and rubbed her finger over the name *Jenny* embroidered on its skirt.

"Mr. Matthews, I really would like them back. Please." Jenny lifted her chin. "They're very important to me."

"You see, Jack," Ophelia began, "Jenny's not my real sister. My father adopted her and—" Ophelia sucked in her breath. Shock coursed through her as if she'd just been punched in the stomach. Her gaze darted from Jenny to Lorelie and back. How could she have been so blind? How could she have failed to see what was right before her eyes?

"I remember when I embroidered this," Lorelie said gently. She raised her gaze to Jenny. "For my daughter."

Jenny's eyes widened. She stared at Lorelie, and for a moment the resemblance between mother and daughter was unmistakable. From their blue eyes, to their delicate build, to their white-blonde hair, Jenny was a younger version of Lorelie.

"I thought you said their child died?" Ophelia turned to Tye.

"That's not what I said." The astonishment in his

eyes reflected her own. "I never said she died. I said they lost her."

"Isn't it the same thing?" Ophelia said.

"Not exactly, Ophelia." Jack's voice was steady, but his expression was intense, his gaze riveted on Jenny. "We were visiting family in St. Louis—"

"That's where Papa found me," Jenny said softly. "Outside the theater."

Jack nodded. "Alma was with us. We were taking separate trains because she was coming back a few days before we were."

"It was my fault." A grim note sounded in Alma's voice.

Jack laid a comforting hand on the housekeeper's arm. How many times had they rehashed this through the years? Each, no doubt, shouldering the blame and the guilt and the sorrow.

"We never could figure out quite what happened, but we thought Alma had the baby and she thought we had her. By the time we all met up in Dead End, realized what had happened and went back to St. Louis, it was too late." Jack shrugged. "We couldn't find a trace of her."

"We tried." Lorelie's voice trembled. "We tried everything. Detectives, notices in the paper—"

"Good Lord!" Ophelia clapped her hand over her mouth. "I saw those, years later. Jenny was maybe six or seven. You see, we left St. Louis the day after my father found Jenny. He assumed she was abandoned and needed a home."

"The notice?" Tye prompted.

Ophelia bit her bottom lip. "It was a newspaper clipping. Old and yellow. And really not much more than the headline." She drew a deep breath. "It said something about a missing Wyoming cattle heiress. I asked Papa about it, but he said it was nothing and threw it away. I always wondered if maybe your family lived in Wyoming."

"My family?" Jenny's voice cracked.

"It sure does seem that way, darlin'." Jack's voice shook with emotion. "When we lost our little girl she had her favorite book—"

"*The Emperor's New Clothes*," Lorelie whispered.

"—and the rag doll." He choked back tears. "Jenny."

"Dear Lord." Alma dabbed at her eyes with her apron. "Who would have ever thought we'd get her back?"

"Ophelia?" Jenny clutched at Ophelia. "I think these are my parents."

"I know, darling." Tears welled in Ophelia's eyes, and Jenny's face blurred. "It does seem that way."

"Does this mean we have a real home now?" Hope rang in Jenny's voice.

A tear tumbled down Ophelia's cheek and she dashed it away and smiled. "I suspect you do."

Jenny leaned closer and whispered in her ear. "What do I do now?"

Ophelia whispered back. "Talk to them. You said it yourself. They're nice people. You'll be very happy with them."

"What about you?" Jenny's eyes widened. "You'll stay here now too, won't you?"

"Jenny, I—"

"Promise me, Ophelia." Panic shadowed Jenny's eyes. "Promise me you won't leave."

"I can't promise, Jenny." Ophelia grabbed the girl's shoulders. "But listen to me. All I ever wanted was for you to have a nice home. I never dreamed I could get you parents as well. This is a fairy-tale ending for you. It's perfect."

"But Ophelia, if you leave—"

"I'll be around for a while." Relief washed over Jenny's face, and Ophelia pulled her into her arms and hugged her tight. No matter what, this girl would always be her sister and the only family she had. Ophelia's gaze caught Tye's. He stared at her as if he knew her very thoughts. How could he? She wasn't at all sure herself what she thought. With a final squeeze she released Jenny. "Now, I'm going upstairs to get some rest. You get to know your family."

"I will see you later, won't I?" Caution edged Jenny's voice.

"Of course." Ophelia smiled in her most reassuring manner and turned toward the door. Behind her, she heard the beginnings of a family reuniting.

"You know," Jack said, "your name isn't Jenny."

"No, indeed," Lorelie added. "The doll's name was Jenny."

"Then . . . what's my name?" Jenny asked.

There was a moment of hesitation, then Jack's voice rang out firmly. "Lora Lee."

"Lora Lee?" Disbelief colored Jenny's words. "Did you say 'Lora Lee'? I'm not going to . . ."

Ophelia laughed through the tears that now freely made their way down her face. Lord, if it hurt this much to lose her sister, how much would it hurt to lose Tye? More? Less? She didn't plan to find out.

A few moments ago she had nearly decided to give in. To Tye and her own desires. Not now. Regardless of what she'd just said to Jenny, or Lora Lee, Ophelia was getting out and getting out this minute. Resolve surged through her. This time, there was no chance she'd change her mind.

The whole family, including Tye, would be so wrapped up in this miraculous turn of events that they wouldn't even notice she was gone until it was too late. The return of their daughter might even distract them from the hell that would surely break loose as soon as the train arrived.

Her things were already packed. Regrettably, she'd have to leave most of the countess's clothes behind. All she had to do now was throw her bag out the window and shinny down the drainpipe. That was the best way to avoid seeing any of the family downstairs. Besides, she'd done it a hundred times before. A sharp pang shot through her.

But she'd never done it alone.

Chapter 19

G<small>AD</small>, she detested this! Ophelia tried to keep in the shadows and stay out of sight to avoid recognition. The train would pull in any minute, and a crowd was already forming to greet the man who would allegedly bestow Big Jack's title.

Why on earth did she feel so guilty about all this? Big Jack's money, minus a few dollars here and there for unavoidable expenses, was still in the bank. So when it came right down to it, what had she really done anyway, short of pretending to be someone she wasn't?

But that was the problem. The visit of a real genuine countess brought a certain degree of respectability and civilization to the town, and Dead End could now proudly call itself Empire City. What would happen to that pride when everyone learned their countess was a fraud? A fake? A two-bit swindler? Wouldn't their respectability be just as bogus? Well, Ophelia wouldn't be here to find out.

The train whistle sounded in the distance and relief surged through her. Just a few more minutes and she'd be gone. She refused to think about Jenny. Her sister was safe and exactly where she belonged. Where she'd always belonged. And as for Tye, well, that was one more thing she simply wouldn't think about.

Wheels squeaked, metal groaned and gears clanged, and the train pulled in, spewing a great plume of steam into the Wyoming sky and chaos in its wake. The crowd gathered on the siding near the station office far down the rails from her position. All eyes were on the disembarking passengers. She lingered for a second and watched Montgomery greet a distinguished-looking gentleman and a tall, elegant woman. Damn that Montgomery, anyway. If he hadn't sent for this lord, Ophelia could well have pretended to be a countess for the rest of her life. In Dead End or even in Empire City, no one would ever have known.

With attention focused on that end of the train, it was a simple matter for Ophelia to slip onto the nearest car. She entered and found it far too crowded for her liking. She preferred to be alone right now. She hurried to the next one, and again there were too many people. Finally, in the third she breathed a sigh of relief. Only one other passenger sat slumped in the car, a cowboy at the far end, and he appeared asleep.

Ophelia dropped into a backwards-facing seat, closed her eyes and rested her head. She could ignore the sights and sounds of the day, but she couldn't stop the thousand thoughts that beat against her mind.

How could she leave Jenny? How could she leave Tye? But how could she stay? It was better this way. For everyone. Jenny had a new life. And Tye, well, Tye was a man, like any other. He might well say he loved her today, but what about tomorrow? No. It was far too frightening to risk.

It's the sheer terror of love that makes it so thrilling. And so very wonderful.

She had to admit that she'd never felt so alive, so complete and so real as when she'd been in his arms. It was as exciting as a standing ovation or a royal flush. But was it a gamble worth taking? Now she'd probably never know.

She sighed and opened her eyes. The sleeping cowboy was directly in her line of sight. Odd. She thought he'd been sitting farther back when she'd come in. She must have been mistaken. Idly, she studied him. His long legs were propped up on the seat in front of him, his hat was cocked forward, covering his face. A wisp of golden blond hair—

Not again! She groaned, and her heart throbbed with emotions too confusing to sort out. "What are you doing here?"

His voice was muffled but unmistakable beneath the hat. "I stopped the train and got on a few miles out of town."

"You can't do that."

"Sure, I can." Tye pushed the Stetson back on his forehead and grinned. "I'm the mayor."

"I keep forgetting."

"You keep forgetting I'm not going to let you go either. I came after you as soon as I noticed you were gone. How did you get into town, anyway? I know you didn't ride."

"I blackmailed Zach into driving me in that little carriage of Lorelie's."

"Blackmailed?"

Ophelia shrugged. "I just mentioned the words *'Big Jack'* and *'and such'* in the same sentence."

Tye laughed. "That would do it, all right."

"It did work rather nicely." She bit back a smile. "I think Zach's conscience is bothering him for going off with Jenny in the first place."

"You know," Tye drawled, "I've always heard confession is good for the soul."

"Well, I've never heard that," she snapped.

He planted his feet on the floor and leaned toward her. "Tell me the truth, Ophelia."

"I have nothing to tell you." She crossed her arms and stared out the window. "Besides, you already know everything, don't you?"

"I want to hear it from you."

"Why? What difference does it make now?" A pleading note sounded in her voice. If he'd just leave her alone, she'd be out of his life for good and safe from him and from herself.

His voice was soft. "Wives always tell the truth to their husbands, remember."

She stared in sheer disbelief. "I'm not going to marry you."

"Yes." He smiled pleasantly. "You are."

"I don't love you!"

"Yes." The smile remained. Her hand itched to slap it off his face. "You do."

"Why don't you believe me?"

"Because you don't lie well." Was it a smile or a smirk?

"I don't lie at all. I—never mind." She glared in annoyance. "You believed me at the creek. Why then and not now?"

"Shock, I think." He studied her intently. "I didn't expect you not to share my feelings. You see, Ophelia, I"—he drew a steadying breath—"I've never told a woman I loved her before."

Her breath caught. Her heart stopped. Time seemed to stand still.

I've never told a woman I loved her before.

"Never?" The word was little more than a whisper.

"Never." A solemn light shone in his eyes.

"How do I know I can trust you?"

"How do you know you can't?" he said quietly.

They stared at each other for a long, silent moment. Hope surged and then sank beneath a fear too long harbored to be denied.

"It doesn't matter, Tye." She shook her head. "I'm leaving. The train will pull out in a few minutes and—"

"And you won't be on it." Tye got to his feet and stepped to her side. With a sure, swift motion he scooped her into his arms and lifted her out of the seat.

"Tyler Matthews, put me down!" She pushed against his chest, struggling to escape.

"Ophelia, ouch, you're making this damned difficult."

"Good! Then put me down."

"Nope." He bounced her in his arms, flipped her around and threw her over his shoulder. "There, that's much better."

"This is humiliating, Tyler. I will never forgive you for this." Gad, it was impossible to keep an angry tone in your voice when you were bobbing along upside down.

He strode toward the car door. "I can live with that."

"I'll shoot you again, Tyler Matthews! I swear I will!"

He carried her through the door and out onto the siding. She tried to ignore the gathered townspeople's shocked gasps and snorts of amusement. "I'll run that risk."

"This time it won't be an accident!"

"I'll just have to learn to duck." He set her on her feet and grinned. "I'll have a lifetime to learn."

She groaned. "Why is it every time I make a decision that's right about you and me, you come along and scramble my mind and my senses?"

"Because, my love"—he took her hands in his—"the only thing that's really right in all this is that you and I belong together. Forever."

"Tye, I—"

"No, Ophelia. I'm not an actor. And I'm not like your father." His gaze bored into hers with an intensity that stole her soul. "I have been with a lot of women in my life, but I have never used the words *I love you*. Not even once. Not even in fun. Never until now. Until you." His jaw tightened. "Damn it, Ophelia, get it through your thick, obstinate, beautiful little head. I love you!"

Ophelia stared, stunned. How could she believe him? How could she not?

"That's her!" a voice yelled from the crowd. "That's the one!"

Ophelia glanced straight into the eyes of—

"Hell and damnation!" Ophelia scrambled to stand behind Tye in a futile effort to hide.

"Who's that?" Tye said.

She groaned. "Hairy Knuckles."

"Harry Knuckles?" Tye laughed. "What kind of a name is Harry Knuckles."

"Appropriate!" She peered over Tye's shoulder. Hairy strode straight for them. She groaned. "You've got to save me."

"Why?" A grin sounded in his voice.

"Because you love me," she said in a fierce whisper.

He sighed in an exaggerated manner. "But you don't believe me."

"I believe you! I believe you!" Desperation colored her words.

"Are you sure?"

"Yes, yes," she hissed. Hairy was only a few strides away. "Now do something!"

"I don't know." Tye shook his head. "Maybe you should agree to marry me first."

She gritted her teeth. "Men who wanted to get married is how I got in this mess in the first place."

"I'd know that flaming hair anywhere!" Hairy pulled to a halt in front of them and pointed. "That's her, all right."

"What do you want with the countess?" a man called from the growing assembly.

"Countess? What countess?" Confusion crossed Hairy's fat face. "I want *her*. Ophelia Kendrake."

"The Countess of Bridgewater," someone said.

"Countess? Her?" Hairy snorted. "She ain't no countess. She's some actor's daughter. And she's a gambler. And she owes me."

"Is this true, Ophelia?" Tye said under his breath.

Ophelia groaned and dropped her forehead onto Tye's back. "Which part?"

"The part about owing him?"

"No. Somebody was cheating, but it wasn't me," she whispered.

"She said she'd marry me." Hairy nodded firmly.

Ophelia's head snapped up. "I most certainly did not."

"I have to believe her on that one, Mr. Knuckles." Tye shook his head. "This woman is not at all inclined toward marriage."

"I don't care." Hairy set his jaw in a bullheaded manner. "She owes me."

"I do not." Ophelia glared from behind the protection of Tye's shoulder.

"What exactly does she owe you?" Tye said quietly.

"Well." Hairy narrowed his eyes at Tye, as if assessing his options. "She took me for a lot of money. A lot of money."

"Now see here, Mr.—"

"Knuckles," Ophelia muttered.

"—Knuckles." Montgomery stepped through the crowd, followed closely by the lady and gentleman Ophelia had seen him with earlier. "You told me just two days ago the pot in question was not significant."

"Yeah, well . . ." Hairy appeared distinctly uncomfortable.

"And you further told me while you had offered marriage, she turned you down." Montgomery raised a brow. "Isn't that accurate?"

"She's really good at that," Tye said brightly. Ophelia jabbed him in the back.

"Yeah." Hairy had the look of a man recognizing defeat.

"So." Montgomery smiled pleasantly. "She doesn't actually owe you much of anything beyond the price of a drink or two. Now, isn't that right?"

"I suppose," Hairy muttered.

"So this can be resolved quite simply. Joe?" Joe Simmons stepped forward. "Joe, would you take this gentleman back to your place and give him a bottle of your best"—Montgomery cast a quick look at Hairy—"your second best"—Montgomery grimaced—"or whatever you have available in terms of whiskey."

Hairy scowled at Ophelia. "All right, I'll take it. But

I ain't happy." He turned and followed Joe, his voice trailing behind him. "Say, why does everybody keep calling me 'Knuckles'?"

Ophelia breathed easier and stepped from behind Tye. Thank goodness Hairy was taken care of. She'd never dreamed the nasty man would actually follow her. Hell, if he'd caught up to her and Jenny alone . . . she shuddered at the thought.

"Well, that's that." She smiled and noted Tye wasn't smiling with her. He nodded at the gathering of townspeople. She turned slowly to meet a crowd of stunned, accusing faces. The silence broke abruptly.

"She's not a countess? Then what—"

"—she's played us for fools that's—"

"—and what about Big Jack? He's—"

"—swindled! She's a liar and a—"

"—cheat and a fraud!"

"And those are my good qualities," Ophelia said under her breath. Tye stifled a laugh. "It's not funny, Tye," she whispered. "These people are mad, and they have every right to be."

He cast her a thoughtful smile. "Do they?"

"Yes," she snapped.

"I think we should hang her!" an unidentified man cried, backed up by a chorus of "Yeah, yeah, hang her!"

She clutched Tye's arm. "Maybe not every right."

"Hold on a minute now." Tye waved his arms to quiet the mob. "We could hang her, I suppose."

"Thanks a lot," she muttered.

"But . . ." Tye shook his head regretfully. "That's not what a respectable town would do. No, sir, a civilized community wouldn't hang her."

"Are you sure, Tye?" a skeptical voice called.

"Pretty sure." Tye shrugged. "They might have

hanged her in Dead End, but remember, this is Empire City now."

"But we still think of it as Dead End," another man pointed out.

"Couldn't we just change the name back? Just for this?" an eager resident chimed in.

"No, no. Afraid not." Tye held up his hands in surrender.

"Well, then, why don't we shoot her?" The suggestion came from the back of the crowd.

"Damnation, Tye," Ophelia muttered. "Caesar's bloodthirsty friends had nothing on the good citizens of Dead End."

"In Dead End, you wouldn't have a chance. They'd definitely shoot you or maybe hang you," he said in an aside. "Luckily for you, this is Empire City now." He addressed the crowd. "Nope, can't shoot her either. It's just not civilized."

"Well, then what are we going to do with her?"

"Nothing." Big Jack's voice rang out over the crowd. He sat on his big, blond horse, his wife and daughter on horseback by his side. "Not one thing."

Big Jack's mount pushed its way through the crowd, parting people and tossing around an occasional smug laugh. Lorelie and Jenny followed. "You see, folks, if there's an injured party, it would be me, not any of you. But the money I paid to Ophelia is still right here in Randolph's bank. Ain't it, darlin'?"

"Most of it." Ophelia smiled weakly.

Tye frowned. "What do you mean, 'most of it'?"

"Expenses," she hissed.

"I didn't get a castle from her." Jack's grin was as big as Wyoming itself. "I got something a lot more valuable."

Lorelie smiled. "And we aren't the only ones."

"I didn't get nothing," someone in the crowd muttered.

"You most certainly did," Lorelie said sharply. "For one thing, you got a new opera house, but even better than that, you got a new attitude. We learned the people in this town can accomplish anything they want to if they simply work together. And that's not all. Why, Anna Rose here learned with a little work she can be queen of the fairies"—a muffled snicker waved through the crowd—"or anything else she wants to be. And I learned that . . . well . . ."

"What did you learn, Lorelie?" a voice called.

She drew a deep breath. "I learned that it doesn't take a new name or a title or even a castle to make people respectable and civilized. It doesn't have anything to do with what you call yourself but rather who you are. We're decent, friendly, very nice people—"

"Nice town, nice people, nice mayor," Ophelia said under her breath.

"—and it doesn't matter if we live in Empire City or Dead End. We are who we are and we have nothing to apologize for. I don't know why we failed to see that. It was right here in front of our eyes all along."

"You didn't mention sophisticated? What about that?" a woman asked.

Lorelie smiled. "I believe we will still have to work on that one."

Enthusiastic nods and muttered comments greeted Lorelie's speech.

"I knew this whole respectability thing—"

"—absolutely right, exactly what I—"

"—manure is what it was. I always said—"

"—more than good enough and better than—"

"—utter and complete nonsense, the entire—"

"—then are we back to Dead End or—"

"—do we keep Empire City?"

The gathering's collective gaze turned to Big Jack. Jack pulled off his hat and scratched his head. "Well, you've got me there. I've always been fond of Dead End, but I find I'm kind of partial to Empire City as well. Tye, what do you think?"

"Empire City has a nice ring to it, but we're all used to Dead End," Tye said.

"And we could hang her then," a voice cried.

"Or shoot her," another added.

Ophelia glared at the mob. Perhaps they weren't quite as nice as she'd thought.

"No, no, didn't you hear what Lorelie just said?" Tye glared at the crowd like a parent chastising a child. "We're already respectable, civilized, decent people."

A rather sizeable groan of regret washed through the assembly. Perhaps they weren't nice at all?

Ophelia nudged Tye. "Why don't you combine the names?"

"To what?" He lifted a brow. "Dead Empire? City's End?"

"Why not"—she narrowed her gaze thoughtfully—"call it Empire's End?"

"Empire's End. Empire's End, Wyoming." He nodded slowly. "It has a nice sound to it. I like it."

"But what does it mean, Tye?" a man called.

Tye deferred to Ophelia with a nod and a barely smothered smile. She slanted him back a scathing glance and drew a deep breath. "It means . . . it means . . ."

"It means that"—the tall, handsome woman Ophelia had seen with Montgomery stepped forward, her voice as imposing as any Ophelia had ever heard onstage—"here, in this glorious country of yours, you have no need for lords or castles or empires. It is 1888, ladies and gentlemen, and you are Americans facing whatever tomorrow may bring bravely and proudly. And right here is where all empires end and freedom rings out over the land. A place where . . ."

"What in the hell is she saying?" Tye whispered to Ophelia.

"I have no idea." Ophelia stared, wide-eyed. "But she's saying it extremely well. Look at that crowd. They're positively spellbound. I'd bet anything she's an actress."

"Not quite." Montgomery stepped up beside them and inclined his head toward the speaker. "That, my dear Ophelia, is the real Countess of Bridgewater."

Ophelia's heart thudded in her chest, and a knot settled in her stomach.

The real Countess of Bridgewater?

Hell and damnation.

". . . hold your chins up and proclaim to the world: yes, world, I am a resident of Empire's End, Wyoming!" The countess held out her arms in a wide embrace and gazed up to the heavens, as if inviting God himself down to earth to join the residents of Dead End/ Empire City/Empire's End, Wyoming.

For a moment the crowd stared, awestruck. Then applause erupted amid shouts of "I like it," "Beats Dead End" and "Let's hear it for Empire's End."

The countess turned to Ophelia and extended her hand. Ophelia grasped it weakly. The older woman's blue eyes twinkled. "You must be the young woman I've heard so much about."

Ophelia swallowed. "You have?"

The countess nodded. "Lord Russelford explained everything."

"Lord who?" Tye stared at his friend.

Montgomery shrugged. "It seems an unforeseen accident has left me as the new earl."

"My condolences, Sedge." Tye studied him carefully. "Does this mean you'll be going home?"

"In very many ways"—a lopsided smile quirked Montgomery's lips—"I feel as though I am home."

"And what of you, my dear?" The countess smiled at Ophelia. "What are your plans?"

"They are, um, uncertain at the moment." She shot a quick glance at Tye, who grinned with absolutely no uncertainty whatsoever. She ignored him. "You were wonderful, Countess. What an impressive speech. I would have thought you were on the stage."

The countess's eyes sparkled. "I was, once, that's where I met my dear late husband—"

"Arthur?" Tye said.

"Archibald?" Montgomery asked.

"Why, no." The countess cast the men a puzzled frown. "His name was Charles."

Tye and Montgomery exchanged glances. Both men appeared hard pressed to keep their amusement under control. It was such a shame Ophelia's gun was in her bag. Who would blame her for shooting either or, better yet, both of them?

"In fact." The countess leaned toward her confidentially. "That little speech of mine was straight from a play I did at the Royal Theater in London back in '68, or was it '69—"

"Hey, Tye," a voice yelled. "What are we going to

do now? We did all this work around town. We got a whole ceremony ready to go and we don't have a count or nothing."

"Actually, we do." Tye nodded at Montgomery. "My good friend Sedge Montgomery is now the Earl of Russelford. We've got our bit of civilization after all."

"He ain't got a castle though," someone muttered.

"I most certainly have," Montgomery said under his breath.

Tye grinned and continued. "And Sedge has brought the . . ."

"The Marquis of Charleton." The gentleman accompanying the countess heaved a long-suffering sigh and mustered a valiant smile.

"The Marquis of Charleton. And here we have . . ." Tye gestured toward the countess with a dramatic flourish. Apparently Ophelia and the countess weren't the only ones who knew how to work an audience. ". . . the Countess of Bridgewater."

The crowd stilled. The countess favored the gathering with a noble smile. Murmurs spread through the assembly.

"Is she really—"

"—don't know if we—"

"—looks pretty genuine—"

"—fooled before, I'd sure hate—"

"—how do we know if—"

"Prove it!" The demand flew out from the mob.

"Prove it?" The countess drew herself up and looked down her nose in a manner so terribly regal that no one could have doubted her for a moment. "My good man. Prove I'm not."

For a long moment nothing happened. Then the citizens of Dead End/Empire City/Empire's End, Wyoming, apparently decided it was high time to stop all this nonsense and enjoy the rest of the day. After all, they didn't have a count to crown, but they did have an earl and marquis and a genuine countess, and in anybody's hand, that was as close to a real live royal flush as you could get. Laughter and excited chatter filled the air, and Ophelia relaxed.

"Tye," a voice called. "We still haven't decided what to do about her." All eyes turned toward Ophelia, and she smiled gamely. "If we ain't gonna hang her and we ain't gonna shoot her, what the hell are we gonna do with her?"

"You know, I've been giving that a lot of thought," Tye said in his best mayoral voice.

"I'll just bet you have," Ophelia muttered.

He ignored her. "And I've decided that we need to put her someplace where she can't do any more harm—"

"I won't go to jail," she snapped.

"—someplace where she can be watched—"

"You wouldn't!" Fear touched her voice.

"—day and night—"

"You couldn't!" Gad, maybe he could.

"—so it seems to be the best thing for everyone concerned," Tye said and shrugged as if he was doing his duty and nothing more, "is for me to just marry her."

A hush fell over the crowd.

A single, awestruck voice broke the silence. "Damn. That is civilized."

Panic surged through her. How could he do this to her in front of the entire town? Honestly, after everything that had happened in the past month it was almost as much her town as it was his. He certainly had a lot of nerve. Thinking he could force her into marriage this way. Well, she was not going to put up with it. "So my choice here is to marry you or hang?"

Tye grinned wickedly. "That pretty much sums it up."

"Very well." She folded her arms over her chest and glared. "Hang me!"

Tye threw back his head and laughed. "Oh, no, you're not getting out of this that easily."

"I'm not *in* anything to get out of," she said pointedly.

"Forgive me for interrupting this"—the countess leaned toward Tye—"would you term it a proposal?"

"More like a shotgun wedding," Ophelia grumbled.

Tye nodded to the countess. "I think proposal is probably as close as you can come. However, the terms *negotiation, bargain*—"

"—*threat, cajole, coerce*," Ophelia muttered.

"—all seem to be equally appropriate in this case."

"I see," the countess said thoughtfully. "Then it surely must be love."

Ophelia gritted her teeth. "I don't love him."

"Of course not, dear." The countess winked. "Whatever you say. Now . . ." She turned toward Montgomery. "I believe something was said about a celebration and a theatrical presentation?"

"Allow me to escort you." Montgomery proffered his arm. The countess linked hers with his and they headed for the opera house.

"Tell me, Lord Russelford," the countess said. "About a month ago, my luggage went astray, and I was wondering if anyone here had . . ." The marquis and the crowd trailed behind them, and Ophelia and Tye were abruptly alone.

Tye narrowed his gaze. "You'll have to give her clothes back, you know."

"I don't—" Ophelia stopped short, her deception finally at an end. "I suppose if I must."

"And you will have to marry me."

"I don't love you."

"Yes, you do."

Ophelia glared in irritation. "Why does everyone in this town keep saying that to me?"

"Because it's true." He cupped her chin in his hand and stared into her eyes with a gaze strong and sure and certain. "It's just like my aunt said about the town. Sometimes you can't see what's right in front of your eyes."

"Like in that silly fairy tale of Jenny's."

"Just like that."

"But I don't believe in love." She wrenched her chin from his grasp. "Why don't you understand that?"

"Ophelia," he said softly, "even Shakespeare believed in love."

"He most certainly did not!" She clenched her fists in a desperate attempt to resist the tender tone of his words and the smoldering depths of his dark eyes. " 'I had rather hear my dog bark at a crow than a man swear he loves me.' *Much Ado About Nothing*."

He stared for a moment, then smiled slowly. Her stomach twisted at the shade of triumph in his gaze. " 'My house, mine honor, yea, my life be thine.' *All's Well That Ends Well*."

Panic fluttered within her. " 'The worst fault you have is to be in love.' *As You Like It*."

" 'Doubt thou the stars are fire, doubt that the sun doth move, doubt truth to be a liar, but never doubt' "—he trapped her gaze with his—" 'I love.' *Hamlet*."

"*Troilus and Cressida*." Her voice rose nearly to a cry. " 'This love will undo us all!' "

"Also from *Hamlet*, 'Forty thousand brothers could not with all their quality of love make up my sum.'" He drew a deep breath and stared into her eyes. "'I loved Ophelia.'"

"You're misquoting again." Her voice trembled. "It's the other way. 'Forty thousand brothers' comes after—"

"Ophelia!" He clenched his jaw.

"Damn you, Tyler Matthews." Defeat flooded her. This was surely a mistake. "Very well, I love you! I've always loved you. And God help me, I probably always will. And you'll break my heart and leave—"

"I will never leave you! Why can't you believe that! I love you."

"Certainly you say that now, but—"

"No!" Frustration washed across his face. "What do I have to do to get through to you? I love you today and I will love you tomorrow and always. And we will be together forever!"

"Forever? Hah!" She wanted nothing more than to believe him, but everything she'd ever seen in her life told her to ignore that nagging voice in the back of her head that cried this was real and forever. How could she take that risk? "You can't help it, Tyler. It's in your nature."

"My nature?"

"Yes!" She glared. "You're just a man."

"You needn't make it sound like a disease!"

"Well, it's not something you can recover from," she snapped. "It's very much like a broken heart. It's incurable!"

"If I break your heart, you can . . . um . . . you can . . ." He pulled his brows together in an obvious effort to come up with something to convince her.

"What? Shoot you?"

"Yeah, you can shoot me."

She snorted in disdain. "I already did that once, and it wasn't nearly as satisfying as I would have thought."

"You claimed that was an accident. This time, it will be deliberate, and you've said it yourself: if you wanted to—"

"I would have killed you." Gad, she didn't really wish to kill him! The realization of what she did want struck her with a force she never expected. All she wanted, all she'd ever wanted, was to be in his arms and by his side for the rest of her days. "And as much as I hate to admit it, I'm not at all certain I'd ever really kill you."

"But I'd deserve it."

"That's true enough."

He picked up her hand and kissed her palm. "You won't have to shoot me, ever."

"Not deliberately anyway."

"Ophelia!"

"Accidents do happen, you know." She forced a pleasant smile to soften the very real threat in her words. "I can't imagine I would ever kill you, but I will not hesitate to shoot—"

He pulled her into his arms. "I'd prefer to avoid any shootings, fatal, deliberate or accidental in the future."

"It's probably best. You don't seem to deal with even minor pain at all well, and who knows what the very nice people of whatever this town ends up calling itself now would do if I actually killed you. Some of them were more than willing to hang . . ." She gazed up at him and her heart stilled. And for the first time, she looked in his eyes and knew, deep down in some secret place she'd always kept hidden and protected, that the love shining in his eyes was right and true and lasting. "Damn, I really do love you."

He grinned. "Then kiss me, Ophelia."

Her lips met his, and joy surged through her. Why had she fought this for so long? Why had she wasted so much time? Why had she denied what she'd known from the moment she'd met him and he'd talked to her of Venice and a moon made for lovers?

She pulled back and studied him for a moment. "If I marry you—"

"When you marry me."

"Very well." She sighed. "When I marry you, will you take me to Venice and show me the moon made for lovers?"

"Ophelia." He laughed. "I don't have that kind of money."

"What do you mean?" A sinking sensation settled in her stomach. "You don't have that kind of money?"

"Jack's got all the money in the family. I'm struggling just to get my ranch going again."

"You don't have any money," she said slowly.

"Nope."

"And I can't keep the money Jack gave me?" A hopeful note rang in her voice.

"Nope."

"Not even a little?"

"Nope."

"You're trying to tell me I went through all this hard work and effort and energy. I helped build an opera house, taught overweight matrons to be fairy queens, confronted laughing horses, threw myself off a porch and lost my sister, and not only do I not get to be a countess anymore but I can't keep any of the money either?" She glared in indignation.

"Not even a dollar." He grinned. "You'll just have to make do on love."

"Love." She smiled weakly. "Wonderful." How ironic. Now that she finally believed in the elusive emotion, it was damn near all she ended up with.

"Is it enough?" he said softly.

Ophelia gazed into his eyes and realized that anyone who'd told as many lies as she had would surely recognize the truth when she finally faced it. And it was indeed the truth. As true as the emotion shining in his eyes. His dark, delicious eyes. And she'd always loved chocolate. "It's enough."

Still . . .

She traced her finger along the side of his jaw. "Have you ever noticed, Tye, how politicians always seem to have a great deal of money?"

"Ophelia." He growled the word.

"I was simply thinking, my love, that you could use your position as mayor as a starting point. I mean, surely it can't be all that difficult to go from mayor of—what is it now—Empire's End to being territorial governor and then on to the Senate and possibly even pres—"

He groaned. "Ophelia."

"Yes, Tye?" She gazed at him with as much innocence as she could muster. He glared down at her with such a profound mix of exasperation and sheer desire in his eyes that she didn't even flinch when he heaved a heavy sigh, flicked a tan finger in the air and said, "Rope."

Epilogue

"**Y**ou're all set." Tye slapped the rump of the horse he'd just harnessed to the surrey and turned to his wife. "Life would sure be a lot easier around here if you'd just learn—"

"I know, I know," Ophelia said in the manner of one who's heard the same speech over and over. "Life would be much easier if I'd just learn to ride. Well, I won't. I don't want to, and you can't make me."

He quirked a brow and pulled her into his arms, his voice low and suggestive. "I thought I could make you do anything."

She gazed into his chocolate eyes and her breath caught. Gad, three years and a baby later and he could still fire a heat inside her that weakened her knees and her resistance. And she hadn't even had to shoot him. Not once.

He nuzzled the sensitive flesh beneath her ear, and she gasped. "Tyler Matthews, stop that! If you don't let me go, I'll be late."

His words tickled against her neck. "I don't see what

you women do every Tuesday and Thursday anyway that's so damned interesting."

"Oh, this and that." She stifled a grin. "Typical female activities, mostly. Nothing you'd be particularly interested in."

He released her and grinned. "Probably not. You'll be home before dark?"

"Always." She brushed her lips lightly against his and let him help her into the small buggy they'd bought after their wedding, a model very similar to Lorelie's. She snapped the reins, the horse laughed in that sarcastic manner all horses seemed to have around Ophelia, and they were off. She'd read recently about the fanciful notion of horseless carriages and did so hope it wasn't simply idle speculation. Eliminating the necessity of those nasty, brutish creatures would certainly make life more enjoyable.

Actually, life in general was proceeding quite nicely, and Ophelia looked forward eagerly to today's meeting of the Every Other Tuesday and Thursday Afternoon Ladies Cultural Society and Theater Troupe. If her luck held in the next few months—and she needed all the luck she could get against the ladies of Empire's End—she'd win enough money to take Tye to Venice and show him the moon. Lorelie said she'd keep the baby, and she promised not to lose her. Of course, Jenny would be around as well. She and Zach hadn't married after all, at least not yet.

It continued to amaze Ophelia how the men of Empire's End hadn't an inkling of the activities of the Every Other Tuesday and Thursday Afternoon Ladies Cultural Society and Theater Troupe. Gad, any idiot could have figured it out if they'd simply paid attention to what was actually in front of their eyes, as opposed to what they expected to see.

She often thought about that very thing. Idly, in the back of her mind, she tried to determine why she'd had such horrible difficulties when those damn tailors in that silly fairy tale had encountered few problems at all. Just like them, she'd tried to sell something that hadn't existed.

Maybe her scheme had been far too grand or a touch too fanciful. Maybe she wasn't as good an actress as she thought. And maybe, just maybe she couldn't have lived happily ever after the way she was now if she'd managed to pull it off.

Still, the notion nagged at her from time to time. Why was it people very often couldn't see what was right in front of them? What made fairly intelligent men believe, in spite of all evidence to the contrary, that wives told their husbands everything? And why would anyone accept an actress's masquerade as a countess when she plainly couldn't even remember her dead husband's name?

And she wondered now and again in odd moments if the tailors had lived happily ever after with their ill-gotten gain. Or if they'd ever realized, like she had, there was far more to life than the mere monetary rewards to be reaped by fabrication and deception and deceit. And she now firmly believed, with a conviction strengthened by the love of one man and the friendship of very nice people, that that fact held true whether you were peddling a castle that didn't exist or duping a town that longed for respectability, or even, or perhaps especially, if you were selling . . . the emperor new clothes.